# COLORADO MORNING SKY

## Cedar Ridge Chronicles Book 3

# A J Hawke

Mountain Quest Publishing

ISBN: 978-0-9834505-8-0

Copyright © 2013 Barbara A. Kee

Cover Copyright © Barbara A. Kee

Layout design © Barbara A. Kee

This book is a work of fiction. Names, character, places, and incidents are either products of the author's imagination or used fictitiously. Any resemblance to actual locales, or person, living or dead, is entirely coincidental. All rights reserved. No part of publication may be reproduced or transmitted in any form or by any means, electronic or mechanical, without permission in writing from Barbara A. Kee.

Edition August 2013

Copyright © 2013 Barbara A. Kee

All rights reserved.

ISBN: 978-0-9834505-8-0

ISBN-13: 978-0-9834505-8-0

## ACKNOWLEDGMENTS

In appreciation to all who have aided in and encouraged the completion of this novel, thank you.

Teresa Hanger, Editor

A-1EditingServices.com

Barbara R. Kee

Editor and Beta Reader

Bill & Jean Ann Edrington

Friends and Encouragers

Janet Grimes

Friend and Beta Reader

Jimmy Thomas Cover Model

www.JimmyThomas.com

Erin Dameron-Hill

Cover Artist

# DEDICATION

In appreciation for the blessings of
the Father, the Son, and the Holy Spirit,

To God Be The Glory

# Chapter 1

Psalm 68:6

"God sets the lonely in families: he brings out those which are bound with chains."

Arizona Territory, 1876

Jeremiah jerked desperately at the chains that shackled him to the floor of the prison wagon as fear crawled through his stomach like a living thing. Indians, whom he recognized as Apaches, yelled and raced their horses on both sides of the iron-barred prison wagon as it bounced across the Arizona desert.

Inside, a guard frantically worked to free the lock that secured the six prisoners' chains through the eyebolts on the wagon floor. The driver whipped the horses, trying to outrun the Indians.

Bile rose in Jeremiah's throat and he fought to keep his breathing under control. The guard released the shackles of the man next to Jeremiah and then turned to him. Without warning, the prison wagon lurched, and they tumbled over a bluff. The wagon rolled over, tossing the occupants inside like rag dolls. Jeremiah winced as blow after blow battered his body until a sudden crack to his head thrust him into darkness.

~

Jeremiah tried to touch his throbbing head as darkness surrounded him but his hands were trapped at his waist. He felt the iron of shackles on his wrist. He tried to move and heard the jingle of a chain between his hands. Pain shot through his shoulders as he discovered his elbows were pulled back, trapped around some kind of bar. He rubbed his face on the ground but could not remove the blindfold. Aches and pains fought for attention all over his body. Gingerly moving his fingers, his toes, he was thankful that he seemed to have escaped the wreck of the wagon without a broken neck. He sensed someone close by and wanted to call out, but his fear of the Apaches whom he assumed had him tied up kept him silent. Yesterday had been his sixteenth birthday. Tall for his age, though not yet filled out, Jeremiah could only hope that he would live to be seventeen.

Suddenly, a rope tightened around his neck. Hanging? Was he about to die? Icy fear raced up his back. The rope pulled upward and he choked. To loosen the pressure on his neck, he got to his feet. Then the rope pulled him along. Unable to see, Jeremiah often staggered and fell. Each time, the pull of the rope on his neck tightened. He soon learned to walk by shuffling. How long he walked, he had no idea, but it was hours. By the time the pull on the rope loosened and he collapsed on the ground, he was so tired and thirsty that all he wanted was to lie down and die.

Someone grabbed his hair from behind and pulled his head back. Even without the blindfold, he probably wouldn't have had the strength to open his eyes and see his captor. A cup pressed against his lips and he eagerly swallowed hot bitter tea.

"Thank you," he croaked and then wretched in pain as he coughed. His body was a mass of raw nerves. His head throbbed relentlessly. His elbows and shoulders hurt from the pole behind his back. His skinned and bruised knees and feet ached from the walking—and falling. At least they intended to keep him alive. He was miserable. And scared.

"Could you just let my arms loose?" he asked the presence he sensed close by. But, no one untied him. Unable to stay awake, he lay down on the bare ground. His body seemed to float, and then he knew no more.

~

Jeremiah woke to a shivering body from the cold and stabbing pain from various parts of his body. He sensed the dampness of the early morning dew. The blindfold still covered his eyes. He tried again to rub his face in the dirt to remove it.

A hand grabbed his hair and jerked his head up. The rope encircled his neck again and tightened. If he wanted to breathe, he had to follow the pull of that rope. He stumbled a few feet and felt the rope pull straight up as if to hang him. He couldn't move away; any step he took tightened the rope. Humiliated and angry, he stood still.

Something pressed against his lips, and when he opened his mouth, he tasted stale cornbread. Almost gagging, he chewed. When he swallowed, his captor shoved another piece of cornbread into his dry mouth. Jeremiah gagged and then chewed again. He tried to swallow until the gravel lump finally passed his throat. He then gulped water from the cup pushed against his lips. At least they didn't want him to starve.

Then the presence went away and left him standing there alone. The rope around his neck threatening to choke him kept him immobile. A burro brayed in the distance. Jeremiah cocked his head at the sound of things moving about. Then the rope loosened for a moment and he could relax from standing so straight. But the moment was brief, for a tug of the rope jerked him forward. Jeremiah sensed someone riding a burro and leading him by the rope around his neck. He could either walk or choke.

~

Four more days of walking followed. The rope guided his every move. His neck burned as the rope carved a raw mass of misery around his neck. Every night, his tormentor fed him cornbread and then poured bitter tea down his throat, which Jeremiah soon realized contained a sleeping potion. Every time he drank it, he fell asleep. He woke every morning to cornbread, water, and a blinding headache. The food sustained his life, but it wasn't enough to take away the hunger. However, as the days went on, he stopped feeling hunger. Would death be preferable to this misery? Where was he being taken? Why did his captor keep him in the darkness of the blindfold? Why wouldn't he talk?

"Tell me who you are. Where you're taking me? Talk to me, please." Only the sound of the burro's hooves clomping ahead of him answered.

"Answer me. Why don't you answer me?" he yelled even though it felt like broken glass was scoring his throat.

"ANSWER ME!" He screamed at the unseen presence and gasped to breathe against the fire in his throat.

The tug on the rope slackened, and the burro stopped. Then the rope jerked furiously and he fell to the ground choking. A hand jerked his head back and stuffed a cloth into his mouth until he was sure he would choke to death. To make it even more secure, hands wrapped something across his mouth and tied it behind his head, and he couldn't push the gag out of his mouth.

The jerking rope on his raw neck and the gag made breathing nearly impossible. Through his thin shirt and on his face, Jeremiah sensed the lessening of the burning sun. As the desert air began to cool rapidly, his captor stopped and shoved him to the ground. The gag was removed. His chest heaved as he filled his lungs. Jeremiah's mouth was dry and his intense thirst overwhelmed him. But he didn't say a word. He had learned.

Jeremiah had kept count of the nights and it was now the fifth day of walking. He staggered and fell often adding to the cuts and scrapes on his already hurting body. He barely had strength to get up after each fall. Finally, he sensed a change in terrain. They climbed. The burro stopped, and then the pull of the rope felt different. The presence walked and pulled him along. Coolness touched his skin. He no longer sensed the desert sun, but rather an enclosure.

The rope jerked hard and he fell. Then someone dragged his body backward—by the pole that held his arms tied—until he sat against a stonewall. Tension on the rope around his neck released.

He sat and waited, afraid to move.

Jeremiah's captor returned after a few minutes and put the cup of bitter tea to his lips. He pulled his head back; he didn't want to go to sleep again. But the hand took his hair, jerked his head back and forced the liquid into his mouth. He gave in and swallowed the tea. It didn't take long for the effect of the drug to take over and he gradually slumped over and slept.

When he woke, he found the blindfold gone and his arms free of the pole, but the irons remained on his wrists and ankles. He looked around at shadowed rock walls of a mine tunnel and he sat on a hard dirt floor. Daylight filtered down the tunnel from one direction. It enabled him to see that a foot of chain connected the manacles on his wrists. The chain between his ankles attached to a long chain that wrapped around a large timber that appeared to support the ceiling of the tunnel.

He stood up and could just touch the ceiling that rose about three feet above his head. He walked toward the light until stopped by the length of chain as he got close to the tunnel's entrance. He sighed as he hoped to be able to at least see out and get a better idea of where he was but the chain was too short. Several smaller tunnels ran off the main tunnel but were so dark he shivered at trying to enter them. One wrong step could lead him into a hole. What was the purpose for bringing him so far across the desert and keeping him here?

In a little while, a short old man with glasses appeared at the entrance of the tunnel wrapped in an oversized coat. A scarf hid his face, along with a red plaid felt hat pulled down over his forehead.

Jeremiah stood up, but the man motioned for him to sit back down.

The man held a plate of food and a cup of water. He stood just beyond the distance of the length of chain. He sat the food and drink on the ground. Then he held up a pick and shovel. He gestured down the tunnel, and then showed Jeremiah some ore and burlap bags. The old man lit a lantern and sat it down on the ground next to the tools. He pointed to the pick and shovel, pretended to fill the burlap bag, and then pointed to the food and drink.

Jeremiah understood. If he wanted food and water then he had to fill the bag with ore. He wasn't going to do it. Then he looked around him. He had no way to get loose from the chains on his own, but maybe with the pick and shovel he could break the chain. So he nodded.

The old man threw the rope at Jeremiah and gestured for him to put it back around his neck.

Jeremiah hesitated, but finally put it back around his raw flesh wincing at the burning sting.

The old man backed away after he put the pick and shovel within Jeremiah's reach. The old man pulled on the rope and Jeremiah started to remove the rope, but the old man held up the cup of water. He let it trickle to the ground.

Jeremiah took his hands away from the rope. He had to have water and he was already so thirsty. This old man didn't care whether he survived or not.

Jeremiah gave in and took the tools, burlap bag, and lantern, then walked toward the back of the tunnel. He soon came to a section of the tunnel that gave evidence of recent digging. It didn't take much effort to see the vein of gold in the granite wall. He used the pick to loosen the gold bearing ore from the wall of the tunnel and shoveled it into the burlap bag until it was full.

As he worked, the rope around his neck rubbed the already raw flesh. His wrists bled from the constant scraping of the irons that encircled them. Each swing of the pick and scoop of the shovel was pure agony. He tied the bag up and carried it down the tunnel until he reached the end of the chain.

The old man had backed away with the rope still in his hand. He threw Jeremiah another bag and gestured toward the far end of the tunnel.

How many bags did he have to fill to earn food and water? He worked several hours and filled ten bags with ore. When he came back with the last bag full, the plate of beans, rice, and cornbread were within his reach as was a full cup of water. He sat down on the tunnel floor, grabbed the water first, and drank it down. He didn't trust the old man not to take it away. He then took the plate and ate the food with his fingers. The old man offered him no utensils, but did place another cup of water within Jeremiah's reach before quickly stepping back. Rubbing his hands together, he watched Jeremiah eat.

Jeremiah considered grabbing the old man, but he always remained just out reach. Jeremiah imaged throwing the pick or the shovel at him. But if he hurt the old man before he could get loose, what would he do for food or water? A slow death chained to the support timber? His stomach clenched and he broke into a cold sweat. For now, he needed the old man.

After he drank the second cup of water and licked the plate clean, the old man jerked on the rope. Jeremiah picked up the shovel, pick, and lantern and trudged back down the tunnel dragging an empty burlap sack. Even if he could break the chains, the old man held the other end of the rope that looped around his neck. It took ten more bags filled with ore before the old man let him rest.

His captor pushed up his glasses and gestured for Jeremiah to bring the pick and shovel to him. Jeremiah took the tools as far as the chain would let him and laid them down.

The old man gestured for him to back away. Jeremiah conceded, and the old man snatched up the pick and shovel. He stepped back out of reach.

Jeremiah might rope his jailor, but he anticipated what Jeremiah would do. He gestured for Jeremiah to take the rope off his neck, then he pulled it out of reach. And he took away the shovel and pick, the only thing that Jeremiah could use to break the chain. The old man left the lantern so Jeremiah had light.

After the old man walked out of the tunnel, Jeremiah examined his wrists. The swinging of the pick and the shoveling caused the irons continually to irritate his wrists, which were already raw. Both of his wrists were bleeding, and they hurt with every movement of the irons. What would he do if they festered? He had no way to protect or treat his wrist. At least for now his boots protected his ankles from the irons around them.

Jeremiah ran his hand through his grubby hair. He had shaved in the territorial prison and washed up. But here there were no facilities of any kind. He didn't even have a blanket. He could barely make it into one of the side tunnels with the length of chain and relieve himself. How long the old man would keep him in the tunnel Jeremiah had no idea, but he couldn't believe it would be long. Of course, as long as he was the old man's prisoner he was alive. He would rather be a prisoner than dead.

The year he had already served in the Phoenix jail had been a breeze compared to just the six days as the prisoner of the old man. Jeremiah had been with various gangs of outlaws since he was a small child. His earliest memory was riding in front of his father with other men chasing them. Then his father had ridden away and never returned. Jeremiah learned years later that he had died in a robbery. A man named George kept Jeremiah with him to help with the horses during robberies. They got caught trying to rob a stagecoach. It hadn't mattered to the territorial judge that Jeremiah was only fifteen. He got the same treatment as the men and received a ten-year sentence.

Five prisoners from the town jail in Phoenix had been in the prison wagon plus the three guards riding with them on their way to the new prison in Yuma. Had anyone else survived? Were they prisoners in other mines? Or was he the only one still alive and a prisoner? This prison was much worse than the year in the Phoenix jail had been. It couldn't last for long. It just couldn't.

It took him about ten minutes to explore the tunnel in all directions as far as the chain allowed him to move. Then he sat down next to the support timber to wait. He was tired to the bone. The days of walking and then working a long day in the mine had taken all his strength.

After what seemed hours, the old man returned and threw the rope back. He waited, rubbing his hands together.

"Please, tell me what you want from me. Is it to mine the ore? I can do that, but I don't have to live like an animal to do it. Just give me a blanket and take these irons off. They're killing my wrists. Please." Jeremiah didn't mind begging. He had nothing to lose, as his pride was gone.

For an answer, the old man gestured toward the rope he had thrown toward him.

Jeremiah picked the rope up and put it around his neck.

The old man then sat a cup of liquid on the ground within Jeremiah's reach.

Jeremiah shook his head and took a step back. "No, I won't drink it. You just want to put me to sleep. Please, let me go."

Instantly, the rope jerked tight and cut into his neck. The fiery pain of the raw flesh rubbing against the rope pulled him to his knees and the rope pulled tighter.

"All right, I'll drink it. Just don't jerk the rope again." Jeremiah reached for the cup and drank the bitter tea.

The old man gestured for him to remove the rope, which he did gladly. He knew from experience now that he only had a few minutes before sleep would descend, so he backed away and sat down by the support timber. He lay on his side and drifted off into a drug-induced sleep.

~

Days of sameness followed. Jeremiah filled the burlap bags with ore and the old man gave him a plate of food in the mornings. It was always the same—beans, rice, and cornbread. Strangely, although he lost weight he wasn't hungry. Every night he drank the tea and slept. He looked forward to the tea as it was the only thing that took him out of his misery for a few hours.

His clothes became tattered and filthy from the work. There were no days off. He used a stone to make marks on the support timber to track the days because one day blended into another.

He barely held on to sanity. No one to talk to and nothing but work and the walls of the tunnel. What if he just didn't work or drink the tea? When the old man showed up that morning, he refused to go to work after he had eaten the food and drank the water.

The old man threw the rope at him and then stood rubbing his hands together.

"I'm not working for you anymore. Just let me go. And forget about me putting the rope around my neck anymore." Jeremiah shouted at the old man

The old man stared at him and then went away, taking the tools and rope with him.

Jeremiah slumped to the dirt floor by the wooden support to which he was chained. So tired, he doused and rested for the rest of the day. That evening the old man came back with the cup of tea.

"No, I'm not going to drink it." Jeremiah trembled and his skin crawled with goose bumps of fear, but he had to do something to change the monotony of his life.

The next morning the old man came back and tossed the rope to him.

"No, I'm not doing your work anymore."

The old man pulled the rope back, went away, and soon returned carrying a cup of water. He slowly poured it onto the floor of the tunnel leaving a mocking wet spot before he left again.

Jeremiah experienced severe thirst by the time the day ended. It had been more than twenty-four hours since he had anything to drink. The thirst was worse than he had imagined. He was having a problem swallowing as his mouth and throat got dryer and then as the day continued he felt his tongue starting to swell. All he could think about was water.

That evening the old man came back. He threw the rope at Jeremiah.

He could hardly talk he was so thirsty. "No."

The old man pulled the rope back and went away.

By the next morning, Jeremiah knew it was hopeless. He had to have water. The old man appeared and threw the rope at Jeremiah. He put it around his neck without a word. The old man placed water and food within reach. Jeremiah grabbed the cup and gulped down the water. He ate the food. The old man brought another cup of water and the tools. After drinking the cup of water, Jeremiah went back to work.

That night the old man brought the bitter tea and Jeremiah drank it without protest.

~

He woke several mornings later to find salve on his raw wrists. The old man had to be close to him while he slept because he sensed other things being different. One morning he woke to find his boots removed, but the shackles were still on his ankles. The shifting irons scraping his ankles soon had them in as bad a shape as his wrists with open sores on both ankles. Although they healed enough to scab overnight, the next day of work reopened the wounds, over and over.

A couple of days later he woke to find his filthy tattered clothes cut off his body. For some reason, that bothered him more than anything else that had happened. If he didn't have clothes then how could he still be a human being?

He looked up and found the old man watching him. "Old man, give me back my clothes! You've no right. I'm a human. Please," Jeremiah begged. "Just give me back my clothes."

The old man went away.

Why wouldn't the old man speak to him? Could it be that he had no voice? That made sense. Maybe he had no tongue. Jeremiah started a mental list of all sorts of reasons why the old man never spoke.

The next morning he awoke to find a large bucket of water and a stack of cornbread and tortillas. The old man didn't appear. The tunnel was empty of the bags of ore. Had his jailor put the water there for him to wash with? Then he looked at the stacked food. Better not to take the chance that his captor was not coming with more water and food. He waited.

Several days passed. He sat watching for the light at the tunnel entrance, wishing to be able to see a sunrise. *What if the old man didn't come back?* Jeremiah had to believe the old man intended to come back. Anything else was unthinkable.

Jeremiah ate only a handful of the cornbread in the mornings and just a few sips of the water. Then when he could tell from the shadows at the end of the tunnel that the day was almost over, he ate a tortilla and took a couple more swallows of water. He got sick the second day after the old man left. He wanted to throw up the little food he had eaten. For hours, he burned with fever, sweat dripping from his hot body. Then he shivered uncontrollably. He wanted to sleep as the long dark nights filled him with dread, but sleep wouldn't come without the bitter tea.

His ability to recall the stories he'd heard and books he'd read kept him sane. He'd always remembered anything he read or heard. His father had taught him to read and write when he was maybe four or five. Reading had been easy and wherever the men had taken him, he had always been on the lookout for books. As Jeremiah quoted everything he could think of aloud, he could see the old outlaw who had let Jeremiah read his Bible. Maybe it would keep him from going crazy in the emptiness of the tunnel.

The Psalms came to him the easiest and comforted him. He took to reciting whole books of the Bible aloud as he waited for the old man to come back. The sound of his voice offered a small comfort compared to the silence of the tunnel.

He tried to conserve the water as he understood the thirst of only two days without it, but it only lasted so many days. Now Jeremiah was out of water and he knew terror.

Between the sickness, lack of water and food, he couldn't get his thoughts to make sense by the time the old man returned. Jeremiah tried to push himself up onto his hands and knees but he had no strength. His captor came over and looked him over. If only he hadn't been so weak Jeremiah could have tried to overpower the old man, but he could hardly lift his head.

The old man pushed up his glasses. He seemed to be assessing just how bad off Jeremiah was, then he turned and left. When he returned, he brought a canteen filled with water and a plate of beans and rice, left it beside Jeremiah, and then backed away.

Jeremiah reached for the canteen with a feeble hand. After several tries, he managed to swallow a few drops of water before his arm fell to the ground. He rested. After a while, he ate a few bites of beans and rice. He drank more water. Then he vomited up the food.

All the while, the old man stood wringing his hands and watching him. After the canteen was empty, the old man gestured for Jeremiah to slide it toward him. Jeremiah hoped that he would refill it and bring it back. Instead, he returned with a cup of the bitter tea. Jeremiah was too weak to protest. Soon he was asleep.

When he woke, he had new clothes on, a blue long sleeved cotton work shirt and lightweight brown cotton pants. Bandages were around his wrists and ankles under the irons. And he had a blanket. He was pathetically grateful for these small favors. Even though the tunnel stayed at a cool temperature that was comfortable for the work, at night he had been cold laying on the hard ground with nothing.

The old man appeared with Jeremiah's breakfast.

Jeremiah rose to his feet. He pressed his palms together as if in prayer. "Thank you for the blanket and for bandaging my wrists and ankles. Thank you, thank you, for the clothes." Stepping to the plate of food, he squatted to eat before beginning his workday. "Just please don't go away like that again. Don't leave me here alone, please."

As usual, he got no response from the old man. He regretted that he couldn't wash before putting on clean clothes, but at least he had on a pair of cotton pants and a shirt. They were of cheap, poor quality, but Jeremiah didn't care. They were clothes.

When the old man appeared with the pick and shovel, Jeremiah understood it was time to get back to work. He filled the bags and carried them down to the old man. The days went forward. The only event that broke the deadly sameness was Jeremiah went to sleep one night chained to a support timber and woke up chained to another one deeper in the mine. Now being too far from the tunnel entrance to see daylight distressed him, and he fought the panic that rose each night. He hated the darkness after the old man took the lantern away each evening. Jeremiah eagerly drank the cup of bitter tea. He longed for the oblivion of sleep.

As he penetrated farther into the tunnel, the old man left timbers for him to shore up the tunnel, which Jeremiah did for his own safety. The gold in the ore sparkled, and just for something to do, Jeremiah took an interest and followed the vein of ore he discovered in his digging. He took a lot of gold out of the mountain.

He woke one morning to find his long straggly beard shaved and his hair cut close to his head during the night. It gave him a strange sensation to know that the old man had been that familiar with his body while he slept. It told him how strong the sleeping potion was that he could sleep through it.

The old man appeared with his plate of food. He wrung his hands as he watched Jeremiah.

"Old man, please give me some water to wash with. Just a bucket, just let me wash. Please, old man." His jailor did the now familiar response of pushing his spectacles up his nose and wrung his hands again.

Though Jeremiah received no water to wash with, he asked for it every day.

He was skinny and lost even more weight during the time in the tunnel. The two small meals a day were not enough to put any flesh on his body. Even so, his shoulders and arms became more muscular from swinging the pick and lifting the bags of ore. The shortening of his pant legs told him he was growing taller.

He woke one morning naked and blindfolded, his elbows pulled back with the pole through them, and the rope on his neck. He sat up with difficulty and felt the rope jerk.

"What now, old man? What do you want me to do now?" The rope jerked again, burning into his neck, then it loosened. He understood he was to follow the pull of the rope.

"All right, I understand. You want me to follow you. Just don't jerk the rope, please." Jeremiah had no choice but to follow. The old man led him out of the tunnel into the cold fresh air. Jeremiah took a deep breath; the smell of the desert filled his nostrils. Then the sound of rushing water filled his ears. He heard the sound of the rope thrown over what he guessed was a tree branch and pulled up tight against his neck. He had to follow the pressure of the rope to keep from choking and it forced him forward into the water.

Jeremiah shivered. "It's too cold! Are you crazy old man?" The rope tightened and he couldn't speak. His calves and feet went numb in the freezing cold water, and with the rope over a branch—which ensured his cooperation—he had to stand straight and still to keep from choking. It was effective at forcing him to obey. He stood still in the freezing water up to his knees.

He wondered what kind of crazy torture this was when he felt hands rubbing his body, scrubbing him with a strong soap from the smell. Freezing water poured over his head to rinse the soap off. It took Jeremiah's breath away. The tight blindfold hurt his eyes, but the buckets of cold water poured over his head didn't dislodge it.

Jeremiah shivered uncontrollably and struggled to breathe. He didn't know how long it went on, but he had to be clean from so much soap. Then the rope relaxed and pulled him back into the tunnel.

"No, I can't go back into the tunnel. Please don't make me. Just let me go. Please, just let me go!" The pull of the rope around his neck gave him no choice. Either he went back into the darkness, or he choked to death. At least it was warmer in the tunnel.

He sat down by the support timber deep in the tunnel shivering from the cold bath, but feeling better to be clean for the first time in months. Then he felt the cup against his lips. He smelled the bitter tea and turned his head away. "I don't want it. Please don't make me drink it," Jeremiah pleaded. "Just tell me what you want and I'll do it. You don't have to drug me."

He didn't want it because it was still day, but the old man jerked Jeremiah's head back by his hair. The cup pressed against his lips so hard he had to open his mouth or have his lips cut. Then he tasted the bitter tea in his mouth and he swallowed to keep from drowning. Maybe the old man was afraid he couldn't handle him with the chains or the rope removed unless he was asleep? He lay down, wrapped the blanket around him shivering uncontrollably, and went to sleep.

~

The two doses so close together left Jeremiah more groggy than usual when he woke. The second one must have been weaker as it didn't put him into a deep sleep, but more of a trance. Hands undid the ropes around his elbows, but he couldn't react. Then hands rubbed his body as if to warm him. He still shivered, then he drifted off to sleep again.

He awoke dressed with the blindfold gone from his eyes. The old man sat down the food, water, pick, shovel, and lantern. Jeremiah ate and drank, then went back to work. His life became a sameness of working the ore and bathing in the freezing water every two weeks. A couple of times he walked through snow to get to the stream. The cold air pricked his bare skin. But just to breathe the cold, fresh mountain air was a break from the drudgery of his life in the tunnel.

~

This numbing routine passed the time in slow motion. One day, Jeremiah counted his marks; he'd been in the tunnel for a year. A birthday passed, his seventeenth. Would he ever take enough gold out of the mountain to please the old man? And if so, would he then just abandon him? Jeremiah lived with this fear, and though he asked questions, the old man never answered.

Jeremiah hated his life, but saw no way out. He kept his mind occupied to ward off the black edges of terror. He talked and sang to himself. He quoted from the Bible aloud over and over. He didn't think of escape, or what was beyond the tunnel. If he allowed himself to think, despair reached down and threatened to devour his                                                                                                         soul.

## Chapter 2

As the second year ended, Jeremiah woke to find himself chained again to the support timber from which he could see daylight. It uplifted him a little to be able to see natural light.

Food and water in buckets stood within his reach, but still he waited. The day ended and the old man didn't come. Darkness descended and fear edged into Jeremiah's mind. Without the tea, he couldn't sleep and his waking nightmares accompanied him into the darkness. He wanted his captor to come back. At least with the old man there he wasn't alone. He covered his face with his hands and sobbed like a baby.

By the third day, Jeremiah was so sick he couldn't lift his head. He doubled over from the cramping in his stomach and vomited. Weakness replaced what little strength he had. He either shivered or sweated profusely. Although Jeremiah rationed the food and water and made it last until the old man returned, the sickness tore him up inside.

~

Jeremiah tried to keep track of the days, and on the tenth day, the old man returned. Immediately, the old man sat a cup of tea down for Jeremiah to drink, and then stood back wringing his hands. Without the drug running through his body the past ten days, Jeremiah realized his mind was much clearer. He didn't want to drink it, but the sickness forced him to seek relief—he drank the bitter addiction.

When he woke without clothes and blindfolded, he got to his feet, ready to be taken down to the stream. After entering the stream, hands scrubbed his body with a bar of soap and washed his hair. As usual, the cold water took his breath away, and he was eager to get back into the tunnel where it was warmer.

He didn't resist the rope that guided him back to the support timber. He sat down without prodding. He had no resistance left in him. Whatever the old man indicated, he did. He didn't know how many more months he could take of his prison. Could dying be much worse?

In a little while, the old man came back with another cup of tea. Jeremiah drank it. It was a small dose as he was aware but couldn't move. Hands on his wrist removed the irons and then put a shirt on him. They returned the irons back on his wrists. Then the shackles on his ankles opened and pants were put on him. For the first time in two years, boots slipped onto his feet.

The old man went away, and then Jeremiah awoke to the pain of a hand in his hair, pulling him up. He sat up and the pole pushed behind his elbows. His arms, tied to the pole, were pulled back tighter than they had been in years. He was now unable to move his hands chained in front of his body. The tight blindfold still covered his eyes. He heard the chain undone from his ankles. The rope circled around his neck. As it tightened, he managed to stand. He followed the rope until he stepped out of the tunnel. The cool breeze tickled his face, and then he walked until he stood next to a burro. He smelled it, and then he felt it.

Jeremiah stumbled when pushed from behind, and he realized that the old man wanted him to mount the burro. He did so with difficulty.

The old man tied his feet under the burro's belly after he put the ankle irons back on. Now he was one with the burro no matter what the burro did. The old man forced Jeremiah to lie down on the burro's back and then he tied a rope around his body. A cup parted his lips, and Jeremiah drank the bitter potion. The burro started walking as he fell asleep.

Several days of traveling passed with Jeremiah drugged most of the time. The hot sun beat down, but they traveled on. Because of the bitter tea, he didn't even wonder where they were going. They stopped for the burro to rest and the old man gave Jeremiah a drink from a canteen. Then just before they started traveling, the old man held the cup to Jeremiah's lips again. He could tell that this cup of tea was very strong and bitter. For some reason the old man wanted him to be in a deep sleep. He didn't resist. Sleep was his refuge.

He woke lying on a blanket in the mouth of a cave, but it wasn't the tunnel. His blindfold was gone along with the irons from his feet and wrists. Jeremiah reached up and touched his neck. The rope was gone. He looked around. The old man was gone. Five canteens of water, three packs, haversack, and two burros stood close by. Jeremiah clutched his stomach as waves of nausea overwhelmed him.

While not physically bound, invisible chains held Jeremiah in place. He waited for the old man. After several hours, he began to think the old man wasn't coming back. What if...? No, the thought was too unbelievable. Jeremiah shook his head. Afraid to hope, he waited. He felt his neck again. Remembered the torturous burn of the rope, and still he waited. Could his captor have set him free? His stomach cramped. He didn't know how to act. He knew he should feel something, but he was dead inside.

He stood up and looked around. He found food, several sets of clothes, a shaving kit, three heavy leather bags of gold, and a note. Jeremiah wiped his sweaty palms on his pants. He sat holding it with shaking hands for several minutes before he unfolded it.

*Jeremiah, go northeast to Phoenix. Five day walk if you follow the map. Watch out for Indians. Remember the law wants you in Arizona. You escaped from the prison wagon. Get out of Arizona Territory. You dug the gold. You have half of it. What you do with your life is now your choice. Forgive me.*

His hands shook and he shouted at the piece of paper, "Forgive you? Old man, you stole two years of my life. I will find you and you will pay. But forgive you? Not in this lifetime!" His hoarse voice echoed back to him with no answer.

Jeremiah opened one of the heavy leather bags and fingered the gold. He didn't know how much was there, but the two burros would have a hard time carrying it out of the desert. If he wanted to take it, he'd have to walk it out. He had earned every ounce of it. After loading everything onto the burros, he began to walk northeast. The five canteens of water would have to be enough to get him to the spring that was his first landmark.

He longed for a horse. It had been three years since he had been on one. He had a lot to get used to again. It was cool, but with a bright sun in the desert. Jeremiah put on the hat the old man left him and pulled it low on his forehead. Though the bright sun hurt his sensitive eyes after so much time in darkness, he took a moment to appreciate its warmth on his skin. He looked to the sky and took in the sound that had gotten his attention. Birds, a sound he hadn't heard in two years. As he walked close to some bushes, he squinted his eyes against the dust that swirled about from the stiff breeze. Birds, crickets, wind among the leaves, every new sound that he recognized were a delight after such a long time of silence.

Dusk was descending as he reached the spring marked on the map. He scanned the area before he made a small fire and boiled some tea in the pot he found in one of the packs. He drank the tea out of habit, but it tasted different. He craved the bitterness. Sleep didn't come for hours and when it did, he dreamed of the tunnel and the old man.

He awoke to a sick feeling. His body ached all over and he had no appetite. He shivered and held his cramping stomach. He got the packs on the burros and started northeast. Several times in the day, he stopped and vomited. With each hour, he grew sicker. His hands shook and he perspired even though the day was cool.

That night he hardly slept, and he longed for the old man's bitter tea. He kept the campfire going all night to drive the darkness away. He got up at first light and vomited again. The stomach cramps racked his aching body. But he kept going.

By the third day of walking, Jeremiah was unable to eat. A nervous restlessness overtook him. His flesh crawled and severe weakness threatened to split him in two. He didn't know what was wrong with him. His mind got clearer as his body got sicker. Each time the old man had gone away he had gotten sick like this. Was it something to do with not having access to the bitter tea?

~

On the fifth day after being set free, he reached the edge of Phoenix. Only fifteen buildings and houses—with several more in the process of being built—made up the town. But it was more town than Jeremiah had seen in several years. He camped outside of town and considered what to do. He found some bushes and rocks where he hid the gold except for a small bag that he took with him. The burros he tied up to the bushes with enough lead rope that they could graze. First, he needed help with his sickness and he was hungry for something to eat besides cornbread, beans, and rice. Strolling into the town, he noticed a big tent with a hotel sign that also offered meals. His hunger pushed him to walk into the tent hotel and find the dining area. He sat at a table next to a wall of canvas.

An older man came up to the table. "What can I get you to eat?"

So wondrous was the sound of another person's voice that it took Jeremiah a moment to realize he needed to answer. "What do you have?" It seemed strange to speak to people who spoke back to him.

"Well, young man, we have beans and tamales, but the best thing today is the special, boiled chicken and dumplings."

"Please bring me some of that and some water." Jeremiah couldn't seem to get enough to drink.

He ate half of it before his stomach started cramping.

The waiter returned. "You all right, young man?"

"You all got a doctor in this town?" Jeremiah fought to hold down his dinner.

"Sure, Doc Jones just moved into town. You go out to the left and you'll see a small tent. That's where he's doctoring until his place is built."

"Thanks." Jeremiah left the man a couple of gold nuggets and walked down to the doctor's tent. He didn't really want to see a doctor, but he also didn't want to continue to be so sick.

He looked in the tent. A short baldheaded man wearing black pants, white shirt, and tie sat behind a desk.

"You the doc?" Jeremiah hesitantly edged into the tent.

The man looked up and adjusted his glasses. "Sure am. Come on in young fellow. What can I do for you?" He stood up and walked around the desk.

"I wondered if you might be able to help me. I been real sick lately and feel pretty sick right now." Jeremiah's body shook as he wiped the sweat from his forehead.

"Sit down in this chair and let me take a look at you." The doctor guided Jeremiah to a chair and looked at his eyes.

"Open your mouth. Tell me about your illness."

Jeremiah obliged, telling the older man about the shakes, stomach problems, and generally feeling miserable.

"Tell me how long you been sick."

Jeremiah cringed when the doctor touched him. It reminded him of the voiceless hands touching him in the tunnel. But he needed relief from the sickness. He took a deep breath. "About five days. I can't eat or sleep. I'm either sweating or shivering. And I got no strength."

"You're awfully thin and your pallor indicates lack of sun. You mind if I ask if you've been in prison? I'm not trying to be rude, but it would help me to know."

Jeremiah hesitated. In a way, he'd just gotten out of the most awful prison one could imagine, but he never wanted to tell anyone about it.

"You're right. I just got out of prison, but I got sick after." Let the doctor think it was Yuma Prison. That is where the prison wagon was taking him anyway.

The doctor adjusted his glasses, and then rolled up his sleeves. "I don't know what the problem is, but I can give you something to take for the cramping." He turned to the cabinet beside him. "I'd suggest that you try to take it easy and eat plain foods like soup, and no meat, beans, or chili peppers. If you're not better in a couple of days come back to see me."

"All right, I'll try that." Jeremiah would not be back as he planned to buy a couple of horses and head out of Arizona Territory. But he took the powder in a little tin box the doctor gave him for his stomach.

"About three times a day mix a tablespoon of the powder in water and drink it before you try to eat anything. That should help." The man seemed kindly enough.

Jeremiah nodded and handed the doctor several gold nuggets.

The doc examined the nuggets. "Thanks, I appreciate the payment. Now, if you're not better in a couple of days come on back and I'll try to help."

Edging toward the flap that was the door to the doctor's office, Jeremiah said, "Good-bye, Doc." He quickly stepped out into the dusty street.

After leaving the doctor's office, he found the livery where he bought a dun gelding, two brown mares, two packsaddles, and a saddle. At the general store, he stocked up on provisions and camping supplies which he packed onto the two packhorses. No one seemed to question getting paid in gold nuggets.

Watching his back trail to make sure no one followed him from the town, he returned to where he had left the gold. He retrieved it and packed it on the two of the packhorses with his supplies. The larger of the brown mares he saddled and packed light as it would also carry his weight. He quietly herded the two burros toward a small adobe house on the edge of town and let them into the pen that already held a small burro. Keeping out of sight of the house, he returned to his waiting horses. Tired of walking, Jeremiah mounted the brown mare while leading the two packhorses and rode east heading for the Arizona border.

~

Jeremiah's weak leg muscles made the first few days of riding difficult. The powder the doc gave him that he mixed a spoonful into a cup of water stopped the cramping and vomiting. After another fifteen days on the trail, Jeremiah sensed his body returning to normal physically. He did not know if he would ever be normal in his mind. As he rode, he couldn't shake the memories of the tunnel.

How would he find the old man? He had nothing to go by. His mind refused to settle down. The craziest of all was that he missed the old man. Most of all he missed the bitter tea. He ached for the numbing sleep where he felt nothing. The bitter tea had freed him even though he had been chained inside the tunnel. He craved an escape from the images and thoughts that imprisoned him.

The nightmares were the worst. He seldom slept, and when he did sleep, he dreamed of waking again alone in the tunnel, forever chained to the support timber with a presence watching him, but never helping. His own agonizing moans woke him. After surviving the two years in the tunnel, was he was finally losing his mind?

Still, he pressed on.

~

Jeremiah rode carefully as he entered the flow of traffic at the outskirts of Austin, Texas. He looked constantly around him as he led his two packhorses down the street with trolley rails down the middle and gaslights along the sidewalks. He had never been to such a large city.

Spotting an older man dressed very smartly in a suit and hat standing on the sidewalk, he slowed his horses and angled over.

Removing his hat, Jeremiah said, "Excuse me, sir."

The man looked up at him, "Hello, young man. Can I help you?"

"Yes, sir. Can you direct me toward a bank?" Jeremiah needed to get some of the gold stored some place, and having helped his father, and then George, rob enough of them, he understood how banks worked.

Pointing down the street, the man said, "Try Bremond's place. Eugene does banking business out of his dry goods store on Pecan Street."

"Thank you and could you recommend a place to stay?"

The man looked over Jeremiah's dusty, trail worn appearance and frowned. "Mrs. Hendrix has a rooming house up the street. She lets people staying with her keep their horses in the barn behind the house."

Jeremiah tipped his hat, "Thank you, sir." Then he maneuvered his horses back into the stream of traffic. When he found the three-story rooming house, he wasn't sure he wanted to stay as it looked confining. But he was tired and his horses needed to be rested.

Taking a deep breath, he dismounted, tied his horses to the hitching post, and walked up the three steps to the porch. After knocking on the door, he took off his hat and wiped his forehead with his sleeve.

The door opened to reveal a grey haired woman dressed very conservatively in a black taffeta dress. "May I help you?"

"Yes, ma'am. A fellow down the street said you rent out rooms." Why Jeremiah felt so nervous with the woman, he couldn't say but his mouth was dry and he wanted to get on his horse and ride out of town.

The woman opened the door more widely and said, "I sure do. Come in. I'm Mrs. Hendrix."

Jeremiah stepped into the cool, dark hallway that for a moment made him think of the tunnel. "Do you have a room with a balcony?" The more open to the sky, the better.

"Yes, one of the back rooms with a balcony is available. I charge a dollar a day that includes letting you keep your horses in my barn. Feed for your horses is fifty cents more a day." The woman led the way up a flight of stairs and opened the door to a small room facing toward the back of the large three-story house. The room was furnished with a double bed made up with a quilt cover, a small chest on which a bowl and pitcher, and lamp sat, and a ladder-back chair by the window. The floor was bare except for a small rag rug by the bed.

Jeremiah walked over and opened the French door to the balcony. "I'll take the room."

Mrs. Hendrix frowned. "I need you to pay in advance."

"Yes, ma'am. All I got until I go to the bank is gold nuggets."

"Oh, well. Bremond's is just down the street. He buys gold."

"May I take care of my horses first?"

She nodded, "Yes, go ahead and leave your horses and pay me this evening. Do you want to eat supper here?"

Jeremiah shrugged. "No thanks, I'll find a place in town to eat." He still was having to be careful what he ate and sitting down with a group of strangers was too off putting.

After taking care of his horses in the barn behind the boarding house, he hid two of the packs of gold behind stacks of hay and packed the other one on the dun horse. Leading the gelding, he walked down Pecan Street to the Bremond store. A placard in the window advertised the availability of banking and currency exchange. Carrying the pack that weighted at least a hundred pounds, he entered the dry goods store.

A tall, thin baldheaded man stood behind a counter. "Welcome, what can I do for you, young man?"

Nervous, but determined, Jeremiah set the pack at his feet. "The banker in?"

The man smiled. "You must mean Mr. Bremond. Let me get him." He walked through a curtained doorway.

Jeremiah could hear a deep voice and then a grey-headed man wearing spectacles came through the doorway, followed by the clerk.

"I'm Bremond. How can I help you?"

Jeremiah liked the solid look of the man. "You buy gold?"

Bremond looked Jeremiah over before answering, "Yes, you got some to sell?"

Jeremiah nodded.

Bremond started walking back toward the curtained doorway. "Come with me."

Picking up the heavy pack, Jeremiah followed the man into the back room of the store and found himself in a cluttered office dominated by a large metal safe behind an old wooden desk. Hoisting the pack onto the desk, Jeremiah waited for the man to sit in the chair behind it.

Bremond looked at the pack and raised his eyebrows. "That pack full of gold?"

Jeremiah opened the top of the pack and took out a handful of gold nuggets. He scattered them on the desk.

The older man picked up one of the nuggets, pushed his spectacles up on his nose, and closely examined the gold. "Where did you get this much gold young man? I don't deal with stolen goods."

Not sure how to answer Jeremiah took a deep breath. "I just spent two years digging in the dirt for this. I didn't steal it. But I'm also not going to tell you where the mine is."

Bremond searched Jeremiah's face as if he was trying to discern the truth of his statement. "I think I will take your word. You seem honest and too young to have gotten into too much trouble. Let me weigh it out and see how much I want to buy from you."

Jeremiah relaxed a bit. If the man only knew whom he was dealing with, but Jeremiah was not going to tell him.

It took the man almost an hour to weigh all the gold and figure how much he would pay for it. Finally, he looked up at Jeremiah and said, "The going rate for gold is $18.94 an ounce. You have a little over a hundred pounds here. I will offer you $17.00 an ounce and handle the sale of the gold. That comes to about twenty seven thousand dollars. If you want, I will bank your money at 1% interest for six months and at 3% interest for a year."

Jeremiah looked at the man. Could he be trusted? Not really caring about the money, he nodded at Bremond. "All right, I accept your offer. I want a couple hundred in gold coins to take with me. I plan to do some traveling. Also, how can I get to my money without having to return to Austin?"

Bremond turned and opened the safe. He took out a tray with gold coins stacked on it. "I have ten and twenty dollar gold coins. When you want to withdraw some of your money from my bank, you wire me the amount and the nearest bank. I will send a bank draft to that bank and they will make the money available to you. It can take a couple of weeks so don't be in a hurry. Of course, if you come in here I can have the money available much quicker."

Jeremiah didn't like the idea of leaving his money behind but he still had two more sacks of gold. Just this one sack was a fortune. He could live off it for years even buy his own ranch. He couldn't say why, but he trusted Bremond.

Filling a small leather pouch with the gold coins, Bremond slid it to Jeremiah. "Give me a minute and I will open your account and give you a receipt." He pulled a ledger out of the safe and began to write in it. "What name do you want on the account?"

"Jeremiah Rebourn." He spelled out the last name as he picked up the leather pouch of gold coins and slipped it into his pocket. Jeremiah Anderson had been the name he was known by in Arizona and had been arrested under. The name Jeremiah Rebourn was what his father had named him and very few people knew the name.

"Address?" Bremond looked up expectantly.

"Don't really have one." Jeremiah had no idea where he would end up.

"For a yearly fee of five dollars I'll act as your contact person. Let me know where you are and if anything comes for you I will mail it on to you."

Jeremiah felt relief that the man could solve the problem so easily. "That sounds fine with me."

"Son, this is a lot of money and it will grow for you. Be wise in how you spend it and it can provide for you and your family." The man's voice had a sincerity that Jeremiah heard.

"Thanks, Mr. Bremond. I'll try to be wise." Jeremiah watched as Bremond hefted the bag of gold into the safe, closed the door, and locked it.

After leaving the store, Jeremiah got the packhorse and led him back to the barn behind the boarding house. Having only two more of the heavy sacks of gold after leaving one secured in the hands of Bremand helped him feel like a small burden had been lifted. What was he to do with the rest of the gold? He took the bridle and harness off the packhorse, fed and watered him, and let him into the small corral attached to the barn. In a way, the gold was a burden. He wanted to get rid of it and be free just to ride. But someday he might want what the gold could buy for him. Not putting all of it in one place seemed like a good idea. After he rested up a couple of days, he would head out for another large town and bank some more of the gold until he had it all stored somewhere making money for him.

After a fitful night trying to sleep in the small room, he ended up making a pallet on the balcony with the lamp on all night. He never wanted to be in a dark place again. Jeremiah wanted to buy some new clothes, get a bath, a haircut, and then head out of town. His uneasiness seemed to grow by the minute and eating was still a problem.

His first stop after leaving the boarding house was John Bremond & Company Mercantile where he purchased two pair of pants, a couple of shirts, underpants, socks, and a new pair of boots. He found a public bathhouse where for fifteen cents he got a tub bath with hot water. It felt so good to sink into the full tub, Jeremiah vowed that he'd never bathe in cold water again. After the luxury of toweling off with a clean towel, he put on his new clothes and went in search of a barber.

He went into a small barbershop. But when he sat in the chair he started breathing hard and broke into a sweat. The wrap the barber put around his neck sent chills of panic down his spine. Then the barber touched his hair, and Jeremiah felt the old man's hand grabbing his hair. He couldn't take it. Jerking the wrap off, he ran from the shop without a word. He walked the streets for hours trying to make sense of his panic. He had to get a grip on himself or he'd truly go crazy.

The next day he went to a different barber. This time he refused the wrap around his neck. He wiped the sweat from his shaking hands on his pants. It took everything he could muster to sit and let the barber cut his hair. It brought back all the feelings of the tunnel. What was wrong with him that he couldn't bear to even have his head touched? As quickly as he could he got out of the barbershop and stopped by the dry goods store to purchase enough provisions for two weeks on the trail. The farther he got from the tunnel, the more things bothered him. He had to get out of the town.

The next day he packed his provisions on the two packhorses along with the rest of the gold and traveled northwest toward Denver. He took his time and rode parallel to the Western Cattle Trail. After three weeks of riding, he came to Denver. He went to the largest bank and again deposited another bag of the gold. After staying only a couple of days in Denver, he headed out again. He really didn't know where he was going, but he was too restless to stay put.

Jeremiah tried to take a good look at himself. He couldn't think clearly as images and feelings of his time in the tunnel smothered the reality of now. He didn't remember being this way before the tunnel. Had the time in the tunnel done something to his mind? What could he do about it if he was crazy? What was he going to do with the rest of his life? He was only eighteen and had the gold. He was rich, but he didn't want anything that gold would buy. What did he want? He was so worn out that he couldn't stop his thoughts. He just wanted to rest and get some peace.

~

Three months after he had been freed from the tunnel, he rode into Cheyenne, Wyoming. At the mercantile, he overheard a couple of old men talking about the high mountains to the south in Colorado. Maybe he could ride into the mountains and get lost. Maybe he would be better away from people and towns. He deposited his last bag of gold in a bank and sold one of his packhorses. He now had large accounts in three different banks any one of which was a small fortune. Jeremiah was wealthy but none of that was important. His mind was so chaotic that nothing mattered.

He bought enough provisions for a month and packed it on one of the horses. He chose the normal amount of provisions for a few weeks of camping, except he packed four lanterns and enough lamp oil for six months use.

He headed southwest into the mountains. At night he camped by streams and kept a lantern lit to keep the darkness at bay. It was crazy and even dangerous, but he couldn't stand the dark. When morning came he sat and watched the sunrise. The lift to his spirits seemed to follow the lightning of the sky as the sun rose in the east and revealed the bright Colorado morning sky. After spending so much time in the darkness of the tunnel unable to see either a sunrise or sunset, he soaked in the glory of a new day.

In the late afternoon of the third day of travel after leaving Cheyenne, he opened a wooden gate and passed through a gap that led into a big valley surrounded by high mountains. For some reason he decided to go into the valley and see who lived there. He wanted the sound of a human voice. Being careful to close and fasten the gate behind him, he rode into valley where he saw log houses and barns, and several smaller buildings. The broad valley went on for miles. Its beauty spoke to Jeremiah's heart and calmed his spirits. He breathed in the magnificence that surrounded him. A large stream ran down the middle of the broad valley. High hills and then snow-capped mountains dotted the landscape beyond the valley. He spent several moments appreciating what this land made him feel inside, a calmness.

Jeremiah rode up to the big house where a tall dark-haired man waited on the porch.

"Welcome to the Rocking ES. I'm Elisha Evans, the owner." Elisha's deep mellow voice put Jeremiah at ease.

"Jeremiah Rebourn. I'm just riding through."

Elisha stepped down from the porch. "Well, we're always happy to have visitors. Get down and I'll show you were to put your horses. You can bunk in the bunkroom if you want to. We'll be called to supper in about fifteen minutes. You're welcome to join us."

Jeremiah dismounted. "That's mighty kind of you. Would you mind if I just sleep on the porch or I can just camp out? I'm used to sleeping outdoors." No way was he going to sleep in a bunkhouse full of strangers.

"Not at all. But you'll eat with us?" Elisha asked as he walked with Jeremiah to the corral by the big barn.

"I'll be glad to eat with you." Jeremiah took the saddle and bridle from his sorrel horse and the pack off the dun gelding.

Elisha showed him where to find some hay for his horses. The corral had a trough with water running into it from a pipe.

As he looked around, Jeremiah liked the tidiness of the place.

Elisha helped Jeremiah carry his pack and saddle to the front porch away. "We'll leave your things here on the porch. If you change your mind, the bunkroom is through that door there on the western end of the house."

Jeremiah nodded but could think of nothing to say in response.

Elisha opened the front door. "Follow me." He led the way through a large front room and into a large kitchen.

Jeremiah almost turned and walked right back out. People filled the large kitchen including three small children. Jeremiah swallowed the lump in his throat. Everyone talked and laughed, around a huge table already set for supper.

Elisha raised his hand for silence. "Folks, this is Jeremiah who's traveling through. He's stopping over for the night."

Jeremiah removed his hat and ducked his head. "Hello."

Elisha put his hand on Jeremiah's shoulder. Jeremiah tensed and gripped his hat to keep from shaking.

Elisha removed his hand as if aware of Jeremiah's reaction and motioned in front of him. "I'll introduce the most important people and the rest will have to introduce themselves later." He pointed to a petite woman with brown hair. "This is my wife Susana."

Jeremiah nodded. "Ma'am."

"It's nice to meet you Jeremiah. And please, call me Susana." The beautiful lady smiled up at him.

Jeremiah fiddled with the bandana around his neck as heat rose to his face. "Thank you, Susana."

Elisha motioned to a rotund man with thick gray hair holding a bowl of potatoes. "This is Cookie. He's in charge of the kitchen."

Cookie set the bowl on the table, and then shook Jeremiah's hand. "Jeremiah."

Jeremiah pulled his sleeve down over his scars. "Nice to meet you, Cookie."

Elisha guided him to the table. "Sit down here by me."

Jeremiah sat in the chair indicated and looked at the smiling faces around him. No one took the food, not even the children. They waited for something. Then Elisha Evans spoke, his mellow voice soothed Jeremiah.

"Our Heavenly Father, we thank you for all that you have blessed us with today. We thank you for our visitor, Jeremiah. Bless him in his travels. Bless this food and the hands that prepared it. Thank you for keeping everyone safe in their work this day. We ask in the name of Jesus the Christ. Amen."

Several said amen and then everyone reached for and passed the bowls and platters of food. Jeremiah took some roast beef, potatoes, gravy, green beans, and biscuits. Elisha poured him a cup of coffee. Everyone ate, and talking reduced to a minimum, which was all right with Jeremiah. He ate almost everything on his plate, but even he noticed the others ate much more.

"Eat all you want," Elisha said.

"Thank you. This is good grub. I don't usually have much appetite," Jeremiah confessed.

Elisha wiped his mouth on his cloth napkin. "You're riding to somewhere? I ask because this ranch isn't on any particular trail."

Jeremiah set his coffee cup down. "No, sir, I just left Cheyenne and started riding and ended up here. I just wanted to see some country."

A slender man with dark brown hair refilled Jeremiah's coffee cup. "Well, if you want to see some of God's good country you came to the right place." He chuckled. "We got lots of country here. By the way, I'm Joe Weathers." He looked at the beautiful woman seated beside him. "And this is my wife Sara."

Jeremiah nodded. "Ma'am."

He stared at this unusually handsome couple. Sara had the prettiest blond hair and blue eyes that Jeremiah had ever seen.

Five attractive women sat around the huge table, although Susana Evans and Sara Weathers were truly beautiful. Staring at the women stirred something inside Jeremiah. He caught himself and looked down at his plate. However, the others didn't seem to notice as they talked among themselves and left the table at the end of the meal.

The low setting sun caused Jeremiah's stomach to lurch. He wanted to get his bedroll set up and his lantern lit before it got full dark. He turned to Elisha. "I'm worn out from traveling. Thank you for the good meal. If you don't mind I sometimes read awhile before I turn my lantern out." Jeremiah prayed Elisha accepted this by way of explanation.

Elisha gave him a warm smile. "We don't mind at all. Go on and get some rest. We'll see you at breakfast." Elisha walked him out to the porch. "And Jeremiah, you're more than welcome to stay a few days."

Jeremiah stopped and turned to him. "But you don't even know me. Why would you do that?" He found the kindness of this man disconcerting.

Elisha slowly brought his hand up and placed it on Jeremiah's shoulder. "Because it gives us pleasure to be good neighbors to all who might come through. God will bless us for it."

"Sort of like 'all those who are heavy laden and in need of rest'?"

Elisha cocked his head. "Exactly like that. You know your Bible. I like a man who knows his Bible." Elisha smiled at Jeremiah.

"Then I may take you up on it." The idea of stopping for a while to rest up and maybe think about what he wanted to do wasn't a bad idea. The man's welcome and his offer seemed sincere.

"Then I'll leave you and see you for breakfast. May God bless you with a peaceful night of rest." Elisha went into the house.

Jeremiah lit his lantern and spread out his bedroll. He didn't require much as the years sleeping on the bare earth of the tunnel had hardened him. The supper has been good and the most relaxed meal he had had in years. What kind of people had he stumbled upon? They seemed too kind and almost gentle. He shrugged. But maybe that was what he needed.

He turned the lantern down, hoping the oil would last through the night. Settled on his bedroll, he prayed sleep would come. It came finally, but so did the dream—the same one of awaking alone in the tunnel. He woke and lay there, waiting for dawn as he did most nights.

## Chapter 3

Elisha went back into the house after getting the boy settled on the porch. He ran his hands through his hair and sank into his favorite chair. Elisha couldn't put his finger on what troubled him about the young man. Jeremiah seemed polite enough, but he was too quiet in a watchful way. Elisha suspected he wanted to be on the porch so he could leave a light on through the night.

Susana came and sat on the arm of the overstuffed chair. "Are you coming to bed soon?" She reached over and rubbed his shoulders.

He slipped his arm around her waist and pulled her onto his lap. "Yes, I think bed would be a good idea." He grinned at her.

"Oh, Elisha," she said, laughing at him. She kissed him, and then straightened. "Did you get Jeremiah settled on the porch?"

He nodded and looked deep into his wife's eyes. "I told him to stay a few days if he wanted to. He seems sort of lost."

Susana toyed with Elisha's hair, wrapping a dark curl around her finger. "Well, we can try to be a blessing for him. Perhaps he just needs a healthy dose of kindness." She put her arms around his neck and looked into his dark eyes. "You can be a big brother to him if that's what he needs."

"I'll ask the boys to let him ride along; they won't ask him any questions. Maybe he just needs to get out and see some country like he said." He cocked his head at Susana. "He quoted scripture when I tried to answer his question of why we would let him stay."

"Then at least we know he's read the Bible. Now Mr. Evans what would you think about taking me to bed?"

Elisha grinned. "Well, Mrs. Evans, I'm right proud to take you to bed with me." With that they got up and, holding hands, walked to their bedroom.

~

During the night, a strange noise woke Elisha. He slipped out of bed and walked barefoot to the front of the house. When he approached the front door, he realized Jeremiah was moaning in his sleep. Elisha's heart broke for this troubled young man. The lantern gave off a soft glow. He decided not to disturb Jeremiah as he sensed that what little sleep that the young man got was uneasy. Elisha stood for several minutes and prayed for him, and then went back to his bed.

Susana held up the blanket for him to slip back into bed. "What is it?"

Elisha snuggled down under the covers. "It's the boy on the porch. He's moaning in his sleep. The lantern is still on as if he's afraid to be in the dark." He pulled his wife to him. "Honey, I feel we need to try and help this young man. I don't know in what way we can help, but I think he's a very troubled soul."

Susana wiggled closer to Elisha. "He seemed sweet and he's awfully handsome with those broad shoulders and thick dark hair. But his eyes look haunted. He reminds me of how Joe looked when he first got here." She fluffed her pillow. "How old do you think he is? One minute at supper he looked younger than Billy who is seventeen, and then the next, something would come over his face and he looked terribly old." Susana turned over and spooned up against Elisha.

He encircled her in his arms, pressed her back against his chest, and buried his face in her hair so that he could smell the sweet scent of flowers from her shampoo. Elisha had bought it for her on his last trip to Cheyenne. "I think he's probably about eighteen. I'm going to suggest to everyone just to let him be. It's kind of like taking care of a wounded bird."

"We know how to do that. Just as Sam Weathers did for you and you did for me at the cabin."

"Hmmm . . . see you in the morning." At peace, Elisha drifted off to sleep.

~ ~ ~

The sky to the east was beginning to lighten the shadows of the valley as Jeremiah woke. He stood at the end of the porch and silently observed the beauty of the sunrise. Such a gift to be able to be free and take time for the sunrise. He never wanted to miss another one.

Jeremiah entered a noisy kitchen where work on the ranch controlled the conversation. He ate his breakfast and tried to respond as people spoke to him. He learned that Joe Weathers was a partner with Elisha and responsible for the horse business.

Bob Fife, the ranch foreman, acknowledged Jeremiah with a strong nod. His wife Minnie greeted Jeremiah as she sat down at the table beside her husband. Bob passed Jeremiah the coffee pot before filling his plate.

"Here, Jeremiah." A young redheaded fellow placed another biscuit on Jeremiah's plate.

"Thanks," Jeremiah managed to say.

"I'm Jeff Kingston, by the way." He turned to the pretty brunette beside him. "And this is my wife Anna." Jeff then passed the plate of biscuits to Elisha.

Anna smiled at Jeremiah. "Jeff is one of the riders, and I help out here at the house."

"It's nice to meet you, Ma'am." Jeremiah ducked his head and examined his plate.

Jeremiah was a rider and knew how to herd cattle, but he had never worked on a ranch. The cattle he helped brand had been ones stolen by the men he rode with. Of course, he wasn't about to tell these people that. The work on the big ranch intrigued Jeremiah.

He looked up when a couple entered the kitchen speaking Spanish.

The man removed his sombrero and nodded at Jeremiah. "*Hola*. My name is Santo and my wife is Mara. We come from *Nuevo Méjico*."

Jeremiah nodded. "Hola, Señor y Señora. Encantado de conocerte."

Elisha sat with his fork in midair. "You speak Spanish?"

"Yes, since I was a child." Jeremiah omitted that he'd learned from Mexicans who had occasionally ridden with the outlaw gang who had raised him. He regretted making the revelation. What if these people asked him more questions? Jeremiah looked down at his plate again, letting his dark brown hair hide his flushed face.

Joe broke the silence by stabbing another piece of ham from the huge platter in the middle of the table. "Santo works with me most days, breaking horses. Mara helps take care of the children."

Jeremiah cast a glance at the three small children sitting between Susana and Elisha. They grinned back at him.

Joe pointed his fork at a young man with a thin face. "Jim here's a rider too."

Jeremiah watched Jim take a bite; his almost delicate hands seemed to caress the fork. Jeremiah imagined the horses responded well to his gentleness.

Jim elbowed the boy who sat beside him. "And Billy's the youngest rider on the ranch. We'll make a cowboy out of him yet."

The round-faced kid, no older than Jeremiah, brushed his brown hair out of his eyes, and grinned from ear to ear.

Jeremiah looked around the table and matched everyone's face to a name. His eyes fell on one man he hadn't been introduced to. He spoke with an accent that Jeremiah couldn't put his finger on. The man caught Jeremiah staring and rose from his chair. He came around the table and held out his hand to Jeremiah. "I am Jacob Blunfeld. I pretend to ride here." He laughed along with the others.

Jeremiah didn't know what to say to the man and had no idea why everyone was laughing at what the man had said, so he just shook his hand.

Elisha seemed to sense his uneasiness. He put his fork down and smiled at Jeremiah. "Jacob comes from Germany. He may not be the best rider here at Rocking ES, but he can build anything out of a piece of wood. You'll see Jacob's handiwork on almost every structure here."

Jacob smiled at Elisha's praise. "*Ya*. You want anything built—" He pounded his chest. "you tell Jacob."

Cookie turned from the stove and wiped his hands on the apron that encircled his broad form. He stepped up and took Jeremiah's almost empty plate. "Oh my. Didn't you like the food, Jeremiah?" Concern washed across his bright, cheerful face.

Jeremiah gave him a reassuring nod. "Oh, yes sir. I liked it very much." The last thing he wanted to do was offend Cookie after he'd worked so hard to feed him. "I'm just not used to eating large amounts at one time." Jeremiah feared that eating too much would provoke the cramping and vomiting he worked so hard to keep under control.

Cookie nodded. "Oh my. Don't you worry none. I'll fatten you up."

As the men drifted out of the kitchen into the ranch yard, Jeremiah could hear the women chatting. The relaxed sense as everyone started their work day was interesting. Jeremiah followed Jeff out into the yard.

Joe stepped out into the yard behind Jeremiah and Jeff. "Jeremiah, I work the horses most days with Jim and Santo. If you want you can come along and watch." He leaned on his left leg. "We're breaking wild horses for the army and also horses that we're breeding here on the ranch."

Joe's smile put Jeremiah at ease. He nodded. "I'd like that. Let me get my horses taken care of and get one saddled."

Jeff raised his hand. "Don't worry about feeding your horses." He adjusted his hat. "I took care of all the horses in the corral before breakfast. Just get your horse saddled and ride out with Joe."

"Thanks, that was kind of you." Jeremiah was proud of himself for responding in a normal way as he had observed others do.

Joe got a funny-looking cart out and hitched up a horse. He winced as he climbed up on the seat of the cart, then he turned to Jeremiah.

Jeremiah realized he was staring and shook his head. "I'm sorry. I've never seen a cart like that."

Joe rubbed his right hip. "Ride alongside me and I'll tell you why I use it rather than ride a horse." Joe clicked twice and started the little Indian Cayuse pony down the trail.

Jeremiah matched his speed as he rode his sorrel. "You don't have to tell me anything unless you want. It's not my business why folks do things."

"No, I don't mind telling you," Joe said cheerfully, though it was clear his hip was hurting him. "I used to be a rider and worked a lot with cattle, but I was injured about three years ago." He clucked his tongue and the pony went into a trot. "After the broken bones healed I couldn't sit on a horse. It damaged my right hip. But with this cart I get around and can still work with horses. Only thing is that one of the riders has to finish off the horses I break. I get it started and they do the riding." He looked over at Jeremiah. "We sell about three hundred horses a year off the ranch. So it works out." Joe turned off the main trail down the valley and rode up to a fence gate at a box canyon. "If you'll open the gate and then after I get through close it back up."

Jeremiah opened the gate and waited for Joe to drive his cart through, and then followed him after he tied up the gate. The box canyon—several miles long—held several corrals with horses of all ages and coloring. Dozens of mares carried foals.

Joe stopped at a fence that enclosed several acres of good grass. He got down from the cart and opened a gate.

Jeremiah tied up his horse and walked behind Joe into the corral.

Joe made a soft cooing sound and the horses all raised their heads and, with their ears pointed forward, looked at Joe. Several of them walked toward him.

"Just stand quiet and still." Joe walked slowly up to the mares.

Joe was about fifteen feet in front of Jeremiah. Several of the mares came right up to Joe and nosed at him. He gave them cubes of sugar and patted them on the neck. Joe examined several of the mares. Then he walked back toward the gate, motioning for Jeremiah to follow him.

About twenty of the mares slowly followed them. The mares stopped when Jeremiah looked over his shoulder and then started again as he looked away.

After they left the corral, Joe tied up the gate and the mares came to the fence and poked their heads over. They paid as much attention to Jeremiah as to Joe. Joe didn't say anything, but Jeremiah tried to understand the strange look he gave him. They went over to another big corral.

"Stay here by the fence. I'm going to choose a horse to break this morning." Joe stepped into the big corral.

Jeremiah stood by the outside of the fence and watched.

Santo on horseback drove about fifteen horses into the corral and got them running in a circle around the outer edge.

Joe stood in the middle and slowly turned, watching the circling horses. He gave a signal to Santo to cut one of the horses, a big red stallion, out of the herd. He ran it toward a gate that Jim had opened into a smaller corral. After he had secured the horse to a post with a rope that gave the horse maneuvering room, Joe went in.

Santo turned the other horses out into the grazing land behind the corrals.

Joe stood quietly and watched the horse for about twenty minutes without moving. Then he slowly walked a few steps toward it. The horse pawed the ground. He lowered his head and shook it as if angry. Joe stood still, and then slowly turned away and took a couple of steps. He stopped, and looked over his shoulder at the horse and took a couple more steps.

The horse calmed down and watched Joe. Then Joe turned and walked back to the horse with slow deliberate steps. He whispered and cooed to the creature. The horse allowed Joe a little closer this time. Joe stopped and looked the horse in the eye for several minutes. Then he took a step forward. The horse backed up. Joe turned in slow motion and took several steps away, before looking over his shoulder. He took several more steps away.

Joe repeated this until the horse followed him and then actually laid his head on Joe's shoulder as he walked away. Joe stroked the horse's head and neck. He pulled a brush out of his back pocket, and for the next thirty minutes, he brushed the horse. The horse stood still and let Joe brush him and even lean against him.

Finally, Joe took a hackamore out of his other back pocket and slipped it on the stallion -all the while cooing at him. Joe walked the stallion around for about an hour with his arm across his neck, putting his weight on the horse's back.

Jim occasionally walked up and then away. Then, confident the horse was used to his presence, he walked up with a saddle.

Joe slowly placed the saddle on the horse and led it around with just the weight of the saddle before he cinched it up. Jim put his left foot in the left stirrup and let the horse walk around while Joe remained on the other side watching, whispering, and cooing. The horse accepted each phase of the process, and before long, Jim lifted his right leg over and sat in the saddle. The horse stopped and looked back at the rider as if to ask what he thought he was doing. Jim gently flicked the rope and the horse walked forward.

Jeremiah stood and watched, not able to take his eyes off Joe, with his heart thumping in amazement. He had never seen anything like it.

Joe walked out of the corral and over to the cart where he had a canteen. He drank thirstily and then offered Jeremiah a canteen.

He took it and drank. "Is that how you break all of the horses?" Jeremiah finally asked.

"Pretty much. Now Jim and Santo will ride him every day, brush him down, and keep gentling him. In another week he'll be trained as good as most horses." Joe wiped sweat off his face with a bandana. "The ones we keep on the ranch we put more work into, but the ones for the army we just break to ride and then they train them to be army horses." Joe poured water on the bandana and wiped his face again.

Jeremiah pulled his sleeve back down over his scars, then handed the canteen to Joe. "Will you get another horse done today?"

Joe squinted at the sky. "I might. I think we need to go get some dinner and then if you want we can come back and work with another horse. If you're willing I'd like to see how a horse would react to you."

Startled, Jeremiah took a step back. "To me? I never worked with horses."

Joe smiled. "Maybe not, but I have a feeling . . . . Let's go get something to eat. My wife likes for me to come in at noon."

"You have a beautiful wife." Jeremiah felt himself blush, then chastised himself for opening his mouth. "I apologize, Joe. That probably wasn't a proper thing to say." There was so much he didn't know.

Joe beat his hat against his leg. "I don't mind. She is beautiful, both inside and outside. I'm a blessed man, Jeremiah."

They rode back to the house and ate with the women, children, and the few hands that had come in. Jeremiah spent some time at the table getting to know the three children. Sam was six, Christine, was four, and little Josh was almost two. Jeremiah had never been around children before and he watched them with fascination.

As the men readied themselves to head back to the box canyon, Sam came up to Jeremiah and handed him a marble. "You can keep it." He put his hands in his pockets and grinned.

"Thanks." Jeremiah made a fist around the marble.

Sam turned and raced out of the kitchen.

Something leaped inside Jeremiah's chest. He'd never received a gift before.

"You've made a hit with that boy. He's never given up one of his marbles before," Joe told him as they walked out to the corral.

"Maybe I should give it back to him?" Jeremiah fingered the green marble.

"No, don't give it back. That would hurt his feelings. He wants you to have it."

"All right, I'd like to keep it. Nobody ever gave me anything before." Jeremiah put the marble in his pocket.

"Well, Sam is a big-hearted little boy and he must have known that and wanted you to have a gift." Joe climbed up on the seat of the cart. "Let's go see what you can do with a horse."

They returned to the box canyon. Joe picked out another stallion. "Jeremiah, come on in the corral and walk behind me. Try to give the horse the same reassure I do with the cooing, walking up to him, and then slowly turn away. Just be my shadow. I'll explain what I'm doing and why."

By the time they had worked for about three hours, Joe slowly backed away and left Jeremiah to work alone. He mimicked what Joe had done throughout the morning. By the end of the afternoon, he rode around on the left stirrup with the horse taking his full weight.

As they passed by Joe, he said, "Go ahead and mount him."

Jeremiah swung his right leg over and settled into the saddle. The horse looked back at him and then kept walking around the corral. Since he hadn't watched Jim finish up with the horse, he was unsure what to do so he just kept riding round and round. He sensed the stallion growing tired. He stopped in front of Joe who sat in the cart by the fence.

"What do I do with him now?" Jeremiah asked.

"Unsaddle him and brush him for awhile. Then let him loose in that pasture over there." He pointed to his left. "Tomorrow ride him again for awhile and brush him. Do that every day for at least a week. By tomorrow you can place a bit in his mouth and then by the next day you can put a regular bridle on him."

Jeremiah unsaddled the horse and brushed him down good. He then let him loose in the far pasture.

The horse ran off, then stopped. He looked back at Jeremiah as if he didn't want him to leave. When Jeremiah started walking back to his horse, the stallion in the pasture walked a few steps toward him, then stopped and looked at him again.

After they left the box canyon, Joe said, "I'm heading over to the creek to take a quick dip. I need to cool off and get rid of this sweat before I go back to the ladies." He nodded at Jeremiah. "You're welcome to do the same."

Jeremiah swallowed hard. He had sense enough to realize that Joe's invitation was a polite way to tell him he needed to wash up. "All right, I'll go with you." Panic gripped him. What had he done? The water would be cold like at the stream by the tunnel. In addition, Joe would see his scars. Jeremiah tugged on his sleeves.

When they got to the stream, Joe got out of the cart, quickly undressed, and jumped into the pool in the bend of the stream.

Jeremiah took his time tying up his horse. Joe wasn't paying him any mind. Jeremiah slowly took off his pants and boots. He left his shirt on and the bandana around his neck. He knew he needed to bathe, but fear gripped him as he walked to the edge of the water.

Joe splashed around, then took a piece of soap, and washed his hair.

Jeremiah took a deep breath and forced himself to walk into the pool. It was cold, but not near as cold as the stream by the tunnel, and he wasn't blindfolded. It made a huge difference. He worked his way farther into the water until it reached his waist.

"Here, catch this." Joe threw the piece of soap.

Jeremiah rubbed his wet shirt and body with the soap. "I may as well do my laundry while I'm here." He hoped Joe accepted his excuse for leaving his shirt on.

"Suit yourself." Joe closed his eyes and dunked his head under the water.

Jeremiah ignored the memories of the old man's hands soaping him down. Then he shook his head and concentrated on quickly scrubbing himself and washing his hair. He ducked under the water and then got out of the pool before the panic threatened to choke him.

"Here, use my towel." Joe tossed the cloth at Jeremiah before drying off with his dirty shirt.

Jeremiah caught a glimpse of Joe's back. A mass of scars crisscrossed down his back. Jeremiah couldn't take his eyes off the scars. Joe had obviously been whipped repeatedly. They were old scars, but brutal.

Jeremiah turned away and put his pants on. He didn't want Joe to catch him staring. Joe had been through some troubles and in spite of the ugliness of the scars still had a beautiful wife. Jeremiah couldn't understand a woman willing to be with a man who was scarred up. But he had to admit he didn't know a lot about women, never having been around one much.

They got back to the ranch in time to put the horses away just as the bell rang for supper. Jeremiah was prepared for the blessing this evening. For the first time in years, hunger pangs gripped his stomach and he ate a full meal. He listened to the talk going on around him. After supper, the hands headed back toward the bunkroom and Jeremiah went to the front porch. No one had said anything about his sleeping arrangement.

~ ~ ~

Elisha breathed in the night air as he walked with Susana. They headed over to Joe and Sara's house while Minnie and Mara put the children to bed.

Elisha settled into a big leather chair. "How did Jeremiah do today?"

"You're not going to believe this. Jeremiah can work with the horses like I can." Joe grinned as he gave the news.

Susana leaned forward. "Are you sure?"

Joe nodded. "I noticed it this morning in how the mares reacted to him. So this afternoon I decided to try him." Joe leaned back in the chair and nodded. "He broke a horse just exactly as he had watched me do this morning. I've never seen anyone else that could do it. It was kind of strange. Like watching myself." Joe shook his head.

Elisha stroked his chin. "How would you feel about him helping you out some?"

Joe looked at his wife, who nodded, and then at Elisha and Susana. "You know I don't talk about my hip much."

Elisha crossed his legs. "And I don't ask much even when I notice you favoring it more."

"I've been having a little more pain than usual. It's getting harder and harder to do a full day."

Elisha didn't know exactly what to say. He never wanted Joe to feel that he considered him less because of his hip injury.

Sara touched Joe's arm. "Do you mind me saying something?"

Joe put his hand over Sara's. "No, honey, you say what you want to Elisha and Susana."

"He's been having a lot more pain. Some nights he can't sleep at all. I've asked him to tell you, but you know how he is." Sara smiled at Joe. "He's got more courage than brains I think."

Joe smiled back at her. "You've always been smarter than me."

Elisha shifted in his chair. "Tell me what you want. There's no need for you to suffer on account of some horses."

"I thought that maybe if Jeremiah wanted to learn and could help me out I could teach him to do some of the work. If I only tried to do one horse a day and when the pain got too bad, not even work a day or so." Joe rubbed his face and shook his head. "Elisha, I don't want to quit. You know me. I got to do something, but the pain—it's getting awful bad."

Elisha reached over and put his hand on Joe's arm. "I don't want you to quit either. But you don't need to suffer. You can manage the horse business anyway you want to. Maybe this Jeremiah has been sent to us by God both for his good and ours." Elisha let go of Joe's arm and sat back.

"Thanks. I should've said something sooner. And you always look at things the right way around." Joe rubbed his right hip. "Maybe this is a way for me to get some relief and to give Jeremiah something to do that'll take the haunted look away."

Elisha hated seeing his friend in pain. "I want to suggest something, but I don't want you to be offended."

"You couldn't offend me. Just say it." Joe shifted his leg.

Elisha hesitated, then leaned forward in his chair. "I think you and Sara should go back east and talk to some doctors. Even go to Europe to see doctors if need be. See if there's anything, anyone can do to help your hip. I know it's a long shot." Elisha folded his hands together. "There's no sure answer, but I keep thinking that we just haven't met the right doctor yet. Even if it can't be fixed you can at least get something done to help with the pain." Elisha held his breath to see how Joe would react.

Joe scratched his head. "I feel two ways about it. I really just want it to stop hurting and go on the way I have been doing. I don't want doctors poking at me. But, if something could be done and I could get rid of the pain that would be worth it." Joe rubbed his eyes. "Course if they could find a way to fix it and I could ride again—" Joe smiled and looked at Sara. "That would be the miracle I'm afraid to pray for."

"Then we'll write some letters to doctors in the east. It might take a few months to work out and that will give you time to train Jeremiah if he's willing." Elisha was decisive when he decided to be.

"I'm going to suggest that we move slow with Jeremiah and only ask him to do one horse a day. He's very skinny, almost like he's starving. And he's got some awful scars. I thought I had some bad ones, but his are more recent and cruel."

Susana leaned forward and asked. "What do you mean, cruel?"

"Well, he's obviously been shackled for months or years. He has barely healed scars on his wrists and ankles. Those scars look recent. He refused to take off his shirt at the pool this afternoon, but I saw his wrists earlier when he raised his arms to stroke the horse." Joe shook his head. "I can't imagine what kind of irons were on his wrists. The scars are about four to five inches wide all around both wrists. His ankles are just as bad. I saw those when he stepped into the water to bathe. To have scars like that he had to have been barefoot otherwise boots would have protected somewhat." Joe stopped and looked at them before he went on. "If he was in prison then it was a terrible place. I can't imagine it, he's so young."

Elisha ran his hands through his hair. "I sensed there was something terribly wrong. That he'd been hurt bad, but nothing like this."

Susana moved to sit by Elisha. "We have to help him."

"Something else happened today." Joe grinned. "Horses and children."

"What?" Elisha cocked his head.

"Sam walked up to Jeremiah and gave him one of his marbles and then just turned away. Jeremiah said it was the first time someone had given him a gift." Joe grinned again. "Horses and children."

"Oh, Joe, wouldn't that be something," Susana said.

"I know you all always say that about Joe, but what does it mean?" Sara looked at them as they smiled and laughed.

Elisha nodded. "I'll try to explain. There's an old folktale that some people are specially blessed with certain gifts. Horses and children recognize these people and respond to them. Joe is obviously one, as the children all follow him around, and the horses respond to him. Now we have Jeremiah with maybe the same thing. Time will tell us." Elisha hoped so for Joe's sake. He was too dedicated to his work and commitment. But Elisha didn't want his good friend working to earn money for them at the expense of suffering.

Joe reached for Elisha's hand. "Would you say a prayer for us? Ask mostly that we'll be able to help Jeremiah in whatever way he needs."

Elisha always felt humbled when his friends asked him to pray with them. He remembered too clearly when he didn't even know how to pray. "I'll be glad to pray for us."

They joined hands as they had done many times before.

"Our Heavenly Father, thank you for the blessing of this day. We have a couple of needs to bring before you. We ask for your wisdom and we accept your answers. We pray for Jeremiah who has come to us. Help us to know how to help him, to be a blessing in his life. And we ask for healing for our brother Joe. Take away his pain and guide us to find help for him. Teach us how to be his help in every step he takes. We know that we are only worthy to come before you with these requests because of the blood of Jesus Christ. And it is through his name that we pray. Amen."

Joe lifted his head and opened his eyes. "Thanks Elisha. As always you know what to pray."

Sara gave Elisha a kiss on the cheek and hugged Susana.

"I need to go to town and I'd like for Susana to get away for a few days," Elisha said. "What would you think about us going to Cheyenne and sending some telegrams? We can get started on finding a doctor. You work with Jeremiah, but only as you feel like it. I'm not going to tell you what to do, but you need to use good sense." He knew Joe didn't want to go to town.

Joe nodded. "All right."

"I'm tired and I think maybe Joe and Sara are too. Let's go home." Susana pulled her shawl around her shoulders.

"We'll see you all in the morning at breakfast." Elisha took Susana's arm and they left for the short walk back to their home. The light of Jeremiah's lantern glowed from the front porch.

"That poor boy. I'm just hoping we can help him." Susana squeezed his arm.

"Yes, we will, my love, and Joe also." Elisha felt responsible that he'd not been able to tell how much pain Joe was in, but Joe had always been good at hiding it.

## Chapter 4

Jeremiah woke from another nightmare. How he hated the dreams. The faint lightening of the sky to the east forecast the coming dawn and the end of another night of fitful sleep. Even though he still felt tired, he might as well get up, as there would be no more sleep. He was proud of how he had worked with the horse the day before. Maybe Joe would let him help again today. And he was amazed that he had gotten into that cold water. Joe hadn't seemed to notice the scars on his ankles. Maybe because of his own scars he was used to them.

A light twinkled from the kitchen, shining through the window onto the porch. That meant that Cookie was up and there might be coffee made. He folded his thin bedroll and turned the wick down to turn off the lantern. After another look at the morning sky bringing the dawn from the east, he turned toward the front door.

Cookie looked up when Jeremiah entered the kitchen. "Morning, Jeremiah. You're up early." He ran a hand through his unruly gray hair. Did it always look like it needed a comb?

"I hoped for some coffee." Jeremiah sat down at the big table.

"I just got it made and here are some donuts to tide you over to breakfast." Cookie poured steaming hot coffee into a cup on the table and then sat a plate of donuts next to it. "Hope you slept all right. That porch can't be too comfortable." He pointed a thumb over his shoulder. "We got plenty of room in the bunkroom."

Jeremiah searched for words to answer. "Outside is fine with me. I don't like to be enclosed."

"Oh my. Let me think what we need to do." Cookie poured himself a cup of coffee and sat down.

"I don't want to be a problem." Jeremiah looked at Cookie and then ducked his head to stare into his cup of coffee.

"You're not a problem. It's a puzzle for me to figure out, which I like to do." Cookie snapped his fingers. "We can set up a bunk on the porch and put up some of the waterproof canvas we use with the chuck wagon. It'd still be open and as airy as you want to make it, but if we have a rainstorm you'd be protected and it'd be your own place." He took a sip of his coffee. "That's the answer. I'll ask Elisha what he thinks. Course I guess I need to ask what you think first."

"That would be fine with me as long as it wasn't too much trouble for everyone." Had he decided to stay on this ranch for a while? Somehow he felt welcomed.

Cookie slapped the table as a smile spread across his weathered face. "All right then." He scooted his chair back "Well, time to start breakfast. Joe will probably be here soon to help."

"Joe? I thought he was a partner with Elisha in the ranch." Jeremiah was confused as to who was really what on the ranch.

"Oh he is, but he's also one fine cook. He doesn't sleep much because of the pain in his hip. You know Joe and I came up from Texas together as cookies with a trail herd. He just likes to keep his hand in." Cookie started mixing batter for the biscuits.

Just as Jeremiah finished his second cup of coffee, Joe came in, put his hat on a peg, and tied an apron around his waist.

"Morning, Jeremiah. I hope you slept well." Joe began to cut up a ham.

"Morning, Joe. I slept as well as I usually do," Jeremiah admitted.

Joe looked over at him and nodded. "I know about not being able to sleep. Between my hip bothering me and my bad dreams I've a hard time getting a full night's sleep."

"You have bad dreams?" Joe's words surprised Jeremiah. Other people had nightmares from the past? He wasn't the only one?

Joe shrugged. "I don't have them as bad as I used to. But some nights it gets really bad. I wake up from a bad one shaking and sweating. For one thing, it disturbs my wife. I hate that. Course she loves me and says it doesn't matter."

It amazed Jeremiah that Joe could speak so matter of fact about something so personal. "Yeah, I know what you mean. I mean, all except the part about a wife." Jeremiah surprised himself by saying anything. These people made it easy to talk.

"You wait. One of these days one will show up." Joe pointed the knife at him. "A good-looking fellow like you will have all the girls at the socials making eyes at you. My wife tells me she knew we'd marry the first week she met me. It took me several months to figure it out." Joe and Cookie laughed.

Cookie set a stack of plates and a box of knives, forks, and spoons on the table. "Jeremiah, put these plates around and the utensils."

Jeremiah got up and put the plates and utensils around the table. Then Joe asked him to stir the gravy. He stood by the stove and stirred the gravy in the big skillet.

Joe and Cookie worked fast and by the time the gravy thickened, they had breakfast on the table. Cookie went to the hallway and rang the bell. Soon the riders and families came in from both doors. Some of the men were yawning, looking sleepy eyed, as did the children. The women seemed more awake. They quietly greeted each other. The calm murmuring and shuffling of the chairs as everyone found their place at the table flowed around Jeremiah. Everyone seemed to accept that he sat down where he had the evening before, as if he belonged.

Jeremiah ate more for breakfast than he had eaten in a long time.

After he finished his breakfast, Joe turned to Jeremiah. "You want to go for a ride this morning and look for horses? We can work with a horse this afternoon."

With a nod and a lift of his spirit, Jeremiah responded simply. "Yes, be glad to." He followed Joe to the corral and caught up his dun and saddled him. Soon he was riding out alongside Joe's cart.

Joe took them to the south side of the valley and up a trail until they could look out over the valley. Joe stopped the cart, climbed down, then went to a large rock, and sat looking over the wide expanse of country.

Jeremiah dismounted and after tying his horse to a tree branch, stood by the rock next to him. The beautiful sight of the valley and mountain beyond took his breath away.

"Look down there. You see that herd of horses?" Joe pointed to the west end of the valley.

It took Jeremiah a minute to spot what Joe had seen. "Yes, I see them."

"I come up here and spot the horse herds and the riders bring them in for me."

"How many horses do you think are here in the valley?" Jeremiah searched the rest of the valley for other herds.

"We think there are at least eight hundred head of wild horses in this valley and in two others that join up with it. We'll eventually get the wild herd under control. We're now breeding our own herd." Joe pointed to a smaller group of horses.

"You got a good eye, Joe. I can barely see them when you point them out."

"Well, I've been doing it a while. I also know the mountains and can spot what is out of place like a running horse." Joe leaned on his good left leg and rubbed his right hip. "Can I ask you a question?"

Jeremiah's stomach tightened. He didn't like questions. He took a deep breath. "Sure."

"I need some help with the horses and I think you could work with me. What would you say to staying around awhile and let me teach you what I do."

Jeremiah turned quickly from where he was standing looking out over the valley and looked at Joe to make sure he was serious. "You think I can do what you do?"

"If I teach you, yes, I think so." Joe looked expectantly at him. "We might give it a try for a few days and see how it goes. If you don't like it you just say so and there won't be any hard feelings."

Jeremiah nodded. "I'd like that. We could give it a try."

COLORADO MORNING SKY

Joe held out his hand and Jeremiah met it. "Then that's a deal."

They got back to the ranch house by noon and Cookie had a surprise for Jeremiah.

"Come on and see." Cookie waved them toward the front porch where Jeremiah had been sleeping. He wiped his hands on his apron. "Take a look at this."

Canvas hung on the end of the porch, down the front edge, and then a canvas across the edge of the porch to the wall of the house. A cord pulled the canvas back and held it in place. The little canvas room held a bunk with a straw-tick mattress, a small bureau and lamp, a table and two ladder-back chairs. A bowl and pitcher sat beside the lamp on the bureau. In front of the bunk was a small round braided rug.

Jeremiah just stood with his mouth open. He didn't know what to say. He felt something stinging behind his eyelids. No one had ever done so much for him and he had never had a place to himself.

"This is a great idea, Cookie. What do you think, Jeremiah? Can you make it with this?" Joe waited for an answer.

Jeremiah swallowed the lump in his throat. These good people evoked strange feelings inside him. "I can make it just fine. It's too much. But I can pay you. I got some money." He reached into his pocket.

Joe held up his hand. "You don't pay when you work for the ranch. If this isn't all right, you let us know." He patted the beaming cook on the back. "Thanks, Cookie, for doing this for Jeremiah."

Jeremiah realized that was what he needed to say. "Yes, thanks, Cookie."

Cookie grinned. "You're welcome. The rug was Sam's idea. He said you needed one and took it out of his room."

Jeremiah couldn't understand these people. Even the children treated him as if he was somebody. He needed to learn more about how to live among normal good people. He suspected it was different from what he knew as a kid growing up around thieves and prisoners. Would they tell him to leave once they figured out that he wasn't like them?

"Well, come on fellows, let's go eat." Cookie led the way to the kitchen.

~

Jeremiah and Joe spent the afternoon working with a horse. Jeremiah watched carefully how Joe picked a horse to break. But Jeremiah still didn't know what he based his choices on. They spent four hours working with the horse and then turned it over to Santo.

Again they went to the creek to bathe and cool off. It was still a major effort for Jeremiah to get himself into the water. He did feel better afterwards, as the afternoon of working with the horse had been hot, and he was dirty and sweaty.

The warm evening forced Elisha and his family, and most of the hands, onto the porch after supper. Jeremiah saw no way out but to join them. He sat on the steps to the side and watched.

They told stories and laughed a lot, and then Susana started singing. The others joined her and sang "Amazing Grace."

Jeremiah had never heard anything like it. The beauty of ten people singing together in harmony was so different from the singers in saloons he'd heard growing up.

Then they took turns quoting scriptures. Even the little children joined in. Without thinking, after Sam had proudly quoted the first verse in the Bible, Jeremiah spoke up and quoted the rest of the chapter. He didn't look at the others, but looked out over the darkening valley. When he finished quoting the chapter, he stopped.

Elisha, who sat on a chair close by, put his hand on Jeremiah's shoulder. "Thank you for quoting that for us, Jeremiah. Well done. Let's try that song we've been learning." Elisha started a song, "A Mighty Fortress Is Our God."

Jeremiah listened in amazement to the strong harmony of the song, and the words penetrated his heart. He wanted a God who would be his fortress. He needed Him, but how could he find Him?

The darkness of the evening approached and Jeremiah felt the panic returning. His breathing grew labored and he started to sweat.

Then a strong hand rested on his shoulder. Elisha said quietly, "If you don't mind, would you go light your lamp so we can have some light out here?"

Jeremiah looked up at him. Elisha's warm smile comforted him. He got up quietly and lit the lamp, trying to control his shaking hands. Then he looked into the bright light and tried to slow his breathing. How crazy was he that he couldn't sit on a porch with some nice people as natural darkness fell?

He went and sat back down on the steps of the porch.

Elisha picked up Christine who stood before him rubbing her sleepy eyes. He gave her a kiss and looked at Jeremiah over the top of her head. "Thanks."

Jeremiah shifted until he could see the lamp. The panic subsided.

Soon Elisha broke up the evening by announcing that it was time for the children to go to bed. Everyone left the porch.

Going back to the little area that Cookie had prepared for him, he took his boots off and lay down on the bunk that seemed unusually soft compared to the hard ground. He turned the lamp down. Sleep was what he wanted, but didn't really expect.

He mulled over the day's events. Joe asking him to try to work with the horses had been a major surprise. But he was hopeful that it might be something he could do. He had seen by the time they left the corral how much Joe favored his right hip. Jeremiah didn't know what the problem was exactly but he could tell the man was in pain.

He looked out toward the stars appearing in the Colorado night sky and drifted off to sleep. He only woke himself three times moaning which for him was a good night.

## Chapter 5

Jeremiah helped hitch the horses to the buggy. Then he stood with the other ranch hands as they bid farewell to Elisha and Susana as they left for a trip to Cheyenne to get supplies and a much needed get-away. The children weren't too happy about seeing their parents leave, but everyone pitched in to make sure they had plenty of care.

Jeremiah worked with Joe every day. He wasn't as smooth as Joe, but Joe assured him that he was doing fine.

Jeremiah liked working with Joe. The calm man gave encouragement rather than getting angry at a mistake. Jeremiah lost his focus a couple of times. For some crazy reason the sensation of being back in the tunnel came over him. Several minutes passed before he realized he was in a corral surrounded by horses and people who seemed to care for him. When it happened, it felt so real that he almost feared that was his real life, and his presence in the valley was the dream. After he snapped out of it, he had difficulty reconnecting to the horse.

Joe told him to be patient and that the next horse would be better.

Jeremiah had almost as much difficulty dealing with Joe's patience, as he would have if he'd gotten angry.

After a week of working side by side with Joe, he let Jeremiah pick a horse and do all the work. Jeremiah worked for four hours getting the horse to trust him. It was with a lift of his head and a quick step when he finished for the day and the horse was ready for Jim and Santo to work with. As he watched Jim and Santo take the horse to the next corral to keep schooling him, Jeremiah finally identified the feeling that was flowing through him. Pride in his work.

Jeremiah fell into the routine of the ranch. After Elisha and Susana returned from Cheyenne, Elisha invited Jeremiah to attend worship service the following Sunday. He explained how the service was conducted and why.

Jeremiah appreciated Elisha's explanation. It was the first worship service he'd ever attended and he enjoyed it. He sat in a chair by the window in the back of the front room by the kitchen door and listened to the hymns, scripture, prayers, and Elisha's simple lesson. Every person on the ranch attended; Cookie sat beside him. Jeremiah smiled when he saw that Cookie's hair was just as unruly on Sunday as any other day of the week.

Jeremiah began to look forward to the services and little by little joined in with the singing. He only had to hear a song once to know the words and melody. Jeremiah liked to sit next to Cookie and gradually began to match his deep bass voice.

~

Jeremiah sat at the breakfast table finishing his coffee with Joe sitting across from him doing the same as he talked over his plans for the day with his wife.

After Sara left the table, Joe turned to him. "Today let's ride to the end of the north valley and look the horse herd over."

"Sure. When do you want to head out?"

"As soon as we can pack a lunch and ready the horses."

"You see to the food and I'll head to the barn to saddle my horse and hitch up a pony to your cart." Jeremiah emptied his coffee cup.

"That sounds fair. See you in a bit." Joe scooted his chair back and went over to the kitchen counter.

Jeremiah grabbed his hat and headed to the barn. He soon had Joe's cart hitched to a Cayuse pony. He then saddled a brown gelding for himself. The gelding belonged to the ranch and Jeremiah had ridden him several times. He liked the easy gait of the horse.

Joe came out of the house carrying a gunnysack. He placed it in the little wagon part of the cart. They rode toward the far west end of the large valley where it branched off into two other valleys that Elisha claimed as his grazing. They then swung to the right to head up the north valley.

They found several small herds and followed them. After a few hours, they stopped by a creek, ate their lunch, and stretched out on the grass for a nap while the horses rested.

They were now a good ten miles from the ranch house. Joe decided they should start back so they could make it before dark, which Jeremiah appreciated.

They rode at a fast trot on the way back to the ranch house. Suddenly the left wheel of Joe's cart hit a large rock and flipped. Joe flew out and lay sprawled on the ground.

Jeremiah caught the horse with the cart overturned and sliding along on its side. After he quickly tied up the horses, he ran to Joe who was lying on the ground, not moving.

"Joe? Joe, can you hear me?" He dropped to his knees and assessed Joe's injuries. Superficial scratches covered his face, but a cut on his head bled profusely. With Joe unconscious, Jeremiah had no way of knowing the extent of internal injuries. He didn't want to touch him for fear of what might be broken and he couldn't leave him to go for help. Jeremiah closed his eyes for a second and took a deep breath. He had to remain calm if he wanted to help Joe.

He went to the cart and righted it, then verified that it wasn't damaged beyond scrapping of the wood on the side. Jeremiah brought the horse and the cart over to where Joe lay on the ground with his own horse tied to the cart. It was an effort to get Joe up into the back of the cart and then Jeremiah got into the back of Joe so he could hold him steady and still handle the reins. He flicked the reins, clicked his tongue, and slowly walked the pony back toward the ranch house. Daylight faded. Jeremiah swallowed the taste of fear that rose in his throat. Joe already bounced around at their current pace. He didn't dare make the pony go faster.

Jeremiah's hands shook. He wiped the sweat from his face. Darkness fell. He struggled to catch his breath. Images of the dark tunnel engulfed him. Jeremiah shook his head to erase the images, then clucked his tongue at the pony. *The old man took away the lantern.* He shook his head again. No. He wasn't in the tunnel. Jeremiah concentrated on Joe. Joe's shallow breathing gave him the courage to keep the panic at bay. He had to get help for Joe.

Jeremiah cocked his head at the sound of horses coming toward them.

"Jeremiah?" Elisha rode up out of the darkness followed by Bob.

Moonlight accentuated Elisha's silhouette. Jeremiah breathed a sigh of relief. "We're here Elisha."

"What happened?" Elisha jumped off his horse and climbed up on the seat of the cart. He took the reins from Jeremiah.

"The cart hit a rock and Joe got thrown out. He hit his head and I don't know what else. He's unconscious." Jeremiah was relieved to hand over the reins to Elisha.

"Let's get him to the house." Elisha shouted at Bob. "Ride quick to the house and warn the women that we're coming in with an injured man."

Bob whipped his horse with the reins and started back to the house at a gallop.

Elisha's presence in the dark comforted Jeremiah. He found it easier to fight the panic. They pulled up in front of the house where everyone waited. All Jeremiah could do was stare at the light pouring from the house. He had to get out of the darkness.

Without a word, Sara reached for Joe. Fear etched across her face.

Bob, Cookie, Jeff, and Santo gently lifted Joe out of the cart and carried him into the house. Jeremiah scrambled out of the cart and to the lamp by his bunk. His hands shook making lighting it difficult. Bob then came back outside to Jeremiah just as he had the lamp glowing bright in his area on the porch. Jeremiah knew the horses needed put away, but he didn't want to leave the light.

Bob walked over to Jeremiah. "You all right?"

Jeremiah sat in one of the chairs and held his hands together to stop their shaking. "Yeah, I'm all right. How's Joe?"

"We don't know yet, but you got him back here. Thanks, Jeremiah. I'll take care of the horses and cart. You go to the kitchen and eat. Cookie saved supper for you."

"All right." Jeremiah's stomach growled. It shocked him and he found it strange that he felt hunger with all that was going on.

Bob took the horses and cart off toward the barn and Jeremiah went into the kitchen. He found plates of food on the table. After pouring himself a cup of coffee, he sat down to eat.

After awhile, Cookie came in and put some water on to heat.

Jeremiah looked up from his plate. "How's Joe?"

Cookie ran his hand through his gray hair. "We don't know yet. He's starting to come around and he's hurting bad in his hip. Did he hit on his hip?"

Jeremiah reviewed the accident in his mind. "He could have." He nodded. "Yes, he must have because he hit on his right side. I didn't think about his hip." Jeremiah shook his head. "I maybe shouldn't have moved him. I just thought it best to get him back to the house."

"You did the right thing, Jeremiah. You did just right." Cookie picked up his medical case and the hot water and went back to the bedroom.

After he finished eating, Jeremiah washed the dishes he had used and went out to his place on the porch. Feeling as if he had done a week of work, he fell into his bunk, his heart heavy for Joe. With Joe injured, would Elisha let Jeremiah work with the horses? He liked working with the men and was learning a lot. Maybe Elisha would need him even more. Being on the ranch these four months had been good and he didn't want to leave. It was a safe place and the people let him be. He didn't dream as much and he slept better. The good food helped him put on weight and he grew two inches. He was as tall as Elisha.

But the darkness still imprisoned him.

## Chapter 6

Jeremiah watched Joe wear down the pain from his head. It took over a week. But he couldn't seem to get over the pain in his hip. He barely made it from the bedroom to the front room. He couldn't sit up for any length of time.

Jeremiah went to the box canyon and worked the horses with Jim and Santo. He often felt unsure that he did what was best with the horses, but he managed to break at least one horse a day. In the evenings, he sat with Joe and reported on what he had gotten done that day.

One evening, Joe was in bed; he hadn't been able to get up at all through the day. Jeremiah wasn't sure he should stay, but Sara asked him to so she could go do something.

Joe pushed himself up on the pillows against the headboard. "Thanks for your hard work and for stepping in for me."

"I hope I'm doing right by the horses. You'd do better."

Joe shook his head. "Not right now, I wouldn't. You're doing it, and I'm glad because we've a contract with the army to fulfill."

"You going to get back on your feet, right Joe?" Jeremiah immediately regretted asking.

Joe didn't act like the question bothered him. "I'm praying so, Jeremiah. But I don't see it happening anytime soon. It comforts me that you're here to help out. God knew that we needed you and so He guided you here."

Jeremiah wasn't sure about God's guiding him to the ranch, but then he didn't know He didn't. "I don't know much about what God wants, Joe. He hasn't been there in my life."

Joe shifted his legs under the covers. "That's what I thought of my growing up years, but I'm glad to confess I've learned better."

"How did you learn that?" Jeremiah really wanted to know. Joe's calm nature inspired Jeremiah and he appreciated Joe's assurance.

"I went through bad times as a child. My mother was crazy." Joe looked hard into Jeremiah's eyes. "And I mean that. She did terrible things to me." Joe turned his gaze to the ceiling. "I know you saw the scars on my back. She did that. I ran away when I was fourteen and made my own way." He adjusted the covers and sighed. "Then I had the fall with my horse, like I told you. God led me here to Elisha and Susana, and God gave me Sara." Joe smiled and nodded. "I had to make a decision to be a man who'd been beaten by his own mother, or move on and just be a man of God. I chose to move forward. I don't know if you wanted to know all that." Joe gazed more intently at Jeremiah.

Jeremiah rested his elbows on his knees and leaned forward. "I do want to know. Maybe it'll help me move forward." How would it be to leave behind the darkness?

Joe pushed himself with his arms to sit up even straighter against the pillows against the headboard of the bed. "Can I ask what you need to move forward from?"

Jeremiah looked at the open bedroom door. He wanted to tell Joe, to tell someone, but he was afraid to trust.

"Go close the door and no one will come in without knocking."

Jeremiah didn't know why he did it, but he got up, closed the door, and sat back down in the chair by the bed. He looked at Joe and decided to trust him.

"I had some hard things happen and I keep remembering them. I dream terrible dreams, even when I'm awake. I'm scared that I might be crazy. Maybe you can tell me as you had a crazy—" He hesitated, not knowing how to continue.

"Just tell what you want. You don't have to tell it all. I still can't tell all that my mother did to me and it was years ago."

That gave Jeremiah courage. He sat up straight and took a deep breath. "I don't remember my ma. I must've of had one, but I don't know anything about her, not even her name." Jeremiah rubbed his hand over his face. Just talking about it was painful. "My pa was an outlaw. He rustled and robbed and then he died. I got left with some men. I was just a kid, but they used me to hold their horses when they robbed banks and stagecoaches." He wanted to stop. Instead, he took a deep breath and continued, "A little over three years ago we got caught and I was sent to prison." Jeremiah couldn't believe he was telling Joe all of this. What would Joe think?

"After a year I was transferred to the new jail in Yuma." He closed his eyes.

"Jeremiah, I haven't heard anything I can't live with."

Jeremiah shook his head. Would it help to tell Joe?

"How did you get out of Yuma?" Joe softly asked.

The wagon accident played across Jeremiah's mind. He took another deep breath. "I never made it to Yuma." He shook his head again against the memories. "We got attacked by Indians and I was captured."

Joe frowned. "I'm sorry, Jeremiah. That must have been rough."

"I don't know who captured me. It wasn't Indians. It was an old man. He took me to a mine and forced me to work it for over two years." Jeremiah stopped. Just talking about it cramped his stomach. He'd never before verbalized the torture he'd experienced. Pain and anguish washed over him as if it happened just yesterday. He rubbed his wrists.

"That's where you got the scars on your ankles and wrists?"

Jeremiah's heart raced. He'd tried so hard to hide his scars. How did Joe find out? Actually, Joe knowing made it easier to talk about. He nodded. "Yeah, from the shackles." Did Joe know about the scars on his neck? He slowly reached up and untied his bandana. "And the ones on my neck came from a rope."

Joe blinked several times as if clearing his eyes. "How did you get away?"

Jeremiah's stomach settled down. Joe accepted him, even with his scars. The realization empowered Jeremiah. He found the strength to continue. "I woke one morning from the sleep potion the old man always gave me and I was alone and free. I never saw the old man again. I walked out of the desert and just wandered around until I got here."

"So he just let you go when he had what he wanted?" Joe wrinkled his forehead.

Jeremiah shrugged. "I guess."

"So that's why you don't like the dark. He left you in the mine in the dark?"

Jeremiah swallowed. The tunnel. His mind wrapped around the darkness. He smelled the dampness, heard the silence. Violent tremors coursed through his body. He searched Joe's face for understanding. "I just can't take it."

"Then you keep the lantern on. You do what you have to in order to get over it and move forward."

Jeremiah found the understanding he needed in his friend's eyes.

"You know we want you to stay as long as you need." Joe's voice was quiet and sure.

Would Jeremiah really be accepted after all he'd revealed? "Even though you know I'm an escaped prisoner?"

Joe folded his hands across his stomach. "It sounds as if you did your time in prison and were let go. That's the way I'm going to look at it."

"Thanks, Joe." Jeremiah swallowed trying to rid himself of the lump in his throat.

"I'd like to tell Elisha. You can trust him the same as me."

Trusting Joe and finding acceptance in his friendship made it easy to trust Elisha. "Will he let me stay and work on the ranch?"

"Yes, he'll let you stay."

"Then you can tell him."

Someone tapped on the door. Jeremiah got up and opened it to find Sara with a tray of cake and coffee.

"I brought you boys a treat. Cookie just made Susana's blackberry jam cake. It's still warm." She sat the tray down on the table by the bed. "Jeremiah, will you help Joe if he needs it?"

"Sure—" Before he could say more, she smiled and walked out of the room, closing the door behind her.

Joe eyed the tray. "Pass me a piece of that cake."

Jeremiah handed him a plate and took one for himself. They both spent several minutes eating the delicious cake. Then Jeremiah took the empty plate from Joe and picked up the two cups of coffee. After handing one off to Joe, he sat and sipped the coffee. He had told Joe enough. He didn't need to know more.

Joe cocked his head and gave Jeremiah a peculiar look. "I don't even know how old you are?"

"Funny you ask. Today is my birthday. I'm nineteen."

"Hey, Happy birthday! We'll consider this your birthday cake." Joe settled back on his pillow and smiled. "Nineteen, that's young. I'm twenty-six years old and Elisha is thirty-two. We aren't sure how old Cookie is. He won't say. You got a lot of life ahead of you." He took a sip of coffee. "Have you thought about what you want to do?"

His question surprised Jeremiah. He couldn't think what he wanted. No one had ever asked him that before. "I don't know. How can I know what I want?"

"If you have to ask that then I would say you don't know yet. You got time. Just let yourself think about it and next year on your birthday we'll talk about it again, all right?"

"That sounds good." Jeremiah swallowed the last of the coffee. "I'll take these things back to the kitchen. You need to rest, and I'm ready to get some sleep." Jeremiah gathered the dishes onto the tray.

Joe put out his hand. "We're partners. Let's just help each other to move forward."

Jeremiah shook Joe's hand. "I can agree to that. Thanks for listening." He took the tray to the kitchen. Joe wanted to talk again on his next birthday. Everyone seemed to just make the assumption that Jeremiah was a part of the ranch. He liked the sense of peace that gave him.

~

Several days later, when Jeff and Jim returned from another trip to town for supplies, they brought a letter from a doctor in New York City stating that he could help Joe. Jeremiah was reading on his bunk on the porch as he heard Elisha and Susana talking in the front room.

Elisha was calm but firm. "We must try every avenue possible to relieve Joe of his hip pain. This doctor may be the one who can do that. I'm just sorry he is so far away. I want to travel to New York with Joe and Sara and help them get settled. Once I know they are in good hands I'll leave them and come home. Do you think you can manage a couple of weeks without me?"

Susana's soft laugh drifted out to Jeremiah. "It will be hard to have you gone for that long but if it will help Joe, I'm willing for you to travel with them."

"I'll ask Joe if he and Sara can be ready to travel by day after tomorrow. There is no reason to put it off. We will take a wagon to Cheyenne and catch the train east from there."

The murmurs of their voices faded as they moved toward their bedroom. Jeremiah didn't really want Joe and Sara to be gone for weeks or months, but that was what it would take to get Joe back on his feet. All Jeremiah could do to help was keep working with the horses.

Jeremiah helped Elisha prepare the wagon and make a bed in the back where Joe could be as comfortable as possible.

With the rest of the folks on the ranch, Jeremiah watched Elisha, Joe and Sara drive out of sight. He couldn't imagine what it was like for Susana to see them leaving. Jeremiah missed them already. How close he'd grown to these wonderful people. He hoped nothing but the best for Joe.

Susana turned to the others. "We've a long wait until we get news back. Let's try to keep our spirits up and the work going. Bob is in charge, of course. But you can all come to me about anything. Other than keep the work going, the only thing we can do is keep praying."

Jeremiah went to the box canyon with Jim and Santo to work the horses. Jeremiah determined to focus and get as many horses broke as he could for Joe. He didn't really know how to pray, but he could keep Joe's business going and help break enough horses to fulfill the army contract.

After he finished for the day, Jeremiah went to the creek. It was the first time he'd been there without Joe. It took an effort for him to enter the water, but he did it. After he scrubbed and washed his hair, he ducked under the water. He climbed out hurriedly and dressed. He was proud of himself for facing his fears.

Somberness fell on everyone at suppertime. Jeremiah supposed that concern for Joe and his travel to get help rested heavy on everyone's mind. After supper, Sam followed Jeremiah out and sat on the porch steps. He brought a piece of string tied into a circle and gave it to Jeremiah.

"We can make things with our string." Sam beamed at Jeremiah as he held up his circle of string.

Jeremiah's heart soared with tenderness for the little boy who was dealing with his father being gone for several weeks. "What can we make?"

"Well, the one I like is Jacob's Ladder. Papa taught me how to make it." Pride for his father showed in his toothless smile. He had recently lost both of his two front teeth. "Now watch and I'll show you how." The boy showed Jeremiah the intricate weaving of string between his fingers and made a Jacob's Ladder.

Jeremiah watched closely and he made one on the first try.

Sam clapped his hands. "Hey, that's good, Jeremiah. I had to do it over and over before I got it right. Want to see something else?"

"Sure, what else can we make with this string?"

"This one is called Moses in a Basket. Watch." He again wove the string and made what resembled a swinging basket.

"All right, my turn." Again, Jeremiah made it the first try.

"You're smart Jeremiah. You learn quick."

Jeremiah tugged on Sam's cowlick. "Some things I learn quick." He followed Sam's direction for making a Cat's Cradle, a Cup and Saucer, a Star, a Moth, and the Outrigger Canoe.

Sam unraveled the Outrigger Canoe. "Do you think Uncle Joe will be back soon?"

Jeremiah wasn't sure how to reassure a little boy. This was the first time he had ever played with a child. "I hope so, Sam. But until then, we've got to keep things together."

Susana came out to the porch. "Sam, it's time to get ready for bed. Thanks for playing with him, Jeremiah. It's a help."

"I'm glad to help anyway I can." Jeremiah held up his string. "Good night Sam, I'll see you in the morning."

"You can keep the string. Bye, see you in the morning." The boy waved as he followed his mother into the house.

Jeremiah went to bed. He lay awake a long time before sleep came. He'd never felt responsible for another person before, but he felt responsible to help the people on the ranch, especially the children. It was a strange feeling.

~

Two weeks passed before they had news, and the news came by none other than Elisha. Jeremiah had gone to bed, but the lantern shone brightly. Jeremiah jumped to his feet when a horse came up the trail from the gap. He grabbed his rifle and waited to see who it was. By the time Elisha rode up out of the dark, Susana and Cookie had come out on the porch. Elisha jumped off the horse and Susana ran out into the yard to be swept up in his arms.

Jeremiah had never seen such a display of public affection. He could only describe it as being allowed to see into a love affair. He had never seen such love between people.

Elisha finally put Susana down, and by then everyone else had come up. "Come on everyone, let's go to the kitchen and let Cookie get me something to eat. I'm starving."

Jeremiah followed everyone into the kitchen where Anna and Minnie had made coffee and started making sandwiches for whoever wanted to eat.

After they were all seated around the table Elisha said, "Pray with me folks."

Jeremiah bowed his head with everyone else.

"Dear Heavenly Father, Thank you for bringing me home to my family and for keeping them safe while I was gone. Bless Joe, Sara, and big Sam in New York. Thank you for this food and for blessing us with such bounty. Thank you for the joy of love. I pray in the name of Jesus Christ, Amen."

They gave Elisha time to eat a couple of roast beef sandwiches and a big wedge of apple pie. But as he was sipping on his second cup of coffee, Susana said, "All right, Elisha, time is up. We can't wait any longer. How's Joe?"

Elisha looked around at all of them. "We got to New York in four days of travel. It was a hard trip on Joe, but you know him. Not a word of complaint." He took another sip of coffee. "We checked into the hotel and as we did who should walk in but Sam Weathers."

Everyone smiled and nodded. Jeremiah sat quietly at the edge of the group. Elisha turned to him. "Sam is Joe's father, Jeremiah. I sent a telegraph and he got on a train and met us in New York. Joe was real pleased."

Cookie leaned forward. "Elisha, get on with it. What happened?"

Elisha put down his cup. "All right, Joe had surgery the second day we were in New York. He was in a big hospital. They used something called ether to put him to sleep. He didn't feel a thing. The doctor cut him open." He leaned forward. "I'm sorry ladies, but I don't know how to tell it nicely. You rather I not tell about the surgery, Susana?"

"I want to know every detail. Don't you worry about us ladies, isn't that right Anna, Minnie?"

The ladies all nodded.

"All right, the doctor told me that he cut Joe open all along his right hip and looked at the bone around the hip socket or maybe it was the hip socket itself, I'm not sure. It took him hours, and Sara, Sam, and I waited and prayed." Elisha rubbed the back of his neck. "The doctor found that when Joe originally broke his hip the bone had grown back in a way that blocked the movement to the side. So the doctor trimmed the bone back to where it needed to be and sewed him all up again." He put his hand up, palm forward. "I know it sounds awful, and I'll tell you, Joe is still very sick from it. He has to lie flat on his back for weeks until it heals. There's still a lot that can go wrong."

Susana started to cry as Elisha talked. He put his arm around her.

"Oh Elisha, I hate to think of the pain Joe's having and poor Sara. She must be exhausted. When will Joe come home?"

"The doctor made sure that Joe had some medicine to take care of the pain. He was sleeping all the time. If everything goes all right, Joe should be back in a couple of months. It may take a while for him to learn to walk again." Elisha smiled at everyone. "The doctor said that he has high hopes that Joe will not only walk without pain, but he's very hopeful Joe will be able to ride."

"Oh my, wouldn't that be something." Cookie rubbed his eyes with his sleeve.

What would it mean to Joe to be able to ride again? Jeremiah guessed that Joe would be pleased, but that if he couldn't he'd still manage to have a good life. It gave Jeremiah something to think about. Could one just decide to have a good life after so much bad?

In the following weeks, it snowed a couple of times. Everyone worried that Joe and Sara wouldn't make it back to the ranch before winter set in for good. Elisha sent someone to town every week to check for news.

Jeremiah and Cookie volunteered to go for the last wagonloads of supplies before the heavy snows blocked the pass. When they got to town, they found a telegram waiting. Joe and Sara would be on the train the next day. They got all the supplies loaded and made a bed for Joe in one of the wagons. The next morning at daybreak, they met the early train coming in from the east.

Cookie and Jeremiah stood on the platform when the train pulled in. Almost immediately, they saw Joe and then Sara at one of the windows of the train.

When Joe and Sara made their way to the door of the train car, Cookie and Jeremiah were there to greet them.

After climbing down the two steps from the train with the help of Cookie, Joe walked slowly, leaning heavily on a cane.

As soon as Joe was clear of the train door, Jeremiah reached up and took the two valises Sara was carrying. She smiled and said, "Thanks Jeremiah. It's good to see you."

Joe shook hands with Cookie and Jeremiah. "It's good to see you Cookie, Jeremiah. Thanks for coming. We didn't know if anyone would be here."

Sara gave the older man a big hug and kissed him on the cheek. "You are a welcome sight, Cookie."

Cookie grinned as he hugged her back. "We hoped you'd be coming in. The snow has started and we're about to get snowed in for the winter." Cookie led the way toward the street.

"Let's go to the hotel and freshen up, get a bite to eat, and then we'll hit the trail for the ranch." Joe put his right arm through Cookie's left one and leaned on his strength as they went up the steps to the hotel.

Watching from behind Jeremiah could tell that Joe was barely on his feet. He wanted to be polite and offer his arm to Sara, but he carried the two valises. She seemed to sense his dilemma and said, "Thanks for carrying those. It's a relief. It's been a long trip."

"You're welcome, ma'am. We'll have you home soon as possible."

~

It took them two days of hard traveling to make it back to the ranch. It was snowing heavily and almost dark when they reached the gate in the gap. Jeremiah tried not to focus on the pending fear that would soon grip him.

Cookie waved to Jeremiah to go on ahead with the wagon of supplies he was driving after they were through the gap. "Go ahead and get your team moving. When you get there tell them we're coming with Joe and Sara."

Jeremiah waved and slapped the reins against the rumps of the horses pulling his wagon. He didn't try to get them into a gallop, but he did get them moving into a good trot. Jeremiah suspected that Cookie knew he wanted to make it to the house before nightfall. Jeremiah wondered if he would ever be able to cope with the dark.

## Chapter 7

When Jeremiah finally pulled the team up next to the barn, dark shadows crept around every corner. Relief flooded Jeremiah when Elisha, Bob, and Jeff came out to help unload carrying lanterns.

"Cookie will be here soon. He has Joe and Sara with him," Jeremiah told them.

"Great news!" Elisha slapped him on the back. "Jeremiah, go on up to the house and tell the women. And get some coffee to warm up. You look cold." Elisha handed Jeremiah his pack and bedroll to take up to the house.

Jeremiah flung his pack over his shoulder. "Thanks, I am cold. By the way, Joe is walking with a cane, but he's walking."

"I can't wait to see him. This is the answer to prayers."

Jeremiah left his things on the porch and went into the kitchen where Susana, Anna, Minnie, and Mara were preparing supper. The smell of steaks frying wafted over Jeremiah and he nearly fainted with hunger.

"Jeremiah, welcome home." Susana came over and gave him a kiss on the cheek. The other women all greeted him with smiles.

Jeremiah never quite knew what to do in situations such as Susana kissing him on the cheek. Fortunately, he had news that would cover his lack of graceful greetings.

He poured himself a cup of hot coffee from the pot at the back of the stove. "Good news, we picked up Joe and Sara and they'll be here in about ten minutes."

Susana clapped her hands together. "Oh, Jeremiah, that's wonderful. Come on, let's get our coats. How did Joe appear to you?"

"He's leaning on a cane and moving slowly, but he's walking." Jeremiah gulped down the hot coffee and felt its warmth throughout his body. He sat the empty cup into the sink.

They all put their coats on and wrapped up the children. Little Josh came up to Jeremiah and held up his arms. Susana walked by, picked him up, and placed him in Jeremiah's arms. She didn't give Jeremiah a choice.

"You can keep track of Little Josh for me. Just don't let him run out under the horses' hooves." Susana helped Christine into her coat.

They all gathered on the front porch with several lanterns. A few minutes later, the big wagon pulled up into the yard. There followed several minutes of joyous greetings as everyone welcomed Joe and Sara home.

Joy and laughter filled the kitchen as they all gathered at the table for supper. Elisha gave a special blessing for their safe return and the delicious food.

When Jeremiah went out to the little canvas room on the porch someone had tied the canvas down tight and put a buffalo robe on his bed. He suspected Elisha.

~ ~ ~

Elisha went to bed with a feeling of satisfaction. He lay in the bed and watched Susana brush her long hair.

It must have shown for Susana looked over at him and said, "What are you so happy about?"

"Our family is all home." Elisha lifted the covers for her to slide into bed beside him.

"I hadn't thought of it like that, but it's true. And thank God." Susana placed her palm against his face and stroked his eyebrow.

"Yes, we don't know what will be the total outcome for Joe, but although he seems weak he doesn't seem to be in pain like he was before." Elisha began to rub his wife's back.

"Sara looked so tired. I'm glad they agreed to sleep here rather than trying to open their house tonight."

"I'm glad Cookie and Jeremiah got in. Jeremiah just made it to the house as it got dark. I wish I knew how to help him get over his fear. One of these days he won't make it back to the house in time."

"Oh Elisha, did you see Jeremiah standing there holding Little Josh? I was determined that he wouldn't see me laugh, but it was so precious. I don't think he's ever held a small child before."

"Probably not. He seems to be doing a lot better. He's not so awkward, but I have a problem I got to take care of." Elisha ran his hand through Susana's long hair now that she'd released it from its customary braid.

"What problem is that? I haven't noticed that he's done anything bad."

"No, it's not something that he's done. It's where he sleeps. I put the buffalo robe on his bed, but it gets colder every night. He can't go on sleeping out there."

"What are you going to do?" Susana lay with her head on Elisha's chest as he played with her hair.

"I think the first thing is to talk to him. We've room in the bunkroom. Since we built houses for Bob and Joe, and Jeff and Anna have the room next to the bunkroom there are only Billy, Jim, and Jacob." Elisha brushed Susana's hair back from her face. "The problem is that lantern. I hate to ask the men to sleep in a room with a lantern on all night. I know it's not usual, but what if we offered the back spare bedroom to him? He could leave the window open and he can leave the lantern on without bothering someone else."

"I think that's the only solution. What'll you tell the other fellows?"

"The truth usually works." Elisha laughed and turned on his side, then pulled Susana closer to him. He brushed the hair back from her eyes and kissed her softly.

~

Elisha couldn't stop smiling the next morning at breakfast. "Joe, Sara, it is so good to see you all back at this table. You have been missed."

Joe laughed. "I'm glad to hear that as Sara and I intend to be around here for some time to come. We both decided that the big city isn't something we enjoy at all. The mountains are much better."

Sara nodded. "There is nothing like coming home and this is home."

Elisha kept smiling. "You both need to take it easy for the next few days and get over that train journey. I remember how worn out I was when I got back."

Joe leaned back in his chair, holding a cup of coffee. "Catch me up on the doings around here for the three months we were gone. I couldn't see much last night."

"You have got to take it easy Joe. I know that will be hard for you. But you need to completely heal and not do any damage to that leg." Elisha knew his friend and if he was left alone would try to get back to work too soon.

Joe squirmed in his seat. "What do you expect me to do with myself if I'm not back at work with the horses? I've got to be doing something or I'll go crazy."

Sara spoke up. "The doctor said he wasn't to do anything extra until at least in the spring. Just walk around some and get his strength back. But nothing strenuous for at least the next five to six months."

"Ah, honey, why did you have to tell Elisha that? Now he won't let me do anything." Joe didn't sound angry, just frustrated.

Elisha laughed. "Thanks Sara. I wanted to know what the doctor told you all. I have a project for you Joe. We've got a lot of harness, bridles, saddles, and other stuff that needs repaired and cleaning by someone who knows what they are doing."

Joe looked puzzled. "You want me to spend my time in a cold barn working on harness?'

"No, I want you to sit comfortably in front of the fire here in the front room. We can bring the work to you. And Joe, it really does need to be done but no one has had the time."

Joe ran is fingers through his hair, frowning. "I know. I'm just frustrated and tired of being sick and tired."

~

After dinner, Elisha asked Jeremiah to walk with him out to the barn.

"We need to talk, Jeremiah," Elisha stood by the corral in the snow and watched the horses.

"Have I done something?" Jeremiah asked as he looked at Elisha.

"No, you haven't done anything, but we need to do something. Winter is upon us and this cold spell is the beginning. You can't stay out on the porch. You've got to come into the house to sleep." Elisha turned and faced Jeremiah with a solemn gaze.

Jeremiah kicked the snow with the toe of his boot. "I don't know as I can do that, Elisha."

"I'm asking you to try. I know it's difficult, but besides my not wanting you to be out in such weather, it'll worry the others, especially the women."

"When do you want me to do this?" Jeremiah's face looked like he had been given a prison sentence, which Elisha guessed was what it felt like to him.

"I want you to move into the house this evening." Elisha gripped Jeremiah's shoulder to offer him support. He knew it was killing Jeremiah even to consider sleeping indoors. "What Susana and I have decided is to give you the back spare bedroom. It has a window that you can open which should help. I'm not going to ask you to sleep in the bunkroom. It's too enclosed and no need for you to have to put up with the fellows. What do you think? I know it's hard, but will you at least try it?" Elisha waited for Jeremiah to respond.

Jeremiah swallowed and looked Elisha in the eye. "I'll try. If I can't do it, do I need to leave?"

Elisha was shocked. He hadn't expected Jeremiah to have such a thought. "Of course not, you give it your best try and if you can't do it we'll work something else out. But I am going to ask you to really try."

Jeremiah nodded. "Yes, sir."

Elisha regretted causing the panic that crossed Jeremiah's features. He prayed the boy could conquer his fears.

## Chapter 8

Jeremiah didn't know how to make Elisha change his mind. Could he force himself to sleep in the house? It had been awfully cold last night even with the buffalo robe. But to sleep night after night in the house, could he do it? He had to try.

When he went back to the house, Susana met him at the door.

"Come in Jeremiah and see the room."

He followed her down the hall. His chest tightened and his hands shook. He concentrated on breathing normally as he forced himself to follow her. Each step he took, he reminded himself that it wasn't the tunnel.

She opened the door into a fair sized bedroom furnished with a bed, and the bureau, table, and chairs from the porch. The open window made the room cold. Even though it was still full daylight, a lamp burned on the table by the bed. Jeremiah knew that Susana had lit it to help him. He looked around. Someone had positioned the bed so he could look out the window.

"Thank you Susana. I appreciate you making this effort for me. I didn't mean to be a problem."

Susana came over to him and kissed him on the cheek. "You're no bother. You're one of the family and we do what is needed for our family. Is there anything else you can think of that you need?"

Jeremiah looked around the room. "No, this is more than I've ever had before."

"I didn't move your pack or rifle. Go get them and put things where you want."

They walked back to the front room. Susana went into the kitchen and left Jeremiah to go to the porch and get his belongings.

He decided he would hold Elisha to his word. If he couldn't do it he would move back to the porch.

Jeremiah got more nervous as evening approached. After supper everyone gathered in the front room and sang together—a celebration of Joe and Sara's return. Jeremiah sat beside the window of the large, spacious front room. It helped ease his anxiety at the idea of sleeping indoors.

Finally, everyone had gone to bed and Jeremiah sat alone in the front room. He made himself stand and pick up the lamp from the small table at the end of the couch. Taking slow steps, he walked through the hallway to the back bedroom. He looked through the open door and found the lamp lit. Susana. She was such a thoughtful person. He put the lamp he carried on the bureau. Jeremiah wiped his shaking, sweating hands on his pants, but it wasn't as bad as he had feared. He couldn't make himself close the door and hoped Elisha and Susana wouldn't mind if he left it open.

He took off his boots, pulled back the covers, and lay down. Unable to calm his labored breathing, he got up and opened the window a few inches. The cold air flowed in through the window, but he didn't care. He climbed into bed and pulled the covers over his shoulders. He stared around his room and admitted to himself that it looked and felt nothing like the tunnel. For one thing with the two lamps it was much brighter than the tunnel had ever been.

Maybe he could cope with it. It took several hours, but he finally dropped off to sleep only to wake from the dreams. He managed to drift in and out of sleep until he woke to the sound of someone puttering in the kitchen. He dressed and took one of the lamps and went to the kitchen.

"Morning, want some coffee?" Cookie greeted him with a cheerful smile.

"Yeah, I could use some." Jeremiah placed the lamp on the table and sat down.

"Rough night?" Cookie poured a cup of coffee and sat it in front of him. Cookie then placed a plate of apple pie and a fork on the table. "Go ahead and have a piece of pie with your coffee. No one ever said you couldn't have pie for breakfast."

"Thanks." Jeremiah ate the pie and drank the coffee.

Cookie watched him from across the kitchen. "I hope you don't mind me saying it. I'm proud of you, Jeremiah. It can't be easy to go against such fear. It takes courage to do something like that." He looped his apron around his neck.

Jeremiah stared at him. "Courage? Just to sleep in a bedroom like a normal person?"

Cookie pulled pots and pans from the hook above the stove. "Yes, I said courage and that's what I meant. You're a strong man. You've overcome some bad things and you're still willing to keep overcoming. That's what a man does." Cookie got biscuits mixed up and nodded his head to emphasize what he was saying. "You want to help get breakfast ready?"

Jeremiah pushed his chair back. "Sure, what can I do?" Cookie's words tugged on his heart. A strong man? While Jeremiah felt it was untrue, it was still a good thing to hear.

~

Winter allowed Jeremiah more time to get to know the others at the ranch. He rode out when he could and when the weather forced them to hole up, he learned to play chess and talked with Joe and Elisha about ranching. He walked with Joe when the weather permitted. The doctor had told Joe to give his leg three to four more months to heal before he tried anything strenuous.

After a couple of months, Jeremiah no longer reacted to the walk down the hall and into his bedroom. Only occasionally did panic at being in the house overcome him. It gave him hope that he continued to move toward being normal, more like the other riders. Without telling anyone, he challenged himself to sleep without the lamps. He would take it one step at a time.

When the snow melted and the grass grew lush and green, Joe got his cart out. Jeremiah saddled a horse and they rode to the box canyon to check on the horses. Through the winter Jim, Santo, and Jeremiah had worked as they could with the horses, but mostly they had kept the herd together with adequate feed and water in the box canyon. The rest of the wild horses had fended for themselves in the valleys.

Joe looked over the horses they had broken and then pointed one out to Jim and Santo and asked them to catch it.

After Jim and Santo had the horse secured with a couple of ropes, Joe looked at the three men and said, "I need your help. I want to try to ride and I think that horse may be the one to try on."

Jeremiah looked at the horse Jim and Santo had caught and realized Joe chose her for the narrow back and small stature. "Let me saddle her and ride her around a bit to get her settled down."

"All right, that's probably a good idea." Joe fidgeted nervously.

After throwing on a blanket and saddle, Jeremiah mounted the horse and rode it round the corral for about thirty minutes. When he sensed the mare getting tired, he pulled up and dismounted. He walked over to Joe leading the mare.

"You ready, Joe?"

Joe hitched up his pants. "I have to be ready. Can you stand by me in case I can't do it, and then help me get off?"

Jeremiah passed the reins to Joe and rested his hand on his shoulder. "You just tell me what to do."

"Give me a minute. I need to be ready to accept it if it doesn't work." Joe stood and looked up at the sky.

Maybe Joe was praying. Jeremiah didn't say anything and waited. He knew fear. The kind where you didn't know if you could do something that you wanted to do with all your heart.

"I'm ready." Joe straightened the reins and put his left foot in the stirrup. Taking a deep breath, he grabbed the pommel and slowly lifted his right leg up over the back of the horse. He eased himself into the saddle.

"Are you all right?" Jeremiah moved closer and rested his hand on the neck of the horse to help keep it calm and to be ready in case Joe needed him. He watched Joe wipe his brow with a shaking hand.

"I think so. It's a little uncomfortable, but it may just be a question of getting used to it again. Let me walk the horse around a bit." Joe settled the reins in his hand and clicked the signal for the horse to start a slow amble around the corral. Joe rode around several times and then he stopped by Jeremiah.

Jeremiah brushed his dark brown hair out of his eyes. "How does it feel?" He could tell that Joe had reached his limit by the haggard look on his face.

"It feels great. I'm riding. But I think I better let that be it for today and take it slow. I haven't any strength in my legs. I'm not in very good shape."

"Give yourself time. This is the first time you have ridden a horse in years. Can you step off?"

"I don't think so. To step off I have to land on my right leg." Joe looked at the ground. "I tell you what, if I can lift my right leg over the horse's back, could you help me from there?"

"Sure, that'll work." Jeremiah helped Joe dismount.

Joe stood still for a moment. "All right, fellows. I need you all to keep quiet about this. I want to work at it until I can ride a horse up to the house and surprise everyone. Your word on it?" Joe looked at Jim, Santo, and Jeremiah.

Santo twisted the end of his moustache and nodded. "*Si, Señor.*"

"Sure Joe." Jim's thin face lit up with a smile. "We understand and we'll help make it a surprise."

"Thanks fellows." Joe grinned at them and went to the cart.

Jeremiah couldn't imagine how Joe must feel. He could ride. It might take him awhile to get back to riding as he used to, but at least it was a major start. Jeremiah felt good to be part of it.

~

Joe easily mounted the small brown mare and grinned. "Jeremiah, I've ridden every day for a month now. I feel ready to ride up to the ranch house. You, Jim, and Santo ride ahead. I will ride up alone. Just have every one out front."

When they got to the ranch house, Jeremiah handed off the reins to his horse to Jim and walked into the house. He found Elisha in the front room of the house with the children. Susana and Sara were in the kitchen helping Cookie prepare supper. Jeremiah wanted them to see Joe ride up. How could he get them all out on the porch without revealing Joe's secret? As he walked into the hallway between the bunkroom and the kitchen, he spotted his answer. He rang the bell for supper.

"What are you doing, Jeremiah?" Cookie was at his side in a moment. "Supper is not ready yet."

"Everyone needs to go to the front porch now, please," Jeremiah said.

"Why?" Susana put a bowl on the table.

Jeremiah smiled at her. "Just trust me and go to the front porch."

Everyone stared at him.

Susana folded her hands as if in prayer. "If Jeremiah is smiling, it must be something amazing. Let's all go to the porch." She led the way.

Jeremiah realized she was right. He had a smile on his face and he couldn't remember the last time.

Soon everyone stood on the porch looking puzzled at one another.

Jeremiah stepped to the front and pointed up the valley toward the west. "Just watch."

In a few moments, a man on horseback came down the trail. The late afternoon sun settled in a blaze of glory behind the rider.

"It's Uncle Joe riding a horse," Sam yelled, jumping off the porch. He pointed and waved.

"Oh my. Will you look at that." Cookie beamed with a suspicious glint in his eyes.

Everyone shouted and waved, except Sara who held a hand to her heart and slowly stepped down into the yard. She walked out to meet her husband.

Joe rode up to his wife. Sara caught his stirrup and walked with him to the group waiting at the porch.

Elisha stepped down from the porch and took the bridle in his hand to steady the horse. "You've done it, Joe. Praise the Lord, you've done it." His whole face was alight with his look of joy.

Jeremiah walked to the side of the horse to steady Joe if he needed help dismounting.

Joe held onto the pommel with both hands while he slipped his left foot out of the stirrup and eased down to the ground. Joe turned and grinned at Jeremiah.

He grinned back.

Elisha gathered up the children and said, "Joe, I have a feeling you had a partner in this surprise. Let's go into the house and you tell me how you did this without us knowing."

~

After that Joe progressed rapidly toward complete healing. He only used the cart when he wanted to take Sara or one of the children for a ride.

Pride filled Jeremiah that he'd taken part and witnessed Joe's return to the saddle. He'd helped Joe get back something important to his life.

## Chapter 9

His third year on the ranch Jeremiah turned twenty-one

"Hey, Jeremiah. Want to go fishing?" Nine-year-old Sam hollered at Jeremiah who was almost asleep in the rocker on the front porch.

Feeling decidedly lazy after eating Cookie's Sunday dinner of fried chicken, mashed potatoes, gravy, biscuits, several different vegetables, and apple pie, Jeremiah wasn't sure he wanted to do anything. But when he looked into the eager face of the little boy hopefully holding a couple of fishing poles, he could only grin. "Sure, Sam. Let's go fishing." He turned to Elisha sitting in the other rocker with his head leaning back and his eyes closed. "That all right with you, Elisha?"

Without opening his eyes Elisha smiled and said, "Please take Sam fishing so I can take a nap in peace and quiet."

"Okay, little man. Where do you want to go?" Jeremiah started walking toward the barn. Unless it was real close he wanted to ride a horse.

Sam skipped to stay up with Jeremiah's long legged stride. "You know where the creek curves at the west end of the valley and makes that big pool? That's a good place to fish. Or, even back up a ways where it slows down just before the short rapids starts ... or, how about we go—"

Jeremiah was laughing so much he could hardly talk. "Whoa, buddy. The pool where the creek curves will do for this afternoon. You fish too much and know all the good places."

Sam grinned. "Yeah, I like to fish."

"That tin bucket got worms in it?"

"Sure does. I dug them up this morning before church. I was hoping you'd want to go fishing with me."

COLORADO MORNING SKY

Jeremiah reached out and ruffled the little boy's hair. He was pleased that the child wanted his company. "Unless I got work to do, I'm always happy to go fishing with you Sam."

They saddled their horses and headed toward the west end of the valley. It was a beautiful beginning of a summer afternoon. Jeremiah soaked up the warm sunshine and peacefulness of the day. He had a home, work to do, friends, and life was good.

Along the creek were Douglas fir, lodgepole pine, and aspen. Farther up the mountains, Jeremiah could see fir and Engelmann Spruce. They unsaddled and staked out the horses in a meadow to graze. They settled on a spot by the pool of gently flowing water under several aspen as the sun was starting to warm the landscape. In comfortable silence of friends, they each took a fishing pole and placed a worm on the hook. Stretching out his long legs, Jeremiah let his fishing line drift on the water, not really caring if he caught a fish or not.

After a while Sam broke the silence. "Jeremiah, kin I ask you a question?"

He turned to the boy to find a serious expression on his young face as he stared out over the creek. "Sure, Sam. Ask me anything you want."

"Well, I noticed in church this morning that all the grown-ups took the Lord's Supper but you and Uncle Joe. Don't you believe in God?" His voice held a tentative puzzlement.

Jeremiah struggled to think how to answer. Little Sam had led such a sheltered, protected childhood. He knew nothing of the evils out in the real world beyond the ranch. Not only his folks but everyone on the Rocking ES made it their responsibility to protect not only Sam, but his younger brother and sister. "I do believe in God, Sam. But I need to be a Christian before I presume to take the Lord's Supper and I've never done what the scriptures tell me I should do to become a Christian."

"Why is that?" Sam glanced up at Jeremiah from where he sat pulling up blades of grass with one hand and holding onto the fishing pole with the other.

"The Lord's Supper is in memory of the sacrifice of Jesus Christ on the cross so Christians can have a way to have their sins forgiven. I need to be a Christian before I take that step." Jeremiah glanced over at Sam to see if the little boy understood what he was trying to say.

Sam looked out over the creek with a frown. "Then why aren't you a Christian?"

"Well, Sam there are some things I need to be willing to do before I can be a Christian and I'm not real sure how to do them." Jeremiah was sharing with Sam what he had never spoken of to anyone before. Maybe because Sam was a child and so quick to accept him that there was no need to hold back trust. "I had some bad things happen to me before I came here and someone hurt me real bad. I can't forget and forgive. But to be a Christian I need to forgive and I'm not sure how to do that."

"Is that why Uncle Joe doesn't take the Lord's Supper?"

"I don't know, Sam. That might be something for me to ask him."

Sam looked up at him with a smile. "I know what you ought to do, Jeremiah. Talk to Papa. He knows everything about the Bible. He can tell you what to do."

Jeremiah had to grin back at the boy. His child like trust in his father's knowing all was delightful to see. What would it be like to have had a father like Elisha growing up? Sam had no idea how blessed he was to have the folks he had, nor how blessed it was to grow up on a ranch like the Rocking ES.

"That's good advice, Sam. I'll do that. But for now let's keep this talk just between you and me."

Sam nodded. "All right. Hey, look! You line is moving."

They ended up catching several good-sized fish. After cleaning them, Jeremiah took them in to Cookie to fry up for supper. After supper Jeremiah walked up the trail back of the house to a point where he had a great view of the valley and the high snow-covered mountains beyond. He needed time to think over his talk with Sam. The little boy had got him to thinking. Jeremiah wanted to be pleasing to God. The more he read the Bible and understood who Jesus really was, the more he wanted to be a part of the disciples. But how could he when he couldn't let go of his memories of the tunnel and the old man. Forgiveness was what the old man had asked for in his note, but forgiveness was something Jeremiah didn't know how to give the old man.

~

After a restless night, Jeremiah rode out with Joe to work with the horses.

"Hey, Jeremiah. You look tired. You doing all right?" Joe rode his sorrel mare with more ease every day.

"Sure, just have a lot on my mind."

"Anything you want to talk about?" Joe kept his horse even with the black gelding that Jeremiah was mounted on.

Jeremiah kept his eyes on the trail. "Can I ask you a personal question, just between you and me?"

"You can ask me anything and it won't even go to Sara." Joe promised.

"Little Sam asked me a question yesterday afternoon that got me to thinking."

Joe laughed. "That doesn't surprise me one bit. That boy is a deep thinker."

Jeremiah chuckled in agreement. "Well, he asked me why you and me were the only ones that didn't take the Lord's Supper on Sunday morning at the worship. I told him why I didn't but of course I couldn't speak for you."

Joe glanced over at him. "You mind telling me how you answered that?"

"No, I don't mind. I told him that I didn't think I should until I became a Christian and I couldn't become a Christian until I could forgive the old man who kept me prisoner in the tunnel. And to be honest, Joe, I don't know how to do that."

With a deep sigh Joe said, "That's my problem too. I don't know how to forgive my mother for what she did to me. I think I have forgiven my pa but she is a different story. And like you, I'm not sure how to do that. That verse that says that God will forgive us as we forgive others keeps resounding in my mind. If I can't forgive her for the torture she put me through then how can God forgive me." Taking off his hat and running his fingers through his hair, Joe let out another sigh. "I know that God wants me to be willing to surrender to Him and accept Jesus as the Christ by being baptized. I know what to do to become a Christian, I just can't see how I can do that and still be so unforgiving of my mother."

Jeremiah heard the pain in Joe's voice. It matched his own when it came to letting go of his feelings toward the old man. "Little Sam had the idea that it might help to talk to Elisha about it. What do you think about both of us together go talk to him?"

Joe pulled back on the reins and said, "Whoa, girl." The horse stopped and Jeremiah pulled up beside him. "Elisha was going to go ride around the south herd. What do you think about finding him and see if we can talk to him now. This is something that has bothered me for years. If he can have another slant to it, I'd be willing to listen."

Jeremiah had not thought about talking to Elisha so soon but did not see any reason for a delay. "All right, if you don't think he will mind."

Joe chuckled. "For this, Elisha will make the time. He loves to talk about God and spiritual things."

It took them half an hour to find Elisha at the west end of the valley where he was riding through the herd that was grazing on the tall summer grass.

As they rode up Elisha turned in his saddle. "Joe, Jeremiah. Is everything all right? Why are you all riding out here? I thought you were heading to the boxed canyon to work with the horses."

Deciding to let Joe take the lead, Jeremiah quietly sat on his horse.

"Jeremiah and I got to talking about something and decided we wanted your ideas on it. It has to do with why he and I are the only ones on the ranch not a Christian." Joe waited for Elisha to respond.

"I got a coffee pot and coffee with me. I had thought to stop with some of the fellows and have a cup later. Let's go find a spot, make a pot of coffee, and talk. Follow me." Elisha turned his horse toward the creek and away from the herd. He found a clearing by the flowing stream and dismounted.

Jeremiah dismounted, found a green piece of wood, and pounded it into the ground under the aspens but away from the creek. He took his rope off his saddle and tied it around the cannon bone on the front left leg of his horse and tied the other end of the rope in a bow line around the stake. Because he had staked out this horse many times the gelding began to graze contently. Joe and Elisha had also staked out their horses nearby and after nuzzling each other the three horses calmly grazed together. With the horses settled, the men quickly made a fire and filling the coffeepot with water from the creek soon had a pot of coffee boiling. After letting the coffee grinds settle, Elisha poured each of them a cup of coffee.

Taking a sip of the hot brew Elisha looked over his cup at Joe. "You want to start?"

Joe wrapped his hands around his tin cup as if drawing the heat of the coffee into his fingers. "Jeremiah and I talked and decided we needed some help with a similar problem. I'll speak for myself and then Jeremiah can add his own questions." He stopped and took a sip of coffee. "You've never pushed me nor asked me why I haven't become a Christian. I know from reading the scriptures and from listening to the Bible studies what to do. I need to believe, repent of my sins, and reenact the death burial and resurrection of Jesus by being baptized. I know from reading the second chapter of Acts that only after I am baptized, understanding what I'm doing, can I have forgiveness of sins and receive the Holy Spirit."

Elisha cocked his head and frowned. "If you know all this and believe, what is holding you back Joe?"

"How can I say I'm truly repenting if I can't forgive my mother for what she did? How can God forgive me if I can't forgive her?"

"Joe, do you hate your mother?"

He looked startled. "No, not really. I can't say I love what she did to me but I want to at least not hold anger toward her. It was a long time ago and I don't even think about her much anymore."

"If she were still alive would you want to hurt her, either with words or any other way?" Elisha kept his voice calm and soft.

Jeremiah had forgotten about his coffee as he listened to Elisha and Joe talk. It all related to his own situation and he wanted answers. He waited for Joe to answer.

"No, I don't want to hurt her. What I want more than anything is to ask her why."

Elisha turned to Jeremiah and asked, "Is this sort of what you're dealing with as to the old man who so badly used you?"

Taking a long swig of coffee, Jeremiah finally answered, "Yes, it is exactly the same. I'm not as knowledgeable about the Bible as Joe but I believe I understand from reading the New Testament what God requires of me. I know for sure I haven't forgotten what the old man did to me."

Elisha reached over and poured himself another cup of coffee. He held up the pot but Joe and Jeremiah both shook their heads to another cup. "Could the problem be, fellows, that you have confused the difference between forgetting and forgiving?"

Joe tipped his hat back. "What do you mean? I don't see a way to forget. I know the scriptures teach us that God remembers our sins no more when we repent and ask for forgiveness, but I'm not God."

Jeremiah chuckled. "Well, you know for sure that I'm not God and have made my share of mistakes. I'll leave running the universe to Him. I'm just trying to figure out my little life here."

Elisha joined in with his humor. "I think we are all relieved that God is in His heaven and all is right with the world. Let me try to explain the difference between forgiving someone for what they did wrong to you and still remembering what they did. We forgive by letting go of the anger and hurt and giving it to God. We give up wanting the person who wronged us to make it up to us. Often they can't make it up to us because they don't have the heart, or because they are dead. They will never do their part to earn our forgiveness so it becomes impossible and will never happen. Our giving it up to God is not an easy thing to do but we keep trying to be able to say, 'I forgive you with the love of God'. Nor is it a one time thing. We do it every time we think about the person."

Elisha paused and looked at his two friends. "Eventually, you will find that you have let it go and forgiven the person. But, and here is the problem, we are humans and we don't forget. The memories come back to haunt us. And when they do we have to actively make ourselves stop thinking about it and let it go." Elisha swung his gaze from Joe to Jeremiah. "That's what God asks of you. He asks that you make the effort to forgive and control the amount of time you spend thinking about it."

Joe leaned forward. "When you put it that way I think maybe I have forgiven my mother. I just can't forget what she did. I can go days and not think about it and then something happens or I have a dream and it's all back, the memories."

"But it is less now than it was even a couple of years ago?"

"Yeah, Elisha, it's much less."

Elisha turned to Jeremiah. "You haven't said much."

Jeremiah smiled. "I learn better by keeping my mouth shut. I don't want to hurt the old man. I'm like Joe. I just want to ask why.

A J HAWKE

Why did he think he had the right to treat me like that? And why do what he did if he knew he needed forgiveness for it?"

Elisha threw the last drops of coffee out of his cup onto the nearby grass. "What I think is that both of you fellows have forgiven and have confused remembering with not forgiving. What you need to be more concerned with is your disobedience by not surrendering to God and accepting the sacrifice of the blood of Jesus the Christ by being baptized to wash away your sins. I'll ask you the same question Ananias asked Paul in the book of Acts, 'What are you waiting for? Rise up and be baptized and wash away your sins.'"

Jeremiah stared at Joe who stared back. "I want to feel clean from my sins and start all over. I want to be baptized as soon as possible."

Joe nodded. "I'm ready. I've been ready for a couple of years and just didn't know it." He turned to Elisha. "I know Sara would like to be there when I confess Jesus as my Lord and get baptized. Will you baptize Jeremiah and me today?"

With what looked suspiciously like tears, Elisha blinked and swallowed before answering. He then stood and held out his hand to Joe. "I would be honored." He then shook hands with Jeremiah.

Jeremiah rubbed the back of his neck. "How do we go about this?"

Elisha slapped him on the back. "Have you ever seen a baptism?"

"No, sir. I've read about them in the New Testament."

"Well, what I suggest is we ride back to the house and get the word out to everyone and just before supper we go down to the creek and I will baptize the both of you. Everyone is going to want to be there as this is a special occasion." Seeing the frown on Jeremiah's face Elisha spoke more softly. "Don't worry Jeremiah. You just wear an old shirt and pants and go into the creek fully dressed with me and Joe. You won't have to say much. If having everyone there is a problem for you it can just be you and me. Whatever you need."

Jeremiah appreciated the explanation Elisha gave him. He was nervous but the people on the ranch were like family to him. The only family he had. If they wanted to see him baptized, so be it. "We'll do it with everyone there as long as I don't have to give a talk."

Elisha grinned. "You don't have to give a speech to be baptized, Jeremiah. Although it might be a good time for me to practice a sermon. Only kidding, fellows. Let's break camp and ride back to the house. We have good news to share."

An hour later they rode up to the barn by the house. Bob was busy helping Jim shoe a horse. Elisha dismounted and walked over to them. "Bob, after you finish shoeing that horse I want you and Jim to ride out and tell everyone to come on in to supper early. I have something to tell everyone and I want to do it before supper."

Bob took the hoof clippers from Jim. "Sure thing, boss."

Jeremiah took care of his horse and then slipped into the house. Going to his bedroom, he pulled an older shirt and pants out of the armoire and changed into clothes to be baptized in. He pulled off his boots and slipped on his moccasins. Taking his Bible he went to the front room to wait for Elisha to tell him it was time to go down to the creek. After sitting in one of the comfortable leather bound chairs, he opened his Bible to the book of Acts and began to read. Every few versus he found his thoughts wandering to the coming event. He wanted to be right with God and believed that what he was about to do was the right thing. But would he be able to live up to what God wanted him to be? All he could do was try.

Soon others started to drift into the large front room until it was full. Elisha came in with Susana. "Let me have every one's attention." Gradually the room became quiet. "Joe and Jeremiah have honored me today by asking me to guide them toward being baptized and becoming a Christian."

Suddenly everyone was smiling and murmuring. "Great news." "Good for you." "Praise God."

Jeremiah felt his face getting hot as his normal reaction of being embarrassed whenever he was the center of attention. He almost missed Elisha's next words.

"Joe, Jeremiah? You two ready to go down to the creek?"

Jeremiah placed his Bible on the table next to the chair. "Yes, sir. I'm ready."

Joe weaved Sara's arm around his. "I'm ready Elisha. Just one thing. Would it be all right if I asked Cookie to baptize me?"

Cookie brushed his hand over his eyes. "Oh my, Joe. I'd be honored to baptize you."

Elisha and Susana each gathered up a child and led the way out the door. It was like a parade as everyone on the ranch made their way down to the side of the creek.

"Jeremiah, if you will follow me into the water, I'll baptize you first." Elisha pulled off his boots and walked into the cold creek water.

Toeing off his moccasins, Jeremiah followed him.

Elisha stopped when the water was swirling around his waist. "This is deep enough. Just relax and I'll take you down into the water and then raise you up. Now, before these friends who care about you, tell me why we have come here this afternoon."

Jeremiah slid his gaze over the men and women of the ranch and the three small children watching with their eyes round and excited. He saw looks of love and respect. Every person there he could count on to be his friend.

Clearing his throat he said, "I believe in and want to surrender to the will of God and the Lord Jesus Christ. I need my sins forgiven and I want to be right with God. I know that God has asked me to be baptized, understanding what I'm doing, and He promises to forgive my sins and make me His child. He promises to be my Father and eventually take me to heaven. Oh, and He promises to give me the Holy Spirit to help me here on earth. I think that is all." He turned to Elisha and this time there was no mistake, tears were running down Elisha's face.

Elisha nodded. "You ready?"

Jeremiah responded, "Yes, sir. I am now."

"Hold on to my arm." Elisha held up his other arm. "Jeremiah, in the name of the Father, the Son, and the Holy Spirit, I baptize you for the forgiveness of your sins and so that you may receive the gift of the Holy Spirit. Amen."

Jeremiah let his body follow Elisha's arm and laid back into the water until it completely covered him and then Elisha's strong arm was lifting him back up. Jeremiah shook his head to get some of the water off. Elisha guided him back up the creek bank to where Susana handed Jeremiah a towel and Bob wrapped a blanket around him. Shivering from the cold creek water that was fed by melting snow, Jeremiah felt a load lift from him and he no longer sensed the dark hole at the center of his being. Instead, he sensed a wholeness he had never experienced before. Was this what it meant to be a child of God and to have the Holy Spirit with him?

Before Jeremiah could really think about what he had just done Elisha spoke up. "I want to welcome you, Jeremiah, into the family of God and to call you my brother in Christ. God has now added you to Christ's body, the church. And now Joe has asked Cookie to baptize him into the death, burial, and resurrection of Christ."

Jeremiah watched as Cookie led Joe into the cold creek water until they were both waist deep. Cookie repeated what Elisha had done and said and within a few minutes, Joe was also baptized. He was clasped into a bear hug by his old friend. As soon as Cookie released him from the hug, Joe turned and sought his wife. Sara was standing on the bank with a look of joy. He walked out of the creek dripping water and caught her up in an embrace that lifted her off her feet.

"Oh, Joe. I'm so happy. God has answered my prayers." Sara had tears running down her cheeks.

Joe gathered his wife into his arms. "I'm just sorry it took me so long to figure out what to do."

Elisha wrapped a blanket around Joe and Sara as they held on to one another.

Soon everyone was hugging and giving manly slaps on the back. The women were crying and Jeremiah saw a glint or two in some of the men's eyes. The children were running around laughing and enjoying the celebration.

Elisha gave a whistle and everyone quieted down. "Let's head back to the house. We need to get into dry clothes and supper is waiting. This evening let's meet in the front room for a time of song and prayer to thank God for today."

Susana wrapped her arm around Jeremiah's and walked to the house with him. Contentment and peace such as he had never felt before settled on him as he walked with his friends and new Christian family back to the ranch house.

## Chapter 10

Jeremiah, Jim and Santo took a trip in the spring to deliver some horses to a rancher near Cedar Ridge, Colorado. They had to lay over in the town for a few days while the rancher arranged payment.

Jeremiah sat in the lobby of the hotel reading the local newspaper. Jim and Santo were down at the local mercantile looking for purchases to take back to the ranch with them. As Jeremiah looked over the ads on the back sheet of the paper, he noticed an ad for a ranch that was for sale just outside of town. It listed a Mr. Novak, Attorney as the selling agent.

Jeremiah had been working for four years on the Rocking ES with Elisha, Susana, Joe, Sara, Cookie, and the others. As he reflected on those four years, he considered how these friends had helped him achieve a level of contentment that he would never have thought possible before he met them. The way they'd taken him in when he hardly knew how to conduct himself around civilized people had made all the difference to him.

Could he make it away from the Rocking ES on his own? He wanted to try. Elisha and Joe had talked often about getting another ranch down in the low country. Partly because he had nothing to do for the rest of the day and partly because of an idea forming in the back of his mind, Jeremiah asked about the location of the attorney's office and walked down to ask him about the ranch that was for sale.

Jeremiah opened the door and stepped from the boardwalk into the small office. A portly man was seated behind a battered desk. "You Mr. Novak?"

The man looked up with a smile, "Yes, sir, that's me. What can I do for you?"

"You the one that put this ad in the paper about this ranch for sale?"

"Yes, I'm handling the sale for the Turner family who are back east. You interested?"

Jeremiah didn't want to seem too eager. "I might be. What can you tell me about it? Why is it for sale?"

The man pushed himself up out of his chair. "The easiest way to tell you about the ranch is show it to you if you got a few hours."

Jeremiah shrugged his shoulders. "I got all day."

"Good, let's go get my buggy hitched up and we can go now. It's only four miles out of town on a good road. What's your name young man?"

"I'm Jeremiah Rebourn. I work on a ranch up in the mountains west of here. I got some money saved and I'm looking to start my own place."

"That's great young man. Let's go see the ranch and see if it will do for you."

Novak had a nice pair of bay horses and at a slow trot it only took them thirty minutes to reach the ranch.

As Novak drove up the long drive from the main road to the ranch house, Jeremiah eagerly looked over the pastureland with a tree-lined creek to the far right. Compared to the size of Elisha's ranch it wasn't large, only 4500 acres, but Jeremiah could envision partnering with Elisha and Joe. The ranch would do very well as a winter range for the horses and in summer, they could take them back to the high mountain valleys. Hay grown and cut through the summer could be stored to feed the horses still on the ranch in winter.

The ranch had a fair-sized house that had only been vacant for six months and a solid barn with a good corral. Several springs trickled across the land and fed into a couple of creeks. Meadows dotted part of the land while canopied forest filled the rest. Four miles of easy terrain separated it from the town of Cedar Ridge.

Jeremiah still had all of the money he had deposited in the banks after selling the gold that the old man had left him from the mine. The asking price was five dollars an acre and the total sale price was only $22,500.00. So on impulse he purchased the ranch.

The purchase price of the ranch hardly made a dent in his bank account.

~

Jeremiah trailed after Jim and Santo as he rode back to the Rocking ES thinking about what he would say to Elisha and Joe. Jeremiah would miss the ranch and the people who had become family. A part of him needed to see if he could function on his own. Four years since the tunnel, fearful dreams still possessed his nights, but the waking daytime dreams almost never happened anymore.

Jeremiah had worked hard at mimicking everyone else. The most difficult had been to sleep without the lamp on. He was able to do that now most of the time. Sometimes when he had a particularly bad nightmare, he lit the lamp for the rest of the night. He never got to where he could shut the bedroom door.

After supper the first night back, he asked Elisha and Joe to stay in the front room and talk. The others went out on the porch to enjoy the spring air.

Jeremiah paced the room, his boots thudding on the polished wood floor. "I have something to tell you fellows and something to suggest." He pushed back the dark brown hair that fell into his eyes.

Elisha leaned back in his chair. "We're listening,"

Jeremiah stopped pacing. "You know how you've talked off and on about finding some winter grazing for the horses at a lower elevation?" He looked from Elisha to Joe.

Joe nodded. "Sure, we've talked about it seriously. It would make a difference in how many of the horses made it through the winter."

Jeremiah took a deep breath and let it out slowly. "Well, when I was over by Cedar Ridge I came across a ranch for sale. I looked it over and it's just what we need." Jeremiah sat in the chair across from Elisha. "It doesn't have lots of acres, only about four thousand five hundred, but that's plenty for the number of horses you want to run." Jeremiah leaned forward and rested his hands on his knees.

"I had some money in the bank and I went ahead and bought the ranch." He paused to allow the information to sink in. "I'd like to talk about me working it, and this fall you drive as many of the horse herds down as you want wintered in the low lands." He pulled the sleeves down on his shirt. "We can talk about what would be my cut when you sell the horses." Had Jeremiah said too much too soon? He waited for Elisha and Joe to respond.

Elisha rubbed his chin. "It sounds like a perfect setup. I just have one question and that is whether you're all right with getting out on your own?"

Jeremiah leaned his tall frame back in the chair. "I feel that I am. It may be harder than I think it will be, but I would really like to try." He ran his fingers through his hair.

Joe turned toward Elisha. "I think we should really consider this if it's what Jeremiah wants to do." He looked at Jeremiah. "I would want it with one condition though. If at any time you feel you need to come back here, you come."

Elisha nodded. "That's right, Jeremiah, this is your home now and we would expect you to come visit and we'd try to visit you." He smiled. "Tell us more about the ranch."

They talked for another hour and Jeremiah shared with them his vision of how their expanding business could work. They finished the talk with a handshake agreement on the partnership and the understanding that Jeremiah would move down to his ranch as soon as he was ready. They would want as much hay cut through the summer as Jeremiah could manage. Then in the fall they would plan to put a horse herd of about 500 horses onto the ranch land.

## Chapter 11

Jeremiah's heart soared when he rode up the lane to his ranch. He'd left the Rocking ES and his family two days before. To leave everyone tore him to pieces, and if he admitted it, he was a little scared. He was also eager to see what he could do. Susana had hugged him and cried as if she was sending off one of her children. Jeremiah had returned her hug blinking his eyes at the strange sensation of tears trying to form. They were his family, the only one he had.

Jeremiah eyed the neglected ranch and saw promise. Four rooms—a kitchen, front room, and two bedrooms—divided the house. Elisha's house on the Rocking ES was more structurally sound. Since Jeremiah only knew the ranch at Rocking ES, he guessed it was normal that he compared everything to it.

Shaking the memories of the leave taking from the Rocky ES, he unloaded his packs onto the sagging front porch and led the four horses to the corral where he turned them loose. Jeremiah stood and looked around him not sure where to start. He had several hours of daylight left and decided to make sure the horses had water and feed. Wood needed to be chopped, and then he would tackle the house.

Jeremiah worked until dusk carrying water from the creek that flowed west of the house to the horses and filling a couple of buckets for the house. He also chopped enough wood to last until the next day. By the time he finished, the sun sat low on the horizon. Jeremiah's stomach tightened when darkness approached. He hadn't felt panic of the darkness for a while and hoped he was past it. Maybe being alone in a new place brought it on. As much as he loved the sunrise, he dreaded the sunset. Darkness was still his enemy.

He went into the house and lit his lanterns, one in the front room and one in the kitchen. The bedrooms could wait until the next day. For the first night in the new place, he put his bedroll on the floor by the open front door.

He fired up the kitchen stove, dug through his pack to find the coffee and coffeepot. He got the coffee ready to brew on the stove, filled a pan with water, and then placed it on the stove to heat. While he waited for the coffee to make, he surveyed the kitchen. Two doors allowed entry into the square kitchen, one from the yard between the house and the barn. The other hung between the kitchen and front room. Three windows provided sufficient sunlight and air into the kitchen. The overabundance of windows was what first drew Jeremiah to the house. Whoever built it had wanted an enormous amount of light, which suited Jeremiah just fine.

A large cook stove with four burners and an oven sat in a corner of the kitchen. Several shelves stood against the wall beside the stove. A rickety-scarred table and three chairs occupied the middle of the room. Furniture didn't concern Jeremiah. Money would buy what he wanted. But he planned to take his time. He had all summer to get the place in shape and cut hay before Joe and the others showed up with the horse herd in the fall.

While his coffee brewed and water heated, Jeremiah got the broom he found in the corner and swept the kitchen. He wiped the dust off everything. With the hot water, he scrubbed the kitchen from top to bottom. Only then did he unpack the kitchen stuff that Cookie had insisted he bring. Those on the Rocking ES didn't know he had money to buy anything he needed. They tried to get him to bring all sorts of things to help him get started. Jeremiah limited what he would accept to what he could carry on three packhorses. It seemed to ease their minds a little to help him set up his home.

Complete darkness surrounded the house by the time he finished. Hunger forced him to pause before tackling the rest of the house. He stood back and admired his clean kitchen. Canned beans heated on the stove would suffice for his first meal in his new home. Jeremiah ate out of the pan, and then he opened a can of peaches. Compared to what Cookie served, he ate a slim supper. He hoped to do better with meals in the coming days. While still unsure about his cooking abilities, preparing breakfast with Joe and Cookie had taught Jeremiah a lot.

He covered a yawn and decided to leave the rest of the house for the following day. He took only his boots and hat off and lay down on his bedroll by the front door. For the first time in months he left the lantern on and during the night woke himself with old nightmares. Elisha warned him that it might be a challenge being off on his own and to give himself time. How Elisha knew so much Jeremiah couldn't figure out, but he was usually right.

Jeremiah woke the next morning after a fitful sleep with dawn just breaking. He rolled up his bedroll and went into the kitchen. There he lit another lantern to chase away the last of the darkness. He started a fire in the stove and heated up coffee left from the evening before. Figuring he would put in a full day of work, he got out the skillet and the small baking pan Cookie had sent and started some salt pork to frying. He mixed some biscuits, put them in the baking pan, and then into the oven. He was grateful now for Cookie and Joe's patience with him. When he had arrived at the Rocking ES he could barely make a pot of coffee.

After he ate and took care of the horses, he cleaned the rest of the house. It took him most of the morning, but he soon had every inch scrubbed and started to arrange things as he wanted.

Jeremiah made a hard decision—hard for him. He wanted to begin life at his new ranch as normal as possible. A twenty-two-year-old man should be able to sleep in his own bedroom without panic seizing him. He chose the bedroom with the largest window. Besides a bunk, an old ladder-back chair made up the furnishings in his bedroom. Jeremiah unpacked his personal belongings and put his bedroll on the bunk. He positioned it where he could see not only out his bedroom window, but also through the house and out the front room window.

He saddled his horse and prepared a packhorse, then rode the four miles into Cedar Ridge. It was strange to be so close to a fair-sized town that one could just ride in, shop, and then be home before dark. This comforted him. He also admitted to himself that he might be a little lonely.

Jeremiah tied the horses to the railing in front of the general store. He pulled his shirtsleeves over his wrists and the wristbands that Elisha had given him as a parting gift. The bands were of black leather with a tan cross woven on the top. Instead of looking at his scars on his wrist from his time in the tunnel, he now glanced at the wristband that was a reminder that he was now a Christian. Except to bath, he never took the wristbands off as they helped hide the ugly scars.

He walked into the mercantile and stopped. A low whistle escaped through his lips. Merchandise stacked high down several aisles of the large store. He reminded himself to act normal and took a deep breath. Fighting back the panic of being enclosed, he walked down aisles to the back of the store. Milburn Black, owner of the store, stood behind the counter. Jeremiah remembered him from his last trip to Cedar Ridge. He had seen the man but had not spoken to him.

Milburn looked over the top of his glasses. "Howdy, what can I do for you?"

Jeremiah leaned his arm on the counter. "Howdy, Mr. Black."

"I'm just Milburn to my customers."

"Well, I'm just Jeremiah to store keeps."

Milburn laughed. "Good enough. Are you new in town?"

"I just bought the old Turner place. I'm Jeremiah Rebourn. A friend of mine told me to say hello and that this was where I needed to do my purchasing."

Milburn clasped his hands around his broad midsection and looked over the top of his glasses. "Who might that be?"

"Elisha Evans, who used to work for Sam Weathers and now has his own place."

Milburn pushed up his glasses and smiled. "I remember Elisha Evans very well and that little wife of his. How are they doing?"

"They're doing fine. They have three children and their ranch is doing well."

"Agnes, come over here. We've news of Elisha and Susana Evans." Milburn waved to a woman putting fabric out. A woman with gray hair pulled back into a braided bun and wearing a blue and red vertically striped dress walked up to the counter.

"I'm Agnes Black." She held out her hand.

Jeremiah shook her hand. "I'm Jeremiah Rebourn. Glad to meet you. Susana Evans told me to give you her greetings. I just left their place three days ago."

Milburn closed the ledger he was working on. "Jeremiah here has bought the old Turner place and will be our neighbor."

Agnes clapped her hands together. "That's wonderful. That place needs someone to come in and get it back into shape." She leaned towards Jeremiah. "Now tell me about Elisha and Susana."

Jeremiah told them about the children and the ranch. Then he gave them his list. He said he needed to go to the bank and then eat. They promised to have the items tallied and ready to load when he returned.

Jeremiah went to the bank and drew out a thousand dollars. He'd transferred a large deposit from Denver when he had arranged the purchase of the ranch. The banker treated him with the respect owed to a successful rancher, something unfamiliar to Jeremiah.

Noontime customers filled half the hotel's dining room. Jeremiah found a table by a window in the back and when the server came, he ordered a large meal. He was that hungry, but he also planned for it to be his main meal for the day.

After his meal, Jeremiah went to Herman Jones' livery and wagon yard and ordered a wagon. When he arrived back at the general store Milburn and Agnes had his purchases stacked, ready for him to pack on the horse.

Milburn pulled a pencil from behind his ear and checked the list he held in his hand. "That comes to fifteen dollars, Jeremiah."

Jeremiah removed five hundred dollars out of his wallet and placed it on the counter. "I'd like to open an account with you. I don't like to pay every time I might have to come in and get a keg of nails or a pound of coffee. So if you're willing I'd like to put five hundred into an account with you and when that runs out you let me know."

Milburn adjusted his glasses and cleared his throat. "That would be wonderful, Jeremiah. You sure you want to do that? That's a lot of money and we would give you credit."

"I'm sure. It just makes it easier for me," Jeremiah assured him.

"Well, it'll certainly help us out. We're always a little behind in having enough cash."

"I've got a lot of work to do at the ranch and will be purchasing a lot more in the next few months." Jeremiah pulled down his shirtsleeves. "One thing I'm going to need is a couple of fellows to help make and put up fencing. If you know of anyone needing work tell them to come out and talk to me."

Milburn opened the ledger and turned to an empty page. He wrote Jeremiah Rebourn at the top and entered five hundred dollars as an opening amount. "I'll keep my ears open."

Agnes leaned forward. "When you write Susana please give her my regards."

Jeremiah hadn't thought of writing. What a great idea. He assured Mrs. Black that he would.

Milburn helped him get the packhorse loaded and Jeremiah headed home. As he rode, he reflected on a name for his ranch and decided to call it the Rocking JR. At home, he unloaded everything into the house and then turned the horse loose in the corral.

He had bought two more lamps, oil for the lamps, a bowl and pitcher for his bedroom, a quilt, and a small rug so his feet didn't touch the bare floor when he got out of bed. Food items, including some eggs, Jeremiah stored on the kitchen shelves.

After he had everything put away, he decided to look around a little to get a better lay of the ranch. He walked back beyond the house until he could look out over the land he had purchased. Green hills dotted the landscape, but he could not see the snowed-capped mountains. He would miss the splendid view at the Rocking ES, but come the middle of winter he knew he would not miss the heavy snow and bitter cold.

Jeremiah took his hat off and fanned his hot, sweaty face. He looked at the sky and judged how many hours of daylight remained. Satisfied that he would have time for a bath, he grabbed some clean clothes, a flour sack towel and piece of soap, and went to the creek. He found a good place to bathe, removed his clothes and crept into the water. He did not think he could ever just jump in as Joe did. Jeremiah had to approach it slowly. The water was cold as he had expected, but by viciously splashing it onto his chest and back, he got used to it. He scrubbed down and washed his hair. A quick duck under the water rinsed him off, then he climbed onto the bank of the creek and dried off. When the hot days of summer arrived, he might be tempted to linger in the water, but not yet.

Once dried off, Jeremiah looked at the scars on his wrists and ankles. They had faded some, but would forever be a part of him as a reminder of the tunnel. Jeremiah admitted that his body had matured and filled out during the four years on the Rocking ES. Physically, he felt strong and healthy. If it hadn't been for the scars, he could have seen himself as almost normal.

~

Jeremiah had been at the ranch two weeks and had worked from sunup until sundown. He got a lot done, but everything he accomplished revealed how much more work remained.

Returning to the ranch house after his daily bath in the creek late one afternoon, he observed a rider coming up the lane from the main road. Jeremiah put his dirty clothes down on the porch and waited. As the horseman got closer, he recognized Jacob from the Rocking ES.

Jeremiah stepped off the porch to meet him. "Hey, Jacob, what are you doing here?"

Jacob dismounted, shook hands with Jeremiah, and grinned. "Elisha sent me. He told me since I am a better builder than rider you could use me more than he could. Of course, if it's all right with you."

Jeremiah slapped his hat on the side of his leg. "All right? Why, it's great!" He realized that it was just what he needed. He wouldn't be alone.

"Well, to tell you truth, I kind of like the idea of working where it not so cold in winter." Jacob looked around at the house and barn. "This is a nice place, Jeremiah."

"Well, it's a start. I have a lot of work to do and a lot of it is building." Jeremiah grabbed Jacob's arm. "Come on in. I was about to start supper."

Jacob grinned. "Let's put my horse in the corral first."

Jeremiah nodded. "Of course, I'm just glad you have come."

After unsaddling and feeding Jacob's horse, they turned him into the corral. Jeremiah then led the way into the house.

"The bedroom on the right can be yours, but I don't have any furniture yet." Jeremiah opened the door to the empty room.

Jacob walked into the bedroom that Jeremiah had cleaned and put his bedroll on the bare floor "You not worry about furniture. You just tell me what you want and I make it."

Jeremiah smiled at the soft-spoken German. Jacob's skills would come in handy around the ranch. They went into the kitchen and Jeremiah started putting a supper together. Before he knew it, Jacob was helping.

Jeremiah cocked his head. "Can you cook, Jacob?"

"Yes, I can cook good. I just never do it at Rocking ES because Cookie is cook. But if you want I can do cooking."

Jeremiah sighed. "That would be a relief. I can cook a few things, especially for breakfast, but it's limited."

"Then I will cook. Can we afford good food?"

Jacob, of course, had no idea of Jeremiah's wealth.

"I have a tab at the general store. I'll introduce you and you can pick up anything we need." Jeremiah put plates and utensils on the table. "In fact, you look around and see what we need and we can go into town tomorrow. I've ordered a wagon and Herman Jones sent word that it's ready. We'll pick it up tomorrow and get what supplies you see we need." Jeremiah grinned. It was great to have help; maybe some things would now get done.

Jacob sat a pan of cornbread on the table beside the ham and greens. "What about tools? You got tools to build with?"

"I got a saw, hammer, shovel, and pick. I also got a keg of nails. Anything else you need you get at the general store. They carry just about anything, and if they don't they'll order it."

"That is good. We will build it strong together. Now let us eat and then we make list of what we need."

They spent the evening talking and planning. Jeremiah drew out some plans of furniture he wanted and then he drew the plans of the fencing he planned to build. He also wrote a letter to Elisha and Susana.

"I realize we're talking about months of work. We need to pace ourselves and not get in too much of a hurry." Jeremiah started a list of projects. "I've asked around for a couple of fellows to work on the fencing. When I find them that'll go faster." He set the pencil on the list and leaned back in his chair. "But you build the furniture for your room and whatever else you want to get done. I've got to plan the haying, but not for another month so we have time to get some of these things done."

"It a lot of work, but it worth it on your own place. We will build it good," Jacob promised.

When Jeremiah went to bed, his mind raced with plans, and without thinking he turned the lantern off. Looking out the window at the moon, he realized it. He could cope without the lantern as the moonlight lit the room. Having Jacob in the house also helped.

Jeremiah woke to the smell of fresh coffee. He dressed and went into the kitchen.

Jacob bent over the oven taking out a pan of biscuits. "Morning, you sleep well?" Jacob greeted him cheerfully.

"I slept real well. How about yourself? The floor not too hard?"

"It was hard and I build a bed today after we get back from town. Sit down." He pointed to a rickety chair. "Breakfast is ready." Jacob set a bowl of scrambled eggs on the table with a bowl of gravy and salt pork. He poured two cups of coffee and sat down. "You want to say blessing or me?"

"You say it, Jacob." Jeremiah didn't mind having a blessing, but he'd not said one yet.

"Thank you, Lord, for our bounty and blessings. Bless all on the Rocking ES and Susana as her time of giving birth is near. Bless us this day in our work and bless Jeremiah for giving me a place here on his ranch. In Jesus' name. Amen."

Jeremiah stared at Jacob. "When is Susana expecting another baby?"

Jacob snapped his handkerchief he was using as a napkin. "She should give birth by end of summer. She get awfully big all of a sudden. You didn't know?"

Jeremiah shook his head. "No, but then I don't pay much attention."

"We need to keep her in our prayers," Jacob said.

Jeremiah picked up his fork. "That we can do. Let's get done with breakfast, saddle the horses, and head to town."

They got to town by mid-morning and went to the general store first to leave their list. Jeremiah introduced Jacob and verified that he could charge on the ranch account. Then they went to Herman Jones' wagon yard to pick up the new wagon Jeremiah had ordered. After they took care of the purchase of the wagon, Jacob and Herman talked about wood for the furniture. Jeremiah told Jacob to buy any wood he needed. For the fencing, they would use trees on the ranch.

He left Jacob with Herman Jones and went to the livery where he bought a team of horses to pull the wagon back to the ranch. He could have brought horses from the Rocking ES, but he'd wanted to travel light and the horses at the Rocking ES were too valuable to be used just to pull a wagon. The team he bought was broke to pull a wagon, but not necessarily for riding.

He took the horses to the wagon yard and hitched them. Jacob drove the wagon while Jeremiah walked back to the general store where they loaded their purchases.

Jeremiah pulled an envelope out of his pocket. "You all still handle the mail?"

Milburn looked over the top of his glasses. "We sure do. You got something you want to mail?"

"Yes, I want to mail this letter to Elisha and Susana." Jeremiah handed them the letter he had written the evening before thanking them for sending Jacob. "By the way, Jacob tells me they are expecting another child by the end of the summer."

"You don't say. You hear that Agnes?" Milburn turned to his wife.

Agnes sat two bundles of fabric down and walked over. "Yes I did. We'll need to start praying for Susana."

Jeremiah nodded. "Yes, please do."

"By the way, you boys are invited to come to church. Elisha and Susana always came when they managed to be here on a Sunday." Milburn shook his head and smiled. "My, but those two can sing."

"What is time of church?" Jacob asked.

Milburn took his handkerchief out of his pocket and wiped his nose. "We meet at ten in the morning. The church building is just down to your left there and over a street."

Jacob shook his head. "I don't speak for Jeremiah, but I would like to come."

Jeremiah tipped his hat up. "I'll be with him."

"Good, we'll look forward to your being there."

After they got back to the ranch and unloaded the wagon, Jeremiah asked Jacob, "Have you been to church at places other than the Rocking ES?"

Jacob took the bags of Arbuckle coffee and put them on a shelf. "Yes, I have been many places both in Germany and in America. Before I was cowboy, I worked in Philadelphia. I went to church every Sunday."

"The only church I've ever gone to is the Rocking ES," Jeremiah confessed. "Will it be a lot different?"

Jacob shrugged. "Maybe some but you just follow me and it will be all right."

"What do we need to wear? Can we just wear clean pants and shirt?" Jeremiah looked down at his jeans that were due for a wash.

"Yes, that will be good. Do not you worry, Jeremiah, God knows our hearts, and it will be all right."

"Thanks, Jacob. You know I'm a little limited on my experience with people and any help you can give me will be appreciated." Jeremiah didn't mind admitting that. It was the truth.

"You do just fine." Jacob patted him on the shoulder, then went to get supper started.

It was a relief to Jeremiah to have someone else cooking. He could do the washing up.

## Chapter 12

The next two years went by quickly and contentedly for Jeremiah. He and Jacob worked hard around the ranch. When Elisha, Joe and the other riders brought the first herd down in the fall, it had been a fun time of showing them around the ranch. The second summer Jeremiah and Jacob built a bunkroom onto the house and two more bedrooms. Jeremiah hired some men from town to dig a well and line it with stones. Water readily available made Jeremiah and Jacob's lives easier.

Jeremiah added a bathing room next to the well room. He did not explain to Jacob his aversion to bathing in the creek. He much preferred to heat water and bathe in the big bathtub he had shipped in from the east. He also installed a potbellied stove in the bathing room—a luxury he could afford.

Jacob tore down the old sagging porch and built a new one across the front of the house only he didn't put a roof on the porch in front of the big window. It let light filter through the front room during the day. Jacob built furniture acceptable even in a fine home back east. He not only built himself a bed, but he built a big double bed for Jeremiah's room with elaborate carvings on the headboard. Then he made matching bureaus. Each room also received a washstand with a mirror.

For the front room, Jacob made Jeremiah a desk and chair out of cherry wood. The bright room also held two couches, two overstuffed chairs, and several small tables. Braided rugs covered the floor. Jacob also built bookshelves on each side of the fireplace. His showpiece was the elaborately carved mantel.

Jacob completely redid the large kitchen. Jeremiah told him to do what he wanted, and Jacob did just that. In addition to the original stove that Jacob kept gleaming, a big pie cabinet now held their foodstuff; shelving built against the walls provided storage and counters; a dry sink under the window drained outside; and a large cedar table with eight matching chairs replaced the original broken-down set.

Jacob built fine furniture and sold the pieces at Milburn Black's store. Jeremiah and Jacob had agreed to a partnership. Jeremiah provided the tools, lumber, and shop. Jacob provided the know-how and labor. Jeremiah insisted they split any profits sixty-forty with Jacob taking sixty.

Jeremiah now ran several hundred head of cattle in addition to wintering the horse herd. Jacob took care of the chickens, a garden, and a milk cow. Jeremiah learned to milk the cow and did so when it was needed, but he preferred to leave it to Jacob. He liked Jacob to cook with the fresh milk, eggs, and butter.

When Elisha and his crew came to get the horses in the spring of the second year, Jeremiah and Jacob learned that Bob's wife, Minnie, had died. She developed pneumonia and died a few days later during a terrible cold spell in February. They had been married a little over five years and had no children. It hit them all very hard, especially Bob.

Elisha asked Jeremiah if he would have work for Bob. The Rocking ES held too many memories of Minnie. Jeff could take his place as foreman of the Rocking ES.

Jeremiah nodded. "Sure, I could do with a foreman myself. Do you think he would want to work for me?" Jeremiah respected Bob Fife as a cattleman and knew he would be fortunate to have him. But Bob had known Jeremiah when he had first come to the Rocking ES and Jeremiah didn't know if that would make a difference.

"Let's ask him. I think it'd do him good to have a place where there's lots of work and he could be a part of building it up. He's at the corral tending to the horses."

The two men walked out to the corral were Bob stood currying his horse. He rode many different horses on the ranch, but he favored the palomino and took special care of him.

Elisha leaned against the railings of the corral. "Bob, you got a minute to talk?"

Bob sauntered over to the corral fence. "Sure, Elisha, what can I do for you?"

"Jeremiah and I've been talking. He needs a foreman now that he's running cattle and taking care of the horse herd. I suggested that you might be willing to work with him awhile and let Jeff take your place at the Rocking ES." Elisha put his foot up on the railing. "If it worked out and you wanted to stay here that would be fine with me, or I would expect you to come back to the Rocking ES. But it's totally up to you. I'm fine either way."

Bob glanced around at the ranch house, barn, and pastures and then looked at Jeremiah. "I'd be foreman?"

Jeremiah nodded. "Yes, I need someone and I don't really feel comfortable with a stranger." Jeremiah shrugged. "Bob, you know me. I'm a little strange in some ways and you understand that. I'd be boss, but I'd leave the cattle business up to you. You'd hire and fire just like you do for Elisha. In fact I like everything I've seen you do as foreman for Elisha and that's how I'll want it."

Bob took his hat off and wiped his face with his handkerchief. "This is a smaller operation than we got at the Rocking ES, but in some ways that might be a relief. I like you, Jeremiah, and I think we could work together." He put his hat back on. "What if I said yes for a year and then if I wanted I could go back to the Rocking ES?"

Elisha shrugged and nodded. "I can agree to that, Bob. I'd ask that you go back for a couple of weeks to help Jeff get started and it'll give you a chance to get your things."

Bob glanced at Elisha and then turned to look out over the land. "I know why you're doing this and you're right. I need to get away from the Rocking ES. Everywhere I look I see my Minnie." Tears clouded his eyes. "Maybe it'll be easier here."

"Then let's say you'll be back here in a month or so. Is that all right with you, Jeremiah?" Elisha turned to him.

"That'll be great. Bob, you mind if I hold off on hiring men and wait until you get back to do the branding? I'd much rather you handled that."

Bob shook his head. "No, I don't mind. In fact it'll give me something to look forward to."

"We've got the room next to the bunkroom empty, or we can build you a cabin," Jeremiah offered.

"The room next to the bunkroom or even the bunkroom will be fine. I'm spoiled at Elisha's place with my own cabin, but for now I don't think I want to deal with having one."

Elisha held out his hand. "Then it's settled. I'll miss working with you but I know you are needed here."

"I'll miss the Rocking ES, too. It's been a good place to work." Bob shook Elisha's hand.

Jeremiah reached over and shook Bob's hand. "Hopefully, this will be as good a spread to work on and I'll try to measure up against Elisha as a good boss." He scratched the back of his neck. "Although, that will take some doing."

## Chapter 13

The door to Emily Johnson's room at the Willard School for Young Ladies in Boston flew open and her best friend swept into the room. Emily put her hand to her chest. "You startled me, Victoria."

Victoria placed her packages and then her hat on Emily's bed. "I am so glad you're here. I've been shopping with the Brownell twins and you know how they chatter on and on."

Emily nodded. She did know, but she also knew that seventeen-year-old Victoria likely did some chattering herself. She folded the letter she had just read and put it back in the envelope along with a train ticket and money that had also come with the letter.

Victoria sat down beside Emily. "Who do you have a letter from?" She smoothed out the lavender dress with white lace trim that she had worn to spend the day in town.

"My grandmother. She wants me to come visit her this summer in Colorado after school is out." Emily braced herself for Victoria's disappointment.

"No, not this summer." Victoria threw herself across the bed. "You're to come to Hampton Beach with me like you did last summer." Victoria's pretty little mouth turned into an instant pout.

Emily sighed and shook her head, which caused some of her light brown hair to come loose. "I know. And I'm sorry. But my grandmother has never asked me for anything." She opened the drawer on her night table and placed the letter inside. "She and my grandfather raised me after my parents died and have sent me to school." Emily pulled Victoria's arms so she sat up beside her. She needed her friend to listen and understand.

"Even after my grandfather died, Grandmother insisted that I stay here in Boston and complete my schooling. I haven't seen her for six years. Besides, think of the adventure of going out west. I will see Indians, horses, and cattle."

Victoria cocked her head and grinned. "And maybe even some handsome cowhands. Now that would be exciting." She ran a hand over her coiffure.

Emily laughed. "Yes, in Colorado there are sure to be some cowhands, but I don't remember them being particularly handsome."

Victoria reached out and tucked a lock of Emily's hair behind her ear. "I will miss you this summer. When will you go?"

Emily toyed with the pleats of her green cotton dress. "My grandmother has sent a train ticket and we only have another week of studies. I'll plan to leave the day after classes end." Emily looked around at her room. She would have to get some trunks and hire someone to help her pack. All of a sudden, she had a lot to do. She enjoyed studying and was an excellent student, but she was ready for a change. "First, I must write Grandmother and tell her when to expect me."

~

The four days and nights on the train left Emily exhausted, but the view left her excited to see what turns her life would take. People she saw getting on and off the train fascinated her. The sheltered life she'd led for the last six years at the Boston finishing school had not prepared her for some of the rough-looking characters she saw from the train window. At Cheyenne, Emily changed trains and headed south. Only a couple of hours later the train pulled into the small station at Cedar Ridge.

Emily stepped onto the platform and looked for her grandmother.

A pleasant-looking plump woman in her fifties approached her with a smile and asked, "Miss Emily Johnson?"

"Yes, I'm Emily Johnson." Emily glanced behind the woman, looking for her grandmother.

"I'm Mrs. Spencer. I work for your grandmother and she asked me to meet you."

Emily shook hands with the woman. "Is my grandmother all right?"

Mrs. Spencer dabbed at her face with a handkerchief as the day had warmed with the June sun. "Yes, she's fine except for her arthritis. She doesn't leave the house much because of the pain and stiffness. She's surely looking forward to your coming. Now, let's get your trunks and valises." Mrs. Spencer took Emily's arm and guided her toward a two-seater carriage waiting at the end of the platform.

"Thank you for meeting me. It was a long journey and I'm glad to finally be off the train." Emily carefully held up her hem so she could enter the carriage without tripping.

Mrs. Spencer waved her hand. "Oh, it's no bother. I know you must be exhausted. We'll be at the house shortly and you can take a hot bath and go to bed." She turned to the rotund man who had taken Emily's valise from her. "Homer, just put the bags in the back." Mrs. Spencer held out her open hand toward the man. "Miss Emily, this is Homer Lumas, he works for your grandmother too."

Homer touched his black felt hat and loaded the bags. "I'll drive you ladies to the house and then come back for the trunks." He climbed in the driver's seat and flicked the reins. The two horses pulling the carriage stepped lively down the street.

Emily leaned back and closed her eyes. She wanted to see the town, but she was too tired to care. All she wanted was the bath and bed Mrs. Spencer had promised.

"Here we are," Mrs. Spencer said.

Emily opened her eyes and realized she had fallen asleep. They had stopped in front of a two-story brick house surrounded by lawn with tall cedar and aspen trees beyond the circular drive. Emily followed Mrs. Spencer through the large double front door into a hallway. Rooms opened to both sides, and directly in front of her a sweeping stairway led to the second floor. Mrs. Spencer guided Emily up the stairs and to a large bedroom at the back of the house where she could look out over fields and meadows.

"Mrs. Johnson thought you would like this room. Her bedroom is on the first floor at the back. She can't maneuver the stairs anymore." Mrs. Spencer pulled the drapes back from the two windows and let the sunlight stream into the room. "Now what Mrs. Johnson recommends is that you take a bath, climb into bed, and sleep as long as you want. I'll bring you a bite to eat. Then if you feel up to it you can have supper with your grandmother."

"Oh, that would be lovely. I am so tired." Emily unbuttoned her travel coat and removed it along with her hat.

"Sally should have your bath ready. The water closet is just down the hall and your grandmother had a nice bathtub brought all the way from the east."

"Oh, my goodness. That must have cost a fortune. I hope Grandmother didn't go to any special trouble for me.

Mrs. Spencer stopped unpacking the two valises that Emily had carried on the train with her. "Now don't you fret none about your grandmother's finances. She cares a great deal for you, my dear." She found Emily's gown and robe and laid them on the bed. She placed her slippers by the upholstered chair.

Emily allowed herself to be cared for by Mrs. Spencer's capable hands. "Thank you, you're being so kind. I'll go bathe right now." Emily sat down in the chair and unbuttoned her shoes. She slipped them off with Mrs. Spencer's help and put on her slippers. It was such a relief as she had worn the shoes for four days without removing them. Emily followed Mrs. Spencer down the hall to the water closet and found the large zinc-lined bathtub already full of hot water.

"Here's the pull bell if you need anything. There's soap, lotions, and towels. I'll go bring you up a bite to eat." Mrs. Spencer left her in the small room and closed the door.

After removing her robe, Emily eased herself into the water. She closed her eyes and sighed. Even back east she had never had such luxury. She stayed in the bath until the water cooled. When she returned to the bedroom, she found a tray with muffins and a glass of milk. It was exactly what she wanted, just something to tide her over until supper. She ate and then slid between the covers and, with a sigh of contentment, drifted off to sleep.

Emily woke from her long nap, realized that someone had come in, and lit the lamp. She got up and found one of her dresses hanging over a chair along with clean petticoats. She dressed, brushed her hair, and tied it with a ribbon. She then made her way downstairs.

Just as she got to the bottom of the stairway, Mrs. Spencer came along the hallway from the back of the house. Her face lit up when she saw Emily. "There you are, Miss Emily. I was on my way to wake you. Did you sleep all right?"

Emily gave Mrs. Spencer a warm smile. "I had a wonderful sleep. After that bath and then to be without the noise of the train, I went sound asleep."

Mrs. Spencer clasped her hands together. "I'm so glad. Mrs. Johnson hopes you will join her for supper in the kitchen. She prefers to eat in there rather than the formal dining room. We all eat together, I hope you don't mind."

"Of course not, it sounds lovely."

"Well, follow me." Mrs. Spencer led the way into a large kitchen.

White cabinets hung on the walls and cedar covered the floor. In the middle of the kitchen, Emily's grandmother sat in an invalid chair at a large table.

Grandmother rubbed her arthritic hands together. "My Emily. Do come in."

Emily walked over and gave her grandmother a kiss on the cheek. "I'm so happy to be here, Grandmother. Thank you for sending the ticket."

"You're welcome, my child." Grandmother pushed up her glasses. "Turn around and let me get a good look at you."

Emily turned, and then curtsied for her grandmother.

Mrs. Spencer laid her hand on Emily's arm. "Miss Emily, your grandmother sits at this end of the table. Why don't you take the seat close by her?" She pointed to the place she had chosen for Emily.

Mrs. Spencer motioned to a girl who sat farther down the table. "This is Sally. She's the one who brought the hot water for your bath earlier."

Emily walked over and held out her hand to the curly headed girl. "It's nice to meet you Sally. And thank you for the delightful bath."

Sally shook her hand and smiled. "You're welcome Miss Emily. We're happy to have you here."

Grandmother held up a wrinkled hand when a heavyset woman in her fifties entered the kitchen. "This is Mildred our cook."

Mildred's big smile warmed Emily's heart. "Howdy, Miss Emily. Welcome."

"Thank you Mildred." Emily inhaled deeply. "Everything smells delicious!"

Mildred shooed her with a dishtowel and blushed. She set a plate of fried chicken on the table then took her place across from Emily who sat in the chair indicated.

"Let's eat." Grandmother reached for a piece of chicken.

For several minutes, they busily filled their plates and passed bowls of green beans, carrots, and corn in addition to the fried chicken, gravy, and biscuits.

Grandmother took another bite of chicken, and then looked at Emily. "How are you feeling after such a long train ride?"

Emily put down her fork and wiped her mouth on her napkin. "I'm feeling well after such a lovely bath and nap. I was very tired when I first arrived, but by tomorrow I should be fine."

"That's good. Such a trip would do me in anymore. Although there was a time when I could walk halfway across the state and did." For emphasis, Grandmother nodded at all the ladies.

Emily wanted to ask her grandmother about her health, but hesitated. Arthritis obviously crippled her, for she had difficulty holding a fork with her knobby hands.

After supper, Mrs. Spencer pushed Grandmother back to her room at the back of the house. Grandmother motioned Emily to come with them.

Mrs. Spencer positioned the invalid chair next to a small round table in front of the fireplace. Grandmother reached over and turned up the lamp, casting light around the room. Emily sat down in the oak rocker on the other side of the little table. She ran her hand over the rich maroon velvet fabric and reveled in its softness.

Grandmother rubbed her gnarled hands together. "Tell me about yourself, Emily. I haven't seen you since you left us as a child, but you have come back a beautiful young lady."

"Thank you Grandmother. If I'm a lady it is thanks to you and Grandfather. My schooling must have cost you a fortune and I'm very grateful."

Grandmother put her hand to her heart. "I'd rather you called me Grandma like you did as a child."

Emily smiled, noting that Grandmother had not commented on her schooling. She decided to keep the conversation light. "I remember. I didn't want to be disrespectful, but I would rather call you Grandma, too."

The old woman smiled back. "It's not disrespectful, but I appreciate you thinking of it." She clasped her hands together in her lap. "Now tell me about your schooling."

Emily spent the next several minutes telling Grandma about the school and her friends back east.

Her grandmother pushed her spectacles up on her nose. "Do you miss them?"

Emily focused on the old wall clock hanging on the wall behind Grandma. "Yes, I do miss them." She brought her eyes back to her grandmother who was responsible for her refined teachings. "But I also look forward to seeing some of this country." She leaned forward in the rocker. "It was so exciting on the train to see the different places and people. It is so different than back east." She sat back and shook her head. "A lot of memories of our time together before I went to school started coming back as I got farther west. I haven't forgotten living in New Mexico and Arizona with you and Grandfather. We had a lot of good times."

Grandma pulled her shawl about her shoulders. "Yes we did. Your grandpa knew how to enjoy life. I miss my George."

A faraway look came over Grandma. Emily rocked softly and waited while the old lady revisited the past.

Grandma dabbed her eyes with a hanky. "I wandered around for the longest time, trying to find something worth living for."

Emily nodded. "Then you settled in Cheyenne. I remember from your letters."

Grandma sighed. "Yes. Four years ago. You gave me something worth living for, my Emily." She pushed her glasses up, again.

The old lady looked at her with love and something else that Emily couldn't put her finger on, almost a look of appraisal.

Mrs. Spencer entered with a tray of china cups and a pot of herbal tea.

"I can't get out and take you about to see things, but Mrs. Spencer here is a nice woman. She can take you to see the town. It's not very large, but it is big enough."

Mrs. Spencer ducked her head as if embarrassed. "I'll be more than happy to show you around, Miss Emily."

Emily set her teacup down. "That'll be lovely. I do want to see the town."

"Mrs. Spencer is a good Christian lady and she goes to church every Sunday. I want you to go with her. It will be a good way for you to meet the best people in town."

"I'd be happy to go with you, if that would be all right. I usually go to church with my friends. I'm glad to hear that there's one here."

"It's perfectly all right. You'll enjoy the folks at church. They're a good group of people." Mrs. Spencer nodded. "I'll be back later for the tea tray." She left the room.

Her grandma sipped her tea. "Well, I've never been to the church, but I hear that it's a good sized one for this part of the country and they just got a new preacher,"

"Is there a school?"

"Yes, but I don't know much about it. Why do you ask?"

"I have my teaching certificate. I thought I might—"

Grandma waved, as if dismissing Emily's words. "You don't have to work. I got money." She looked at Emily over the top of her glasses. "And what I got is yours."

Emily reached for her tea. "Grandma, I thank you for your generosity. It's not so much the money as it is to have something to do with my time. I like to stay busy."

"I can understand that. Time weighs heavy on me sometimes. Can you cook and keep house?"

"I can cook a little and do ordinary cleaning, but I'm sure I have a lot to learn."

"Do you intend to marry and bear him lots of children?" Grandma smiled and blinked several times.

Emily laughed nervously at Grandma's bluntness. She'd never known the old lady to be so unsophisticated. "I would love to find a husband and get married. Do you think that will happen out here?"

"Well, since we have about four cowhands to every pretty girl, I think you'll be kept busy swatting the fellows away." Grandma winked at her.

"That sounds like fun."

"I don't know about fun, but it'll probably be true." Grandma sat her teacup down. "I was thinking that maybe you would like to spend some time with Mildred and learn to really cook. And I can teach you to make a mean cornbread." She nodded. "Then you could spend time with Mrs. Spencer and learn how to keep a house and to sew. I figure that finishing school taught you a lot about reading and writing, but maybe not so much about how to do the daily things that make life easier."

Emily set her cup back on the tray. "I hadn't thought about it, but I think it might be fun to learn how to do some of those things. If I did get a job teaching school it wouldn't be until school starts in three months."

"Good, I'll tell Mildred and Mrs. Spencer to plan out how to teach you. And then you can tell me what you're learning. You might even bake me a pie."

Emily smiled at her Grandma. "I'll be glad to bake you a pie."

Grandma shooed her. "Now, go on to bed and get a good night's sleep. Tomorrow being Saturday is a good day to shop. Mrs. Spencer is planning to go and pick up some things for me. You can also spend part of the day getting your things arranged and deciding what to wear to church."

Emily stood. "Goodnight, Grandma. I'm so happy to be home." She kissed her grandma on the cheek and went up to her room.

When she entered her room, she found her trunks. And someone had straightened her bed. She assumed it was Sally. As she prepared for bed, she wondered at her grandma wanting her to learn how to cook and keep house. Emily wasn't opposed to it, but hadn't thought of it as something she needed to do immediately. She had sensed an urgency in Grandma.

~

The next day Emily woke feeling refreshed. All her young healthy body needed was a good rest after the long trip. After breakfast, she and Mrs. Spencer walked the short way to the main downtown street to shop in the big general store.

A bell chimed when they entered and a gray-haired lady behind the counter looked up. "Mrs. Spencer, how are you today?"

Mrs. Spencer made her way to the back counter. "I'm doing fine. Let me introduce you to Mrs. Johnson's granddaughter, Miss Emily Johnson."

"Glad to meet you, Miss Emily. I'm Agnes Black. That's my husband, Milburn, over there with the men." She pointed to a round man with glasses.

"I'm happy to meet you, Mrs. Black. Please call me Emily."

"Then you must call me Agnes. Are you going to be with us for a while?"

Emily nodded. "As far as I know."

Mrs. Spencer set her basket on the counter. "She'll be coming with me to church tomorrow."

Mrs. Black stood with her hands folded and a bright smile. "Well, that's wonderful. Milburn and I will see you there. But, for now what can I help you ladies with?"

Mrs. Spencer pulled two pieces of paper out of her handbag. "Mrs. Johnson gave me her list, and then this list from Mildred."

Emily turned and regarded the store. "I'd like to look around if I may."

Mrs. Black waved toward the merchandise. "By all means. We have a great many items, but if you want something you can't find just ask."

Emily wandered up and down the aisles. Books and items to stock a house cluttered the shelves, and farm tools stood on the floor. She reached up and ran her hand across the colorful stacks of fabrics that lined the shelves along the wall. The abundance of supplies amazed her. How did they keep stock of everything? She spotted some aprons with pretty flower insertions. If she was going to learn to cook, she needed her own apron. She put one of the aprons over her arm and continued to browse.

Bolts of fabrics lay scattered on a nearby worktable. Emily tugged on the edge of a green cotton print that caught her eye.

The bell at the top of the entrance door tinkled and a man's boot heels clomped across the wood floor, drawing her attention away from the material. A young man removed his Stetson, allowing dark brown-colored hair to fall across his eyes.

Emily released the fabric and studied the tall stranger. Dressed in rough dark pants and a colorful plaid shirt with worn boots, he gave the look of a cowhand. She raised her eyebrows at the cowhand's shirt that fought to cover his broad muscular shoulders. Her eyes traveled up to a bandana that circled his throat. Her breath caught in her throat. She'd never been this close to such masculinity.

"Morning Jeremiah. How are things out your way?" Milburn greeted the ruggedly handsome young man.

*Jeremiah.* His name rang through her ears. As he turned his head toward her, she glanced down at the fabric, but kept the man in the corner of her eye mesmerized by his handsome face.

"Morning Milburn, here's a list if you don't mind." He pulled a piece of paper out of his shirt pocket. "I'm headed to the barber to get a haircut, and then to the hotel for a bite to eat. I'd like to pick this up after dinner and head back to the ranch."

Emily made her way to the counter with her apron. She wondered where Mrs. Spencer and Mrs. Black had gotten to.

"Ma'am, have you found what you want?" Milburn Black turned to her and smiled.

"I'm Emily Johnson." She smiled back at the pleasant-faced man. "And I would guess that you are Mr. Black. I'd like to purchase this apron." She glanced toward the cowboy who stared at her.

Mr. Black adjusted his glasses and cleared his throat. "Jeremiah, let me introduce Miss Emily Johnson." He looked over the top of his glasses. "This is Jeremiah Rebourn who owns a ranch outside of town."

"Miss Johnson." Jeremiah gave her a little bow.

His dark brown hair curled over his ears and down his neck. Yes, he needed a haircut. She also noted that he did not wear a ring.

She held out her hand. "Mr. Rebourn, please call me Emily." She smiled at him surprised at her forwardness.

His eyes opened wide and she swore he blushed as he briefly took her hand and then quickly released it. Was he shy?

"Ma'am, Emily, I'm Jeremiah." He almost stammered.

Emily turned back to the storekeeper. "I didn't mean to interrupt, Mr. Black. Continue with Mr. Rebourn. I have to wait on Mrs. Spencer anyway. I'll just look around a little more. It was nice to meet you, Mr. Rebourn ... ah, Jeremiah. I hope we see each other again," Emily said in her best finishing school manners.

He definitely blushed.

Emily wandered off to look at other things and left Mr. Black and Jeremiah to talk.

"I'll be back about one this afternoon if that's no bother," Jeremiah said.

"The items will be ready," Milburn said.

As the two men talked, she saw Jeremiah, out of the corner of her eye, turn and his eyes followed her movements.

Soon he left the store and Mrs. Spencer and Mrs. Black came into view from the other side of the store. Emily went back up to the counter to pay for her apron.

"Jeremiah seems like a very nice man, Mr. Black," Emily said with her best wide-eyed innocent look.

Mr. Black looked at her over the top of his glasses. "That he is, Miss Johnson. He's been here a couple of years." He paused and wrote in his ledger. "He bought the old Turner ranch. He and a big rancher up in the mountains are partners and raise horses. He attends church regularly with his ranch hands. He doesn't have a wife yet." He tucked his pencil behind his left ear.

"What are you going on about, Milburn?" Mrs. Black asked.

"Jeremiah Rebourn was just in and left this list. I was just telling Miss Johnson a little about him." He held out the list to his wife.

Mrs. Black ignored the list and smiled at Emily. "Oh, you met Jeremiah. He's real shy, but very nice. You'll see him tomorrow at church." She leaned against the counter. "Well, maybe you'll see him. He sits in the back and can be gone at the end of the service faster than a plate of donuts around cowhands."

Mr. Black cleared his throat. "Here's your purchase and that will be twenty-five cents."

Emily handed him a few coins, took her package, and waited for Mrs. Spencer to finish her shopping.

They arrived at the house just in time for the noon meal. Then Emily spent the afternoon unpacking her trunks and arranging her things. After supper, she visited with Grandma, who brightened at Emily's account of meeting Jeremiah Rebourn.

Emily fell asleep that night thinking of the tall handsome cowboy.

~

Emily woke the next morning feeling as if she had butterflies in her stomach. She dressed carefully for the church service, deciding on her light green dress with a hat to match. She debated what to do with her hair but settled on a French knot at the base of her neck. She put it up loosely so it framed her face instead of pulling it back into a severe bun. With her soft gray gloves, she knew she looked stylish but not too much. She suspected that most of the church women would be dressed in plain cotton dresses and possibly without a hat.

Sunshine peeked over the horizon, promising a pleasant June day. Toward mid morning, the women walked to the church building located on South Street, four blocks from Grandma's house. Emily walked between Mrs. Spencer and Sally. Mrs. Spencer's light blue cotton dress brought out the color of her eyes. Silk flowers dotted the brim of her straw hat. Sally's plain gray dress and bonnet concealed her beautiful features. Emily thought of all of her beautiful dresses and determined to give a couple to Sally if she could do so without offending her.

Emily scanned the people entering the church building as they walked toward it. She hoped to spot the handsome ranch owner. Just as she had decided he wasn't there yet, she spotted him tying a horse to a rail at the side of the building. Just before she crossed the threshold, he sauntered toward the entrance, looked up and their eyes locked. She nodded and followed Mrs. Spencer into the building, down the aisle to a pew in the middle of the church. Mrs. Black waved at her from across the room where she sat beside her husband.

A bearded young man stepped up to the pulpit. "Good morning, everyone. My name is Jim. Let's all sing *Amazing Grace* together."

The congregation followed his strong tenor voice.

The churchgoers' harmonious singing impressed Emily. From behind, a deep bass blended perfectly with her soprano. It made it easier for her to sing as she matched the voice behind her.

Milburn Black got up after Jim sat down at the end of the hymn. "I want to welcome everyone today. We have Miss Emily Johnson with us for the first time. She's the granddaughter of Mrs. Maude Johnson who, as you all know, is unable to attend because of her arthritis. Be sure and welcome Miss Emily after services.

"Today our preacher, Brother James Quinn, will be talking about the *All Sufficiency of Christ*." Milburn motioned to a reddish-blonde headed man seated on the front row. "Preacher."

Milburn sat down and a man in his thirties got up. Brother Quinn's bright smile assured Emily that he led his flock with love and understanding. His blue eyes held a spark of mischief. Emily didn't know if etiquette allowed her to think of a preacher as looking mischievous. But nonetheless, he did and it made Emily smile.

"Welcome, everyone. Today I want to talk about what it means to have Christ be all that we need in our lives."

Emily's thoughts wandered to the young rancher. She forced herself to listen to the sermon instead letting her thoughts rest on a tall handsome cowhand. What was wrong with her? She was not so usually taken with a good-looking man, a stranger at that.

Brother Quinn ended his lesson. "We need to practice forgiveness of ourselves and others. If God chooses to forgive us through the all sufficiency of Christ, then who are we to question it?"

Brother Quinn closed his Bible. "I've put enough of you to sleep this morning. In the coming weeks I will speak more about this topic and how we can see forgiveness at work in our daily lives in our actions, love, and obedience. Brother Jim will have a song in a minute. Then we will have the communion service. Anyone who needs prayer, encouragement, salvation through baptism, or any other need that we can meet, just come down front during the song. Let's stand and sing."

Jim walked to the pulpit. "Let's sing the Charles Wesley hymn, *A Charge To Keep I Have."*

After the congregation sang the song and sat down, two men went to the front and took a white linen cloth off the small table to reveal a communion set. One of the men picked up a silver plate with some flat bread on it. He asked everyone to bow and pray with him. He then passed the plate to the audience. Each person who chose broke a small piece and ate the bread. When it came to Emily she took it, broke off a small piece and passed the plate on to Mrs. Spencer. Emily placed the piece of unleavened bread on her tongue and thought about the Christ's broken body on the cross.

The two men returned to the front and took two tall silver cups. One of the men prayed over the cup and then it passed from person to person with each adult taking a small sip. Emily took a small sip of the fruit of the vine and passed it to Mrs. Spencer. Emily closed her eyes and thought of the blood flowing from the body of the Christ for her.

She opened her eyes to see Jim at the front. "We will take a collection for the preacher's pay. All who want to give do so by placing it on this table before you leave. Any amount is helpful." Jim nodded. "If you can't give money but can give food, meat, or anything else then just take it by the preacher's house this week. We'll sing, *Christ Above All Glory Seated*. Then Jeremiah will give us a scripture, and Cullen Ferguson the dismissal prayer." Jim raised his hand to give the downbeat. "Let's sing."

Jim led the powerful praise song to the Christ. Emily had never heard it before, but the man behind her sang it with force and familiarity.

Then the man behind her stepped into the aisle and walked to the front. It was Jeremiah Rebourn. Emily's stomach tightened. For some reason, knowing she'd blended her voice with his, sent shivers up her spine.

Jeremiah brushed the hair out of his eyes. Emily wondered why he didn't get his hair cut the day before like he said he'd planned to.

He cleared his throat. "Our closing scripture, Galatians 2:20, I am crucified with Christ: nevertheless I live; yet not I, but Christ liveth in me; and the life which I now live in the flesh I live by the faith of the Son of God, who loved me, and gave himself for me."

His clear deep voice rang through the church like a tolling bell. He paced himself as the elegant scripture rolled from his lips. The fact that Jeremiah didn't have his Bible open intrigued Emily. After he finished he sat down on the front pew.

A tall gray-headed man walked up to the front. "Let's pray.

"Almighty God, be with us this week as we serve you. Help us to keep Christ as the all-sufficient one in our lives. Keep everyone safe and bring them back to us next week. In the name of the Christ. Amen."

Immediately, people came up to Emily and welcomed her to the service. She appreciated the friendliness and spoke to each one. They gave their names, but after the third one, she gave up trying to remember. Then Jeremiah Rebourn stood in front of her. Her heart leaped to her throat.

He brushed his hair back. "Welcome to the congregation. I hope it helps you as much as it has helped me."

"Thank you, and thank you for the scripture. It was nicely done." Emily smiled at him but he didn't smile back, but he did blush. She couldn't hardly imagine being so shy and so handsome at the same time.

"I hope we see you again next week," he said.

Emily nodded. "Yes, God willing. I hope you have a good week."

He ducked his head and gave way for someone else to speak to her.

When Emily finally got outside the little church she looked around for Jeremiah, but he had already left. She tucked her disappointment away and went to find the other ladies.

As they walked back to the house, Emily asked, "Mrs. Spencer, have you talked much with Jeremiah?"

Mrs. Spencer waved her handkerchief to get a breeze as the day was warm. "No, he never stays around for us to visit much. He's always polite and the preacher has asked him several times to give the scripture. He never opens his Bible, he just knows it."

Emily put her arm through Mrs. Spencer's arm as they walked along. "I enjoyed the service. I liked the preacher and I feel a sense of peace for having gone."

Mrs. Spencer patted Emily's hand that rested on her arm. "I'm glad, and that's the way I feel too, dear. Let's get home and see what Mildred has for dinner."

~

Emily spent the following week with Mildred, learning to bake bread. Mrs. Spencer also showed her how to keep the furniture clean and polished. Under Homer's watchful eye, Emily worked in the garden, learning to hoe and tend to the plants. In no time at all, she'd be able to take care of a home by herself. Each evening after supper, working her needlepoint, she sat with her grandma, and told her of her day's activities.

She looked forward to Sunday. Only to herself did she admit she secretly hoped to see Jeremiah Rebourn again. She felt more than a little drawn to the shy young rancher. Why she was so attracted to him was a puzzle.

Sunday morning Emily was up early and took special care in how she did her hair. She decided to wear her dark blue dress with the lace at the neck and the sleeve cuffs. White lace tied into a bow decorated her pretty hat and matched the lace on her dress.

As she and the ladies from the house approached the little white church building, Emily searched for Jeremiah Rebourn. Just as she was about to enter the front door, she spotted him as he rode up with two other riders. After she took her place in the pew, it was all she could do not to look around to see where he sat. Several people shuffled into the pew behind her.

It only took a few chords of the first song for Emily to know that Jeremiah had again sat behind her. As she listened to his strong bass and matched it with her soprano, contentment soared through her. Another simple but rich worship service followed with meaningful songs, prayer, communion, and Brother Quinn's sermon. Again, at the end of the service, Jeremiah gave them the ending scripture. This time he quoted the eighth chapter of Romans. Emily could have listened all morning to his deep smooth bass voice. She marveled at his moving eloquence as he shared the scriptures.

Emily stepped out from between the pews just as Jeremiah made his way down the aisle from the front of the meeting room.

"Miss Johnson," Jeremiah said with a nod.

"Mr. Rebourn," Emily responded.

AJ HAWKE

"Call me Jeremiah, everyone does."

"Only if you call me Emily, everyone does." She smiled at him as she watched his face blush.

He walked out of the building with her and stood in the yard. He tugged on his shirtsleeves and looked at the ground. "How was your week?"

Emily sensed his struggle to make conversation, not that he did not want to, but that he was shy. "I had a lovely week. It was relaxing after my long train trip from Boston." She tucked in a curl that had escaped from under her hat. "And how was your week?"

He brushed his hair out of his face. "It went well. We're branding cattle and getting ready to start the haying."

He still hadn't gotten a haircut.

"How big a ranch do you have?" She stepped closer to show her interest in what he had to say.

"I have four thousand five hundred acres with about five hundred prime beef." He relaxed a little and as he managed to look her in the eyes, he seemed to enjoy their conversation.

Emily shaded her eyes in the bright summer sun as she looked up at Jeremiah's face. "I'm afraid I don't know much about a ranch. I spent the last six years in school back east."

He tugged on his sleeves again and glanced down at her. "Do you ride?"

She laughed. "I do but not like these western folks. Why do you ask?"

Jeremiah looked down and kicked the ground with the toe of his boot. "I just wondered."

Emily couldn't help but smile at his awkwardness. He tried so hard. She sensed that he wanted to invite her out to his ranch. Her heart soared at the possibility. Would he ever gather the courage to ask? She doubted it.

Taking a deep breath, she said, "Maybe if you're free sometime you could show your ranch to me and Mrs. Spencer."

His face turned as red as the bandana around his neck. "Uh, yeah. I mean, yes, actually that's why I asked if you rode." Jeremiah looked at her intently. "Would you—"

Emily smiled, hoping to put him at ease. "I would like that. Homer, my grandma's driver could bring us out in the buggy."

He pulled a handkerchief from his back pocket, wiped his face, and returned his attention to the small hole in the ground he was digging with his boot. "When?"

His directness caught her off guard, but she secretly admired the courage he showed.

"When would be convenient for you?" Emily reminded herself she wasn't back east anymore. Besides, she had no intention of going anywhere without Mrs. Spencer.

"How about next Saturday morning? We could do some riding and then have the noon meal." He stopped digging and looked at her with hope in his eyes.

Emily nodded. "Yes, we could come next Saturday morning."

"I'll look forward to seeing you next Saturday, Emily." Jeremiah bowed, put his hat on, and strode off toward his horse.

Emily turned to find Mrs. Spencer had waited for her. Emily rushed over. "I'm sorry I kept you waiting."

Mrs. Spencer patted her arm. "Don't you worry. Jeremiah Rebourn is one handsome young man. And he has good sense to pay attention to you."

"Well, he invited me out to see his ranch next Saturday and I told him yes and that you would be coming with me, which is only proper. Is it all right that I said that without asking you?" Emily slipped her arm through Mrs. Spencer's as they walked toward the house.

"Oh, you did, did you?" Mrs. Spencer laughed and gave Emily a wink. "I guess I can manage that, dear. Of course, we'll ask your grandma if it's all right with her."

"I hope she'll approve. Besides getting to know Jeremiah, I am interested to see a ranch."

"Now don't you go getting all caught up with this young man because he is the best-looking one around these parts. He's a little strange in some ways." Mrs. Spencer pointed her finger at Emily. "You be careful and get to know him."

"Oh, Mrs. Spencer, I'm not getting all caught up as you put it." She looked at Mrs. Spencer quizzically. "But, why do you say he is a little strange?"

"Not really strange, he's just so shy and quiet, almost like he's never been around people much. He obviously can read and write, but he doesn't seem to have an ease socially about him."

"I'd have to agree with you. Maybe he just needs someone to teach him."

Mrs. Spencer's eyes twinkled. "And that someone would be you?"

Warmth spread to Emily's cheeks. "Well, why not? I am a graduate of one of the best finishing school in the east. If nothing else they taught social politeness." Emily laughed. She could teach the young man, but at the same time she had an idea he had a few things he could teach her too.

When they got back to the house, Mildred had dinner ready and they sat down to eat. Neither Mrs. Spencer nor Emily mentioned the conversation with Jeremiah. Immediately after dinner, Grandma went to lie down for the afternoon.

Restless, Emily went out and walked up past the barn. Homer sat on a bench outside the barn reading the newspaper.

"Hello Homer. Lovely day isn't it?"

Homer straightened his posture and looked up. "Hello, Miss Emily. Yes, it is."

"Homer, does my grandma have any riding horses?" Emily had seen the matched pair of black horses that pulled the carriage.

"Yes, Miss Emily, she has an old mare, but no one has ridden her in quite awhile."

"May I see her?" Emily followed Homer to the corral at the back of the barn. A sleepy-looking brown mare stood nibbling grass beside an old burro. The old nag would not win a horse race any time soon, but she looked just right for Emily to get some riding practice before next Saturday.

"Here, Molly ole girl," Homer said as he offered the old horse a sugar cube. The horse ambled over to the fence and took the cube from Homer's hand.

Emily reached through the fence and rubbed her neck. "Do you think Molly would let me ride her?"

Homer' face lit up. "Oh, yes. Molly's a gentle old horse." He rubbed the horse's head.

Emily looked toward the barn. "Do you have a saddle?"

"We have a couple of saddles. I think one was your grandfather's and the other one belongs to your grandmother. I keep them oiled and rubbed down. They're both in good shape even if they haven't been used for a while."

"If I went and changed into my riding outfit do you think I could ride in the corral this afternoon?" The idea excited Emily. She hadn't been on a horse in months.

"Of course. You go get changed and I'll have old Molly here saddled by the time you get back."

Emily hugged the old man. "Thank you Homer."

It only took her a few minutes to run back into the house, change, and return to the corral. Her riding outfit was a black shirtwaist jacket and a long, full divided skirt. She also had on her boots, a straw hat with flowers on the brim, and gloves. When she walked her skirt swung full and did not appear divided. She was glad she had the outfit because she much preferred to ride astride than sidesaddle.

Homer helped her mount the horse with the help of a step-up stump and handed her the reins. She urged the old mare into a walk and spent an hour going round and round the corral. By the time she dismounted her legs trembled. If she was going to ride with Jeremiah over at his ranch, she had to do better.

That evening after supper, she went into the back bedroom with her grandma.

The old lady wrung her hands and looked at her granddaughter expectantly. "Did you have a nice service at church this morning?"

"Yes, it was lovely." Emily sat in the glider rocker and turned to face her grandma. "I do like the preacher, the songs, and the scripture reading. All of it."

Grandma set her cup of tea down. "Did you talk to anyone especially?"

Emily gasped at her, then smiled. "Now, how did you know that? Did Mrs. Spencer tell you?" Emily asked with a laugh.

Grandma adjusted her glasses. "No, Mrs. Spencer didn't say anything, but you were all rosy cheeked when you came in from church." She shrugged. "I just suspected."

Emily blushed, thinking back to the talk she had with Jeremiah. "Well, Grandma, Mr. Jeremiah Rebourn and I spoke after services."

Grandma sloshed a bit of her tea as she sat down her cup, but quickly wiped it up with her napkin. She looked at Emily with wide eyes behind her spectacles. "Tell me more." She leaned forward and cupped her ear toward Emily. "What did you all talk about?"

Emily told her about the conversation as much word for word as she remembered.

Grandma picked up her cup and took a sip of tea. "And he wants you to come out to his ranch?"

"Yes, next Saturday. Of course, I included Mrs. Spencer otherwise it might not be proper."

"Splendid! You did just right. Yes, go and see his ranch. I will be mighty interested to hear what type of place he has."

The idea of Emily getting to know a man seemed to energize her grandma. Emily studied the old woman's face and found serenity. "So you think it's all right if I get to know Jeremiah?"

"Yes, Granddaughter. I think it is a very good idea." She reached over and patted Emily's hand. "A very good idea indeed."

~

The week flew by for Emily with lessons in cooking, housekeeping, and gardening. She also rode old Molly every day. By the end of the week, she was riding out over the back pastures. On Friday afternoon, she asked Sally to wash her riding outfit and press it carefully. Sally also filled the bathtub and helped her wash her hair. She lay back in the warm bubbles and daydreamed about visiting Jeremiah's ranch the next day.

## Chapter 14

Jeremiah rode back to the ranch. She'd said yes. Now what would he do? What had he gotten himself into?

Jacob had dinner on the table. After he said the blessing, they filled their plate and ate in their usual silence. Jeremiah's stomach knotted up. When Jacob served apple pie and poured fresh cups of coffee Jeremiah couldn't stand it any longer. He needed help. He cleared his throat. "Fellows, I need your help with something."

Jacob put his fork down. "What can we do?"

Bob looked up from his dessert.

Jeremiah cleared his throat again. "I asked a young lady to come to the ranch on Saturday to have dinner, she and her friend." He waited for their reactions.

Jacob bobbed his head up and down, a huge grin plastered on his face. "Now that is nice, Jeremiah. You need to know a young lady and to have a wife."

"Whoa there, no one said anything about a wife." Jeremiah protested.

"Of course not, just a friend who visits." Bob grinned.

"That's right and that's all." Jeremiah wasn't even sure he and Emily were friends but at least she had said yes.

Bob stuffed another bite of apple pie in his mouth. "What do you want us to do?"

"Well, one thing is help me get this place looking good. And Jacob, would you prepare a meal for us? I mean something special." Jeremiah searched the German's face for understanding.

Jacob refilled Bob's plate with a second piece of pie. "Of course, you not worry. We have a great dinner for the ladies."

Jeremiah sighed with relief. "Good. Now I invited her to come and ride out to see the ranch. I need to decide on a horse. Do we have a nice extra saddle or should I go into town and buy one?" He looked from Bob to Jacob. They continued eating like this wasn't the most nerve-racking moment of their lives. He ran a hand through his long hair. Why had he invited Emily out to the ranch?

Bob pushed his now empty plate to the middle of the table. "Relax, Jeremiah. Don't worry. You'll do fine. Get a haircut and bath on Friday. Saturday, put on a clean set of clothes that you would wear to church." Bob picked up his cup and swallowed some coffee.

A haircut? Jeremiah's anxiety grew. "What if I don't know what to talk to her about? What if I act completely stupid?" He knew there was a real possibility of it.

Bob drained his coffee cup, looking at Jeremiah over the rim. "Then you will be acting normal. That's how most of us men act around a pretty girl."

Jeremiah took a deep breath and leaned back in his chair. "All right, I'll try to be calm about it. I don't know what got into me to even invite her out."

Jacob beamed from across the table. He clearly enjoyed Jeremiah's discomfort. "Just who is this person?"

"Oh, I forgot to tell you. It's Miss Emily Johnson and her friend Mrs. Spencer."

"Emily Johnson! You sure know how to aim high. And she said yes?" Bob slapped Jeremiah on the back.

Jeremiah felt sick. "Yeah. You think I shouldn't have asked her?"

"I think you did just right and we all work to make it a good time, both for her and for you." Jacob waved his hand around. "I clean kitchen. We have nice dinner." He pointed to the door. "You go riding and show her ranch." Jacob placed both palms on the table. "And I stay right here and visit with Mrs. Spencer. It will be a good visit."

Jeremiah took a deep breath. He could count on his friends. They wouldn't let him down. "Thanks, fellas." Jeremiah meant it.

~

Jeremiah worked all week to make the place look acceptable. He also branded cattle. By Friday he knew he had done enough. He went into town and got a haircut—it took every ounce of strength he had. Then he bought a new pair of jeans and a blue cotton shirt. About to leave the general store, he spotted some flowery china dishes and thought about the plain blue enamel ones at the ranch. He bought the flowery set. When he unpacked them with Jacob, he discovered a damask tablecloth came with the dishes.

Saturday morning he woke at daybreak and knew he had at least three hours before Emily arrived. After breakfast, he helped Bob clean the barn and corral and then took a quick bath before putting on his new clothes.

For some reason Bob and Jacob kept grinning at him.

At nine Jeremiah gave the house one more glance before he heard a horse and buggy coming up the lane. He went to the front porch and waited. His heart raced. He took a deep breath and willed his hands to stop shaking.

An older man drove the buggy up to the house. Jeremiah stepped off the porch to meet them.

"Welcome, Emily, Mrs. Spencer." He gave Emily a hand as she stepped out of the buggy wearing a nice-fitting jacket and full skirt. He then turned to Mrs. Spencer and lent her a hand. He'd watched Elisha helping Susana out of the buggy back at the Rocking ES and mimicked what he had seen.

"Good morning, Jeremiah. It's a beautiful day for us to be out in the countryside." Emily stood on the porch and looked out over the ranch. "This is really a nice place."

Mrs. Spencer waved at the elderly man driving the buggy. "Jeremiah, do you know Homer Lumas? He drives for Mrs. Johnson."

Jeremiah reached up and shook the older gentleman's hand. "Homer."

"It's nice to meet you Jeremiah."

Bob and Jacob had come out of the house and Jeremiah introduced them.

Bob went over to the buggy. "Homer, let's take the buggy up to the corral and unhitch your horses." He led the horses toward the corral.

Jacob bowed to the women. "Ladies, come into the house." He held the screen door open.

Jeremiah followed them into the front room and watched as they looked around.

"This is a lovely room." Emily walked over to the fireplace. "And this mantel over the fire place, it is magnificent." Emily ran her fingers over the intricate carvings.

"That's Jacob's work." Jeremiah said.

"Jacob! You did this? It's beautiful." Emily gave Jacob a brilliant smile.

"Jacob made all the furniture in the house."

"You are a very talented man, Mr. Blunfeld," Mrs. Spencer said as she sat down on one of the couches.

Jacob bowed again. "Thank you." He stood with his hands behind his back. "Jeremiah, if you and Miss Emily are to ride you go now. Mrs. Spencer can keep me company while I prepare dinner." He turned to her. "That is, if you agree?"

Mrs. Spencer untied her hat. "Only if you'll let me help with the dinner preparation."

"Emily, are you ready to ride out and see the ranch?" Jeremiah asked.

"I'm ready." She pulled lightweight leather gloves on her slender hands.

Jeremiah led her out to the corral where two saddled horses waited tied to the rail.

"I saddled the sorrel mare for you if that's all right."

"That'll be fine." After walking up to the mare, she paused with a light frown.

"Is something wrong?" Jeremiah looked around wondering what was causing her to frown.

"You don't have a step up and I can't reach the stirrup."

"May I just lift you up?" Jeremiah didn't know if that was improper, but knew he could do it easily.

Emily gave him a warm smile. "That would be helpful."

Jeremiah stood behind her, placed his hands around her small waist, and lifted her up in one easy motion.

Emily put her left boot in the stirrup and easily swung into the saddle.

Jeremiah mounted his black gelding and led the way up the trail.

They spent a couple of hours riding the trails of the ranch. It was with pride that Jeremiah showed her the pastures and hay fields. He had dammed up several creeks and created large ponds that he used both to water the horses and cattle, and to irrigate the hay fields.

They followed the trail to the top of a ridge and he pulled up next to some large boulders at the edge of the overhang.

Jeremiah looked at her and smiled. "This is my favorite view of the ranch. We can dismount and let the horses rest a few minutes."

"I'd like that. It is beautiful up here." She waited for Jeremiah to dismount and then lift her down from where she stood on the left stirrup.

She gazed out over the ranch land. "I really like your ranch. It's a comfortable place, peaceful."

"Thank you. It's the first place I've ever had. I've worked hard to make it nice with the help of Bob and Jacob." He found the conversation easier than he thought it would be, especially as he got his breath to calm down and to stop shaking. He gazed at Emily rather than the view of the ranch. "You can see several miles from up here. Look yonder at the horses running in the far pasture. Those are mostly young colts, all born here on the ranch."

They settled into a comfortable silence as Emily took in the breathtaking view.

Emily sat down on a large rock and gazed out over the rolling hills. She closed her eyes and breathed in the fresh air. "It's so refreshing up here."

Jeremiah agreed, though his eyes focused on Emily's face, not the landscape. She turned and found him staring. He immediately looked at the ground, fearing he'd crossed the line. She surprised him when she scooted over and patted the spot next to her on the large boulder. He walked over and sat beside her. The breeze carried her soft, flowery scent to him. He didn't know a woman could smell so nice.

"Where did you grow up?" she asked.

Jeremiah hesitated. Panic crept up his spine. He hadn't thought about her asking questions concerning his early life. He swallowed and took a deep breath before he answered. "We moved around a lot and didn't have a settled place. I've lived in Arizona, New Mexico, and Colorado."

"You said you had only lived here for two years. Where did you live before?"

Jeremiah relaxed a little. That was a safe question to answer. "I worked for a rancher up in the mountains west of here, Elisha Evan's ranch, the Rocking ES. I broke horses with Joe Weathers. Joe's in partnership with Elisha."

"That sounds like fun and a lot of work. Are the horses that come here each winter from the Rocking ES?"

Jeremiah nodded. "That's right. They bring them down for the worst months of the winter. It's hard for the horses to get enough feed with all the snow they have. We don't have as much snow and I can grow hay through the summer. It's working well. In three or four months they'll bring a herd of about five hundred horses down."

"I would love to see that. I mean all the horses running onto your land. It must be an amazing sight."

Jeremiah agreed it was, but not near as amazing a sight as Emily seated on the rock with the breeze blowing little curls of her hair loose from the coiled twist at the nape of her neck. He stared at her and she looked at him as if waiting for him to say something.

"Do you mind if I say how pretty you look?" As soon as he said it he wished he could take it back. What if she thought he was being too forward?

"Thank you, Jeremiah. That's a nice thing to say." Emily turned so she could look more directly at him. "Do you mind if I say you're a handsome man?"

He hadn't expected her to say something like that. "I don't mind you saying it, I just question that it's true."

"You don't know that you're handsome?" She seemed surprised.

He dared not look at her. "I've never given it much thought." Self-conscious, he tugged on his sleeve. The scars sure weren't handsome, and he wasn't about to let her see them.

A lock of her hair blew softly across her face as she studied him. "When you've gone to socials have none of the girls ever told you that you were handsome?"

He shrugged. "I've never been to a social."

Would she think him strange knowing he preferred staying at home to socializing? He didn't have a lot of the experiences that other people had and he didn't even know where to begin to make up for it.

She reached up and tucked the wayward strand of hair behind her ear. "Did you ever go to school?"

He wondered if all girls asked so many questions. "No, I never went to school. My Pa taught me to read, write, and do figures. I've read a lot of books."

"I can't imagine not going to school, but that helps explain why you never went to socials. And if you moved around a lot that makes it hard to have friends."

"My only friends are at the Rocking ES and here. Men like Bob and Jacob."

"Did you go to church as a child?"

Jeremiah began to understand that she was trying to get a handle on what his life had been like. But, he knew that nothing about his life was like the life she had growing up.

"The only church I ever went to was at the Rocking ES. The one Elisha Evans has on his ranch."

"It's like your life didn't begin until you got to the Rocking ES?"

Her question held so much truth. "You might say that. It was the first good thing that ever happened to me. Maybe one day you can meet Elisha and Susana Evans. They are the finest people I know. I'd give my life for everyone on that ranch."

"I'd like to meet them. They sound like people worth knowing." Emily cocked her head. "Other than the people on the Rocking ES do you have other family?"

Jeremiah shook his head. "No, there's no one."

"We're alike in a way. I only have my Grandma and she's getting old. When she passes on I won't have anyone."

He hadn't realized that she didn't have family. "What happened to your folks?"

"My mother died soon after I was born of a fever and my father went back east and died in the war. My grandparents raised me. Grandpa died six years ago just after they sent me back east to go to school. What about your folks?"

How much to tell her? He wanted to tell her everything, but it was too soon. "My mother died when I was born and my Pa died when I was about eight." He had decided that his mother must have died giving birth to him. But, the truth was he didn't really know.

"Who took care of you after your pa died?"

Should he tell her the truth? "A friend of my pa's took me in and I stayed with various friends of his until I was fifteen. Then I went out on my own." Which was sort of true. But, he for sure was not ready to tell her about the tunnel. He didn't know if he would ever be ready to tell anyone other than Joe and Elisha and it still surprised him that he'd told them.

"It sounds as if it was a rough life for you." She looked at him in a soft gentle way.

Did she care what his life had been or was she just being kind? He had no way to know. But, he liked the way she looked at him. They needed to start back to the house. Jacob and Mrs. Spencer would be waiting. Even with her questions, he liked sitting and talking to her. It hadn't been near as hard as he had feared.

"We better get back to the house for dinner. Jacob has gone to a lot of trouble and he'll want us to enjoy it."

"You're right." She stood and brushed off her riding skirt. "This has been nice. Maybe we can do it again sometime."

"I would like that. There are some other trails we didn't ride today." Jeremiah took Emily by the elbow and led her to the horses they'd left tied to some branches.

"Would you mind helping me mount?" she asked, turning her back to him.

He didn't mind a bit. He stood behind her and placed his hands around her—he almost completely encircled her waist. She put a hand briefly on top of his as if to secure his hand. He lifted her easily and held on for a moment longer than he had to, and it seemed to him that she rested her weight in the left stirrup a moment longer before she swung her right leg over and settled into the saddle. Jeremiah mounted his horse and led the way back to the ranch house.

Dinner was a pleasant time with Mrs. Spencer, Bob, Homer, and Jacob carrying the conversation. Jeremiah mostly just watched Emily who returned his looks.

The new damask tablecloth displayed the new dishes beautifully. Wildflowers added a dash of color, their petals splaying from a jar in the middle of the table. Jeremiah stood back and admired the table.

Jacob had outdone himself with both the table setting and the meal. Brown sauce dripped from the succulent beef; gravy ran in rivulets down peaks of mashed potatoes; fresh green beans and carrots tasted like summer, while applesauce gave every bite a tangy sweetness. Fresh baked bread lay in slices on a platter with homemade butter smeared on top. And just when Jeremiah couldn't hold another bite, Jacob brought an apple torte to the table. Both the beef recipe and the torte were dishes his mother had made back in his homeland of Germany.

After dinner, they sat and talked while drinking coffee. Then Mrs. Spencer said they needed to get back to town and Bob helped Homer hitch up the buggy.

"It was a lovely dinner, Jacob," Mrs. Spencer said. "Thank you so much for having us."

"Yes, Jacob." Emily praised Jacob with a warm smile and he bowed in return. "I especially liked the apple torte." She put her gloves on, then her hat. "Jeremiah, I want to thank you for the ride and for putting up with all my questions."

"You're welcome." He took her arm and led her away from the others. "When can we do this again?" Jeremiah saw no reason not to go ahead and ask.

"How about next Saturday?" Emily grinned.

Jeremiah found himself grinning back. "I'll plan on it."

Mrs. Spencer put her shawl on. "We'll see you men at church tomorrow. You all feel free to sit with us. It would be an honor." Mrs. Spencer climbed into the buggy.

As they watched the buggy disappear down the lane, Bob and Jacob looked at each other and then at Jeremiah.

"Well, Jeremiah, how did ride go?" Jacob asked for them both.

"The ride?" Jeremiah looped his thumbs through his belt loops. "Oh, it went all right."

"Did you talk any?" Bob asked.

"Yes, we stopped up on top of the ridge and talked for about thirty minutes."

"Well, what did you talk about? You must tell us, Jeremiah. Did she seem to like you?" Jacob was more direct than Bob.

"How can I know if she liked me? She asked a lot of questions, mostly about when I was a kid and she told me about losing her folks. Does that mean she likes me?"

Bob slapped him on the back. "I think maybe it means she would like to get to know you better. And she said she would come back next Saturday to go riding again. That has to mean something."

"And Mrs. Spencer said you could sit with Emily at church. Now that definitely means something." Jacob nodded.

Jeremiah kicked at the dirt. "You keep saying that it means something. But what does it mean?"

Jacob said. "I think it mean you have permission to court her."

"You know, Jeremiah, spend time with her and get to know her," Bob explained.

Jeremiah threw his hands in the air. "Well, why didn't you say so in the first place?" All this talk of women and courting drained him. "I think I'm going to take a nap." Jeremiah went back into the house and lay on the bed. The visit had left him exhausted.

He missed Emily now that she was gone. Did that mean he wanted to court her? If courting a woman didn't have something to do with branding cows or riding horses, he was clueless. He would have to take his time and get to know her, and most important, let her get to know him.

Would she be able to put up with his strangeness? While better than when he'd arrived at the Rocking ES, he still had nights where the bad dreams woke him up. Sara dealt with it for Joe. Would Emily ever be able to deal with it for him?

## Chapter 15

When Emily and Mrs. Spencer returned from their visit with Jeremiah, Emily wanted to rest in her room and read. She took off her riding outfit, put on a light summer robe, and lay barefoot on the bed. She tried to read, but all she really did was go over the day in her mind.

Jeremiah, so manly and strong, and yet in some ways, he reminded her of a little lost boy. His shyness at times appeared almost too painful to watch. Handsome, yes, but also someone that she was coming to care for—a lot. She had asked him too many questions, but she wanted to know everything she could about him. And she felt that he had similar thoughts about her. She would enjoy the friendship and see what path it would take.

After supper, she went in to tell her grandma about the visit. Grandma asked many more questions than Emily had with Jeremiah. Emily guessed it ran in the family. Jeremiah's house interested Grandma and she wanted exact details. Emily had only seen the front room and the kitchen, but she told her grandmother everything she could remember about those rooms. She also described the ranch. Grandma seemed pleased that Emily planned to go back for another visit the next Saturday.

Sunday morning Emily forced herself to sit up in bed. Every muscle in her body ached from the ride the day before. She determined to keep riding Molly until she was in better shape. She remembered the feel of Jeremiah's hands around her waist and the strength that enabled him to lift her so easily. With anticipation, she dressed for worship services.

Emily was a little late coming downstairs and found that Sally had already left for church services. She and Mrs. Spencer walked quickly. As they approached the building, they found Jeremiah and Jacob standing outside.

"Good morning, Mrs. Spencer, Emily. May I have honor of sitting with you ladies this morning?" Jacob offered his arm to Mrs. Spencer.

Mrs. Spencer accepted Jacob's arm. "Good morning, Jacob. It is we who are honored."

Jeremiah shyly offered his arm to Emily as he saw Jacob doing for Mrs. Spencer. Emily slipped her hand around Jeremiah's arm and let him escort her into the building.

Emily tried hard to pay attention to the service. Jeremiah sat so close to her; his nearness was powerful. His shaving soap smelled manly and Emily caught herself breathing deeply just to get a whiff. She especially enjoyed his singing. He knew all the songs and sang with a rich deep bass. When she knew the song, she sang soprano as if she sang a duet with Jeremiah.

She tried to concentrate on the lesson. Was this what falling in love felt like? To want to have every sense filled by the other person? She shook her head and tried again to concentrate on the lesson. Jeremiah shifted positions several times. Was he having trouble paying attention? She glanced at his face, but she couldn't tell what he might be thinking.

After services, they stood outside the building and talked until almost everyone else had left. Emily finally said she must go and not keep Mrs. Spencer waiting. Emily held her hand out for Jeremiah to shake it as a goodbye. She was almost afraid he wasn't going to give it back he held it for so long.

That evening when she talked with her grandma about Jeremiah, the elderly lady clapped her hands together and smiled from ear to ear. Emily omitted the parts that exposed her feelings about Jeremiah.

~

The weeks passed as Emily tackled her lessons with zeal. While she worked around the house or in the kitchen, her thoughts often drifted to the tall, shy rancher and the time they were spending together. Mildred and Mrs. Spencer gave her pointed looks, but Emily's heart soared. Should she marry Jeremiah, she would need to know everything the women taught her about keeping house, cooking, and gardening. She tried not to have such thoughts, but she did. She didn't know what Jeremiah was thinking because he never said.

Emily invited Jeremiah over to the house for Sunday dinner. They ate in the kitchen with everyone else and then retired to the front parlor and talked, and then later they went for a walk. They soon fell into a comfortable routine of Emily going out to the ranch on Saturday with Mrs. Spencer, and Jeremiah coming to the house for Sunday dinner and spending the afternoon with Emily. The only disappointment for Emily was her grandma's worsening health. Every time Jeremiah had come to the house, her grandma had not been able to leave her room nor have visitors, but she encouraged Emily to see as much of Jeremiah as she wanted.

On Emily's birthday in August, Jeremiah gave her a beautiful Appaloosa horse. He'd broken and gentled the horse himself. His gift touched Emily's heart and tears filled her eyes. Jeremiah pleased her more than she knew how to say.

~ ~ ~

Jeremiah could hardly wait to introduce Elisha and Joe to Emily, and she seemed excited to meet them. September would soon be upon them and then in another six weeks they would arrive with the horses.

After breakfast one morning near the end of August, Bob headed out early to meet the crew of men from town who were coming to cut hay. Jeremiah sat at the table, enjoying a second cup of coffee.

Jacob poured himself another cup of coffee and sat at the table. "Jeremiah, have you decided what you do with Miss Emily?"

Jeremiah rubbed his chin. "What do you mean?"

"Are you going to marry her?"

Jeremiah put down the coffee cup and stared at Jacob. "Do you think I should?"

Jacob held up his hands and shook his head. "It is not what I think that matters. What do you think?"

"How can I know if I should ask her? How can I know if that's something she would consider?" Dare he hope? He didn't know how to ask her.

Jacob raised his eyebrows. "Do you love her?"

"I want to be with her all the time. I'm miserable when she goes home on Saturdays. I can't stop thinking about her. Does that mean I love her?" He thought he did, but he had never been in love before and didn't trust himself to know.

"If someone want to hurt her would you give your life to save her?"

Jeremiah looked surprised at such a question. "Of course."

Jacob took another sip of coffee, then smacked his lips. "I think you are in love. But do you love her enough to stand by her for rest of your life. To make yourself change into what she needs you to be for her good?"

"I'm willing to try." He didn't know what to do to be what she needed.

"That is what important, that you willing to try. None of us can promise completely." Jacob filled his cup again and offered to refill Jeremiah's cup.

"So are you telling me I should ask Emily to marry me?"

"If that is what you want, you should do. Why wait?"

"What if I ask and she says no?" Jeremiah covered his face with his hands. He didn't want to think about that. But, if she said yes, did he know how to be a good husband? Both answers scared him.

"Then you will know and will make right decisions." Jacob nodded with a wise look.

Jeremiah ran his fingers through his hair and looked at Jacob. "How do I ask her?" For someone who could quote whole books it frustrated him to be so ignorant about so many things. He rubbed the back of his neck. He had so much to tell her he didn't know where to begin.

"You tell her you love her, and then if she say she loves you also, you ask her to marry you."

"I can do that?"

"Of course, you can," Jacob said with a nod and a smile.

Hope filled Jeremiah one minute and then the next he told himself not to be foolish. How could he expect Emily Johnson to want to marry him?

Sleep was almost impossible. His thoughts ran in a constant circle. Finally, he asked himself what would Elisha tell him to do? Calmness washed over him as he heard Elisha's voice in his mind. Elisha would tell him to pray about it and follow his heart.

Jeremiah rode up to the ridge and dismounted. He slipped to his knees by the large rock. Looking out over the ranch, he prayed for God's wisdom. How long he prayed he never remembered for sure, but it was hours. A rainstorm passed south of the ranch. As he watched the storm in the distance, a rainbow appeared. Could it be a promise of God's blessings? He wanted to think it was. Yes, he would tell Emily he loved her and ask her to marry him.

~

The next Saturday Emily arrived at the ranch with Mrs. Spencer. Jeremiah kept the Appaloosa for her at his ranch. He had the Appaloosa mare and his big black gelding saddled. They rode together to the top of the ridge and he helped her dismount. Jeremiah tied the horses up to a tree. Emily sat on the big rock. He walked over and sat next to her.

"Emily, I have something I want to talk about and I just ask that you listen to me for a bit." Jeremiah pushed aside the panic that threatened to engulf him. He had to do this. Emily meant more to him than all the pain he harbored from the past.

"Of course I'll listen, Jeremiah. You should know that." She looked up at him with a puzzled look.

"I want to tell you some things about myself. I haven't told you before because it never seemed to be the right time." He looked down at his hands. "I haven't meant to deceive you but you may look at it that way."

Emily reached over and placed her hand on Jeremiah's arm. "Just tell me."

He looked out over the valley and the hills beyond. He had to do this no matter what happened after. He took a deep breath, then turned back to her and said, "When I was a boy my father was an outlaw. He was killed robbing a stagecoach. The men he left me with were also outlaws. I helped them rob and rustle until I was fifteen when we were caught by the law." Jeremiah swallowed. "I went to prison. During a transfer a year later to Yuma Prison, Apaches attacked the prison wagon. We went over a cliff and everyone else was killed." He stopped. Clenching his trembling hands into fists, he concentrated on breathing in and out until the wave of nausea left him. Sweat covered his body.

He couldn't do it—but he had to if he wanted Emily as his wife.

He tucked his hands under his armpits to stop the trembling and continued. "I got hit on the head, and when I came to an old man had captured me. I never discovered who he was. I had shackles on my wrists and ankles. The old man had put a pole through my elbows across my back, which made it impossible for me to raise my arms. He blindfolded me, put a rope around my neck, and made me walk for five days to a mine tunnel." Jeremiah leaned forward and rested his hands on his knees. Darkness clouded his mind as his stomach cramped. But he pressed on. "He made me work the mine for two years chained like an animal, and then one day, he set me free."

Jeremiah sat up straight and lifted his sleeves and removed the wrist bands Elisha had given him. He hated to have to show her, but he also had to know how she would react to such ugliness. He'd expose his scars one at a time to make it easier for Emily. Raising his head, he made himself look at her face. The compassion and concern he found gave him strength to go on. He slowly took off his bandana.

"Oh, Jeremiah." She reached out and touched his neck. She took one of his hands and raised it until she could kiss the scarred wrist. Tears trickled down her cheeks.

He'd prepared himself for every reaction except this one. Did she really care? He tried to swallow the lump that formed in his throat. He couldn't believe she would even touch the scars but she had kissed them. Hope surged through his veins.

"There's more. After he let me go, I was awfully sick for a long time. I don't know from what, but I suspect it was the bitter tea the old man made me drink that made me sleep. After he left I didn't have it anymore and I was sick for days and days." Jeremiah put the bandana back around his neck. "But, the worst is what being in the tunnel had done to my mind. I can't stand enclosed places. I'm better after the four years at the Rocking ES. That's what saved me. The old man left me days at a time in the dark tunnel chained up. I can't stand the dark."

Emily had been so quiet that he feared what must be going through her mind.

"I'm so sorry, Jeremiah. It must have been awful. I cannot imagine, and I don't think you've told me but a surface telling." She shook her head. "What kind of evil would make a person do that to a boy?"

"Do you think you want to be friends with someone who has all that behind them?"

Her eyes widened. "Of course, you just said it. It's behind you." She touched his arm.

"I'm not a completely whole person. There's a lot that I just don't know about being with people. Elisha told me it was because I had never been shown anything about how to be with people as a boy. I just grew up, but I didn't have a home or family. But, he also told me that he thought I could learn and catch up to other people. That's what I've been trying to do."

"And you are doing well. You really are." She still held his hand and was now stroking it.

He blinked the tears back. He wouldn't cry in front of her. He just wouldn't. "Thank you. I want to be like other people. And I want to have what other people have."

"What do you want?"

"I want you." That wasn't what Jeremiah had planned to say, but it just came out. "I want to be with you. I want to love you. I do love you. And I want you to love me."

"I do love you, Jeremiah. I have for some time." She placed the palm of her hand along his scarred neck.

He took both her hands in his. "Emily, do you love me enough to put up with me? Do you love me enough to marry me and be with me forever?" He wanted her to say yes. As he looked at her, he couldn't bear the thought that she might say no.

Then, she nodded.

"Yes, Jeremiah, I'll marry you." Emily smiled radiantly.

He couldn't think what to say so he simply took her into his arms. He didn't intend to do more, but Emily placed her hand behind his head and pulled him toward her until she could reach his lips with hers.

He learned to kiss that day.

Emily leaned back and took his hands. "When do you want to get married?" She put his hands to her flushed face.

Jeremiah held her face in his hands and wanted to kiss her again. "I haven't thought about it. When would you want to get married?"

Emily released his hands. "We need to talk about what type of wedding we'll have." She put her arms around him and leaned her head on his chest. "I want it to be simple, but I do want it in the church with our friends and family there." She looked up at him.

"I would like for Elisha to marry us. He's a preacher." He raised an eyebrow. "Would you mind?"

"Do you think he would come?"

"I can ask him and Susana to come." Jeremiah stroked her hair. "I can't believe it. Will you truly marry me?"

Emily nodded several times. "Yes, I will." She laughed and hugged him. "Yes, Jeremiah Rebourn, I will marry you."

He just looked at her, speechless. Her answer filled his heart with so much joy that it silenced him.

~

Jeremiah wrote to Elisha and Susana about getting married. He asked Elisha to come and perform the wedding. He also invited everyone at the Rocking ES to come and celebrate with him. When he got their response, he showed it to Emily when she came out on Saturday.

"Elisha wrote that all of the Rocking ES is coming for the wedding. Susana and the children, Joe and Sara, and even Cookie."

Emily radiated with happiness. She held his hand. "I'm so glad, Jeremiah."

"You know, Emily, I've never met your grandma. Will she make it to the wedding?"

"I know you haven't and I'm sorry." Sadness filled Emily's eyes. "She's getting more and more feeble. She tells me that the wedding is too much for her. I want her there, but I guess it's not meant to be."

Jeremiah took her soft hand and held it with his large rough hand. "I promise to be there for you. If I'm not you tell me." He felt her disappointment that her grandma was so ill and couldn't come to her wedding. He wanted to have the right words for her.

"I will and I'll be there for you." Emily laid his palm against her cheek.

"Elisha is bringing the herd and will stay for a couple of days after the wedding to help take care of things. We can go to Denver for a wedding trip if you want." Jeremiah did not want to go to Denver, but thought he should offer to take Emily.

Emily pulled back and searched his face. "I don't think you really want to go to Denver. Where do you want to go, Jeremiah?"

He kissed the tip of her nose. "I want to go where you want to go."

"I want to go somewhere quiet, just you and me. Do you think we could find a place close by?"

"There might be a place. Let me ask around and I'll let you know."

Emily smiled. "We only have two weeks. I know it's hard for you, Jeremiah. I want to thank you for being willing to go through with a wedding for me." She wrapped her arms around him.

Her smiling at him in that special way filled him with so much joy he couldn't get enough. Jeremiah didn't dare tell Emily that he just wanted all the planning and the ceremony to be over. She was so excited about it. He shook the thoughts from his mind and inhaled the flowery scents from her hair.

"I'm glad to do it for you. If it makes you happy then we will do it. Elisha and family, Joe and Sara will stay at the ranch. Jacob is getting it all ready."

"Oh Jeremiah, we are going to be so happy. God is blessing us at every turn."

## Chapter 16

Emily rose early on her wedding day. It had been such a busy time of preparation that she was glad to have a couple of hours to herself before the rest of the household stirred. The events of the last few days crossed her mind and made her smile.

She'd met all of Jeremiah's friends from the Rocking ES. They had arrived with the horse herd two days before. Elisha and Joe impressed her. They were such fine Christian men for Jeremiah to have as his friends. She bonded immediately with Susana and Sara. She could tell they all loved Jeremiah by the way they greeted him. His greetings had been more restrained, but she knew him well enough now to know he was pleased with their coming so far for him. Emily laughed when she remembered watching the children run up to Jeremiah and hug him.

Mrs. Spencer knocked on her bedroom door then poked her head around it. "Emily, Sally has the bath ready for you. You go ahead and then go downstairs for breakfast."

"I don't know that I can eat anything." Butterflies danced in her stomach. Food was the last thing on her mind.

Mrs. Spencer entered the room and closed the door. "I know, but you'll do better if you go ahead and eat something. Believe me." Mrs. Spencer slipped Emily's slippers on her feet and then held out Emily's robe for her to slip into.

Emily gave her a hug. "You're probably right. I will get my bath and then eat breakfast. And I am going to spend some time with my grandmother." She slipped into her robe. "How is she this morning?"

Mrs. Spencer cast her eyes to the carpet. "She's not too strong today. But she will be happy to see you."

Sally had brought plenty of hot water. Emily took her time with her bath and washed her hair. When she got back to her room, she found that Mrs. Spencer had brought up a tray with coffee, scrambled eggs, ham, and biscuits. She did her best to eat, but only managed about half of what was on the tray. Still in her robe and with her hair loose so it would dry, she went down to her grandma's bedroom.

Grandma lay in her big four-poster bed. Emily was struck by how much her grandmother had aged since she had arrived in June. Of course, she reminded herself, her grandma was ill.

"Hello, Grandma." She kissed her wrinkled face.

Grandma pushed her glasses up. "My Emily, let me look at you. Oh my, you have grown up to be so beautiful. I'm thankful you have come to see me this morning." She squinted at something in the distance and wrung her hands. Emily turned, but found nothing peculiar.

"What is it, Grandma?" Emily straightened the covers and helped her sit up more on the pillows.

"It's the boy, always the boy," The old lady saw something that Emily couldn't see.

"What boy? Was it a dream, Grandma?"

"Yes, a bad dream," she gasped, barely able to get her breath.

"What can I do?"

"Sit here on the side of the bed, honey." Her grandma patted the bed. "Tell me what your wedding dress looks like. How will you fix your hair?"

Emily recounted everything she'd planned for her perfect day, right down the number of flowers at the church and layers of cake that would feed the guests. Grandma only half listened, adding appropriate comments as if on cue. Emily left her with concern. She had never seen her grandma so feeble and feared that her days were numbered. When she returned to her room, she found Mrs. Spencer laying out her wedding garments.

"Oh, Mrs. Spencer, I've just been with Grandma. She seems so much worse."

Mrs. Spencer took Emily into her arms and gave her a warm smile. "Dear, you shall not worry that pretty little head one bit about anything other than becoming Jeremiah's wife." She tucked a strand of damp hair behind Emily's ear.

Emily kissed her cheek and thanked her for her support. Then she let Mrs. Spencer help her do her hair and put on her wedding dress. Homer pulled the polished buggy up to the front of the house. Emily and Mrs. Spencer rode the short distance to the church for her wedding.

~ ~ ~

Words had failed Jeremiah as he had watched Elisha, Susana and the others arrive at his ranch. Bob directed Jim Finely, Santo, and Billy where to trail the horse herd. Cookie drove up in the chuck wagon and the women and children arrived in the big buggy. Everyone was excited to see Jeremiah's ranch and to be there for his wedding. With the house so full, he slept on the porch. It brought back memories of his beginning at the Rocking ES.

He was amazed at how much the children had grown. Susana looked wonderful. The newest member of the family who was two-years-old was already walking. Little Daniel held out his arms toward Jeremiah and he had no choice but to hold him.

Susana smiled at him. "Horses and children."

Jeremiah smiled back at her as he then turned his attention to the black-haired little boy. "Hi Daniel. I'm Jeremiah."

Daniel patted his face. "Miah."

At different times Elisha, Susana, and Joe spent time talking with Jeremiah on how to be married. He appreciated each bit of advice they gave. Jeremiah didn't want to admit it, but the truth be told, he was scared that he couldn't be the husband that Emily deserved. He wanted to have her as his wife with all his being. That desire overrode his fear.

The morning of the wedding, he dressed in the new black broadcloth suit with a tie and white shirt. And a cravat to hide the scars on his neck. At the church he waited up front with Joe beside him and Elisha, who was to conduct the wedding service.

Emily entered the church escorted by Milburn Black. Jeremiah blinked and his breath caught in his throat. A simple, but elegant white silk dress flowed around Emily like a cloud. Her white gloved hands clasped a small bouquet of flowers, and a white hat with veil adorned her lovely head. She seemed to float up the aisle toward him. Her radiant face carried a smile just for Jeremiah.

As he took her hand and turned to face Elisha, Jeremiah whispered in her ear. "You are so beautiful. I love you with all my heart."

Emily whispered back. "And you are truly handsome and the love of my life."

The ceremony was short and simple just as Jeremiah had requested. Elisha introduced them to the guests as Mr. and Mrs. Jeremiah Rebourn.

Jeremiah had rented the hotel dining room and everyone who attended the wedding came for dinner. He could hardly stand the next three hours as they greeted everyone and accepted congratulations, but finally it was time for them to leave their wedding dinner.

They rode in the buggy back to the ranch. Jeremiah had asked Elisha to give them an hour before any of the others returned. He still had not told Emily where he was taking her for their wedding trip.

"Just change into your riding clothes. We have a ways to ride this afternoon," he told her with a grin.

"Oh, you're too good at keeping secrets. Are you sure I'm taking what I'll need?"

"I told Mrs. Spencer where we're going and she said she could pack what you needed."

He let her go into his bedroom to change and he went into the other one. The idea of changing in front of her scared him. Being married would take some getting used to that was for sure. He changed and went to saddle the horses. He already had a couple of packs ready and put one behind each of their saddles. When he brought the saddled horses up to the house, Emily came out onto the front porch in her riding outfit. He helped her mount and then mounted up himself.

"Emily, if you don't like where I'm taking you we don't have to stay."

She reached for her husband's hand and squeezed it. "I know I'll like whatever you have chosen for me." She smiled at him.

"Then follow me, Mrs. Rebourn." He started up the trail that led west toward the hills. They rode at a steady pace for more than two hours. Jeremiah didn't want to stop and rest because he needed to get to the cabin before dark. He had told Emily about his problem with darkness, but he wasn't sure she truly understood how big a problem it still was for him.

After climbing up a steep ledge, the land opened up into a high valley. It wasn't a large valley and a forested cliff covered the other end of it. A waterfall fell and ran into the creek that flowed through the valley. In a glade by the waterfall, stood a cabin and corral.

Jeremiah stopped his horse and let Emily ride up beside him.

He stretched out his arm and pointed toward the cabin. "What do you think Emily? Will this do for the night?" He could hear the anxiety in his voice. He so wanted her to like it.

Her eyes opened wide and a bright smile appeared. "Oh, Jeremiah, it's beautiful. Whose place is it?"

"It's mine. I bought the land and cabin. I know it's isolated, but we don't have to stay but a night."

"We'll stay as long as we want to. Let's go see what it's like inside." She kicked the Appaloosa in the ribs and looked back at Jeremiah as if daring him to catch her.

He urged his big black horse into a gallop to overtake her and they rode up to the cabin together.

After they dismounted, he led her into the cabin. The small room held a double bed, side table and lamp, table and two chairs, washstand, two-burner box stove, and a fireplace. A bright-colored quilt covered the bed. Dishes, cookware, and food filled crates on the floor beside the stove.

"This is lovely. How did you get all this ready?" Emily stood in the middle of the cabin holding Jeremiah's hand. Her eyes darted to every corner and a smile spread across her face. He'd truly surprised her.

"Jacob got it ready for us." Jeremiah planned it but he sent Jacob up to the cabin to have it clean and ready for them. "I'll bring in the packs and take care of the horses."

He set the two packs down inside the cabin and then unsaddled the horses. He took the saddles into the cabin, as there wasn't a barn. Then he let the horses loose in the big corral where there was plenty of grass for the horses to feed on.

He went down to the creek and filled the big water bucket. He hurried back to the cabin as darkness was approaching more nervous than he wanted to admit. As he entered the cabin and sat the bucket of water down, Emily lit the lamps and the darkness disappeared, along with some of Jeremiah's anxiety. They unpacked and got the food organized. Jeremiah built a fire in the fireplace, as the late September air was cool in the mountains.

"We have roast beef sandwiches, apple pie, and coffee for supper." Emily set the food on the table and then brought out the dishes. She had a fire going in the little stove and had coffee made.

Jeremiah rubbed his hands together. "It sounds good. I'm hungry." He sat down at the table across from her.

"So am I. Would you say a blessing for us?" Emily asked as she offered him her hand.

Jeremiah thought she would ask him to say a blessing. He was prepared. He took her hand and bowed his head.

"Heavenly Father, Thank you for the blessing of this day. Thank you for the food that we have. Bless us as we are here in this place. Help me to be the husband that Emily deserves for the rest of her life. In the name of Jesus the Christ. Amen."

"Thank you, Jeremiah." Emily smiled at him with that particularly radiant smile of hers.

"I am the one who should be thanking you. Thank you for becoming my wife."

"And thank you for becoming my husband."

They ate the roast beef sandwiches and apple pie that Jacob had prepared. Then Emily put the dishes in the washbasin and washed them. Jeremiah dried them with the flour sack towel. He took his time, but eventually he ran out of things to dry. He thought the silence would eat him alive. He didn't know what to say or do next. He toyed with the fringe on the towel and watched Emily out of the corner of his eye.

She laid the dishcloth down, turned, and put her arms around him. Her touch gave him courage and he took her into his arms and kissed her. He pulled the pins from her hair and tossed them on the table. Finally, he was weaving his fingers through her waist length hair that felt like silk. Her fragrance tickled his nose and he craved more of her. "Come to bed with me, wife."

"Lead the way, husband."

~

The next morning they hiked to the top of the waterfall just after sunrise. Sitting on a large stone with his arms around Emily's waist they faced the rising sun. "Emily, thank you for sharing this Colorado morning sky with me."

She pressed his arms tighter around her waist. "I hope we get to share several thousand sunrises together. This is nice."

Over the next week they talked for hours. For Jeremiah it was a time of quiet contentment. He'd never felt so at ease with another human being before he met Emily.

She teased him and got him to have fun. They chased each other in the meadow in the front of the cabin and raced each other up the hill to the top of the waterfalls. Then she coaxed him into going swimming with her in the middle of the day in the pool below the waterfall.

He was amazed that he got into cold moving water and enjoyed himself. But Emily by his side made that possible. He couldn't wait to explore other possibilities that until now seemed unreachable.

He slept without the lamp. When he woke in the night and felt her warm body close to his, he tightened his arms around her, and the night terrors receded. They stayed at the cabin for five days. He didn't want to leave, but he knew they had to get back to the ranch.

They started back to the ranch after eating the noon meal and rode at a leisurely pace. They arrived at the ranch house by late afternoon. Jacob came out of the house to greet them.

"Welcome, home." Jacob held the reins of their horses while Jeremiah helped Emily dismount.

"Thank you, it is good to be home. Did Elisha, Susana, and all the others get off all right?" Jeremiah asked as he untied the packs.

"They went home in high spirits," Jacob said. "After the wedding they all came to front room and talk and laugh and tell stories about you Jeremiah when you were just a boy and came to live with them. Susana cried when she left. She said to tell you that she loves you both and will pray that you have the best marriage ever."

Bob came up from the corral. "Hey, boss, Miss Emily. Glad you're back." He reached for the reins. "Here, let me take care of the horses. You all go on in the house."

Jeremiah picked up one of the packs and held the door for Emily to enter the front room. "Go on back to our room. I'll bring the packs." He followed his wife into what was now their bedroom. It already looked and felt like a different room. With a sigh of contentment, he knew he was ready to start this new part of his life.

## Chapter 17

Emily returned from their marriage trip rested and content. She was so glad that Jeremiah had arranged the time at the cabin and that they had not traveled to Denver. She had gotten to know Jeremiah much better after five whole days and nights with just the two of them. She often thought how God had known what they needed even before they did.

She walked into the front room of the house that was now her home and into the back bedroom.

Jacob had brought her trunks from Grandma's house. He had also made another bureau for the bedroom and built a tall armoire for her to hang her dresses.

She changed into a cotton dress and hung her riding outfit in the armoire. She was going to have to get the seamstress in town to make her some more riding outfits if she kept riding as much as she had lately. She stood in front of the mirror, redoing her hair when Jeremiah walked into the bedroom and up behind her. He slipped his arms around her and kissed her on the neck.

"Jacob just told me that he moved out of the bedroom next to this one while we were gone. He's going to stay in the bunkroom. He said newlyweds needed privacy. Do we need privacy?" He grinned at her in the mirror.

"That was very thoughtful of him. Will he be all right in the bunkroom?" She covered his arms with hers and leaned back against him.

"He'll be fine. It's actually bigger and we don't have any hands. Bob stays in the room next to the bunkroom. We also have another room at that end of the house that's empty. So it won't hurt anyone for us to have this part of the house to ourselves."

Emily straightened. "Should I go help Jacob with supper? I'm not sure yet what I should do."

"No, not this evening. He had everything started and told me that supper would be ready in about an hour. Do you mind if we all eat together, Bob, Jacob, and the two of us?"

She continued to lean back against him. "Of course not, that will be fun. I can spend the time getting my things unpacked." Emily glanced up at him with a mischievous grin. "I looked in the bureau there and you only use two of the five drawers. May I use the others?" Emily could tell that Jeremiah, while always clean, didn't worry about his appearance or clothes. But he only had the one suit and three other sets of clothes. She was already planning to buy him more shirts and pants.

"You use whatever you want. I can put all my stuff in one drawer if need be."

Emily laughed. "No, I can manage with the armoire, a full bureau, and three of the five drawers of the second bureau. You did understand that when we got married I would bring all my clothes."

Jeremiah laughed with her. "I'll beginning to understand that a little better. Unless you need me to help you, I'll go get some work done in the barn before supper."

"I'll need help putting the trunks somewhere later." She turned around and kissed him soundly. "Maybe that will hold me in the kissing department until bedtime."

"Mmmm . . . I think I need a couple more." He kissed her again on the lips and then on the cheeks.

Emily pushed him toward the door. "Go on with you, how can I get unpacked if you stand around kissing me all afternoon."

Grinning, Jeremiah left the bedroom.

Emily hummed to herself as she unpacked and placed her things. She had one trunk of books, but would get Jeremiah help her to unload them into the shelves in the front room later.

They had an enjoyable supper with Bob and Jacob. The men talked of the ranch work. Emily didn't mind as she enjoyed listening to the masculine voices. Ranch work was much more complicated than she had realized. She hadn't understood that Jeremiah spent a lot of his time in the winter months breaking horses. Mares that foaled during their time at the ranch meant Jeremiah had the responsibility of making sure a stallion covered the mare within twenty days. As Emily listened to the men talk of the work, she wondered how they kept it all straight.

In the middle of the night, Emily woke to find Jeremiah moaning and thrashing about on the bed. He had warned her about his nightmares.

"Don't leave me alone, please, don't leave me in the dark," he mumbled, repeating the same phrase over and over.

She hesitated. Should she wake him? The nightmare evidently worsened for he moaned even louder and his face twisted in fright. She decided to wake him.

"Jeremiah, Jeremiah, wake up, wake up, it's only a dream." She spoke softly and then gently shook him on the shoulder.

He woke abruptly and stared at her as if he didn't know where he was.

"It's me, Emily. You're having a bad dream." She rubbed his back, trying to soothe him.

"I'm sorry I—"

"No, don't you be sorry. You told me about your nightmares. I just want you to know it's all right and I'm here with you now."

He gasped and sobbed. "Thank you."

"Is it the same dream over and over?" If she got him to talk about it maybe it would help it to go away.

"Yeah, it's the same."

"Do you want to tell me about it?"

"No, I just want to forget about it and go back to sleep. Sorry I woke you."

"Shhh, just close your eyes." She cuddled his head to her and stroked his hair. He gradually relaxed and was soon asleep again. She lay beside him wide awake. It happened twice more during the night. Her heart ached for her husband. The nightmare tormented him and she couldn't help stop it.

The next morning Jeremiah was exhausted and so was she.

"I'm sorry. I had hoped they were gone. I haven't had a night like that since I was at the Rocking ES." He rubbed his eyes and then the back of his neck.

"Did anything happen yesterday that upset you?" Emily wanted to find a key to his nightmares in hopes of stopping them.

"Not that I can think of. You were with me. I didn't really want to come home and get to work, but that's nothing to upset someone."

"Well, let's just hope you don't have any more. But, if you do we'll face them together." She wished now that she had thought to talk to Sara about how she responded when Joe had nightmares.

"What do you plan to do today?" Jeremiah finished his breakfast.

"I need to go into town and see Grandma. I'm worried about her."

"Do you want me to come with you?" Jeremiah picked up his hat.

"No, you have work to do. I'll just go in, see her, and then come back." Emily reached up and kissed him. She appreciated his offer.

"You know I'll help if I can." He put on his hat. "Be safe. Get back as soon as you can." He kissed her and went out to hitch up the buggy for her.

Emily drove the buggy up to Grandma's barn. Homer came out with a hammer in his hand.

His face brightened when he saw her. "Miss Emily, good to see you." He took the reins. "Here, I'll take care of your horse. Your grandmother will be so happy to see you." He offered his hand as she stepped out of the buggy.

"Thank you, Homer. I'm anxious to see Grandma."

She went into the house and into the kitchen where she greeted Mildred.

"Oh, Miss Emily, look at you. You just look lovely. Mrs. Johnson will be so glad to see you." Mildred gave her a hug.

Emily took off her shawl and hat and laid them across the back of a chair. "How is my grandma?"

Mildred looked down at the table where she had dough ready to roll out for a pie. "She's not doing too well. She stays in bed most days now. I keep trying to think of things to fix that she can eat but she doesn't eat much."

Emily hugged the kind woman. "Well, I'm going in to see her." Emily went from the kitchen, down the back hall, and into her grandma's bedroom.

Mrs. Spencer sat next to the bed and smiled at her warmly. "Mrs. Johnson, look who's here, it's Emily."

Emily hugged Mrs. Spencer and then kissed Grandma on the cheek. She looked so frail and even smaller than before. "Hello, Grandma, it's me, Emily."

Grandma perked up and gave Emily a weak smile. "My Emily, how are you?" She pushed up her glasses and patted the bed. "Sit down. I want to hear all about your wedding and wedding trip. Where's Jeremiah?" Her face tensed, as if in pain.

Emily smoothed her forehead and Grandma relaxed. "He's at the ranch, working. With us having been gone for a week he has work to do. He would have come if I had asked him to." Emily took her fragile hand and held it gently.

Grandma held her hanky to her chest. "Was he handsome for the wedding?"

"Oh, yes, he was very handsome in a black suit and new boots. He was nervous but determined." Emily accepted the teacup that Mrs. Spencer offered. "I don't know if I told you, Grandma, that he gets very nervous sometimes and doesn't like crowds." She blew on her tea. "So for him to go through with the wedding like I wanted was a true gift."

"I've always known he was a good boy."

Sometimes Grandma said the strangest things. But Emily felt it best to agree and avoid agitating her. "Yes, he is."

"Where did you go for the wedding trip?" The elderly woman's eyes bore into Emily's.

She wondered at the intensity of her grandma's behavior. "Jeremiah planned it. He has a beautiful little cabin near the foot of a waterfall in a valley about two hours by horseback from his ranch." Emily took a sip of her tea, then set her cup down. "We went there for five days. He'd stocked it with food, the bed was made, wood cut, and the quiet and peacefulness of it took my breath away. It was wonderful." Emily smiled at the memory of their time there. It had been perfect.

Grandma looked at Emily over the top of her glasses. "Were you good to him?"

Emily stared at the old lady in shock. "Of course, Grandma. Why would you ask such a thing?"

Grandma settled back on her pillows. "I'm so glad. Just be good to the boy." She patted Emily's arm. "You owe him." Her voice grew faint as she closed her eyes.

Emily leaned closer. "What did you say, Grandma? I don't understand."

When Grandma didn't answer, Emily quietly left the room and let her sleep. She returned to the kitchen.

Mrs. Spencer and Mildred sat at the table drinking coffee and eating red velvet cake.

"Would you like to join us, Miss Emily?" Mildred asked.

"Yes, I would, thank you." She sat down at the table across from Mrs. Spencer. "I just had the strangest visit with my grandma. I know she's ill, but is she all right in her mind?"

Mrs. Spencer cut a generous portion of the red velvet cake, slid it on a plate, and handed it to Emily. "She's weaker and the doctor comes every day now. But, I haven't noticed anything wrong with her mind. She has just been asking if you were back." She leaned forward and patted Emily's hand. "You got to prepare yourself. I don't think your grandma will last the winter. She's a tough old lady and she might, but she is so much weaker. You have to remember that she is getting old."

Emily took a deep breath. "Thank you for being honest with me. It's a comfort to know that you two ladies are with her. Let me know if there's anything I can do."

Mildred poured more coffee in her cup. "We do the best we can. There's just not much we can do to make her more comfortable."

"I'll try to come every few days. If you think I need to come, you send Homer and I'll be here at once." Emily drank her coffee and ate the piece of cake. She talked a few more minutes with the two ladies and then left.

The drive back to the ranch went swiftly. She thought so hard about what her grandma had asked, that she hardly noticed the passing countryside. For someone who had never met Jeremiah, her grandma had a strange interest in him.

~ ~ ~

Jeremiah fell back into his work routine of breaking horses every day. In addition, he worked with about a hundred mares that would deliver in the next three months. Between the young foals and making sure the right stallion covered the mares, Jeremiah worked full, hard days.

He took great delight in coming home to find Emily there to greet him lovingly at the end of the day. He tried to think of things to do for her. He wanted her life to be an easy one. The only problem she had was her grandma's illness. She went into town three or four times a week to spend some time with her.

Jeremiah enjoyed getting up on Sunday—the only day of the week when no work pressed on him—and leisurely have breakfast with Emily. And then they went into town to the worship service at ten o'clock. After church services, they went to Emily's grandma's house for dinner with Mildred, Mrs. Spencer, and Sally. With Mrs. Johnson bedridden, Jeremiah never saw her. It puzzled him that she could visit with Emily but was never able to be introduced to him. After Emily visited with her, they went back to the ranch and enjoyed the rest of the afternoon and evening together.

Jeremiah had always been a listener and he liked to listen to Emily. He encouraged her to talk about anything she wanted. He just listened and looked at her loveliness.

Of course, sometimes he got caught when she said to him, "Are you listening?" and he had no idea what she had said because he was watching the way she tossed her head back and bounced the curls around her face. He never got enough of her.

## Chapter 18

Emily found herself busy every day. She did more and more of the cooking, which she enjoyed. She appreciated that Jacob got up early and had breakfast ready for them. She then began dinner and supper preparations. Her cooking skills had vastly improved under the tutelage of Mildred and now Jacob.

She sometimes felt a little exasperated at Jeremiah after she would spend hours in the kitchen and the only comment he would make was that the meal was good. He liked all foods and ate anything put in front of him.

When she told Mildred and Mrs. Spencer about her frustration, they told her to be grateful as some women only heard complaints from their husbands. Emily couldn't imagine that; Jeremiah never complained.

Some days Jacob stayed and helped her, but other days he busied himself in his workshop at the back of the barn where he made fine furniture pieces to sell.

Emily liked to go out to the shop and watch Jacob work; his skill amazed her. Their home constantly received a new little table or cabinet on the walls. If Emily mentioned something that might make it nicer or handier, in a few days Jacob walked in with it made. He did the same thing in the barn. They were blessed to have someone as talented as Jacob on the ranch.

Emily really liked Bob but found him hard to get to know. He was almost as quiet as Jeremiah. Jeremiah told her that he had not been that way before he lost his wife. Bob was a hard worker and managed the ranch well for Jeremiah. Jeremiah didn't want to be boss and was happy to turn it over to Bob.

Emily did everything she could to make things lively. Jeremiah seemed to enjoy himself when she initiated some fun, but he never initiated any himself. He told her he never had any fun until the Rocking ES. She wanted to make up for such a barren childhood with lots of laughter in his life now. How she loved that man.

~

Emily prepared for Christmas and baked cakes and cookies for days. When Jeremiah came into the kitchen after she had just taken a pan of cookies out of the oven he ate the hot cookies as fast as she could ladle them onto the platter to cool. She grinned indulgently at him and started another batch. He had never had cookies as a child and she didn't mind trying to make up for it.

The day before Christmas, Jeremiah helped her load the buggy with food and toys. They drove into Cedar Ridge to the little wooden house where the preacher James Quinn lived with his wife Charlotte and three small children.

Jeremiah was about to knock on the front door when it opened. He removed his hat. "Mrs. Quinn, we've come to visit for a few minutes."

Mrs. Quinn smiled at them and opened the door wide. "Call me Charlotte, Jeremiah. Emily, come on in out of the cold."

The house was tiny with only three rooms. Charlotte led them through what was a sleeping room into the kitchen. "Have a seat at the table and I'll prepare some coffee. James should be back any minute."

Jeremiah and Emily set packages on the table. "We have toys for the children. Where should I put them?" Jeremiah asked.

"Oh, bless you. Will they fit under our bed there in the front room?" Charlotte smiled without a hint of embarrassment.

Emily sat at the table while Jeremiah went back to the buggy and carried the rest of the packages into the house. He slid them under the bed.

As he was taking his coat off, the preacher came in the house.

"James, Jeremiah and Emily have brought food and toys for the children."

Emily rose to greet him. "Preacher Quinn."

"Call me James. I appreciate your thoughtfulness for my children. Christmas was looking a little slim and then you bring all this." He waved at the table on which was sitting a ham, a basket of vegetables, cakes, cookies, and loaves of homemade bread.

Jeremiah pulled out a chair and sat down. "Well, we had to do something with all that Emily has been baking."

Emily smiled at him. "Yes, I hope it's all right. This is my first year to bake for Christmas. You'll have to tell me if it's any good."

Charlotte poured the freshly made coffee. "I'm sure it will be wonderful, Emily. We'll have to exchange some recipes. I love to bake."

Emily drew her shawl tighter across her shoulders as cold air rushed in from the back door that didn't fit properly in its frame. The house was cold but the warmth of the couple more than made up for it.

It hurt Emily to see the small, poorly built house where this good family lived without complaint. As she and Jeremiah sat at the small kitchen table and had a cup of coffee with James and Charlotte, Emily determined to do something to help this family.

They didn't visit long as they had several other stops to make including Milburn and Agnes Black. Emily had baked a large fruitcake for the Black family as their two married daughters and families had come for the holiday. Emily knew their youngest was a son, but Milburn and Agnes never talked about him.

By the time they arrived back at the ranch, the buggy held several gifts for Jeremiah and Emily from their friends.

Emily loved seeing the look of pleasure and surprise on Jeremiah's face as he gave and received gifts. It made the days of hard work of baking more than worthwhile.

Christmas Eve they had a special supper at the ranch with Jacob and Bob. After supper, they gathered in the front room, popped popcorn in the fireplace, and drank hot apple cider. Bob gave Jeremiah a horsehair lariat he had made. For Emily, Bob had a soft wool shawl. Emily suspected that Agnes had helped pick it out as it matched her new winter dress.

Jacob brought in a beautiful little bookstand that he had made to hold a big family Bible.

Jeremiah and Emily gave Bob a new saddle and two new shirts. For Jacob, Jeremiah had ordered a special set of tools for working with wood. Emily gave him two new shirts.

Emily gave Jeremiah a warm winter coat and a new Stetson. He gave her a silver-plated brush set and several new combs for her hair. He also gave her a new saddle and boots. She wanted to tell him he had given her too much but he seemed to enjoy the giving so much. She rewarded him by kissing him under the mistletoe in front of Bob and Jacob.

For Christmas dinner the next day, everyone from the ranch went in to her grandma's house. It was a fun time, but her grandma lying in bed unable to participate was a sorrow to Emily. Her grandma had ordered gifts for everyone. Including a beautiful gold necklace and earring set for Emily.

Jeremiah wanted to go into her grandma's room to thank her for the fancy, silver mounted expensive saddle she gave to him. But Grandma said no. Emily wondered about it. Did her grandma not want anyone seeing her so sick and old looking?

Emily and Jeremiah had gifts for all the ladies. Emily had carefully chosen gifts she thought they would enjoy. She was finally able to give Sally a couple of pretty dresses. Mrs. Spencer received a new hat and gloves. The gift for Mildred was a warm shawl and slippers. It warmed Emily's heart to see such true appreciation for what in times past she would have considered small gifts.

~

April arrived in a flurry of activity. The men came from the Rocking ES to take the horse herd back to the mountain range.

Elisha and Joe praised Jeremiah several times on the great job he had done with the herd. With Jeremiah's work, they would sell four hundred horses before the fall. Over a hundred foals had been born and over a hundred mares carried the next year's offspring.

With most of the horses gone Jeremiah and Emily took a week and went back to the cabin by the waterfalls. Jeremiah slept a lot which only proved how hard he had worked to have the horses ready for Elisha and Joe.

When they arrived back at the ranch, Jacob came out of the house to meet them. "Emily, Homer just left. He came to tell that your grandmother she is very ill. The Doctor says for you to come."

Emily turned to Jeremiah. "I have to go now."

He nodded. "I'll ride with you. Let's get these packs off the horses and go on into town. The horses are still fresh enough."

Emily's eyes blurred as tears threatened. "Thank you Jeremiah. I didn't want to ask but I'd like for you to come with me. I'm so afraid that I'll soon lose my grandma."

Jeremiah took her into his arms and held her. "I know, honey. Don't worry. I'm going to be with you."

At a fast trot they made it quickly to her grandma's house and left the horses for Homer to put into the barn.

After they went into the kitchen, Mildred gave Emily a warm hug and then wiped her eyes with her handkerchief. "Oh, Miss Emily, I fear this is it."

Emily untied her hat. "Did she have a spell or something?" She placed her things on a side table.

Mildred wrung the dishtowel she held in her hands. "We couldn't wake her yesterday and then the doctor came. She roused this morning and asked for you. You better go on in." She turned to Jeremiah. "Jeremiah, have a seat and I'll get you a cup of coffee."

Emily went into her grandma's bedroom where Mrs. Spencer sat by the bed.

"Emily, honey, I'm glad you're here." Mrs. Spencer looked tired. She stood and gave Emily a hug.

"Go get some rest. I'll sit with Grandma." Emily didn't know how strong she was to sit and watch her grandmother die, but she knew she couldn't leave.

Mrs. Spencer ran a hand over her hair. "Thank you, I could use a few minutes. I've been up all night." She closed the door quietly behind her.

Emily sat down in the chair next to her grandma who looked even more fragile than the last time she had seen her. She took the thin bony hand in hers and prayed.

Emily looked up and found her grandma's eyes open.

"Is that you my Emily?" she whispered.

"Yes, Grandma, I'm here."

The old lady closed her eyes, then quickly opened them again. "Is Jeremiah here?"

"Yes, Grandma, he's in the kitchen. Would you like to meet him?"

"Yes, but let me talk to you a bit first."

Emily was surprised as she had reconciled herself that Jeremiah would never meet her. "What would you like to talk about?"

Grandma swallowed, then looked at her. "I'm dying, my Emily. Soon and I want to tell you some things. You know I'm leaving most everything to you. Mildred, Mrs. Spencer, Sally, and Homer will have a little money." She paused and took a couple shallow breaths before continuing. "They have been good to me. You get the house and other property."

"You don't need to worry about all that. If you left everything to these lovely people who have taken care of you, I wouldn't mind. Jeremiah is taking care of me."

"I know he is, but I just wanted you to know."

Grandma drifted off to sleep, but Emily remained at her side. Emily refused the dinner tray that Mrs. Spencer brought to her. Emily asked if Jeremiah had returned to the ranch. Mrs. Spencer assured her that Jeremiah was fine and spending time in the barn with Homer.

Several hours later, Grandma woke again. Emily held a glass of water to her dry cracked lips. Grandma took a sip before settling back on her pillows. Emily adjusted the blankets to make her more comfortable.

Grandma held up her hand. "Don't fuss over me dear. Sit down. I need to tell you something."

Emily placed a clean hanky in Grandma's hand and sat back down.

"In my chest at the foot of my bed is a carved wooden box. What's in that box is for you alone. Don't open it until I'm gone. I couldn't stand it if you did." She grasped Emily's arm in a tight grip. "Promise me."

"I promise, Grandma, of course I do."

"I've done some bad things and I need forgiveness. I'm leaving it for you to deal with as you decide. I'm sorry honey." Tears ran down her wrinkled cheeks. "Please forgive me," she pleaded.

"Of course, but there is nothing to ask my forgiveness for."

Grandma smiled weakly and shook her head. "Anyway, Mrs. Spencer knows where the box is. You promise me that no one but you will look inside it. You promise." The old lady gripped Emily's hand so hard that it hurt.

Emily gently pried her hand away. "I promise, Grandma."

"You be good to Jeremiah. He deserves it. Promise me that you will always be good to him."

"Of course, Grandma, I'll always be good to Jeremiah. I love him."

"I'm so glad. We owe him." Her voice faded as she fell back to sleep.

"What do you mean by that, we owe him?"

Grandma jerked back awake and took a ragged breath. "Let me see him while I got time. I don't want no lamp on me. Light one there on that table and have him come in and stand in the light. Turn this one by the bed off."

Emily grew more concerned about Grandma's strange wishes, but she did as her grandma asked.

~ ~ ~

Jeremiah had just finished eating a sandwich and a piece of cake when Emily came back into the kitchen. He got up and took her in his arms. "Is your grandma bad?"

"Oh, Jeremiah, she's really dying." She blew her nose on the handkerchief Jeremiah pulled out of his pocket. "She wants you to come in and meet her."

Jeremiah took a deep breath. "All right, I can do that." He followed her into the bedroom.

Emily led him into the light of the lamp. "Just stand here so she can see you." She went over to the bed and stood by the old lady. "Grandma, Jeremiah's here."

Uncomfortable, Jeremiah shifted his weight to his right leg and put his shaking hands in his pockets. The spotlight made him feel on display. He couldn't make out the old lady's face in shadows.

"Jeremiah, is that you?" the old lady asked, her voice but a raspy whisper.

Jeremiah shifted legs. "Yes, ma'am. I'm here."

The old lady coughed several times before she continued. "Tell me about yourself," she said between shallow breaths.

Jeremiah crossed his arms. "I was born down in New Mexico. My ma died when I was too young to remember her and my pa died when I was eight. I lived all over until I found a place on the Rocking ES with Elisha Evans and his family. Then a couple of years ago I bought the ranch here and met Emily. You know about that."

He intentionally left many details out of his story. The old woman made him uncomfortable. Or did death make him uncomfortable? He shook his head. Something stirred at the edge of his mind. He felt trapped. Caged. Like at the tunnel. He glanced around the suffocating room. The hairs on the back of his neck raised in panic. He needed air.

## COLORADO MORNING SKY

"Where did you get your gold?" she asked.

Jeremiah held his breath. He hadn't told anyone about the gold. Not even Emily. How did this old lady know about the gold? Had one of the bankers talked?

He finally released his breath and said, "I dug it out of a mountain."

"Do you love my Emily?"

"Yes, ma'am, I love Emily with all my heart." He said it without hesitation.

"Do you promise before God to be good to her no matter what?"

"Yes ma'am, no matter what." He could promise that as it was his goal for the rest of his life.

"Then that's all right. I'm glad to have met you again, Jeremiah."

Jeremiah took that to mean he could leave the bedroom. He couldn't get out of there fast enough. The old lady had asked some of the strangest questions. And how did she know of the gold? And what did she mean about meeting him again?

He went out into the backyard and wore out the ground walking back and forth. What would he say to Emily if she asked what he thought about her grandmother? What a strange old lady. He didn't want ever to see her again. He shuddered and wished that he and Emily could just leave and go back to the ranch.

About an hour later, Emily came out the kitchen door. She ran into his arms and sobbed.

"She's gone, Jeremiah, she's gone. After you left she told me to take good care of you, and then she told me she loved me and for me to forgive her. She closed her eyes and now . . . now she's gone." Emily looked up at Jeremiah, tears streaming down her face. "What do I have to forgive her about?" Then she buried her face into Jeremiah's chest and cried for her grandma.

A J HAWKE

Jeremiah held her and let her cry. He would never tell Emily, but he only felt relief that the old lady was dead. He didn't have the attachment to her that Emily had and could be removed from her death. He needed to be there for Emily, but the old lady? She scared him.

After a while he walked Emily back into the house and sat with her in the front parlor. The doctor came and said he would make arrangements. Mr. Powers, a representative of the bank, called on Emily after the doctor left.

He pulled some papers out of a case he had brought with him. "I'm the executor of Mrs. Johnson's affairs. I know this is soon after her death but she insisted that I waste no time." Mr. Powers handed a document to Emily. "It is her request for burial. She wants to be taken back to Arizona and be buried by her husband. She requests that you not accompany her. She has made all the arrangements and it's all paid for." He looked down at his copy of the document. "She has written here that you may have a service if you want, but she didn't see it was necessary. She had already put her property in your name, Mrs. Rebourn, as well as all of her bank accounts. So basically, except for monies that are going to the staff, you inherit it all immediately."

Jeremiah spoke for Emily as he sensed that she didn't want to deal with all of this. "Let me talk to my wife alone, and then I'll let you know if we'll have a service." Jeremiah escorted the banker to the front door.

He went back and sat down next to Emily. "What do you want to do?"

Emily looked up at him, her eyes swollen and red from crying. "There's only a few of us who knew her. But I think Mildred, Mrs. Spencer, and Sally would like to have a service."

"What if we had a service here at the house at ten in the morning and asked Brother Quinn to come and anyone else who wants to. I think Jacob and Bob will. Then they could take her on the train at noon. Are you all right with her being buried in

Arizona?" Jeremiah was and he could have skipped the service, but he knew Emily needed it.

Emily dabbed at her eyes and nodded. "All right. I feel like I need to stay here tonight. I don't want to leave her alone." Emily started crying again.

Jeremiah held his wife and rocked her gently as she grieved. "I'll send word out to Bob and Jacob, then I'll go talk to the preacher and tell the banker your decision. Will you be all right if I leave for a while?"

"Mrs. Spencer has my old room ready. Walk up there with me and I think I'll lie down. I feel so tired."

He lifted her up in his arms, carried her up the stairs, and into the room that had been hers before they married. It was a bright cheerful room. He laid her on the bed and pulled a cover up to her chin. He kissed her lightly. "I'll be back as soon as I can. I'll be with you until we can go home."

She wrapped her arms around his neck and hugged him tight for several minutes. "Thank you. It would be unbearable if you weren't here." She let him go and closed her eyes.

He sat for a few more minutes until she was asleep. Jeremiah tiptoed from the room and went to the kitchen where Mildred, Sally, and Mrs. Spencer sat at the table crying.

"Mrs. Spencer, I have some arrangements to make with the preacher and Mr. Powell. Would you go up and sit with Emily? She's asleep, but I don't want her to wake up alone."

Mrs. Spencer nodded.

Jeremiah looked around the table at the three women who had cared for Emily's grandmother. "Mrs. Johnson had made arrangements for her body to be taken back to Arizona. We're going to have a service here at the house at ten in the morning, then they'll take her body and put it on the train for Arizona. Mrs. Johnson requested that no one travel with the body."

"Should we plan a meal for after the service?" Mildred asked.

"I hadn't thought about it. Do you think we should?" He didn't know about such things.

"I think we should," Mrs. Spencer said. "You'll be surprised how many people will come tomorrow out of respect for you and Emily and it's customary to have a light meal ready. In fact I wouldn't be surprised if people didn't bring food starting this evening."

"Can you ladies handle that without bothering Emily?" He wanted her to rest if she could.

Mildred walked to the counter and opened a drawer. She pulled out a tablet and pencil. "We can handle that if you'll go talk to the preacher." Mildred said. "We'll also take care of preparing Mrs. Johnson. Her casket is out in the barn. She bought it a couple of years ago."

"Her casket! I hadn't thought about such a thing. Will Homer be able to bring it in?"

"Oh, yes, he'll get a couple of fellows to help him. We'll take care of it. You go talk to the preacher and the banker, then come back and sit with Emily."

"Thank you, ladies. I know Emily appreciates it." Jeremiah went out to the barn and saddled his horse.

The next couple of days were a blur for Jeremiah. He helped Homer build a stand for the casket and place it in the main parlor. Mrs. Spencer draped a cloth over it and then he helped carry the casket from the bedroom to the parlor where it was placed on top of the stand. He spent time just sitting with Emily near the casket as various people came by to express their condolences. The main parlor of the house barely held all the people who attended the simple service—most of whom had to stand. Mildred and Mrs. Spencer, with Sally's help, served dinner buffet style in the formal dining room. As the meal was being served, Mr. Powers had men come and take Mrs. Johnson's casket to the train depot.

Jeremiah talked Emily into saying goodbye to her grandma at the house instead of the train station. To relieve Emily's concerns

Jeremiah asked Homer to accompany the body to Arizona and make sure it was buried properly with a headstone.

After the wagon left for the train depot, Emily took a deep breath, squared her shoulders, and went back into the house to be hostess to her guests.

Jeremiah was proud of how she handled it. He spent most of the afternoon in the backyard talking to the men.

After everyone had left late in the afternoon, Jeremiah and Emily sat around the kitchen table with Mrs. Spencer, Mildred, and Sally.

Although her eyes were red and swollen from crying, Emily was calm. "Ladies, I need to tell you some things. My grandmother has left me the house but for now I want you all to keep it open and in a few days I will come and we will decide what to do with all her things."

Mrs. Spencer reached over and patted Emily's hand. "You know that we loved your grandma and we love you and Jeremiah. Whatever you need us to do we will do." Mildred and Sally both nodded their agreement.

"Thank you. For now Jeremiah and I are going home, but I'll be back in a couple of days. I'm not up to making any decisions right now."

Mrs. Spencer nodded.

Mildred stood up and moved to the kitchen counter. "I'll make you up a basket of food to take home with you."

Jeremiah went out to the barn to get the horses saddled and to give Homer instructions.

Emily and Jeremiah returned to the ranch in the late afternoon, arriving just before dark. Jeremiah was relieved finally to be home with his wife.

A J HAWKE

## Chapter 19

Emily squinted in the mirror at her puffy eyes. It had been a week since the service and she'd awakened with a sense of dread. She guessed the looming decisions about her grandma's house and belongings caused her gloom. Grandma's death had affected her more than she ever imagined it would. She thought she'd prepared herself for it. But when her beloved grandmother died, the grief swooped down on Emily like a dark cloud. Other than Jeremiah, she had no one in the world.

Emily struggled to dress and comb her hair. Wanting to climb back into bed and cover her head, she forced herself to leave her bedroom.

In the kitchen, Jeremiah put down his coffee cup and held out his hands to her. "You look so sad this morning."

Jeremiah had such a direct way of saying things.

She let him take her into his arms. "I am sad this morning. But I know it'll get better." She rested her head on his chest. His heartbeat in her ear gave her courage. "I need to go into town and spend the day with Mrs. Spencer and Mildred. We need to make some decisions." She looked up at him. "Is that all right with you?" She asked him, knowing he would be all right with it.

He kissed the top of her head. "Do you need me to come?"

"You've work to do. I'll be all right. I'll take the buggy in case there's anything I decide to bring back from the house."

"I would rather get some work done here, but you know I'll come if you want me."

Emily smiled at him. She never had to wonder what Jeremiah wanted as he just said things straight out. "I'll be back by suppertime."

She arrived at her grandmother's house by nine and found everyone but Homer in the kitchen.

Mrs. Spencer scooted back her chair and stepped to the cabinet for a cup and saucer. "Sit down, honey, let me get you some coffee." She poured the coffee into the cup and placed it on the table. "You look tired."

Emily sat down and put her elbows on the table. She felt so drained she could barely hold her head up. "I am tired. I haven't been sleeping very well. What do we need to do this morning?"

Mrs. Spencer sat at the table. "If you'll tell us what you want to do with your grandmother's things we'll take care of it. But we need you to make the decisions." She pulled a tablet and pencil toward her on which she had started a list. "She doesn't have a lot of personal things like clothes. There's no jewelry or other fine things. She was a plain lady in lots of ways." Mrs. Spencer shook her head. "The grandest things she had was this house and furniture."

"You all take what you want of her personal things and donate the rest to the church to give to the poor. As you go through her things if you find anything of my parents—pictures or letters—I would like to have those. I don't know of anything else I want. We will deal with the furniture and the house later."

Emily didn't even want the furniture, as Jacob created simpler pieces that better suited her tastes. She guessed she would eventually sell the house. She couldn't think why she would want it.

Mildred coughed and said, "Mr. Powers came by yesterday and told us of the bequests that Mrs. Johnson had left for us. We were so surprised but pleased. It was so like her to be so generous."

Mrs. Spencer quickly agreed. "She left Mildred and me enough each that we can retire if that is what we want."

Sally chimed in. "And she told the bank to keep paying me from now on, no matter what. Isn't that wonderful."

Emily knew that was wise as Sally was only sixteen and not well educated. Emily didn't know for sure if she could read.

Mildred shook her head. "She also took care of Homer. He's more surprised than we were."

When Mr. Powers had explained the will to her she had been surprised at just how wealthy her grandmother was and Emily was more than happy to share it with these fine people who had made the elderly woman's last days so comfortable.

Emily finished her coffee and Mrs. Spencer came back into the kitchen with a carved wooden chest about two feet in length, height, and width.

She placed the chest before Emily. "Your grandmother made me swear that I would give this to only you. I was to make sure you opened it alone." Mrs. Spencer handed Emily a little key. "So I thought maybe you could go up to your room and open it while we pack up her clothes and things from her bedroom down here."

Emily ran her fingers over the chest's intricate carvings. "I might as well see what it is and then I'll come help you all." She carried it up the stairs to her old room. She placed the chest on the bed, slipped out of her shoes, and climbed up on the bed. Sitting cross-legged in front of the chest, she put the little key into the lock and opened it.

At first, she thought Mrs. Spencer had given her the wrong chest. It contained the oddest assortment of things. She used two fingers to pick up a long rope, which had stains around a loop at one end. Pieces of black silk cloth rested in one corner, a key, and iron rings and chains of some kind covered the bottom that explained why the chest was so heavy. Emily pulled out a leather book—a journal written in her grandmother's handwriting. Emily settled back and started on the first page.

*My name is Maude Johnson. This is a record of a most difficult time in my life. I have done some things that tell me that evil rests within me. I don't know who all will read this after my death, but I feel a need to confess to you, Emily. You need to know.*

*Let me tell a little about myself. I was born in Pennsylvania and came west with my family. We traveled the trail to Oregon. It was hard, and I knew my folks worried, but for us kids it was an adventure. I have always been ready for an adventure. I met my* husband George Johnson when I was fifteen and we were married by handfasting. Later we had a preacher say words for us. I had our first child the next year. A baby girl that died when only a year old. I grieved so much for that child. And then I had a baby boy, Johnny. George and I loved him. I kept house and took care of the baby.

George wanted to find gold. He worked for a while and then he would go off and look for gold. He just knew he would find some. We moved down to Tucson and he looked for gold in the desert. One day he came home and told me he'd found it. It wasn't a big vein, but he could mine enough for us to live on. The only problem it was right in the middle of the Indian trouble. He was careful and he only brought out a little of the gold at a time.

Our boy Johnny met the sweetest girl, Callie. They married and had Emily, but Callie was sickly and soon after the baby was born she died of a fever. Johnny grieved so that he left the baby with us and went off to fight in the war going on back east. We never heard from him again. But we had little Emily. When my Emily was fourteen we sent her back east to a finishing school. It was what George thought we ought to do. George went to the mines more often so we could afford it. He came home one day and took sick. He told me where to find the mine and how to get the gold out. He even drew me a map. He told me never to trust no one and never ever take anyone to the mine. George didn't want to leave me, but he died.

I had to take care of my Emily. So I dressed up like a man, took George's tools and his burro and went to find the mine. I found it all right, but I'm a small woman and I couldn't work it very good. I wasn't hardly getting enough gold to support myself much less support Emily in that expensive school. I needed money to get her the nice dresses so she wouldn't feel ashamed. I had to get that gold out.

I'd been back to Tucson to close up the house and get provisions. I planned to work the mine as best I could and then live in the house when I had to go back. I couldn't go to the same town all the time to get rid of the gold, so I started going to different towns to get supplies and put the gold in the banks. It was on the way back to the mine that I found the boy, Jeremiah, and I kept him.

I saw the vultures first and then I smelled death. I was cautious, you better believe it. I wasn't about to let some Apache take my gray scalp. At the bottom of the bluff was the wreckage of a wagon that had come over the bluff. Wagon was all broke up. As I looked at it I saw that it was a prison wagon with bars and bolts to attach chains. There were two guards in uniforms and six prisoners. At first I thought they were all dead. I went through their pockets to see if there was anything of value. I didn't think of it as stealing because they were dead and no one was going to find them for a long time. It was out in the middle of nowhere. When I moved some splintered wood to get to the pockets of a couple of men and I realized that a boy lay there breathing. Well, I didn't know what to do. He had irons on his wrists and ankles so I knew he was a prisoner. He looked to be about sixteen, much younger than the other men. I had already found a key that unlocked the chains and shackles.

I started to undo the irons on the boy, who wasn't awake. Then I looked at him. He was about six feet tall and muscled. Good looking, I'll say. Dark curly hair, deeply tanned skin, the build of a rider with slim hips and wide shoulders. A healthy strong-looking boy. I needed a strong young man who could swing a pick. If I hadn't come along he would have just died. I could ask him to help me, but why would he agree. No, I decided it would be better if he had no choice and had to help me. But how could I do that? He was so much bigger than me. I looked at his shackles and thought of a way. In my pack I had a black silk petticoat that my George had given me. I tore it and made a blindfold. The boy mustn't see me as a woman if I was to control him and force him to help me. I tied the blindfold around his head and I tied it tight. His wrists had an iron ring locked on each one and a link chain across that was about twelve inches long. I studied on how to tie him. I couldn't put his hands behind him and expect him to do much, but how could I keep him from grabbing out at me. So I got one of the poles that had been a bar on the prisoner wagon and threaded the pole through his elbows behind his back which pulled his arms back and left his hands free but with no maneuvering room. He was starting to come around and I wanted to get out of there as I didn't know when some Apaches might come back. I couldn't carry him and I couldn't make him want to come with me. I puzzled on that as I got ready to leave and then I found a rope that had fallen out of the wagon. I tied it with a knot so it would slide up and down easily and I slipped it over the boy's head. I got on the burro and pulled on the rope that was around his neck. He didn't want to come with me, but only for a few moments, and then he got on his feet and followed me as I pulled the rope tight around his neck. I didn't start out to make him a slave or a prisoner and would never have thought of it except he was just lying there. I had no right, but once I did it I couldn't go back. As I led him across the desert I wondered if it was a mistake. He might be more trouble than he was worth. But I kept thinking about that gold and my Emily and how he was a strong boy—if I could make him work.

When I stopped for the night I tried to think what was I going to do with him. I was so tired and had to sleep. Then I remembered the big bottle of laudanum I had in my pack. George would never travel without it. It killed pain, but it also made you sleep. So that first night I made a cup of tea and put a cap full of laudanum in it. I made the boy drink it. He thanked me for it and I almost answered. Poor boy. He had no idea.

It took me five days to get to the mine. I got him into the mine and then jerked hard on the rope. He fell to his knees. I grabbed the pole and dragged him to the support beam while keeping the rope tight on his throat. He didn't try to fight me. I think he was pretty tired and weak by then. I could tell he was losing weight fast. After I got him to sleep I fastened the chain I had brought from the prisoner wagon around a support beam and I ran that around the chain between his legs. Then I removed the blindfold and the pole. I left the wrist and ankles shackled. I was sorry about the mess his neck was with the rope burns, but I had him at the mine and he was going to help me get the ore out for my Emily.

The next morning I went back to the tunnel. I had a plate of food and a cup of water with me. Between the threat of pouring the water on the ground and the fact that he had no way to get loose, he finally understood what I wanted him to do. I had him put the *rope around his neck. It was the best control I had. He talked to me and begged me to talk to him.*

*The first several days were hard for him as he adjusted to the work and the dark tunnel. I comforted myself with the thought that he was on his way to jail for a reason and I was just going to let him do his time at the mine instead of Yuma Prison. He talked and sang to himself. I learned his real name was Jeremiah Rebourn, but as I listened to him talk to himself I learned the law knew him by John Anderson. I guess he was lonely. I know I was. I missed George and I missed my Emily. Jeremiah didn't know that I would sit just outside the tunnel and listen to him. He could quote scripture like no one I had ever heard.*

*Every night while I was getting supper ready I would let him sit and rest after a day of work. Most of the time I didn't leave a lantern for I didn't have enough oil, so he was in darkness. A few times I heard him crying and I felt bad, but then I'd remember my Emily and hardened myself against him. But we got the gold out. While he filled the sacks of ore I separated the gold from the dirt and rocks. He was too afraid I wouldn't give him food and water and so he worked. He kept a calendar of sorts by marking off the days. It also helped me keep track of the time.*

*After a while we ran low on food and laudanum. I left him there in the tunnel with food and water while I went to a town to get supplies. I was gone longer than I had planned and when I got back he was in a bad way. I got him water and food. He was so grateful. He thanked me three times. I found it odd that he would thank me when I was torturing him. But, I couldn't stop. I had to get the gold for my Emily.*

*I never saw him smile or heard him laugh. Well, why should he? I kept him in misery. I wondered what kind of person he would have been if this had not happened to him. And what kind of person he would become when I gave him his freedom. I wondered if he would hate me as much as I was growing to hate myself. But he wasn't getting his freedom yet. Not until I had enough gold for my Emily.*

*I finally decided that I had enough gold to take care of Emily and myself for the rest of our lives. Then I thought of Jeremiah.*

*What would he have when I let him go? So I kept him at it for another six months to have enough gold to give some to Jeremiah. He was only sixteen when I took him into the tunnel and he was eighteen when I took him out of the tunnel.*

*I tied him blindfolded to a burro, gave him the tea and took him the three-day journey to a cave George had told me about. I didn't want him to be able to backtrack me. Just before we got to the cave I gave him an extra strong dose of the laudanum because I wanted to be miles away when he awoke. Before I left him I took the irons and chains off him, took the rope away, and the blindfold. I kissed him on the forehead and asked his forgiveness and I rode away. Two years I kept the boy. And it's been six since I let him go.*

*But I couldn't get him out of my mind. So I hired a Pinkerton man to let me know what the boy did. When he finally got to Phoenix five days later he was terribly sick. I didn't understand at the time but I've since learned a terrible thing. Laudanum is a potion that one becomes used to having and you develop a craving for it. I didn't know. I just knew he went to sleep if I gave him enough of it. I'd given it to Jeremiah for two years every night. I made him crave it. When I left I didn't leave any laudanum and Jeremiah didn't know what I'd been giving him. Even if I had known what the laudanum would do to Jeremiah, I still would have given it to him.*

*Then Jeremiah just sort of drifted for several months. He couldn't get settled and he didn't seem able to be with people. Then he found a ranch southwest of Cheyenne, over in Colorado and was there for several years. By all accounts they were good people at the ranch and they helped Jeremiah. Then he got his own ranch, the Rocking JR, just outside Cedar Ridge, Colorado.*

*The Pinkerton man wrote in his last investigation that Jeremiah was healthy, had people he knew at a church he went to regularly, and was thought of as too quiet, but a hard worker by the towns people. He didn't have a wife or children and seemed lonely and when he was asked about his past he wouldn't talk about it. He may think he is still wanted by the law, but the law thinks he's dead. I asked the Pinkerton man if he thought Jeremiah was happy. He said he didn't think Jeremiah knew what that was.*

*My last writing—I'm an old lady now and my Emily completed her schooling. I'm happy she came to live with me as I don't know how long I will last. I've lived a hard working life and I was loved by one good man, my George, my boy Johnny loved me, and my little Emily loves me.*

*But, oh how I do regret what I had to do to Jeremiah and long to hear him say he forgives me. I think about him every day and I can still hear the sound of his voice coming from the tunnel. I wish I could have seen him smile or heard him laugh, but I know it is my fault that he did neither in the two years I held him prisoner. I wronged him terribly. I had good reasons and when I think of my little Emily I know I'd do it again. But it doesn't make it right.*

*They say God can forgive anything, but I don't know if he will forgive me for what I did to Jeremiah. I try to watch over Jeremiah in a way. If he ever needed anything that I could provide I would.*

*Emily, I ask that you be good to Jeremiah. Just make sure he's all right. I feel like we're responsible for him. I might should of told you, Emily, before you married Jeremiah but we owed him and if he wanted you then I had to let him have you. By all accounts he treats you good.*

*I'm getting very tired and think I better put this away. I'm going to put this journal in the box with the rope that is stained with Jeremiah's blood, the blindfold, and the wrist and ankle irons and chain. I kept all of it. I don't know why. Emily, I want you to give Jeremiah the love that I didn't show him. And ask him to forgive me. Lord knows, I did it for love of my Emily.*

*Maude Johnson*

A J HAWKE

## Chapter 20

Emily's hands shook uncontrollably, yet she couldn't move the rest of her body. Her mind refused to believe what she'd just read. No, she wouldn't believe it. She started shooking her head violently and rocked back and forth. *Oh, Jeremiah.* Tears blurred her vision and ran down her cheeks to pool in her lap. She again looked at the contents of the box. These shackles had made the horrendous scars on Jeremiah's wrists and ankles. Emily shuddered. Pain, unbelievable pain pierced her heart for her husband. This chain had kept him a prisoner for two years. His blood stained the rope. Her mind drifted back to Grandma's final days. Emily now knew what her grandma had meant when she'd said, *"We owe him."*

She reached out her hand to touch the rope and couldn't. What was she to do? How could her grandma have done such a horrible thing. Yes, she was evil. Only someone evil could have tortured a boy like that. Nausea rose inside Emily. Part of her died inside. She grieved her grandma's death all over again, only this time she grieved for—the good person she'd thought her grandma had been. What was she to do? Should she show all this to Jeremiah? Would he stop loving her?

*Oh, God, help me, please, help me.*

Emily put the leather book with the horrible words back into the chest and locked it. What should she do with it? How could she go home to Jeremiah with what she now knew? But she feared to tell him. What if he left her? There wasn't room for both her heart and the pain in her chest. She wiped her eyes. This was an agony beyond tears. She wanted to scream. Why hadn't her grandma let this die with her? Why give it to Emily to bear?

*Oh, God, help me know how to bear this. What should I do?*

Someone tapped on the bedroom door. Mrs. Spencer looked into the room. "Emily, are you all right?"

All right? She would never be all right again. Her world was broken.

Mrs. Spencer came over to the bed. She placed her hand on Emily's arm, "Emily? What's wrong?"

Emily took a deep breath and slowly let it out. "I'm all right. It has all just kind of gotten to me. What time is it?"

"It's almost four. Do you plan to spend the night?"

Emily shook her head. "No, I've got to get back to Jeremiah. Mrs. Spencer, I need you to do something very important for me." She thrust the box into Mrs. Spencer's hands. "Will you keep this chest and don't tell anyone about it. Not ever. I'll get it from you in a few days."

"Of course, I'll keep it for you. Are you sure you're all right to drive home?"

"Yes, I'll be fine." Emily put her shoes on and descended the stairs. She went out and got into the buggy after saying goodbye to the women at the house. Before she had her mind ready the ranch house came into view.

*Oh, Jeremiah, I'm so sorry.*

She shook herself. She would just act as if nothing had changed—but she knew everything had changed.

~ ~ ~

Jeremiah's heart soared to see the buggy back in the barn when he returned from branding the new calves. He was eager to see Emily. He didn't like for her to be away from the ranch.

He went into the kitchen, expecting her to be there. "Hey, Jacob. Where's Emily?"

Jacob looked up from the stove where he turned the steaks he had frying. "She got back not looking good and went to lie down. I take care of supper. It should be ready in about thirty minutes."

"I'll go check on Emily." Jeremiah went into the bedroom and found Emily lying on the bed.

"Emily?" Jeremiah knelt by the bed and took her hand. "What wrong, Emily?" Her eyes were big and staring.

"Nothing is wrong. I'm just tired." Her eyes searched his face as if trying to find something there.

Jeremiah took her hands into his. "Your hands are like ice. Are you sick?" The change in her behavior from this morning scared Jeremiah.

"I love you so much, Jeremiah. Will you hold me?" She held out her arms like a child.

He lay down beside her and gathered her into his arms, holding her close. He couldn't figure out what was wrong, but if holding her helped ease her pain then he could do that.

She took a deep breath and it came out a shudder, like a child who had cried deeply for too long. Jeremiah looked at his beloved wife and didn't know what to do.

Jacob rang the bell for supper. Jeremiah stirred and looked at Emily. Her pleading eyes were open wide and unblinking. What could she be pleading for?

"Emily, tell me. Did something happen today?" He stroked her back.

"You go eat. I'm not hungry. You go eat." She pulled away from him.

"I don't understand. Something is wrong, but you won't tell me."

"Please, Jeremiah. Let me be."

He gave in. "I'll go eat and then we're going to talk." He got up from the bed and went into the kitchen.

"How's Emily?" Jacob asked.

Bob was seated at the table. He raised his eyebrows in question.

Jeremiah ran his hands through his hair. "I don't know. She won't talk to me. Don't wait, she said she wasn't hungry." He sat down at the table.

Jacob said a blessing in which he prayed for Emily.

Jeremiah ate, but he didn't taste the food. All he could think about was Emily. What could have happened to upset her so much?

He went back into the bedroom after he ate and found Emily asleep on top of the covers. He gently pulled them back and covered her. He undressed and slipped into bed next to his wife and prayed.

Jeremiah woke the next morning to find Emily's side of the bed empty. He dressed and looked for her. He found her in the yard watching the sunrise.

"Emily?" He asked tentatively as he walked up behind her.

She turned and looked at him her face void of the ready smile she ordinarily had for him.

"Are you all right?"

"I'm all right. I apologize for last night. I wasn't myself." Her voice sounded tight as if it was an effort to speak to him.

"Have I done something wrong, Emily? Is it me?" It had to be something he'd done, though he searched every corner of his mind and found nothing.

Emily shook her head. "Oh, no, Jeremiah. Don't you dare think that. You haven't done anything wrong." She appeared to be holding in a dam of misery, but no tears fell.

"Then what is it?"

"If you love me, Jeremiah, you'll let it alone. Just trust me. You did nothing wrong. I'll be all right in a day or so." She stepped up close to him and put her arms around his waist and her head on his chest. "Let's just watch this Colorado morning sky."

He did love her and as he put his arms around her to pull her tight against him, he decided to do as she asked and let it go.

Emily remained just as caring and loving, but Jeremiah missed her spirit of fun. She didn't laugh and smile as she used to before—and that worried Jeremiah. He didn't know what had caused the change.

He tried every way he knew to let her know of his love. He gave her more attention and tried to be with her every minute he didn't have to work. Gradually, they settled into a new way of being with each other.

~ ~ ~

Emily tried to act as she had before she read her grandma's journal, but every time she looked at Jeremiah, she thought about what that time must have been like for him in the tunnel. She almost hated her grandma for leaving the journal. Emily wished she didn't know.

Her constant guilt ate at her spirit. Guilt consumed her for what her grandmother had done; guilt weighed heavy on her shoulders for the easy life she had led while Jeremiah had been tortured into digging for the gold that paid for that life; and guilt robbed her sense of honesty for not being able to tell her husband what stood between them. She lost weight. She lost sleep. And most of all, she lost her joy of living.

She tried to live her outward life as if the inner turmoil didn't exist. How could she make up to her husband all that she was guilty of? Jeremiah didn't understand, and she could tell he tried to make up for something without knowing what he needed to do. It broke her heart.

She brought the wooden chest to the house and hid it in the bottom of her armoire. She didn't know what to do with it. She wanted to burn it, but something held her back. It was a part of Jeremiah's life and she didn't feel she had the right to destroy it. But it terrified her that he might find it.

~ ~ ~

At the barn, Jeremiah checked on a colt with an eye infection. Flies, attracted to the infection, swarmed around the miserable colt's inflamed eyes. Jeremiah pondered what he could do to protect the eyes until they healed. He thought about the net thing that Emily sometimes wore with her hair gathered in it at the base of her neck. The net, if tied around the colt's head would prevent the flies from irritating its already sensitive eyes.

He went into the house to ask Emily if he could take the netting. Then he remembered that she had gone up the creek to pick blackberries. Jacob and Bob were in town getting supplies and wouldn't be back for hours.

Jeremiah went into the bedroom and looked for the netting. He would get Emily a new one and didn't think she would mind if he used it. He looked first in the bureau, but didn't find it. He then opened the doors of the armoire and rummaged through the boxes and bags underneath the hanging dresses.

His hands touched a wooden box at the back of the armoire and he lifted it out. It was heavier than he expected. It had a key in the little lock. He sat it down on the bed and eased it open.

Flashes tore through his mind. Memories. The tunnel. He jumped back as if bitten by a rattlesnake. His mind recognized the rope and shackles at the same time his body responded to them. The rope tightened on his neck. He fell to his knees, choking. Jeremiah closed his eyes. The rope jerked and he cried out. Shackles once again clamped down on his ankles and wrists. His body froze and his heart no longer beat, and then his breath exploded from his lungs where he had been holding it.

His mind refused to process the contents of the wooden box he had found in the bottom of his wife's armoire.

*How ... ?*

He couldn't even form the question in his mind. He found himself seated on the floor in the corner of the room with his knees drawn up and his arms locked around his legs, just as he had sat day after day in the tunnel. He shook all over. He rocked himself and tried to think.

These items were real. He rocked. Daylight. Sweet daylight poured through the window. His heart beat with hope. Not the tunnel. His bedroom. Jeremiah looked around. Yes, the bedroom of his ranch house. Not the tunnel. That much he knew.

*But how had the things in that box gotten there? It made no sense.*

He didn't know how long he sat there. He finally got up, lifted the box to the floor, and sat down again. He slowly pulled the rope out and knew that his own blood stained it, he lifted the shackles out with the chains, and then the black silk material that he knew was the blindfold. Then, he found the journal.

Jeremiah stared wide eyed at it for the longest time. He forced his shaking hands to reach out and pick it up. Cramps twisted through his stomach. What would it reveal? His breath came in quick gasps as his lungs labored to take in air. He opened the journal and began to read.

It was like being back in the tunnel again except that he saw it from the other side of a veil. As he read, things began to make sense that he had puzzled over for years. Why the old man had never spoken. It was hard to comprehend. His captor had been an old woman — Emily's grandmother. He remembered how he felt the day he met her. The day she died. He'd sensed something about her.

How long had Emily known? *Emily—*

Jeremiah wanted to stop, to throw the journal away, but he couldn't. He had to read it, he couldn't stop. When he read the part about the laudanum so many things began to make sense. Why he'd been so sick and why even now he sometimes longed for the bitter tea.

Then he read the end of it and realized that Emily had not known before they had married. That gave him a little comfort—very little. Why hadn't she told him when she discovered it?

He lost all track of time as he sat in the corner on the floor. A presence brought him out of his nightmarish reverie. He looked up.

Emily stood in the doorway of the bedroom, her face a mask of fear.

Somewhere deep inside of him he wanted to help her. To take that look away, but an invisible force held him to the floor.

"Jeremiah?" Her voice, small and childlike, broke the silence.

"When did you know?" His voice was harsh, brutal.

She jerked her head to the side as if he'd slapped her. She took a couple of steps into the room.

"Tell me, when did you know?" he shouted at her. Jeremiah got to his feet and dropped the journal. He suddenly towered over her.

"After my grandma died, I swear I didn't know before, Jeremiah, I didn't know before."

"Why didn't you tell me?" He was so angry that spit flew from his mouth.

"Please, Jeremiah, you're hurting me." Her eyes stared into his with a look of horror.

He held her arms and was shaking her. He let go of her and stepped back.

With the sudden release of her arms, Emily stumbled back and fell against the doorframe, hitting the side of her face. Blood ran down her cheek, and she pressed her hand against her eye. She looked at Jeremiah with disbelief.

All of the anger drained away, Jeremiah stood in shocked disbelief. He couldn't believe he had hurt her. He never intended to.

She got up from the floor, picked up a towel from the washstand, and pressed it to the side of her face.

In a small voice she said, "Because I was afraid of just this, of your anger. And I can't blame you for your anger. I deserve it for what my grandma did to you. All I can do is ask your forgiveness and for you to believe me when I say I never knew."

Jeremiah looked at her agonized face and wanted to take her into his arms and make it better. Then he saw the things on the floor and he turned away from her without speaking. He didn't know what to do. He didn't know how to survive this.

*Elisha, Elisha and Joe, they would help him.*

He turned back to her. "Can you ride?"

"What?"

"We're going to the Rocking ES if you can ride. We're going to see Elisha and Susana. I can't handle this by myself. They'll help."

She nodded. "Yes, I can ride."

"Make a pack of your things. We leave for the Rocking ES as soon as I can get some horses saddled."

He turned and threw the things back into the box as fast as he could before his mind registered what he was doing. Jeremiah slammed the box closed, then threw some clothes and his shaving kit into a pillow case. Putting on his holster and revolver, he then grabbed his rifle.

Before he left the bedroom he turned to Emily and said, "You be ready to ride in fifteen minutes."

Jeremiah chose two horses that could stand a fast pace and saddled them. He then chose two others and put bridles on them. His mind worked fast on what needed to be done to leave for the Rocking ES. He went back into the house, made up two bedrolls, packed food and a coffee pot, two lanterns and a can of kerosene. In fifteen minutes, he had everything they needed for the trail. He wrote a note to Jacob and Bob simply saying that he and Emily were making a trip to the Rocking ES and he didn't know when they would return. He put what monies he had in the house on the kitchen table so that Bob and Jacob would have money for expenses. At the moment, he didn't know if he would return.

Emily came out of the house carrying a small valise and dressed in her riding outfit. He placed the packs on the back of the saddles. He put the wooden box in a burlap sack and tied it on one of the extra horses. He helped Emily mount and then mounted himself. Leading the two extra horses, he went down the lane toward the road at a fast trot.

They left the ranch at mid-morning and rode all day with no stops except to change horses. As night approached, Jeremiah found a likely camping place and let the weary horses finally rest. It had been many years since Jeremiah had ridden a horse in such a cruel way.

Emily was barely hanging on and he had to help her dismount. He got the camp set up and lit a couple of lanterns. His old fear of the darkness returned full force. He didn't talk to Emily. She tried a couple of times to say something, but the look he gave her put her into silence.

He could hardly bear to look at her. The right side of her face was swollen and bruised with an ugly cut running perpendicular to her eye. His disgust with himself for hurting her warred with the sense of betrayal he felt from finding the box.

Jeremiah tried to sleep and he could tell that Emily, on the other side of the campfire, struggled as well. If he hadn't been so afraid of the dark, they would have kept riding into the night.

At daylight they headed out again. It took all day of riding the horses to exhaustion and changing back and forth, but they reached the Rocking ES just before dark. The horses stumbled as they rode up to the house.

Elisha was the first one out of the house. He started to greet them with a smile, but he took one look at their faces and walked up to lift Emily out of the saddle.

Jeremiah said in a harsh voice. "Elisha, we need help."

## Chapter 21

"I see that. Go on into the front room, Jeremiah." He carried Emily into the house past Susana and the others. He put her down on a couch where she sat like a statue.

Susana followed them in and knelt by Emily, and took her hat and gloves off.

Jeremiah untied the wooden box and carried it into the front room where he placed it on Elisha's desk. He then just stood and stared at Emily, unable to think what to do.

Cookie came into the front room. "What do I need to do to help?"

Susana put a cushion behind Emily's back. "Get me some hot water to help Emily wash up and make us some strong hot coffee."

Cookie returned to the kitchen.

Elisha had gone back out onto the porch and Jeremiah heard him tell someone to take care of the horses and someone else to take care of the children. Jeremiah hated to cause problems, but he had nowhere else to turn.

Elisha came back into the front room and walked over to Jeremiah. "Let me have your hat, and why don't you take a seat, Jeremiah." Elisha guided him over to a chair.

Susana sat on the couch with her arm around Emily. "Elisha, I think Emily needs to go to bed. She's exhausted, hurt, and seems ill."

Emily shook her head. "No, Susana. We need to talk first. I'm all right. It's Jeremiah—" She sniffed back a sob

Cookie carried in a tray of coffee cups, sandwiches, and cake. He sat it down on a side table before handing a cup to Jeremiah and one to Emily. He then slipped out of the room.

Jeremiah sipped on the coffee that Cookie had loaded up with sugar and cream. It wasn't the way he preferred it, but maybe he needed it. Safe at the Rocking ES, he now felt drained.

"Can you tell me what this is about?" Elisha whispered.

Jeremiah didn't know how to start.

Emily did it for him. "Jeremiah found out something horrible yesterday morning. All he could think to do was come to you all. I'm glad he did. We need your help." Emily began to cry.

Jeremiah's heart ached for her, but he couldn't say anything to comfort his wife. He felt too stripped and torn. The long ride had only made it worse.

Susana sat beside Emily with her arm around her holding her close.

Elisha pulled a chair up next to Jeremiah. He sat down and leaned forward. "I'm here, Jeremiah. Whenever you're ready."

"I don't know where to start," he managed to say.

"Give him the journal." Emily pointed at the wooden box.

He heard Emily as if through a wall. He almost recoiled at the idea of Elisha reading the horrible words of his time in the tunnel, but Elisha had to know.

Jeremiah rose and went to the desk. He picked up the box, walked back on leaden feet, and fell into the chair. He handed the box to Elisha. "The journal's in the bottom."

Elisha accepted the box and placed it on his lap.

"While you read it maybe Susana could take Emily and let her lie down. I didn't mean to hurt her." He bowed his head.

Susana helped Emily get up and together they walked toward the bedrooms.

Elisha began to read the journal.

Jeremiah sat with his head bowed and waited.

A couple of times Elisha sighed and said, "Oh, Jeremiah, I'm so sorry," and continued to read. When he finished, he sat the journal down on a table. He looked at Jeremiah calmly. "When did you read this?"

"Yesterday morning. I was looking for something and found the box in the bottom of Emily's armoire. I didn't know what to do. I shouted at Emily and grabbed her to make her tell me why she hadn't told me. She fell back against the door. I hurt her." The anguish in Jeremiah's voice was plain even to him.

"When did she know?"

Jeremiah wrung his hands. "I think she found out about two months ago. She went into town to take care of her grandma's things after she had died." Jeremiah had to stop and try to breathe. He could hardly bare to mention the old woman. "She went into town her normal self and came back changed." He shook his head. "She hasn't been the same since."

"Is what is written in the journal true? Is that the way it happened?" Elisha pointed to the journal

"Yes," Jeremiah whispered, not able to look Elisha in the eyes. It shamed him that it was true.

"I'm so sorry. I'm sorry that you had to go through such horror. I'm sorry that Emily had to find out what her grandmother had done. And I'm sorry that you all are going to have to work through this."

Jeremiah looked up at Elisha. "Can we work through this, Elisha? Is that possible?" He wanted to believe it. He needed to believe it.

"You're both still trying to figure it out right now. It'll take time, but if you both turn to God and let Him help you, you can move past this. The old woman is dead. Don't let the evil she did continue to destroy you."

Jeremiah shuddered and tried to take a deep breath. "That's what Joe told me one time about his mother. He said he had to decide that she was dead and that any damage he still got from her was from within himself. He had to stop carrying his mother around with him, to keep hurting him. Is that what you're saying?"

Elisha nodded. "Yes, you have to let it go and move on with your life with Emily. From what I can see she's innocent even though she'll bear the guilt the rest of her life for what her grandmother did to you." Elisha waited for Jeremiah to say something.

"Why didn't she say something when she found out?"

Elisha shrugged. "Because she feared you would react just as you have. She was afraid of you."

Jeremiah closed his eyes. She had been right to be afraid. He felt even more ashamed. "What can I do?"

"You've done the best thing for Emily and yourself by coming here. You don't need to deal with this by yourselves. It's too big and hurtful. We're going to face it together." Elisha leaned forward. "I'm going to ask your permission to let Joe read the journal and Susana. I don't really want Susana exposed to it, but she can deal with it." Elisha rubbed his face with his hand as if to wipe out the images from the journal. "They can't really help you or Emily unless they truly understand what you're dealing with. If you had just tried to tell me, without me reading the journal, I don't know that I would have understood. It's just too awful to believe."

Jeremiah sighed. "I'd like for you to share it with Joe. He might be able to tell me how to deal with the craziness. If you think it'll help Emily then share it with Susana and Sara, but it is so ugly and I'm ashamed."

"Ashamed? What do you have to be ashamed of?"

"I'm ashamed of what happened to me in the tunnel and now to know that it was a woman and I couldn't help myself." Jeremiah clenched his fists and hit the side of the chair.

"I can understand that, but from what I read she was one crafty old woman. She gave you no way to beat her. I don't know of anyone who could have escaped from her. You have nothing to be ashamed of. She was too evil for you or anyone else."

Jeremiah knew that Elisha was right, but the knowing and how he felt didn't match. "You are probably right, but I can't shake the feeling that I should have been able to do something to help myself."

"I think what will help is for us to talk about it. To talk about it a lot, it will be difficult and will wear you out, but you came to us for help and that's what we are going to do." Elisha had put his hand on Jeremiah's shoulder and gripped it tight as if to give strength to him.

"We had to come. I didn't know where else to go. I love Emily and I don't want to lose her, but when I read the journal I couldn't separate her from her grandmother in my mind." Jeremiah looked at Elisha with pleading in his eyes. "It made me crazy. I thought I was back in the tunnel again."

"And I can't think of anything more horrible for you. But, I'll say this to you now and many times over the next few days, Emily is not her grandmother. You hear me, Emily is *not* her grandmother."

Jeremiah nodded. He knew. In his head he knew, but in his gut, old feelings still crawled around.

"I can't believe I hurt her. I would rather have hurt myself. I was just so angry." He buried his face in his hands. He wanted to rid himself of the horrible sick feeling that rose up in his throat every time he thought of Emily's face. He had done that to her.

"I know. You didn't mean to do it, but you did and now you live with it. Her forgiveness will be easier than you forgiving yourself." Elisha's gentle voice held concern without condemnation. "You're exhausted and need to eat something and I'm sure Emily does too. Let's get you two settled and have a night of rest. In the morning we'll talk more." Elisha put his hand out to Jeremiah. "I'm so thankful that you trusted us enough to come. We're honored to be asked to help. Thank you, Jeremiah."

Jeremiah took the hand that Elisha offered and the two men shook hands. "You're amazing, Elisha. Here we have just showed up and given you all our burdens and you thank me." Jeremiah remembered when he had first arrived at the Rocking ES and how he'd wondered what kind of people they were. He still tried to understand fully.

"You know why we are able to be here for you?" Elisha looked at him expectantly.

"Yeah, I guess I do now. It's because you accept the all sufficiency of Christ."

"That is exactly right, but it's so much more of an answer than what most people could have given me. You've grown so much since you first rode up almost seven years ago."

"Well, it's about time I grew up."

"How about we go check on Emily and get you all settled for the night." Elisha got up and carried the tray with the uneaten food down the hallway toward the room where Jeremiah stayed before. He tapped on the closed door.

Susana opened the door and motioned them inside. She took the tray from Elisha and set it on a table by the bed where Emily lay.

Jeremiah's heart caught in his throat at the sight of Emily lying so small and fragile in the big bed. She had on a lady's wrapper and her hair splayed loosely over the pillow. Before he could stop himself, he went over to her and knelt by the bed.

She touched his face with her fingertips, just a feather of a touch, but it was all he needed to know she had forgiven him.

He heard Elisha and Susana depart from the room, leaving the door slightly ajar. He knew they did it for him.

He took Emily's small, soft hand and kissed her palm. "Can you ever forgive me for hurting you and frightening you?"

"Can you forgive me for not telling you?" She asked in that little girl voice he now knew meant she was frightened.

He didn't want his wife frightened of him. That hurt as much as anything. That she should be afraid of him who loved her with all his heart.

"You've nothing to be forgiven for. You were right to be afraid of how I would react. Look at what I did." Jeremiah wanted to go back in time. But he couldn't, so he would just have to make it up to her.

Emily took his hand. "What are we going to do?"

"We're going to stay here as long as it takes for us to get over this. I don't want to lose you, Emily. I can't lose you, but I don't know how to face this." Jeremiah gently stroked her hand. "Elisha, just in the little bit we talked, has already helped me understand better. I want us to stay here and talk with Elisha, Joe, Susana, and Sara. They can help us." He pleaded with her to understand.

"It's all right. You know them much more than I do, but I trust them. We do need help with this. It's been eating me up inside. I couldn't have stood it much longer."

"For this evening let's eat a bite, get some sleep, and then tomorrow we face it."

"All right, I think I could eat a little now." Emily sat up in the bed. "Bring the tray over and climb into bed with me."

"Are you sure you want me here? You're not afraid of me?" He had to ask. "If you want I can stay out on the porch were I stayed when I first came here."

She stroked his cheek. "I want you here with me. You did scare me and I might be scared again, but I need you here with me now."

Jeremiah's knees almost buckled with the relief that she still wanted him in her bed. He got the tray and put it on the bed. He went around to the other side, undressed, and climbed in with her. They each ate a little of the sandwiches and cake. He then set the tray on the floor.

"Emily, may I leave the lamp on?" He had been able to sleep with the lamp off for months, but this night, just as he had the night before, he couldn't face the darkness.

"You leave the lamp on if you need to. I don't know if I should say this—"

"You can say anything to me." He brushed a curl of hair back from the cut by her eye.

"Until I read the journal I hadn't understood why you were afraid of the dark and needed the lantern on all those years. But, now I understand better. Just reading about it made me want to throw up. It amazes me that you can ever sleep in the dark. The courage you have to go on after all of that—it makes me so ashamed."

"No, Emily—I don't want you to feel that way. It wasn't your fault. It wasn't you." Jeremiah realized he was saying just what Elisha had said and he believed it.

Emily yawned. "I'm so unbelievably tired." She removed the wrapper she wore, displaying a shift nightgown underneath. She did it without thinking, but it revealed the terrible bruises on her forearms where Jeremiah had grabbed her.

Jeremiah was shocked and grieved at what he had done. He touched her bruised arm and started to say how sorry he was, but Emily touched his lips with her fingers before he could speak.

"Shhh, we're not going to talk about it. I know you didn't mean to hurt me. You had just been hurt yourself." She snuggled up to him. "Just hold me for a while."

Jeremiah took her into his strong arms, but with gentleness, his strength under control. As he buried his face in her hair and smelled the faint flower scent of her shampoo, he wanted to hold her forever. He pulled her closer to him and let her fall asleep in safety.

## Chapter 22

Elisha and Susana left Jeremiah and Emily alone and went back to the front room.

Susana stood in the circle of his arms and laid her head on his chest. "Oh Elisha, what is going on? Emily looks like she's been beaten and there are some terrible bruises on her arms that I suspect Jeremiah did."

Elisha held her close and smoothed her hair. "I want you to read something. It's ugly but without reading it I don't think you can understand what Jeremiah and Emily are going through. I need to go get Joe and Sara and I don't want you to read it until I get back."

Susana looked at him with trust. Elisha knew she wouldn't go against his request. "All right, I'll go up and check on the children and meet you all back here."

Elisha arrived at Joe and Sara's and knocked on the front door. The light was on in the front room so he hoped they hadn't gone to bed.

Joe opened the door. "What's the problem?"

"Can you and Sara come over for a while? We need to talk and I need to stay at the house."

"Sure, let me get Sara." Joe went inside, and a few moments later, he and Sara came out. They walked back to the main ranch house with Elisha.

"Something really difficult has happened to Jeremiah and Emily and they need our help. But to help you understand, there's something I want you to read. It's pretty bad."

"All right Elisha." Joe matched Elisha's stride, limping slightly.

When they got back to the front room, Susana sat waiting for them.

Elisha picked up the old woman's journal from the table. "Since it is a nice warm evening let's take a couple of lamps and go out on the porch. We can have more privacy yet be available if we're needed."

They placed a couple of lamps around for light and sat in the rockers that lined the porch.

"As I've thought about it, I want to suggest that I read this aloud to you all at once. But, only if you want to hear it." Elisha looked at each one in turn.

They each nodded their willingness. Joe and Sara held hands.

"Before I begin to read I want to have a prayer.

"Our Almighty Father, who knows our every need and provides it for us. We ask that you bless Jeremiah and Emily. They are hurt and broken. Give us wisdom to help them. We all are in need of your healing and all come to you broken. But you are our healer through the name of the Son, Jesus the Christ. Amen."

Elisha picked up Maude Johnson's journal.

It took him an hour to read it aloud. Some parts he had difficulty getting through as his own tears burned his throat. It was bad enough if he had not known the person that it happened to, but Elisha was sure they all remembered how Jeremiah had come to them almost seven years earlier a broken, wounded boy trying to be a man.

Susana and Sara cried without trying to hide it.

Joe wiped his eyes on his sleeves. "We knew when he first came that he had been through something awful. But I never imagined it was so bad." Joe rubbed his eyes as if to wipe out memories. "In some ways, I think that for him to read about it from the person who did it to him makes it worse. Almost like it's happening all over again. I know that's how I'd feel if I found a diary that my mother had written, trying to make it sound as if she had a right to do it."

Susana pulled her chair closer to Elisha who reached out and held her hand. "It explains so much of why he does what he does. Just hearing about it makes me want to keep the lamp on tonight."

Elisha leaned forward. "Emily found out after her grandmother died, about two months ago and has been carrying it as a burden.

Jeremiah found out yesterday morning that it was Emily's grandmother who did all that to him. He hasn't had time to really think it through."

"What can we do to help them?" Sara asked.

"Yes, that is the main question." Susana agreed.

Elisha bowed his head, then he looked at each of them. "Here's what I suggest. They need to stay here a few days or even weeks. We need to let them talk about it. Let them get it all out and then talk to them about how to go on with their marriage. This lady was Emily's beloved grandmother and yet, Emily now has the burden that all of her good life was paid for by Jeremiah's torture." Elisha shifted in his chair. "But, Jeremiah doesn't want a wife who only stays with him and does for him because she feels guilty. There are a lot of problems they have to work through to be able to move forward." Elisha waited for their response.

"Then we need to take the next week or two and help them. How do we do that?" Susana wiped her eyes with the handkerchief Elisha handed to her.

"I can get Jeremiah to work the horses with me some. Not much because he needs to be with Emily and to talk to you, Elisha," Joe nodded.

"We just need to be with them and let them talk," Sara wrapped her arm through Joe's.

"And we pray," Susana leaned forward with her palms together.

"And we pray," Elisha agreed.

## Chapter 23

Jeremiah woke not sure where he was. He looked over at his wife asleep beside him. The bruised and swollen right eye and the memory of the last two days flooded back. It comforted him to wake up in his room at the Rocking ES. Daylight peeked through the curtains and he slipped out of bed, dressed, and went to the kitchen where he found Joe and Cookie preparing breakfast.

Cookie kneaded the biscuit dough. "Hey, Jeremiah, you ready for coffee?"

Jeremiah stood by the table. "Sure am."

"Sit down and let me pour it for you." Joe got a cup and poured the coffee. He set it down in front of Jeremiah. "I'm glad to see you."

"Wish it was just a visit." Jeremiah sipped some of the hot coffee.

"You did right to come." Joe went back to the stove to stir the gravy.

"I didn't have any other place to go."

Joe turned toward him, but kept stirring the gravy. "The Lord brought Cookie and me here when we didn't have any other place to go. We know how it feels."

"We just didn't go away." Cookie chuckled.

"Later, I'm going up on the south ridge to look for horses. Want to ride up with me?" Joe poured the gravy into a bowl.

"I'd like that, but let me check with Emily first."

Cookie put the pan of biscuits in the oven. "How are Jacob and Bob doing?"

"They are both doing well. Working hard as they always do." Jeremiah got up and poured another cup of coffee.

Cookie wiped his hands on his apron. "And that Mrs. Spencer and also, Mildred?"

"For all I know they're fine. You should ask Emily about them. Well, thanks for the coffee. I need to check on Emily."

Cookie began to set the dishes on the table. "Breakfast will be ready in about fifteen minutes. If she doesn't feel like getting up I'll be glad to fix her some breakfast later."

"Thanks, Cookie." Jeremiah went back to the bedroom and quietly entered.

Emily lay awake on her side facing the door.

Jeremiah went over to the bed and sat on the edge. He bent down and kissed her. "How are you this morning?"

"I'm tired and my stomach hurts. I don't want to get up and face the day." Emily closed her eyes and sighed deeply.

"Then you don't. Cookie said to tell you he would prepare breakfast whenever you wanted. I've never known Cookie to fix breakfast special for someone." Jeremiah rubbed her back and shoulders.

"Mmmm . . . that feels good," Emily murmured.

"Joe asked me to ride out with him. Would you mind? If you want me here I won't go."

Emily peeked at him through long lashes. "Would you be gone all day?" She closed her eyes again.

"No, just a couple of hours. We'd be back by dinner." He continued to rub her back. It pained him to see the bruises blacker than the night before on her face and arms.

She opened her eyes and studied him. "How are you doing?"

"I'm tired. We had a couple of hard days."

"I'm sorry." Tears clouded her eyes and threatened to spill over.

"No, I'm sorry. It didn't have to be as hard a trip up here. I just felt I had to get here or ... ."

Her tears receded for the moment. "Or what Jeremiah?"

"I've never told you. Since the tunnel, I've feared I was crazy. A lot of strange things and feelings kept happening that made no sense. I tried to be normal, but sometimes—" He looked away.

"And you saw all that stuff in the box and you thought you were going crazy."

"Yes. For a minute, I thought I was back in the tunnel. It can seem so real when it happens."

"It has happened before?" Emily sat up and looked at him intently.

"It used to happen all the time the first couple of years after I got here. Yesterday was the first time it has happened since—" Since he met the old lady.

"What Jeremiah?"

Jeremiah looked away. "The last time before yesterday was when I went into your grandmother's room. I'm not trying to upset you, but it's true."

"No, I need to hear you talk about it. You never told me about any problem when you met her. What was it?"

He looked back at her. "I don't know. I just had a bad feeling and I had to get out there." He rubbed his aching head.

Jeremiah jumped when someone tapped on the door. He turned to see Susana holding a large tray.

"I've brought breakfast and I insist that you both eat something." Susana handed the tray to Jeremiah.

Emily leaned against the headboard. "Thank you, Susana. I'll try, but my stomach is cramping."

"Well, try to eat and we'll see how you feel after."

Jeremiah sat the tray in the middle of the bed so Emily could reach it. "Thank you, Susana. Will you tell Joe that if he can wait a little while I'd like to ride out with him."

"I'll tell him, and Emily, we're heating water for you a hot bath. We're going to pamper you this morning." Susana went over and kissed Emily on the forehead. "I'm so glad you're here. Let me know when you're ready for your bath." Susana kissed Jeremiah on the cheek and then went out of the room.

They both sat on the bed. Emily picked at her food while Jeremiah ate all of his. He drank a couple of cups of coffee and it helped ease his aching head.

"I better go and meet Joe or he'll leave without me. I'll be back by noon." He kissed Emily and went to find Joe.

~

Jeremiah and Joe rode up the trail on the south side of the valley until they came to the overlook. They dismounted and sat on the large rocks looking out over the valley and the mountains beyond.

"Tell me how you survived that time in the tunnel."

Though a little surprised at Joe's bluntness, it relieved Jeremiah that he didn't have to start the conversation. Joe had always been straight with him.

Jeremiah took a deep breath. "You read the journal."

"Yes, I read the journal and most men wouldn't have survived such isolation. How did you find the courage to do it?"

Jeremiah looked out over the horizon. "I was a kid. I'd just spent a year in the city jail crowded up with a lot of others. Never alone and then I woke up in the tunnel. The old man, I mean woman, I don't know what to call him—"

"Just talk about it as the old man. That's what it was for you at the time," Joe suggested.

"All right, the old man not talking to me was so hard to take. I couldn't understand why he wouldn't talk to me. So I decided that he couldn't talk. That he didn't have a tongue. Then I could deal with him not talking. I just talked to myself."

Jeremiah rubbed his forehead with the back of his hand. "I sort of shut down and tried to take it one day at a time. I wouldn't let myself think about what was going on outside the tunnel. I was so scared that it would go on and on. I lost hope. Then toward the end I wanted to die . . . . It was bad."

"I'd have been scared. Especially when the old man went away and you ran out of water."

"Yeah, that was a real scary time. I was so sick. You know, it's kind of funny, but being so sick pushed aside being so scared."

"And then you were free?" Joe asked.

"I was out of the tunnel, but something happened to my mind and I was still a prisoner in a way. You remember how I first tried to work with the horses and lost focus?"

Joe nodded. "Sure, I remember. You would be standing and maybe for fifteen minutes you stared off into the distance. I could tell you were somewhere else, but I had no idea."

"It was like waking dreams. I would be back in the tunnel and when I came to or whatever it was, it would seem so real. I questioned at times which was the real world, the tunnel, or here on the ranch."

"You never said anything."

Jeremiah shrugged his shoulders. "I was strange enough to you all. I didn't want to admit to being totally crazy."

Joe shook his head. "That's what you thought was going on? That you were crazy?"

"Yes, wouldn't you think that?" Jeremiah asked.

"Yes, I probably would have. When did the waking dreams stop?"

"I haven't had one for several years until I walked into the room where Emily's grandmother was. The day she died. I walked into that dark bedroom with all the room dark except the one lamp where she wanted me to stand. I had the worst feeling, and I was back in the tunnel." He rubbed his hand over his face. "It didn't last very long. And then it happened two days ago when I found the box and saw the things in it."

"Are you all right talking about it? Does that bring up the feelings?"

Jeremiah paused and took a deep breath. "I'm surprised, but talking about it is a relief."

They sat and looked out over the valley for a few minutes. Jeremiah sighed. "Joe, what do I do about Emily?"

"What do you mean?"

"I hurt her. I shook her and caused her to fall and cut her face. What kind of man does that to his wife?" Jeremiah swallowed the bile that rose in his throat.

"You didn't mean to hurt her. She knows that, but still something like that can scare a woman. You're so much bigger than she is and so much stronger. That's why it's so important for a man to be gentle, to keep his strength under control."

Jeremiah nodded. He understood now in a way he hadn't before. "Will she want to stay with me?"

"A bigger question might be can you live with her without blaming her for what her grandmother did?" Joe leaned forward and waited for Jeremiah's answer.

"I think I can. She didn't know. I want to think that if she had known she would have stopped it. She's such a kind person."

"You're right, she would have stopped it."

"I love her, Joe. I don't want to lose her and I'll do what I can to keep her."

"Love her for herself and live beyond what happened in the past."

"Move forward?"

"Yes, move forward and leave the tunnel behind completely. That's what both of you need to do."

"I can try, but what about my dreams? They won't leave it behind."

Joe rubbed his face. "Yeah, I know. That's my problem. When I'm awake I do fine, but my dreams betray me."

"What do you do about it?"

"I make sure I know the difference. A dream is just a dream, but I'm in control of what I decide to do when I'm awake."

"I can understand that. You're saying that's what I have to do?"

"A little at a time, you can't deal with this all at once. Give yourself and give Emily time."

"I'll try. I want to move forward with Emily. I can't not do it."

Joe gripped Jeremiah's shoulder. "Well, what do you say we head back? It's almost dinnertime." Joe stood up and mounted his horse.

Jeremiah watched him mount the horse and remembered what Joe had gone through to be able to ride. Maybe this was his learning to ride again.

~ ~ ~

Emily's face and head hurt, but she did feel better after a hot bath.

"Let me brush your hair for you." Susana motioned toward a chair and picked up a brush from the bedside table.

Emily tied the lady's wrapper around her waist and sat in the chair. She closed her eyes as Susana brushed her long hair. She really didn't care that she hadn't gotten dressed yet. She just didn't feel well.

A sharp pain in her abdomen caused her to double over.

Susana dropped the brush and knelt in front of Emily. "Emily, what's the matter?"

Emily gasped. "I don't know. A bad pain. I think I better lie down." Emily made it over to the bed with Susana's help.

"Lay here a minute. I'll get Jeff's wife. She's a nurse."

Susana returned shortly with Anna.

"Oh Susana, I'm bleeding." Emily tried to control the urge to cry.

Anna took over and spent several minutes checking Emily. She finally sat back and smiled at her. "Emily, are you aware that you're expecting a child?"

"A child?" Emily looked from Susana to Anna. "Truly?"

"I think so and we have to be careful now. You may not be able to carry it, which wouldn't surprise me after what you've been through. I want you in the bed. No getting up, no worry, just be quiet and let your body recover if it can."

"A baby! Oh, I pray so. But, you think I may lose it?" Jeremiah's baby! What she had been praying for. But what if she lost the baby? That hurt worse than learning the truth about her grandmother.

Anna pulled the covers up to Emily's shoulders, then patted her on the arm. "You just stay in bed and take care of yourself. Go to sleep if you can. But, if the pain comes back you must let me know," she said. "We'll pray that everything will be all right."

"Thank you, Anna." Emily closed her eyes and let herself relax.

Emily woke to see Jeremiah seated by the bed watching her. She smiled at him. "Hello, my love."

He leaned over and kissed her softly. "How are you, sweetheart?"

Emily paused to think. She wasn't in pain. Her heart soared with hope that maybe the life inside her continued to grow. Then she realized that Jeremiah didn't know about the baby—unless Susana had told him.

"Have you talked to Susana?" Emily took his left hand and rubbed the wedding ring on his finger.

Jeremiah shook his head. "I came directly to the bedroom when Joe and I got back." He straightened and furrowed his eyebrows with concern. "Should I have talked to her?"

## COLORADO MORNING SKY

Now she had to tell him or he'd worry. "No, but I have something to tell you."

Fear darkened his face and she realized what he thought.

He took a deep ragged breath. "What do you want to tell me?"

Emily stroked his arm to reassure him. "I just found out something this morning that you need to know. I hope you'll be as pleased as I am." She wasn't sure how to tell him. What if he didn't want a baby yet?

Jeremiah closed his eyes. "Just tell me." He held his breath.

"Anna told me this morning that she suspects we're having a baby." Emily couldn't stop the grin that spread across her face.

Jeremiah released his breath and his eyes sprang open. "A baby?"

Emily nodded as tears filled her eyes. "A baby. You're going to be a papa."

Jeremiah cradled her hand between his and held it to his lips. "How do you know?"

"I've got all the signs and this morning I was bleeding. Hopefully, the baby will be all right, but I need to stay in bed for now."

"Did I cause the problem?" His face twisted with pain and fear.

"No, of course not." She didn't really know if the fall or the hard ride had caused the bleeding, but she didn't want Jeremiah to take responsibility.

"How can you know for sure?"

"I just know. Don't you want us to have a baby, Jeremiah?"

His eyes lit up. "Yes, I want us to have a baby. But only if you're all right."

She held out her arms to him. He gently embraced her as if she was fine porcelain.

She put her hand behind his head and pulled his head down so she could kiss him. "I love you, Jeremiah. Thank you for giving me your baby."

"I love you, Emily." Jeremiah gathered her up in his arms. "Don't leave me."

Emily pulled back. "Why would I leave you? We're going to have a baby together."

"But I made you afraid of me."

"Yes, but only for a while. We'll be all right. I promise." She wanted to take his pain away. "Please be happy about the baby."

"I am happy about the baby. It's just such a surprise."

"For me also, I knew we would eventually have one, but not this soon." She thought of Jeremiah with a baby and she smiled. "Have you ever held a baby?"

Jeremiah smiled at her. "I've never even seen one up close, not a newborn." His smiled faded. "I don't know if I'll be a very good father. I didn't have a good example growing up and I'm not sure what you do to be one."

"I've never been around babies either. I think we better look for someone to help us." Emily wished that the Rocking ES was closer. She trusted Susana and Anna.

Jeremiah snapped his fingers. "Maybe Mrs. Spencer and Mildred could help us."

Emily thought of Mrs. Spencer and Mildred and agreed. "Yes, we'll ask them."

Jeremiah lay down beside her and cradled her in his arms.

"I talked a lot with Joe this morning," Jeremiah told her as he smoothed her hair back from her brow.

Emily didn't know how to respond. "Was it helpful?"

"I think so. I was able to tell him some things that I've never talked about before. He gave me hope that we can move forward from all this. But he said we had to give it time."

"We are going to more forward from all this. That's what I want with all my heart. But Jeremiah—" Emily snuggled closer to her husband.

"What?" Jeremiah held her closer.

"I'm not sure how to do it or how to help you."

"We just got to hope. Elisha, Joe, Susana, and the others here can help us. The hardest part for me right now is to figure out how to let God help us."

"Why is that the hardest part?" Emily felt that was the easiest for her.

"I have to figure out why he let it happen to me in the first place. Why he didn't protect me if he is so all loving? If I can figure that out maybe I can figure out how to move forward."

"I can understand your question, but I don't have an answer. It sounds like a question for Elisha." Emily looked at her tall, muscular, husband. She wished she had the answer for him. She wondered if the pain of knowing what her grandmother had done to him would ever go away—for both of them.

"Yeah, that's a question for Elisha."

## Chapter 24

Emily found Sara wise about how to help Jeremiah with what Sara called his "demons." Emily learned that Joe still had frequent nightmares about his childhood. It had been several years since Joe found out that his tormentor was dead, but he still hadn't gone back home to the house where it happened. Sara said that when Joe got quiet and didn't want to talk, she let him alone, and in his own timing, he came to her. Emily vowed in her heart to learn the lessons from Sara and help Jeremiah.

Emily and Jeremiah spent the next two weeks at the Rocking ES. They talked to each other and they talked to Elisha, Susana, Joe, and Sara, who remained available to listen and pray with them any time of the day or night. Nothing was expected of Jeremiah or Emily and if they wanted to talk it was all right, and if they wanted to be quiet that was okay too.

~ ~ ~

After two weeks, Jeremiah wanted to go home, but he didn't know how to gauge if they were ready. He had almost gotten used to the idea that his tormenter had been a woman—Emily's grandmother. In some ways, he wanted to move forward without dealing with the past—just brush it all under a rug and pretend none of it had ever happened. But he knew that wasn't best. In some ways, he'd already done that for seven years.

He asked Elisha if he could go with him to check on the cattle. They rode out toward the second valley. As they rode, Jeremiah wondered how to start what he wanted to ask him.

"You got something on your mind. Just spit it out." Elisha rode easy in the saddle.

Jeremiah glanced at his friend. "How do you think Emily and I are doing? How will we know we're all right to go back home?" Jeremiah twisted in the saddle slightly so he could watch Elisha's face.

"An easy response would be to say that only you and Emily can answer that question. But that's not what you need."

"No, I want to know what you think."

"All right, I'll tell you. We've talked about what happened to you in the past and to both you and Emily two weeks ago. You're able to talk about it with Emily, which is good. She has talked a lot to Susana and Sara which is also good." Elisha stopped his horse and turned in the saddle toward Jeremiah. "Now, you need to look, not at the past, but at the future. What do you have to do to make the future work for the two of you?"

Jeremiah had also reined up his horse. "The future is what I am most concerned about. I want it to be the two of us. I'm just not sure how to do it." They had to be able to move on together. He couldn't bear to think of any other future.

"Can you look at Emily and not see her grandmother?"

Jeremiah saw Emily as she had looked walking down the aisle at their wedding, her mischievous grin when she teased him, and how she radiated such joy when she told him about the baby. He knew the right answer Elisha was searching for, but Jeremiah wanted to be honest. "I think I can mostly. I won't lie to you and say I don't sometimes look at her and thoughts come up. It's less and less every day."

Elisha pointed at him. "Can you be Jeremiah Rebourn, husband, father, rancher, and most of all Christian? Someone who just happened to have something bad happen a long time ago, but who doesn't let it tell him who he is today?"

Jeremiah nodded. "Again, I know what I should be able to answer. I can't say it's never a problem."

Elisha stroked his chin. "I know it's all been brought up in the last two weeks, but can you let it go? Can you go days and weeks without thinking about it except as something that happened a long time ago?"

Jeremiah leaned forward in the saddle. "You mean, let it slide into the past and stay there?"

"That's a good way to put it. What about going back to your ranch and being so close to the house where the old lady lived? Will that be a problem?"

"I don't think so. The good thing is that Emily's grandmother never came to the ranch. All my memories of the ranch are good ones. But I want Emily to get rid of the house. Is that wrong of me?"

"No, that's normal. Do you think she'll have a problem doing that?"

"No, she'd already planned on it."

Elisha settled his hat. "You got another problem on your mind?"

Jeremiah took a deep breath and looked up at the sky. He watched the rolling clouds against blue for a moment before he answered. "What do I do with the box?" He returned his gaze to Elisha. "What do I do with the journal and other stuff in the box?"

"What do you want to do with it?"

"I want to burn it or bury it. I don't want those things around. But is that just wanting to pretend it didn't happen?"

"I can only tell you what I would do. I'd find a place and either burn or bury that box and never look at it again." Elisha shook his head. "I don't see any good in keeping it. I'd not want it around for my children to see. I wouldn't want it around, not because I was ashamed, but because it symbolizes evil and I wouldn't want it in my home."

Jeremiah rubbed the back of his neck. "What if Emily wants to keep it?"

"I don't see it as something she should decide. I know her grandmother left the box to her, but it is about your life. My gut feeling is she wants it gone too."

"How do we thank you for what you've done for us these past two weeks?"

Elisha smiled. "That's easy. You go forth and live a life worthy of the calling. You raise this child that is coming in the sight of the

Lord." Elisha shrugged. "You know, easy stuff like that." He chuckled and patted Jeremiah on the back.

Jeremiah found himself smiling back. "Yeah, real easy."

Elisha flicked the reins and settled his horse into a walk.

~

The next day Jeremiah borrowed Joe's little cart and drove Emily up to the look out over the valley. He didn't want her to ride a horse in case it might hurt the baby.

He helped her out of the cart and they sat on one of the larger rocks and looked out over the valley spread below them and the tall mountains beyond. It reminded him of the good times they had up on the ridge back at their place, looking out over the ranch.

Jeremiah sat behind her and encircled her with his arms. She leaned back against his chest and rested her head on his shoulder. He made sure he held her firmly yet gently. He never intended to be rough with her again.

"I wanted to bring you up here to see this. You know this is where Joe asked Sara to marry him."

She twisted around and looked at him. "Is it really?" She straightened up and leaned against him once again. "What a lovely romantic spot to choose for such a wonderful event. They won't ever forget it."

"I wanted to ask you something and thought this was a good place to talk about beginning again."

"Yes, you thought right." She settled more securely against his chest.

"What do you think about us beginning again?"

"How do you mean?"

She wasn't going to make it easy for him so he might as well spell it out.

"Emily, I want to take you home and for us to begin our lives anew. I want to put the past behind us. I know neither of us can forget it. But, can we move forward?"

"Can you forgive me for what my family did to you?"

He knew what she was really asking. "I have nothing to forgive you for because you did nothing to me. But, you want to know can I forgive your grandmother for what she did?"

"Yes, I guess that's what I'm asking."

He sighed. "I wish I could say yes. I'm trying, but I don't think I have yet."

Emily looked up at him. "That's all I ask, both of you and of me. I'm not sure I've forgiven her and I'm trying."

"Maybe we can try together."

"I would like that."

"I want to go home and I want to go home with you. I worry that you won't feel safe with me."

"Am I safe with you?" She placed her arms and hands over his and caressed the scars as they encircled her waist.

"Yes." He said it simply, but with a promise in his voice.

"You've never lied to me. I believe you."

Jeremiah kissed her neck. "What do we do next?"

Emily twisted around and kissed his lips. "Take me home and let's have our baby."

"That's what we'll do then. I'll borrow or buy a buggy from Elisha. I'll not have you ride all that way."

"Thank you Jeremiah."

Jeremiah stroked her hair. "I do have one more thing I want to ask you. What should we do with the box from your grandmother?"

"I have to give this one to you. You decide. I never want to see it again in my life."

"What if I ask Elisha to get rid of it for us?"

A J HAWKE

"I think that's a good idea."

~

Elisha offered to loan them his small buggy and he would pick it up when they brought the horses down in the fall. He also agreed to dispose of the box.

Gratitude to God for providing him with his family at the Rocking ES lifted Jeremiah's spirits. He truly understood the imagery of soaring on the wings of eagles.

As eager as he was to get on the road to home, there was a definite tug on his heart when he thought of the Rocking ES. His strength was renewed and he was ready to do battle to put his marriage back together. As he looked at Emily seated next to him in the buggy as they made their way home, he vowed to himself that he would be the man of God she deserved and that he wanted to be with all his heart.

They took three days to travel in the buggy with early stops in the evening to camp. He determined that Emily would arrive home as rested as possible.

~

Bob and Jacob, while pleased to have them back, refrained from asking questions. They took excellent care of the ranch in their absence.

Jeremiah fell back into his rhythm of ranch work, but with a difference. He divided his attention more evenly. He went to the house several times a day to check on Emily.

One day, Jeremiah worked on the dam of one of the creeks and got his clothes wet. He came back to the house to change.

"Jeremiah, you're all wet," Emily said as soon as he walked into the kitchen.

He laughed. "Thanks for noticing. I had to repair the dam on the north creek." He went to the bedroom and found dry clothes to put on.

When he came back into the kitchen, Emily had set two places at the table for dinner. "Where's Jacob and Bob?"

Emily stood at the stove, stirring the gravy. "Jacob took a sandwich to the shop with him. He said he wouldn't be back until late afternoon. Bob told me he needed to go to the blacksmiths in town. So there's just you and me for lunch." She looked over her shoulder at him.

"That's fine by me." Jeremiah walked over and took her into his arms. He kissed her long and hard.

"What was that for?" she asked with her arms around his shoulders.

"For being here with me." He gave her another kiss. "I am a blessed man to be able to kiss the most beautiful woman in the world in the middle of the day."

"Oh, go sit down." She laughed and pushed him toward the table.

He reluctantly let her go.

"Ohhh!" She placed her hand over her stomach.

"What's wrong?" Had he been too rough in his embrace?

"Here, give me your hand." She guided his hand to the side of her stomach. "Do you feel that? That's our baby moving."

Movement fluttered under his hand. "I feel it!" He smiled down at her.

"Susana told me to expect it about the fourth month and that it would get harder and more often. She said by the time he was born there would be times we will think he is doing a dance."

"So we're at the fourth month?"

Emily slowly nodded. "I think so which means we have five more to go. We may have a Christmas baby. I better get to sewing."

"You know Jacob is making a cradle and a crib." He didn't know what else they needed for the baby.

"That's wonderful. Knowing Jacob it will be the most beautiful cradle ever made." Emily smiled one of her radiant smiles.

Jeremiah couldn't help but respond with a smile of his own. They seemed to be back to their old selves and that relieved him.

They sat down at the table and Jeremiah prayed a blessing for the food and the miracle of the coming birth.

Emily cleared her throat. "I want to ask you something but I don't want to upset you."

Jeremiah put his fork down. "You won't upset me. Just ask."

"I've thought a lot about what to do with my grandmother's house and furnishings. I don't want to profit from it and we seem to have enough money." She paused.

"Yes, we have all the money we need." He poured milk into Emily's glass. "If we live simply and make some money from the horses and cattle, we have enough to last for many years. That's what I have. I'm not counting what you have."

"What I thought about is to give the house and furnishings to the preacher and his wife. James and Charlotte don't have much and the congregation can't pay them a lot. That little house they live in is terrible." Emily took a drink from her glass of milk. "What do you think?"

"Do you want to give it to the preacher or to the congregation?"

"I want to give it to the preacher and his family."

Jeremiah thought about what it would mean to have someone he knew living in the house. It was really just a house and Emily was right, the preacher and his family didn't have much.

"That would mean that when they invited us over we would have to go to that house."

Emily looked blank for a moment, and then a look of realization crossed her face. "Would that be a problem for you?"

Jeremiah cut into his steak. "It might be at first, but I would make an effort for it not to be a problem." He ate the bite of meat.

"I didn't think about that. I don't think it will be a problem for me because they would have their own things. It would be different." Emily took another biscuit and broke it open. She smothered it with the steak gravy.

"That's right, it would be different." He tried to image how it would look with other people's belongings in the house but he really couldn't.

Jeremiah also grabbed another biscuit. "If that's what you want to do then it's fine with me." He hoped it would be all right.

"The other thing is I would like to ask Homer to keep up the place and take care of the yard and barn. I would pay him out of my money." Emily dabbed at the corners of her mouth with her napkin.

Jeremiah watched her dainty movements. "That's a good idea. If the preacher is doing his job he's not having a lot of time for upkeep."

"Would you tell the preacher and have it come from both of us?"

"You don't want to do it?"

"No, I want it to come from us as a couple. I want it to be our gift as a family to their family."

Jeremiah cleaned his plate and set the fork down. "All right, I'll tell him, but first you need to decide what you're going to do about Mrs. Spencer and Mildred." They had been living in the house with Sally since the old lady's death.

"With everything I need to do to get ready for the baby—plus curtains and such I'd like to make for the house—I could use their help now. How would you feel about them moving in?"

"I can get used to it. I got used to so many people at Elisha and Susana's place." He understood she needed help, but he'd have preferred to be alone in the house with Emily. The child coming would be another addition and he wanted to be prepared. He was glad that Elisha and Joe would be coming in the fall with the horse herd. He hoped to ask Elisha many more questions about being a father.

Emily scooted back her chair and went over to the stove. She took a peach cobbler out of the oven and placed it on the table. "Then we are in agreement to ask Mrs. Spencer and Mildred to come work for us here?"

He took a moment to answer. "Could we say that we will try it until after the baby comes and then talk about it again?" He watched as she spooned two helpings of the hot cobbler into bowls.

"We can do it that way. Thank you for not just saying yes and then regretting it." Emily placed a bowl of the hot cobbler in front of Jeremiah.

"Well, I try to be honest with you." Was he too honest with her? She always knew what he thought because he didn't try to come at things sideways.

Emily scooped up a peach slice with her spoon. "I'll talk to Mrs. Spencer and Mildred. Then when you're ready we can talk to James and Charlotte."

Jeremiah paused a moment to swallow the sweet dessert. "We don't have to be in a rush do we?"

"I don't see any reason to be."

The last of the cobbler disappeared from Jeremiah's bowl. "Good. I need to talk to Bob and Jacob. This will make a difference for them also. But until I can talk to them, I'm going back to work for this afternoon." He got up, gave her a kiss, put on his hat, and went out the door.

~

Jeremiah talked to Bob and Jacob later that afternoon about Mrs. Spencer and Mildred coming to work at the ranch. Bob didn't care as long as the ladies stayed out of his room. Jacob made the suggestion that he move to the shop and that they have the bunkroom.

Jacob nodded. "I can make a nice place for me. I eat at the house, but work at the shop." He pulled his tablet and pencil to him. "The bunkroom is big room and be good for the women. Then we think about how we add onto the house. There be other babies and you will need more bedrooms."

Jeremiah watched as Jacob designed an addition for the house. "I'm still worrying about this first baby. Don't talk to me about more babies." Worry seemed to be hanging around at the edge of his mind. What if Emily had problems with the birth? The thought of it twisted his insides. And would the baby be all right? He held his breath every time he thought about it. And then the worry of how to be a good father. He sighed deeply. He just had to be a good father. His baby deserved that.

~

Jeremiah looked forward to spending an afternoon with the preacher and his family. They invited James, Charlotte, and their three children to dinner the next Saturday. After eating a full meal prepared by Jacob and Emily, Bob and Jacob took the children for a walk along the creek. The two couples sat in the rocking chairs on the front porch.

"You have a nice place here, Jeremiah," James said as he looked out over the front pasture.

"Thanks, Emily and I are quite comfortable here."

Emily nodded. "Jeremiah has worked hard to build the ranch to what it is today."

James scratched his beard. "It shows. I remember when old man Turner lived here. It's really a different place. How long have you been here?"

"I bought it three and a half years ago. I'd been here two years when I met Emily."

James leaned forward. "A question I'd like to ask is how you became a Christian. I'm always interested in that."

"Elisha Evans baptized me into Christ four years ago at the Rocking ES. He and my other friends there taught me about being a Christian." Jeremiah nodded.

James smiled. "I remember meeting them at your wedding. Elisha Evans is the one who conducted the ceremony."

Emily laid her hand on Jeremiah's arm. "That's right. He and Joe and their wives have been very good friends to us."

Charlotte smiled. "And what about you, Emily? When did you become a Christian?"

"I was blessed to have a friend at school who invited me to her home for the summer when I was sixteen. Victoria's parents were Christians and guided me into belief and obedience. I was baptized into Christ that summer. It took me a while to decide to really grow as a Christian though." Emily shook her head. "I think Jeremiah was more serious about it." Emily looked over at her husband and smiled. "Over the last year and a half we have both gotten more serious about following in the footsteps of Jesus."

Jeremiah shifted in his chair. "That works into what we wanted to talk to you all about."

James leaned forward. "Is everything all right?"

"Emily and I have talked about it and we've decided to give her grandmother's house to you all." Jeremiah reached over and took Emily's hand.

James held his hand up, palm forward. "You mean you want to give it to the church?"

Emily shook her head. "No, we don't want to give it to the church. We want you, Charlotte, and the children to have it."

James reached over and took Charlotte's hand. "You don't mean it." His voice was gruff with emotion.

Jeremiah nodded. "We don't have a need for it and don't plan to use it. We felt that with the work you do and with the children you could use a bigger, nicer place." He leaned forward toward

James. "You work hard and expect little. This is something we can do to thank you for doing the Lord's work."

James wiped his eyes. "All I can say is thank you and God bless you."

Emily looked at Charlotte. "The house is in good condition and ready for you when you wish. Mrs. Spencer and Mildred are there, but they will be moving here in a couple of days." She leaned forward and put her hands on her knees. "Sally would like to stay and work with you all. My grandmother left her money to live on, but she needs a home."

Charlotte looked at her husband who nodded. "We would be happy for Sally to stay with us and with that big house there will be plenty of room."

Emily nodded. "She can be a big help with the children. I'm not sure she's a cook, but she can clean and care for children. The house has six bedrooms upstairs, and a front parlor, dining room, kitchen, pantry, and back parlor downstairs."

Jeremiah nodded. "The barn is in good shape and there is about ten acres with the property."

James looked at each in turn. "Would you all pray with me?" He bowed his head.

"Heavenly Father, You have blessed us so continually and again, with the blessing of this new home you have brought us another reminder of your care for your children.

"We give you grateful thanks. Please give a special blessing on Jeremiah and Emily for their wonderful generosity. Help us to be worthy. In the love of Jesus the Christ, Amen."

Jeremiah put his hand on James arm. "Thank you, James, we need God's blessings. With the coming birth of the baby, we need God's grace." He looked at Emily. "We need to be grateful also. God has helped us through a bad time the last couple of months, but I think we're through it." Jeremiah turned to Emily. "Are we through it?"

"Yes, I think we are," Emily smiled.

James shook his head. "We don't need to know any details, but was it a serious time of testing?"

Emily slowly nodded. "Serious enough that we could have lost our marriage if we hadn't worked it out with God's help." Tears sprang to her eyes. "I think we are stronger now as Christians and in our marriage."

James took Emily's hand. "I'm sorry that you had to go through a testing, but I'm so thankful that you have made it through to the other side."

Jeremiah heard the happy shouts of children, which told him they were back from their walk with Bob and Jacob.

Charlotte looked in the direction of the children as they came around the corner of the house. "We need to gather the children and head for home." She turned to her husband. "You still have to work on your sermon for in the morning."

James smiled and nodded. "Yes, we need to make a move toward home. Thank you for a delightful day that we will never forget."

Charlotte gave Jeremiah a kiss on the cheek and hug, then she hugged Emily. "I suspect this was your idea. On behalf of my family I thank you."

"You are so welcome. I look forward to seeing you raise your family in that house."

James shook hands with Jeremiah and then gave him a bear hug. "Thank you, my brother."

"Why don't we plan to meet in town on Monday morning and arrange the transfer of the deed to the house and give you all the keys?"

James shook his head. "I'm having trouble believing this blessing. But I'm willing to accept for my family's sake. Yes, Monday morning will be fine."

Jeremiah watched as James listened to his children tell him about their walk along the creek. He treated each child as if their comments were the most exciting. Jeremiah admired James' ease with his children.

James and Charlotte finally had the children in the buggy and started the four-mile trip back to town.

Jeremiah had been blessed so much by Elisha and Susana, when he was in need, and Joe and Sara's friendship had blessed him even more. To give to another family with the help of Emily was another sign to Jeremiah of God working in his life.

"I feel good about being able to help them." Emily gave Jeremiah a hug. "Now we need to concentrate on getting ready for the baby."

"I'm going to get to know James better." Jeremiah hugged her back. "I have wanted someone to talk to about how to be a father. I watched how he dealt with his children. I think I can learn from him."

Emily looked up at him. "That's a wonderful idea. You can learn from him while I learn from Charlotte."

## Chapter 25

Jeremiah worked hard preparing the ranch for the horse herd. With the use of irrigation, he had several more fields of hay ready to harvest. He would need to buy very little hay through the coming winter. He also continued to build and repair fencing. He now had most of the main pastures secure for the horses with fences along the boundaries of his property.

Even with the work that he put in on the ranch, he spent time with Emily. Their relationship grew and strengthened. Jeremiah made an effort to talk to her in addition to listening. Now that she knew all that had happened to him in the past, he felt free to share his deepest darkest secrets with her. It liberated him to truly speak his mind and heart and trust that it would be received with love.

The first week of October, Elisha and the crew arrived with the horse herd. To Jeremiah and Emily's surprise, Susana and Sara came with them. They didn't bring the children which disappointed Jeremiah.

Cookie drove the chuck wagon behind the house and stopped by the creek.

It was like a family reunion for Jeremiah. The only ones missing were Santo, Mara, and Anna. Mara and Anna each expected a child and didn't want to travel and Santo didn't want to leave Mara. They had already lost three children and he was frantic about Mara being careful. Elisha and Susana's children were old enough now to be of help and Anna could take care of them by herself.

The first evening Cookie, Jacob, Mrs. Spencer, and Mildred cooked supper at the house and had all the hands eat in the kitchen. After supper, everyone gathered on the porch to visit and share stories.

Jeremiah rode out the next morning with Elisha to look over the horse herd.

Elisha shifted in the saddle. "Jeff and most of the boys will head back in the morning. Jeff wants to get back and be with Anna." He looked over at Jeremiah. "We're going to stay a couple of days.

Susana and Sara can't be here for the birth of the baby so they wanted to come now and visit with Emily."

Jeremiah nodded. "I'm glad. That will give Emily a chance to talk to the ladies and me a chance to talk to you." Jeremiah hoped to take advantage of Elisha being there and ask him some questions about being a father.

"Let's ride up to the top of the ridge and talk a while," Elisha said.

After they got to the top of the ridge, they dismounted, tied up the horses, and found a couple of rocks to sit on. They looked out over the ranch and could see most of the horse herd.

Elisha turned toward Jeremiah. "How are you doing these days?"

"We're doing well. I'm amazed at how easily we've been able to move forward. In a way, Emily and I are able to talk more now that we both know the full truth. As much as I didn't want her to know about what happened in the tunnel, now that she knows she understands me so much better." Jeremiah tipped his hat back.

"I'm glad to hear something good came out of all that."

Jeremiah nodded. "I'm still having the nightmares, but Emily is able to cope with them. She knows now what the bad dreams are about. I still leave the lamp on at night. I hate that, but I just can't take the dark." Jeremiah rubbed his face with both of his hands. "I'd gotten to where I could sleep fine without the lamp and then I had to go and read that journal."

Elisha slowly nodded. "You need to give yourself time. You got to the place where you didn't need the lamp once, and you can do it again."

Elisha's caring voice soothed Jeremiah and reinforced his will to keep trying to sleep without the lamp.

"Your words always make me feel better."

"All you can do is try."

"I'm trying as hard as I can, but those dreams. Trying doesn't make a difference." Jeremiah tried to stop the shudder.

"I know you're trying and that's why you're doing so well. And you're right, you can't control the dreams, but like Joe says, just make sure you know what is a dream and what is real life."

They sat for several minutes in silence watching the horses in the distance.

Jeremiah turned to Elisha. "Tell me how to be a good father."

"You don't ask an easy thing. Let me think. How to be a good father?" Elisha scratched his head and laughed. "There are so many things to being a father. Most important is just love them, each child for himself." He smiled. "I try to keep my expectations of each child within their capabilities. I try to spend time with each child each day. I tell them the truth. I let them know that I love them, I love their mother and most of all, that I love God."

Jeremiah plucked a piece of grass and began to chew on it. "That's a lot to keep up with especially since you have four children."

"Think about it. Is there any of that you can't do?" Elisha challenged.

"I can do that. Are there other things I need to know?" Jeremiah had no problem with the idea of loving his child. He already had such a strong sense of wanting to protect this child. And he loved the child's mother. He was still growing in his knowledge and love of God.

"With a child it is the same as with someone, like Emily, you need to be gentle, kind, just, and firm. It depends on what the child needs. You won't have to worry about it for the first three months as the baby mostly sleeps and eats." Elisha got up and stretched. "You will do well as a father. I'm not worried about it."

"Thanks, I appreciate your confidence. I'm glad you come down to the ranch twice a year. If I do have problems I'll know I can ask you."

"I look forward to watching you with your children. They are going to be blessed to have you and Emily as parents." Elisha rubbed his back. "Let's start back to the house. I told Susana we'd be there for dinner." Elisha walked over to his horse.

"Everyone keeps talking about us having lots of children. I'm more worried about this first one." Jeremiah untied his horse and mounted.

Elisha laughed. "Well, you'll probably have several children by the time you're old and gray. I don't know that Susana and I planned on having so many children, but they just come. And I love each one for who they are." Elisha guided his horse down the trail toward the house.

"How does Susana manage with the births? I don't mind confessing to you that it scares me."

Elisha nodded. "When Little Sam was born I swore she would never go through a birthing again. I have never been so scared in my life." He rubbed a hand over his face. "Susana really did fine and told me to trust God and love the babies. You won't believe how quick Emily will forget about the pain of the birth. It will haunt you and you will be scared every time, but when you look into your child's eyes it will be worth it." Elisha smiled. "Your prayer time will increase, that's for sure."

"Thank you, Elisha. I wish you all could be here. I know you can't, but I can wish for it."

Elisha pulled on the reins and turned in his saddle to look directly at Jeremiah. "You will do fine when the baby is born, Jeremiah. Inside you'll have tremendous fear, but outwardly, you'll be strong and confident for Emily because that's what she'll need from you. Just trust God to see you through it." He held out his hand to Jeremiah.

Jeremiah reached across and accepted the hand Elisha offered. "Thanks, Elisha. I needed to hear those words."

They talked about the ranch work as they made their way back to the house. Jeremiah went over the words Elisha had shared. He was blessed to have such a friend.

~

Jeff and the other riders left the next morning. Jeremiah was surprised that Cookie didn't leave with them. Elisha explained that Cookie wanted to stock the chuck wagon with supplies for the ranch before leaving. When Cookie went into town to place his order with Milburn Black, Mrs. Spencer rode in with him.

Each time Jeremiah passed by the front room, he caught Emily, Susana, and Sara talking about plans for the baby. Emily's sewing machine sat in the middle of the room and the women cut and sewed for hours. Jeremiah couldn't imagine what they were so busy about, but they seemed to know what the baby was going to need. As Jeremiah watched his wife happily chatting with her two friends, he thought about how rich their lives were.

Joe and Jeremiah spent hours talking about the horse herd and planning for next years' crop of foals.

"Your plan to build another barn is a good one," Joe said as he leaned against the corral fence watching several mares that would foal in the winter. "It'll be better for the mares and easier on you all to have a barn for the foaling."

"I've thought about it for a while and I'm going to try to get it built by Christmas. I want to place it in the meadow back from the house a ways. I don't want it too close to the house." Jeremiah leaned against the corral railings.

"Wish we could be here to help you. That's one of the problems of the ranch being up so high in the mountains. I love it and don't want to live anywhere else. But the winters can be tough."

"Joe, how long have you and Sara been married?" Jeremiah asked abruptly.

"Well, let me think. Sara could tell you in a heartbeat." Joe rubbed his chin. "I guess it's coming up on eight years now."

"Do you mind me asking why you don't have any children? If that's a rude question don't answer." Jeremiah still didn't know what was considered rude. "With Emily having a baby in the next few months, it's sort of on my mind."

"From you I don't mind the question. From someone else I probably would." Joe looked out over the horses in the corral and remained silent for a few moments. "We want to have children, but it just hasn't happened." He shook his head. "And it's probably my fault. I don't know why, but the doctors in New York told me it might have been part of the injury when the horse fell on me. I was so hurt and in such pain that I'd believe anything is possible."

"I'm sorry, Joe, I didn't think." Jeremiah regretted asking.

"Don't be sorry. It is one of those things that happened. God never promised me that I would be a father. It hurts me worse to see Sara look longingly at Elisha and Susana's children. She tells me she can cope with us not having children, but I know she wants her own children." Joe turned and looked at Jeremiah. "It's one of those things that how we handle it reveals more about our character and our faith in God than the actual thing. Like you and me having to choose to move forward or choosing to be trapped in the past."

"I never thought about it like that, but it makes sense." As usual, Joe was giving him a lot to think about.

"I can think of worse things. I look at Bob and think about his loss. He loved Minnie with all his heart and in just a couple of days she was gone. I compare that to Sara and me not having children. At least I still have Sara." Joe shook his head and looked at the ground.

"I can see the change in Bob from before. He carries a lot of sadness with him now." Jeremiah didn't want to think about what it would be like to lose Emily.

"He seems to be doing much better since he came to work with you. It was the right move. I miss working with him though. You know, we came up the trail together." Joe looked at Jeremiah.

"I hadn't thought about that, but you two have been friends for a lot of years." Jeremiah began to know the comfort of having friends who knew his past and still wanted to be his friend.

"I pray for Bob that he will find another wife. But he needs time." Joe nodded.

Later when they went in for supper Jeremiah looked at Sara with a different appreciation. She laughed and talked to everyone with an obvious contentment. He noticed that she often looked over at Joe even when she was talking with someone else. Joe gazed back at her with the look of love. Jeremiah wished things could have been different for them, but he admired how they handled their disappointment.

At supper that night, they received a surprise. At the end of the meal, Cookie stood up and asked for everyone's attention.

"I want to make an announcement." He looked around the table. "Mrs. Spencer and I have decided to get married in the spring." Cookie reached down and took Mrs. Spencer's hand. "We have been writing to each other for a year. I asked her today to be my bride and she has agreed."

Everyone talked at once and got up to shake Cookie's hand and to give Mrs. Spencer a hug.

Cookie got their attention again. "I haven't asked Elisha if it's all right for me to have a wife at the Rocking ES. I just told him we were getting married." He looked expectantly at Elisha and Susana.

"Of course, it's all right," Elisha gave a broad grin.

"Oh, Mrs. Spencer, we'll be so happy to have you with us." Susana said.

"We'll wait for spring because I don't want Ruth to begin her life at the Rocking ES facing one of our winters. And she wants to wait because she has to see Emily through the birth of the baby."

Jeremiah had never heard Mrs. Spencer's given name. It relieved him to know she'd be with them through the winter and the birth of the baby. He looked over at Emily and found her wiping tears. He reached over and took her hand, not sure what caused her to cry.

"Oh, Mrs. Spencer, I am so happy for you. And thank you for staying through the winter. We need you." Emily smiled through her tears. "You just caught me off guard. I had no idea, but I should have suspected with all the letters going back and forth."

"Well, honey, you know I wouldn't leave you during your time, but you have to admit that this big old man needs me." Mrs. Spencer looked up at Cookie and beamed.

Jeremiah could see that they went together perfectly. Why he hadn't seen it before he didn't know, but they just looked right as a couple.

"If you all don't mind we'll plan to come down like we did for your wedding, Jeremiah," Elisha said. "Cookie asked me this afternoon if I would conduct the wedding for them next spring. Of course, I told him it would be an honor."

The rest of the evening, they planned for next spring. Jeremiah guessed that Cookie had already told Joe, as he hadn't seemed surprised at the news. They had had a special friendship ever since they'd come up the Chisholm Trail together almost ten years ago. Cookie's attitude toward Joe was that of a father watching out for an adult son.

The next morning the visitors from the Rocking ES started home. Jeremiah stayed close to the house and spent time with Emily.

"Oh, Jeremiah, it was so good to have them here." Emily wiped tears away.

"But, honey, they'll be back in the spring. Don't cry."

"I know and I'm all right. I just feel like crying today." Emily let him put his arms around her and hold her for a few minutes. Then she pushed him away. "You go on with your work. I have things to do."

He went out to find Bob to talk about plans for the new barn. He didn't understand what was going on with Emily, but it didn't seem to be anything he'd done.

## Chapter 26

The next two months passed quickly. Jeremiah put Bob and Jacob in charge of getting the new barn built. The huge structure—at least three times as large as the barn by the house—would be used only for the horses. He had his hands full dealing with breaking the horses and checking on Emily several times a day.

Emily was so big that she could barely get around and stayed in the house most of the time. Jeremiah was more thankful each day that they had Mrs. Spencer and Mildred with them. He talked to the doctor in town and he came out and visited with Emily. Doctor Hendrix kept a close watch on her size and said he would be available when the baby came.

Emily had thought the baby would arrive around Christmas time, but Doctor Hendrix told them to be prepared by the first week of December.

~

Jeremiah woke from one of his nightmares the first of December. He lay there shaking and sweating, trying to get his mind away from the nightmare and back to what was real. The lamp burned low by his side of the bed and offered a comfort.

"Are you all right, my love?" Emily reached over and stroked his face.

He hadn't realized she was awake. "Yeah, did I wake you?" He hated that part of the nightmares, knowing that it disturbed Emily's sleep. The feel of her hand on his face pushed away the horrors.

"No, I was awake. I could tell it was another bad one." She sounded tired. "Since you're awake, would you mind rubbing my back? It's really hurting."

Jeremiah sat up in bed and rubbed her back. It was the least he could do for her. She had been so uncomfortable for several days.

"Is that helping?" He moved up to her shoulders.

"Not really. I think you better go wake Mrs. Spencer. Something is not right and the pain is getting really bad."

Jeremiah swung out of bed, wide awake. "What's wrong?" He pulled on his pants, shirt, and boots.

"I don't know for sure, but I think maybe the baby's coming. I guess after you get Mrs. Spencer you better send someone for the doctor."

Jeremiah took a moment to kiss his beloved Emily. Then he lit the other lamp, and carrying it, ran to the bunkroom on the other side of the house. He pounded on the door and Mrs. Spencer opened it in her gown and nightcap.

"Emily needs you. She thinks the baby is coming." Jeremiah gasped barely able to speak.

Bob opened the door of his room as Mrs. Spencer pushed past Jeremiah.

"What is it?" Bob asked, pulling his shirt over his head.

"Can you ride to town and get the doctor? Emily thinks the baby is coming. I would go but—"

"You go back to Emily. I'll get the doctor and I'll also wake Jacob to help." Bob took Jeremiah's arm and turned him back toward the kitchen. "Don't worry Jeremiah. We're all here to help Emily. We just need to be praying."

Jeremiah went back to the bedroom where Mrs. Spencer sat wiping Emily's face with a wet cloth.

"Here, Jeremiah, you do this while I go get dressed. Did you send for the doctor?"

Just then he heard a horse leaving the yard toward the lane at a gallop. "Yes, that was Bob that just left for town."

Jeremiah took the wet cloth from Mrs. Spencer and laid it on Emily's brow.

"I'll be back in a few minutes, as soon as I get dressed."

Emily opened her eyes and looked up at him. She gave him a weak smile. "Don't look so worried, my love. I'll be all right. Just be here with me if you can."

"Why wouldn't I be here with you?" Jeremiah had no plans to be anywhere else but by her side.

"It may get pretty bad. Susana told me to scream all I wanted. If it's too much for you don't stay."

"You want me to be here and I will be here. If you can take it, I can take it." Jeremiah promised, hoping it was true.

"Thank you. Oh, here it comes—" She closed her eyes tightly and grabbed her stomach.

Jeremiah could tell from the way she stiffened and drew up her knees that it was a bad pain. He let her squeeze his hand in her pain and when he felt her loosening her grip knew the pain was lessening.

"That wasn't so bad," she said weakly. "Just be prepared. Susana said they start out with about five minutes in between and then they come quicker and quicker."

"Do the best you can and the doctor will be here soon," Jeremiah said, just to have something to say to try to reassure her. He wasn't feeling reassured at all.

He was grateful when Mrs. Spencer and Mildred came in. They sent him to the kitchen to get some hot water and a basin. He found Jacob there making coffee.

"So it is time that you become a father." Jacob grinned.

"How can you be so cheerful? Emily's in awful pain and it's barely started." Jeremiah felt a need to fuss at someone.

"I know, it will be bad for her, but then the joy of having a child." Jacob put his hand on Jeremiah's shoulder. "I pray, all the time I pray."

"Thanks, Jacob, I haven't even stopped to pray," he admitted.

"You take care of Miss Emily and I will pray for both of us," Jacob said with a smile.

"All right, you be sure and ask God to help Emily first and then help me find the courage to help her."

"I have already prayed that. God is with us, no matter what happens."

Jeremiah felt a cold sliver of fear run through his being. "Surely God won't let anything happen to Emily."

Jacob gripped his shoulder "We have no guarantees, but we do have God's promise to be here with us. You do not let fear rob you of strength to be what Miss Emily needs you to be for her this night."

Jeremiah nodded. "You're right. I want a guarantee, but I know I can't have it." He took the hot water and basin into the bedroom. Emily was now in a different gown and all the covers were gone. Only a sheet remained. They had put all the pillows behind her and she sat up, cushioned by the pillows.

He went to the chair close by the bed and sat down. Emily immediately took his hand and held on.

The next forty-five minutes the pains continued to come more often and harder. By the time the doctor arrived, Mrs. Spencer had given Emily a piece of leather to bite on to keep her from grinding her teeth.

Even though Jeremiah wanted to stay, the doctor made him go to the kitchen for breakfast while he examined Emily. Jeremiah drank some coffee, but he couldn't eat. Jacob sat down at the table with him. In just a few minutes, Bob came into the kitchen carrying a load of wood.

As the three men sat at the table, Jeremiah heard his wife cry out and he headed toward the bedroom.

Jeremiah thought he couldn't bear it as hour after hour he held Emily's hand until his own hand was bruised and swelling. He could tell that the doctor was worried as well as Mrs. Spencer and Mildred. Finally, after what seemed unending torment, as Jeremiah held Emily's head as she strained to birth the baby, a small cry of protest echoed through the room.

The doctor shouted. "You have a son!"

Jeremiah held Emily's head up to look at the tiny infant; she was so exhausted. She grabbed Jeremiah's hand and groaned as another pain started. Jeremiah looked at the doctor.

The doctor was looking from Emily to the baby he was checking. He handed the baby to Mrs. Spencer and sat down again at the foot of the bed.

Emily pushed as hard as she could and screamed.

Jeremiah held on to her hand and looked to the doctor. "What's wrong? Why is she still in pain?"

"Hang on, Jeremiah." The doctor examined Emily.

She took a deep breath and then started pushing again.

Jeremiah wanted to go and shake the doctor to tell him what was going on but he couldn't leave Emily's side. "I know it hurts, but it has got to be over soon." He wanted to reassure her but didn't really know how.

The doctor spoke. "Now, Emily, let's have another push."

Emily pushed with what Jeremiah was sure was the last of her strength.

"Good, good . . . ah, you have another son." The doctor smiled.

It took a moment for the doctor's words to sink into Jeremiah's mind.

Another son?

He pulled away from Emily's grip enough to look down the bed at the doctor handing a second baby to Mildred as Mrs. Spencer stood there holding the first.

*Two babies?*

Jeremiah looked at Emily who was smiling through tears. "We have two babies."

He couldn't believe it. No one had mentioned the possibility of twins to him.

"Can you see them?" Emily asked, trying to sit up.

"Hold just a minute, Emily," the doctor said as he attended to her. He then looked each of the babies over as Mrs. Spencer and Mildred cleaned them and wrapped them up in the swaddling they had ready. Both babies cried heartily until the swaddling comforted them.

In a few minutes, the doctor placed two tiny infants on the bed next to Emily. "They both appear to be fine, just small. That's normal with twins and they may be a couple of weeks early."

Jeremiah looked down at the tiny bundles and had trouble believing that these small people had just left his wife's body. Fearfully, he picked up one of the babies and held it in his hands.

"Hand him to me, please." Emily held out her arms.

Jeremiah carefully laid the baby in its mother's arms. He then picked up his other son and held him.

"Oh, Jeremiah, they are beautiful." Tears ran down Emily's cheeks. She looked up at Jeremiah. "Say something, my love. What do you think of your sons?"

He looked at her and then at the two babies. He couldn't speak. Taking a deep breath, his voice quivered. "Thank you and thank the Lord that you're all right." He turned to the doctor. "She is all right?"

"She's fine. Because its twins, she's more tired and will have to take it easy for a while. Emily, you stay in bed until I tell you different. You've got help and you need to get your strength back. Mrs. Spencer knows what to do and I'll come back out tomorrow morning." He packed up his bag and put on his coat. "Jeremiah, you go somewhere else and get some sleep. Emily needs quiet. Come on and walk me out to my buggy."

After the doctor had some coffee and cake that Jacob had ready, Jeremiah accompanied the doctor to his buggy. As he walked back to the house, he realized darkness surrounded him. The day had passed and he hadn't realized it. The fatigue of the day descended on him and he could barely walk to the kitchen.

Bob met him at the door, took his arm, and guided him. "Use my room and get some sleep. Lie down and let me pull your boots off. You can rest an hour or so."

"Thanks Bob, I'm feeling awfully tired all of a sudden. Did you know we had two babies?" Jeremiah asked him in wonder.

Bob laughed. "Yeah, boss, I heard. Now go to sleep."

Jeremiah smiled back at him as he closed his eyes and slept.

~

Daylight streamed through the window and woke Jeremiah. It took him a minute to realize he was in Bob's bed. He felt much better and was hungry. But first, he had to see Emily. He pulled on his boots and walked into the kitchen.

Jacob stood at the stove, frying bacon. "Morning, Jeremiah. You look better."

"I feel better. How is Emily?"

"She is fine. She asked for breakfast so I fix. You go see her and I bring her breakfast."

"Thanks." He left Jacob in the kitchen and went to the bedroom. As he passed through the front room, he saw Mrs. Spencer asleep on one of the couches. He felt a little guilty as he guessed that she had stayed up through the night with Emily.

He stopped at the door of the bedroom and looked at his beautiful wife sitting up in the bed holding an infant to her breast.

Emily looked up and saw him. "Good morning, my love." She motioned him in. "Come look at your sons." She looked refreshed and rested. He couldn't believe it. After what he'd seen her go through the day before, he thought she would be barely awake.

"Are you all right?" He carefully sat on the side of the bed. His second son, all wrapped up and sleeping, lay by her side.

"I'm doing well. I'm not ready to get up and do anything, but I don't have to with all the help I have." She took the baby from her breast and held him out for Jeremiah to take.

Jeremiah felt the weight of his son in his hand and tried to balance him properly while glancing back to Emily. He sure didn't want to drop this fragile package.

"Don't hold him like that," Emily reached over and repositioned the baby so he was resting in the fold of Jeremiah's arm up close to his heart. "That's better."

The baby looked up at him, blinked a couple of times, and then softly went to sleep. Jeremiah held his breath.

"We have a problem," Emily said with a smile.

He took a deep breath and looked up at her quickly. "What problem?" Her smiled reassured him.

"We have two babies to name."

"We decided on one name, Elisha, if it was a boy. Would you mind if we named the other one Joseph?" Jeremiah thought that was a good solution as he had wrestled with whether to call his first-born son after Elisha or Joe. They both meant so much to their lives.

Emily settled back on her pillows. "That's what I thought too."

"Can you tell which is which? They look just alike to me."

"Of course, can't you?"

"Not really. They do look alike." He might as well admit it.

Emily laughed. "Don't worry, honey, I noticed something last night. This baby has the tiniest little red place on his neck just below his right ear and the doctor said he was born first, so this baby is Elisha. The one you're holding is Joseph."

Jeremiah looked down at the sleeping bundle in his arms. "Hello, Joseph." He rubbed the soft little cheek with his finger.

His sons. He was a father. The need to protect and provide rose until he thought he couldn't contain it. So this was the feeling of love for his children, the need to stand against the world for them. He looked at his beautiful wife and his two sons and the bareness of his life before he met Emily filled completely with the love he felt for his little family.

He wondered if his father had felt the same thing about him. Jeremiah would never know. He vowed that his sons would know how he felt about them.

Jacob came in carrying a tray, followed by Mrs. Spencer.

"Thank you, Jacob, I'm really hungry." She looked at Jeremiah. "Have you eaten?"

"No, he has not eaten in two days," Jacob said in a stern voice. "You make him come to kitchen and eat."

Jeremiah started to protest, but before he could say anything, Mrs. Spencer took the baby from his arms. "Now, you go with Jacob and eat. You're going to have these babies here for a long time and you got to stay well and strong to provide for them."

He smiled at her. "Yes ma'am."

"Jacob, Mrs. Spencer, do you see this little red mark below his ear?"

They both leaned over the bed and peered at the baby in Emily's arms.

"I'd like to introduce you to Elisha." She reached up and placed her hand on the baby in Mrs. Spencer's arms. "And this is Joseph."

Jacob nodded several times. "That's good strong names for babies. Now come on Jeremiah. I fix you good breakfast." Jacob guided Jeremiah out of the bedroom and toward the kitchen.

## Chapter 27

Emily took time getting back on her feet, fortunately she had help with the babies. Charlotte sent Sally out to help them; the laundry alone was a full-time job.

Jacob made a second cradle and started on the second crib.

The horses kept Jeremiah busy. They hired extra men and got the new barn completed before Christmas.

Every time Jeremiah went into town that fall, he listened to the men talk about the signs that forecasted a severe winter. Larger spider webs hung everywhere. Thick, tight husks enveloped ears of corn. Squirrels scrambled to store nuts instead of eating them. Thick bark covered the trees. Starlings and geese migrated earlier. And hoot owls called late into fall. Jeremiah shook his head. But when winter descended with a vengeance and didn't let up, he began to believe their predictions.

The men spent Christmas Day moving horses in foal into the new barn. Jeremiah bought several stoves and put them in the barns. He didn't like the increased fire danger, but with the unrelenting cold, the men working with the horses needed the warmth. With the extra space of the new barn, and using the old barn as well, Jeremiah was able to get over a hundred horses under cover. He put the mares carrying foals and the best stallions into the barns. He also sheltered his two best bulls.

For the rest of the animals he tried to find some sort of sheltered forested pasture. As they went from January into February, Jeremiah experienced the worst cold spell in his life. Helplessness paralyzed Jeremiah as he watched cattle and horses freeze to death. Many ranchers lost their entire herds. Jeremiah feared for Elisha and the Rocking ES. He hoped he could at least save the best of the breeding stock from the horse herd.

The hands and Jeremiah worked every day, including Sunday. By building feed troughs down the middle of the barns and tying the horses to a line, they crowded many more horses into the barns, but then the barns had to be mucked out.

Jeremiah spent every minute he could with his sons. The first time little Elisha wrapped his hand around Jeremiah's little finger and held on, it was as if his son had wrapped his hand around Jeremiah's heart. The next night, Joseph did the same thing. It provoked such a feeling of protectiveness that he knew he would never be the same.

Jeremiah fell into a routine of going in just before dark, eating the supper that Mildred cooked, and rocking his sons for a few minutes before falling into bed exhausted. He wished he could spend more time with the babies for they grew so fast. The babies were three months old at the end of February and responded to those around them. Jeremiah couldn't get enough of holding one of his sons in his hands, looking him in the eyes, and cooing at him until the infant responded with gurgling, smiles, and kicking feet. Both of the boys would turn their heads and stare at Jeremiah when he came into the room and talked to Emily. When he realized his sons recognized his voice he felt his heart give a thud.

The cold lasted until the middle of March. When Jeremiah finally did a count, he had lost over two hundred horses. Most of the cattle had died. He had saved a hundred fifty horses in the barns along with his bulls and the milk cows. Of the three-hundred-fifty horses not in the barns only one hundred-fifty survived. He knew it could have been worse.

What was happening up on the Rocking ES he didn't want to think about. It had to be much worse. As March went into April, they all held their breath, waiting for news from the ranch up in the mountains.

Mrs. Spencer was especially anxious as she and Cookie had thought they would be married by the end of March.

Finally, as the second week of April came to an end, Jeremiah looked toward the lane as he had been doing for days. Riders and the chuck wagon followed by two buggies appeared on the horizon. Jeremiah let out a whoop as he ran toward the house to alert the women.

Jeremiah couldn't believe it. Everyone had come, all the families and children. Several minutes of chaos erupted as everyone greeted one another. Jeremiah wanted immediately to ask Elisha and Joe about their herds, but he refrained. He would find out in good time.

The visitors planned to camp out as they had done on the way down from the mountains, but Emily would not hear of it. Mrs. Spencer and Mildred solved the problem of where to house everyone by moving into Bob's room and giving their room to Elisha, Susana, and the four children. Bob said he could manage out in the barn for a couple of nights. Joe and Sara took the empty room next to Bob's. No one had ever stayed in that room, but Jacob had built furniture for it anyway. Jeff, Anna, and their little baby settled into Elisha and Joseph's room and the twins slept in Jeremiah and Emily's bedroom. Santo, Mara, and their two-month-old baby took over Jacob's room out in the barn. Jacob also said he could manage in the barn loft. All the others camped out by the chuck wagon by the creek.

The kitchen became a beehive of cooking, visiting, and general bedlam. Emily just smiled and Jeremiah tried to stay out of the way. He regretted that they didn't have the extra bedrooms they planned to build, but he knew it would only be for a few days.

People ate supper that evening in shifts. The children ate first and then the riders. The couples all sat down at the table together with Jacob, Cookie, and Mildred serving them. Mrs. Spencer sat at the table holding one of the twins while Sara held the other one.

Elisha stood and asked for their attention. "Let's pray.

"Dear Heavenly Father, We come to you with grateful hearts to be together around this table. We thank you for the births that have occurred and the safety of the mothers and babies. We have suffered terrible losses this hard winter, but through it all we never forgot that you were there with us. Help us be thankful for what we have left. We are thankful for the occasion we have before us to witness the wedding of our beloved Cookie and Mrs. Spencer. Bless this food and the hands that prepared it. We are so grateful for your love and care. In the name of Jesus the Christ. Amen."

Jeremiah covered his eyes to stop the tears that threatened to fall. He looked around the table he noticed several others with tears. He was just so glad to have everyone in his home, safe.

~

The next morning after breakfast Jeremiah, Elisha, and Joe rode out to survey the horse herd. They ended up at the lookout at the top of the ridge. It was an intensely sunny spring day. They tied up their horses after dismounting and sat on the rocks as they looked out over the ranch. They could see the main part of the horse herd below them.

Elisha took off his hat and ran his fingers through his thick black hair. "Well, Jeremiah, we have to hand it to you. You saved the best of the horse herd. I don't know how you did it."

For the first time Jeremiah noticed the gray along his friend's temples. He tried to remember how old Elisha was. He thought he was only about thirty-seven, but the last year had been a hard one.

"It was getting that barn built that made the difference. We put over a hundred head of horses in there. I tried to put the best stallions and the mares carrying foals." Jeremiah waited for their comments on his decisions.

Joe stretched out his legs. "You did the right thing. We still have the breeding stock and we can begin again."

"How bad was it up at the Rocking ES?"

Elisha rubbed his hand over his face. "We lost almost all of the cattle, probably a couple of thousand at least. And we lost over half the horse herd. We kept our riding stock up in the barns, but there wasn't any way to get more under cover. And the cold was too much for too long." He sighed deeply. "I'm just grateful that we didn't lose any riders," Elisha said in a calm voice tinged with sadness.

The news of the devastation of Elisha's herd, both the cattle and the horse herd, left Jeremiah feeling all twisted up inside. Considering how he felt finding dozens of horses frozen to death.

What must it have been like for Elisha and Joe? His heart ached for his friends.

Jeremiah removed his hat and held it against his leg. "I'm sure sorry, Elisha. I can't imagine how hard the winter was on you all."

Elisha straightened up where he sat on the rock. "It's not all lost. We have the land and the breeding stock here. I can buy more cattle, although I have a feeling that I need to hold off." He turned to Jeremiah. "I have a strong sense that the coming winter may be as bad."

Jeremiah wondered how Elisha knew, but decided not to ask. "What do you think we should do to start building up again? We aren't going to meet the contract with the army unless we can put them off a few months." He shook his head. "I haven't been able to work with the horses. We had our hands full just keeping them alive."

Joe nodded. "I know what you mean. We lost so many of the horses that were already broke and then we couldn't work outside and break any others." He rubbed the back of his neck. "If we worked all summer we might get enough broke to fill the contract, but most of the horses here are breeding stock. It will have to be horses up at the ranch that we catch and break. It'll be like doing a year of work in three months."

"And what about the grass, feed for the horses this summer and next winter?" Jeremiah asked.

Joe rubbed his hip. "That's a good question. Will the shorter summer, especially if it stays cool, grow enough grass?"

Elisha leaned forward. "Here's what I suggest. Jeremiah, you build a couple more barns. I'll help pay for it. We take the horse herd back to the mountains for the summer as usual except for ones that you can break here." He paused and then continued. "And then Joe, you break what you can. I'll talk to the army and tell them the contract will be filled the best we can by the end of September." Elisha looked from one to the other.

Jeremiah nodded. "That sounds workable and then next fall with the smaller herd you bring all the horses down where I can keep them up in the barns if need be." Jeremiah put his hat back on. Elisha's plan began to take shape in his mind.

Joe put his hands on his knees and leaned forward. "You may have to buy hay, but we can manage."

Elisha looked out over the horse herd below them. "I'll think about it, but I might sell the rest of the cattle this summer. The market is going to be way down. But I would rather get something for them this summer than have them die next winter."

Though Elisha said it, Jeremiah felt he didn't really want to.

Jeremiah shook his head. "But you still got the land, and everything I've heard indicates this is not the normal weather. If we can survive a couple of bad years, then we can pick up again." Jeremiah wanted to encourage his friends just as they had always been there to encourage him.

Elisha nodded. "You're right and I need to thank God for that."

"If you need any cash, Emily and I have plenty. I don't want you to lay off any hands," Jeremiah offered, not sure if he would offend.

Elisha looked at him and smiled. "That's kind of you. If we run short, I'll let you know, but for now we're all right. If we have several more winters like this we won't have enough to survive."

"What Emily and I have is yours if you need it and don't you forget it," Jeremiah said forcefully.

"So, do we have a plan?" Joe asked.

Jeremiah and Elisha nodded.

"Good, I'm hungry. Let's head back to the house for dinner." Joe got up and untied his horse.

~

Two days later, they all gathered at the little church in town for the wedding of Malcolm "Cookie" Smith and Ruth Spencer. The crew from the Rocking ES helped fill the building. Elisha performed the ceremony with Joe and Billy standing up with Cookie and Mildred and Sally standing up with Mrs. Spencer.

It was a joyous time of celebration. Jeremiah enjoyed it in a way that he would never have believed possible. He barely remembered his own wedding, he had been so tense, but for this wedding, he just let himself enjoy.

Elisha and Susana stayed for another day. Then they rounded up the horse herd, except for the ones that Jeremiah planned to break over the summer, and headed back for the mountains.

Joe and Sara rode with them and then planned to head south toward his father's ranch. Joe was worried about his father and felt he was ready to face going home. He had run away as a young boy and this was to be his first visit back. His father had been to the Rocking ES every year, but Joe had not been able to make himself return to a house where his mother had treated him so badly. He told Jeremiah that this was a part of his being able to move forward.

Jeremiah prayed for his friend.

It was quiet at the ranch after everyone left. After a light supper, Jeremiah and Emily went to their bedroom to care for the twins. Nursing two growing babies took most of Emily's time. She sat in one rocker nursing little Elisha, and Jeremiah sat in the other rocker holding little Joseph.

"It's almost like I can't believe they were all here," Emily said as she held her little son.

"I know and to think that Cookie and Mrs. Spencer, I mean Ruth, are married." Jeremiah smiled at stumbling over what to call her. She had asked them to call her Ruth after the wedding, as Mrs. Cookie didn't sit right with her.

"Yes, I'm so glad they found each other."

Jeremiah looked at his wife holding his son and then he looked at the baby in his lap, his other son. What if he hadn't found Emily?

"You're going to think this a strange thing for me to say. But if your grandmother keeping me in the tunnel was what it took for me to be with you now, then I would do it again." He looked up at her.

Emily smiled at him with her radiant "I love you" smile. "That is the sweetest thing you've ever said to me."

He smiled back at her. "And I think I can finally say I forgive the old lady. I can move on with my life and leave all that behind." Jeremiah looked first at one son, and then the other. "Look at these two babies. Why should I waste any more time on bitterness when I have all of this to live for?"

"I love you, Jeremiah," Emily said softly as she rocked their son Elisha.

"I love you, Emily," Jeremiah responded as he rocked their son Joseph.

The End

# A J Hawke Books

# Inspirational Western Historical Romance

# Cedar Ridge Chronicles Series

### CABIN ON PINTO CREEK, Cedar Ridge Chronicles 1

Elisha Evans is out of luck. By the age of twenty-five, he'd planned to have his own ranch. Instead, a series of losses forces him to beg for a job at an isolated mountain ranch. The loss of his parents at a young age has left Elisha longing for a place of his own and a family to provide for and to protect. But betrayal and loss have left him fearful that he will never attain his dreams. The only job he is offered is the line rider out of the isolated cabin on Pinto Creek. As he hunts for cattle alone in the high Colorado Rockies, he discovers a broken-down wagon in the snow with an old preacher and his granddaughter, Susana, stranded inside. Elisha manages to bring them to the cabin just ahead of the winter snows that blocks the way out of the valley.

The old man's dying wish is that Elisha should marry his granddaughter. The old man knows that the two young people will be snow bound for the next five months and the grandfather wants to spiritually protect his granddaughter by leaving her married. Elisha wrestles with the dilemma of consenting to a marriage he did not plan. He understands the reasoning of the old man. Although he does not know much about God, he respects what this grandfather is trying to do for his granddaughter. Is he man enough to take on the responsibility? But will marriage to a stranger change his life for better or worse?

Only sixteen, Susana Jamison has no choice but to marry this stranger, although he is an unbeliever. Faced with the brutal conditions of frontier living and the dangers she encounters alongside her new husband, she is challenged to the limit of her strength, hope, and faith. Can she hold on to her faith in the midst of this desperate situation? An inspirational historical Western romance, *Cabin On Pinto* is the first in the Cedar Ridge Chronicles.

### JOE STORM NO LONGER A COWBOY, Cedar Ridge Chronicles 2

If a cowhand can't ride, what can he do? Joe Storm can no longer ride a horse—and that hurts more than his injured hip. Swallowing his pride, he takes a job as cook's helper on a cattle drive. There he meets the daughter of the owner of the trail herd. In spite of the opposition of her father, Sara befriends Joe. When the herd is sold to a rancher in Colorado

Joe wonders if there will be a place on the ranch for a man who can't ride. And he watches as Sara and her father head for California and out of his life.

Facing life without the woman he has come to love, Joe must also confront his past when his father, whom he hasn't seen in twelve years, arrives at the ranch. As Joe struggles to build a place for himself on the ranch, he longs to go to Sara in search of a happy forever. Only with the help of God and friends will Joe be able to achieve his dream.

## COLORADO MORNING SKY, Cedar Ridge Chronicles 3

### Swift Justice in the American West.

At age 16, a guilty verdict hurls Jeremiah Reborn across a hot Arizona desert in an iron prison wagon. The year is 1876.

Left for dead after an Apache attack on the wagon, Jeremiah alone survives. He wakes to find himself blindfolded, shackled, and enslaved to a cruel, mute taskmaster.

His only companion becomes the ever-present noose around his neck that forces him to do its bidding. He labors hard in a gold mine for days, months, years. He awakes one day to discover his irons and blindfold gone...and an unexpected message. Now equipped with uncommon strength and a deep distrust of his fellow man, he sets out to begin a life.

### Balm from a Gentle and Quiet Spirit.

Emily Johnson, at finishing school in Boston, is summoned west by her ailing grandmother. She arrives in town and soon attracts the attention of Jeremiah.

This strong, silent rancher stirs Emily's interest as no other man has ever done. Will her love break the chains that enslave his heart? Will Jeremiah grasp that God is using the evil done to him and his present trials for a grander purpose?

## COLORADO EVENING SKY, Cedar Ridge Chronicles 4

Thomas Black is offered parole from Yuma Prison after twelve years of a fifteen-year sentence spent paying his debt to society for rustling cattle. But, there are conditions to his release. He must serve the last three years of his sentence working as an unpaid cowhand on the ranch of Jeremiah Reborn. The ranch is located in Colorado, which is a long way from Yuma Prison. Anything is better than Yuma Prison, especially as

Thomas meets the pretty woman running the local cafe in Cedar Ridge, Colorado.

Catherine has struggled to make ends meets running the little cafe that her mother had left to her. She has no intention of getting involved with a cowhand still serving a sentence for rustling. But, after meeting the shy young man, who is the son of her best friends, she cannot help an attraction. Myles McKinley owns the biggest ranch in the area and the local bank. He has his eyes on Catherine and has no plans for a rustler and prisoner to cut him out of the running for her hand, even is he has to break the law.

## Other Novels

### MOUNTAIN JOURNEY HOME

Rock Corner, Texas. 1877.

Life couldn't get much better for Dave Kimbrough. He has a beautiful wife in Jenny, a fine young son in Jonathan, and a small ranch with which to build their future. But when Jenny suddenly dies, the heartache is more than Dave can bear, so he leaves his son with his wife's family and rides off into the rugged Texas country alone. After several years Dave is wrongly accused of murder, and when he sets out to find the man who can clear his name, he runs instead into a posse that has set out to kill him. Wounded, he holes up for the winter in a cave. It is not time wasted, however, as he is given time to contemplate the mistake he made in abandoning his son.

Once spring arrives, Dave returns to make things in his life right. Things rarely go as planned, however, and Dave's plans are no different. Beset by a trip to jail, Jenny's spirited sister Rachel, and the heartache of taking away the only life and family his son really knows, Kimbrough makes a promise he thinks is the right thing to do. But a fateful winter followed by a deadly spring storm changes the course of their lives in ways that no one—least of all Dave—could have ever imagined.

### Inspirational Contemporary Western Romance

### CAUGHT BETWEEN TWO WORLDS

People from completely different worlds can find a connection in the most unsuspecting places. For Stephanie Wellbourne, it was when she went off on a walk in the woods to relieve some stress from an executive retreat gone awry. Being a New Yorker, she found herself being alone in the Colorado woods unprepared and with a broken ankle. Fear starts to set in and then, out of nowhere, Flint Tucker comes walking through the woods.

Stephanie is not in any position to be strong and independent at the moment. She immediately takes the noticeably handsome Flint's help to get her back to the retreat center. She tries to thank him with a reward and is surprised that he declines. It inspires her to find out more about this ruggedly handsome Colorado man. There are no men even similar to him around New York City.

A rancher, Flint is working as an accountant to stay afloat financially. He has the business expertise that Stephanie needs for her business, Wellbourne Group. She hires Flint's firm and Flint is made an offer he cannot refuse. He agrees to go to New York, a place that is definitely not like home, because he'll have the opportunity to make the money quickly—something he desperately needs.

Flint's daughter, Allie, was born with a serious heart condition and may not even make it to her fourth birthday if she doesn't get the heart transplant she needs. To get on the list, Flint needs money he doesn't have. Through faith and love for his daughter, Flint agrees to take on the challenge of working with Stephanie. In many ways, it was not a difficult decision because he was drawn to the dark-haired beauty the day they met in the Colorado mountains.

A close friendship develops that Flint knows cannot go any further. Stephanie can tell Flint is attracted to her and cannot figure out what is holding him back. As with all things that are meant to be, the events in both Flint and Stephanie lives unfold and amazing opportunities begin to weave the connections that open the way for love.

## About the Author

Born in Spur, Texas into a multi-generational Texans family, A J Hawke has lived and traveled throughout the American West as well as other parts of the world and enjoys reading, writing, friends, family, and being a Christian.